VICIOUS PROTECTOR

MAFIA WARS - BOOK FOUR

MAGGIE COLE

This book is fiction. Any references to historical events, real people, or real places are used fictitiously. All names, characters, plots, and events are products of the author's imagination. Any resemblance to actual events or places or persons, living or dead, is entirely coincidental.

Copyright © 2021 by Maggie Cole

All rights reserved.

No part of this book may be reproduced in any form or by any electronic or mechanical means, including information storage and retrieval systems, without written permission from the author, except for the use of brief quotations in a book review.

PROLOGUE

Skylar Scott

FAIRY TALES AREN'T REAL. I LEARNED THIS LESSON THE HARD way. Looking back, I curse myself for ever wanting to find true love. Everything I assumed about it is wrong. It's not the amazing feeling I expected.

It's one hundred percent soul-crushing, delicious at times, painful in ways you never imagined, addicting beyond measure, all-consuming torment. Love grips and holds on to you, stabbing you any chance it gets.

Or maybe it's only like that if you love Adrian Ivanov.

Why didn't I bring a date?

Did he?

I didn't see anyone with him.

She could have been in the bathroom or talking to someone else.

Why was I even looking? We're finished.

"It's time. Everyone, please take your places," the wedding planner tells us. It's Kora and Sergey's wedding. She's been my best friend for longer than I can remember. She's so happy, she's glowing. It gives me joy and creates a jealous flare in my bones. I hate feeling envious of her happiness. Kora deserves every morsel of delight. She and Sergey have been through so much. They are perfect for each other, and you can feel their love.

I hug her again. "You look stunning."

Her beaming smile only grows. "Thank you."

I take my place behind Aspen and Hailee. I'm Kora's maid of honor. When I walk down the aisle, I try to avoid Adrian's cocky stare, eating me up, as if I'm going to be his dinner. I take controlled breaths to attempt not to blush. I can feel him checking me out with his piercing, icy-blue orbs, even though I'm avoiding him.

My insides shake. Before last night, I hadn't seen him in several months. Our last encounter was at the hospital. Kora and Sergey got abducted, and something went down. I still don't have all the details. I'm tired of asking for them. Kora and Aspen hide issues concerning the Ivanovs in a secret vault. I've fought with them so many times to tell me things, but they won't. I finally decided I needed to let it go. I already lost Adrian. I don't need to lose my friends, too.

Last night, I stayed on the opposite side of the room from Adrian. We were at a restaurant for the rehearsal dinner. My heart raced similar to what it's doing now. Somehow, I got through the night without talking to him. Earlier today, I saw him across the room when I went to the bathroom. I

VICIOUS PROTECTOR

ignored him, and when I came out, he was gone. Disappointment and relief swirled through me.

Focus on the ceremony, not him.

The peek I allow myself only makes my pain expand. Adrian Ivanov is the epitome of sex on an average day. In a tux, he's a demigod. Adonis himself would be jealous. Fabric stretches over Adrian's hard, chiseled body, with just enough tautness to tease any female who glances his way. Assumptions about his body will make your panties melt, but firsthand knowledge is what makes everything even more unfair. Until you see and feel Adrian's naked body against yours, you assume he's ripped, no different from other fit guys.

All hypotheses of Adrian and what an experience with him is like are wrong. Other men may have good bodies, but they don't know how to use them. Adrian can dominate you in the bedroom in the smallest of ways. His eyes alone can bring you to your knees. I'm convinced no other man on the planet knows how to use his tongue or fingers, and I'm not even referring to the most intimate acts.

Sex with Adrian is filthy ecstasy. There's no boundary of how he'll please you. His smug arrogance drew me to him. Each cocky expression is well-earned. Everything he does with his hands, mouth, or eyes turns my insides to hot lava. There's masculinity about him other men don't possess, along with a thick Russian accent growling in your ear.

Focus on Kora. Focus on Kora. Focus on Kora.

He's staring at me.

Don't look at him.

My eyes dart to his sculpted features and verify my feeling

was correct. He's got his hardened, cocky expression pinned on me. Heat rushes to my cheeks. I quickly refocus on Kora.

No one is next to him.

Is his date hiding somewhere?

Why am I even thinking about this?

A pulse of paranoia creeps from my toes and crawls up my body, torturing me. When I was with Adrian, I loved how his mere presence sent my loins into overdrive. Right now, I detest how much he still affects me.

If he could only trust me enough to tell me the truth about what he does and where he goes at night, or what happened to Kora and Sergey, we could be together.

He chooses not to let me in.

I can't help myself. I gaze away from Kora and catch Adrian's eyes again. The heat on my face intensifies.

Someone should tell him it's rude to stare.

The ceremony continues. I miss what's going on. All I can think about is Adrian and how much I miss him. His ongoing arrogant poker face gives me the impression he wants to do naughty things with me. It's not helping my current predicament.

I've missed that look.

Not helping!

The officiant announces Sergey may kiss the bride. I snap out of my thoughts when the room erupts in cheers. My reaction is a mix of tears and a smile. I'm happy for Kora, but having Adrian this close, keeping his intense eyes on my body, only reminds me how I fooled myself I could have the happily ever after.

No man is ever going to match up to Adrian in any department. Not the looks, sex, or way he made me feel when I was with him. Besides all the fights about where he was and who he was with, everything about us seemed to sync. He made me laugh. I felt safe with him. We just got each other.

Most days, I feel like I can't breathe. I keep trying to convince myself it'll get better. Somehow, I'll get past Adrian.

It's a lie. How do you go from a five-star resort with luxurious amenities you never knew existed to a cheap, dingy motel?

You can't. It's impossible not to remember what you once had.

Over the last few months, I've had good-looking men from every walk of life hit on me. I attempted to date to move on. I keep thinking if I find someone else, I'll forget Adrian. It's another lie.

I couldn't get past dinner, coffee, or whatever else we were doing to get to know each other. I hoped enough time passed that I could move on. Each date only reaffirmed my suspicion. There is no getting over Adrian Ivanov.

I follow the happy couple down the aisle and go through the motions. When the photographer tells us we can all go and for Kora and Sergey to stay, I hightail it to the bathroom.

No one is inside, except me. I wash my hands with cold water and refrain from putting it on my face so I don't mess up my makeup. I give myself another pep talk to stay away from Adrian.

Straightening my shoulders, I step out of the bathroom. My gut flips. Adrian is standing against the brick wall, as if waiting for me.

Blood pounds between my ears. My heart hurts, looking at the man I love whom I can't get over. I think the pain can't get any worse, but I overestimated the ache that keeps growing. It's nothing compared to what lies ahead.

1

Adrian Ivanov

Several Months Prior

"Cat's Meow," Hailee announces.

I turn from the passenger's seat. It's not a place I expected Hailee and Aspen to frequent. Hailee seems way too innocent to go anywhere near the co-ed strip club. Maksim won't like Aspen there, but my job isn't to stop her from going places. Maksim didn't give me orders to report to him her whereabouts. Plus, it's Dmitri's rehearsal dinner, so I'm not interrupting. My assumption is they're in the middle of a lover's tiff, or she would be there with him. Whatever their situation is, it prevented me from going to the dinner and having a night off, so I'm not overly excited to be babysitting two women who have no business stepping foot inside the seedy bar. I raise my eyebrows. "Cat's Meow?"

"Is your job to judge me or guard me?" Aspen snaps.

Great. Looks like I'm going to have an awesome night with Ms. Pissy Pants.

What the hell happened between her and Maksim?

I snort at her, biting my tongue, and she rolls the divider glass up.

As we approach the heart of Chicago's south side, the metal bars covering every window and door don't give me any comfort. I'm not worried about my safety. I can handle myself in any situation. But these women don't stand a chance of surviving in this neighborhood if they were to be out of my eyesight. Now, I don't only have to watch Aspen, I have to make sure Hailee is okay as well.

We pull up to the building. There's a line snaking around the corner. I get out of the car, holding in my groan. It's packed, which means my job got even more complicated.

I open the door to hear Hailee say, "At least we have Mr. Russian Badass in case things get dicey."

Neither of you should be here.

Why are you voluntarily choosing to go somewhere that could put you in a bad situation?

I stay quiet and reach in the vehicle to help Aspen out, but she pushes past me. She's been angry all night about me following her. Hailee ignores me as well, and they go to the back of the line.

Good thing I know everyone in this city.

I make a clucking noise to get under Aspen's skin. If she's going to be nasty all night, I'm not going to sit back and take it without a bit of push back. I place my hands on both their backs.

"What are you doing?" Aspen accuses.

"Not standing in the cold. Let's go inside," I direct.

"Do you not notice all the people?" She motions toward the line, which is at least fifty feet long.

"Yep. But I'm a man who makes things happen. Let's go."

"We better not lose our place in line," she grumbles but lets me lead her toward the front.

We pass her friends, Skylar Scott and Kora Kilborn halfway to the bouncer.

And my night just got more interesting.

"Ladies, you come, too," I demand while checking Skylar out. It's not the first time she's looked me over like a hungry wolf. I've only seen her one other time. It was during a lunch Aspen had with her friends. Her long, curled, magenta hair made me notice her. All the women are beautiful, but Skylar has a flair to her. Nothing about her looks ordinary, including her bee-stung lips I want all over my body.

She blinks her long lashes a few times. Her deep-blue eyes meet mine. Her lips twitch, and she confidently eyes me over.

She takes Kora's arm and saunters in front of me, swaying her hips.

"You might want to keep your eyes on our surroundings instead of my friend's ass," Aspen hisses.

I smirk and refocus on Skylar's backside again.

When we get to the front, I high-five the bouncer, then speak Russian. "Pavel, how are you?"

"Good, man. Long time since you've been here."

I grunt. The Cat's Meow isn't my cup of tea. It's one of those places I only go to on an as-needed basis. "Mind letting us skip ahead?"

"Not at all. Nice entourage you have there." He scans the ladies then motions for us to go in. There's a cover charge, so I slap cash down.

"You need to go," Aspen orders.

Trust me. The last place I want to be is here with you tonight. Your friend, on the other hand, I'll give you points for inviting.

"Wasting your breath," I bark out above the music.

She stomps off into the club, and I follow, hoping the women don't decide to split up. Then I can't watch them as closely.

A red glow illuminates the dark bar. Poles, cages, and small stages surround the perimeter. A dance floor is in front of a bigger stage. Private booths, VIP areas, and bars are expertly laid out. Three floors get more exclusive as you go up.

Topless strippers, both male and female, dance in cages and swing on the poles. A new show starts every half hour on the main stage. Shot girls wearing lingerie so skimpy they might as well have nothing on roam through the club. Several of them I know and say hi to, while Skylar sneaks curious glances at me.

The women find a table and Skylar orders shots. She asks me, "You want one?"

Only if I'm licking it off your body.

I let my eyes trail over her, lingering on different parts of her anatomy. She blushes, and I lean into her ear. "Not while on duty." I pull back and study her some more.

"Go away," Aspen orders.

Skylar smiles. "What time would you be getting off?"

I lick my lips. *As soon as you all decide this isn't the place for you to be.*

Come to daddy.

Aspen rises and jabs my chest. "Leave. Now."

"Aspen, cool it," Skylar says.

She angrily accuses, "Are you here for him or me?"

She scrunches her forehead. "You, of course."

"Then he goes, or I do."

I hold my hands in the air. "I'll be against the wall if you need me."

"I won't," Aspen assures me.

Maksim needs to give me a different job after tonight. This is getting old.

I walk away, but I'm only several feet from their table. I still don't know what happened between her and Maksim, but she's obviously taking out some of it on me. If Skylar wasn't here, I might give Aspen a bit more lip.

Aspen orders several rounds of shots, and the four women pound them hard. She motions for a male stripper to come over.

Maksim is going to be pissed when he finds out she's here.

He didn't say to update him.

It's Dmitri's rehearsal dinner.

I debate for several more minutes but decide if he wanted updates, he would have told me or texted me.

More male strippers join the table, which doesn't amuse me. Aspen, Kora, and Skylar stuff dollar bills in their pants while Hailee smiles politely, looking mortified.

How is she even friends with these three?

Typically, I would peg Aspen as more reserved than her actions tonight display. Kora and Skylar are more free-spirited. Hailee reminds me of a goody two-shoes. It's almost as if they are corrupting her in front of my very eyes.

After several lap dances and more drinks, Kora, Aspen, and Hailee move to the dance floor.

Skylar steps in front of me. She's a bit tipsy. The scent of salted caramel and pears mixes with the sweaty bar air.

Jesus, this girl has it going on.

I could smell her all day.

She reaches for my face and drags her finger over my jaw. "Do you always look so serious?"

"Only when I have to watch over four women in a bad part of town and in a seedy establishment."

"Seedy?" she repeats, looking amused.

"What would you call it?"

She purses her lips and leans closer to my face. "Are you a prude?"

I study her facial features, the way her chest rises and falls, then pin my gaze on her eyes until her cheeks turn red. "What do you consider prudish? Nakedness? Sex? Porn? I can guarantee you, printsessa, I have no issues with any of those."

"Is that your way of calling me a snob?"

"What?"

"Printsessa?"

I grunt. "No. What makes you think that?"

"The way you said it. It sounds like the word princess."

"It is. Something wrong with princess?"

She furrows her perfectly plucked eyebrows. "I always get the sense a man is being derogatory when he calls a woman princess."

"Why?"

She shrugs. "I just do."

"Well, I didn't say princess. I said printsessa, which is Russian. And it's anything but derogatory in Russian."

She bites on her plump lips. I resist grabbing her and taking her outside to the car.

I'll show you exactly how not prudish I am.

The truth is, she's crossed my mind a few times since I met her a few days ago. It didn't help my wandering thoughts when Aspen got a text from her asking if I was single. She clarified it was Skylar and not Kora or Hailee, so I told her I was single. Kora and Hailee are nice, but I don't have a problem getting a date or laid. Hailee isn't a woman I think would be able to handle the things I'm involved in, not that I tell my women anything personal regarding my criminal activities. I'm sure Kora would be a good time, but I'd probably spend most of my time arguing with her. Her strong personality and mine wouldn't last more than a few fun nights.

Skylar seems like the perfect mix of fun, able to stand up for herself but not as apt to butt heads as I assume Kora might be. Plus, she's smoking hot in an eclectic way, right down to her earrings.

She suspiciously assesses me. "Do you call all women printsessa?"

"Did you hear me call your friends it?"

"No."

"There's your answer."

Her lips twitch, torturing me. She's got the most amazing pair I've ever seen. All I've thought about since meeting her are those naughty lips.

I spin her so her body is flush against mine, put one arm on her waist, and my other arm flat across her shoulders. She inhales sharply. I brush my cheek against hers and nod toward one of the strippers. "See that guy you got a lap dance from?"

She turns her head slightly. Her lips are so close to mine, I can taste her breath. She teases, "Were you jealous?"

"No. I'm confident enough about my dick and my abilities."

Her face heats with a blush and she glances at my mouth. I cup her jaw and turn her back toward the stripper. "He was in jail for armed robbery. See that stripper." I motion to a woman wearing nothing but a thong.

"Yeah."

"She got caught hooking six months ago."

I turn her chin to the corner of the room. "See the guy in the hat?"

"Yeah."

"He'll sell you whatever drug you want."

"How do you know all these things?"

"That's the wrong question to ask."

Amusement passes in her face. "What's the right one?"

"Why am I telling you this?"

She smiles. "Okay. I'll bite. Why are you telling me this?"

I rub my thumb over her lips, unable to hold myself back. She closes her eyes briefly. I position her mouth right next to mine, and her hot breath tempts me further. "I don't think this is the type of place for you, my printsessa. You're here for fun, but you should be careful where you look to amuse yourself."

She reaches up and pats my cheek. "Appreciate the concern, but we can handle this place."

I'm not happy she isn't heeding my warning. The other women come over. I release her and step back.

"Are you allowed to grope my friends when you're harassing me?" Aspen slurs. She glares at me, hands Skylar another shot, and downs hers.

"Might want to slow down on those," I advise.

"Whatever, Dad." She turns, grabs another four from a server's tray, and passes them out.

"Aspen," Hailee quietly says.

"What?"

"Maybe we should—"

"Don't, Hailee!" She clinks the tubes with Kora and Skylar, and they down them. When Hailee doesn't drink hers, she grabs it out of her hand and takes it.

"Aspen!"

She puts her arm around Hailee's shoulders. "Come on, Hailee. Let's go dance and shake your amazing little booty."

"Yes! Shake your ass and show us what you got, Hailee!" Skylar eggs her on.

"Twerk! That's what we need to do. Let's all go see if Hailee can twerk!" Kora adds.

"What? No!" Hailee's face turns the color of a beet.

They pull her out to the dance floor, continue to take more shots, and a combination of bar guests and strippers join them on the floor.

I need to get them out of here. Being in the Cat's Meow is dangerous enough. Downing shot after shot is a recipe for disaster.

My phone vibrates.

Maksim: *Is she at her apartment?*

Me: *No. She went to her friend's, and they went out.*

Maksim: *Which friend?*

Me: *The blonde. But now, all four of them are together.*

Maksim: *Where?*

Me: *Cat's Meow. They aren't in the best shape, either.*

The phone rings, and I send it to voicemail.

Me: *Too loud to talk.*

Maksim: *What did you mean?*

Me: *They're pretty hammered. I think I'm going to need some back up to get the four of them out of this place. Aspen is pissed I'm here, and the more she drinks, the more I can't do anything right. I'm pretty sure if I have to drag her out of here, it's going to get super ugly.*

Maksim: *Don't leave. I'm on my way.*

I look back at the dance floor. The four women are suddenly in different parts of the bar. I try to keep my eyes on all of them, but it's too hard. I reprimand myself for spending most of my time watching Skylar and attempt to keep cool over the drunk college student trying to get in her pants.

Suddenly, I can't find Aspen or Hailee. I scour the bar looking for them, but they are nowhere. When I focus back on the dance floor, Skylar and Kora are gone as well.

Panic sinks its claws into me and grows. When I look up and see all four women on the third floor, I avoid the elevator and run up the stairs. I use the VIP card to get past security. I always have it on me for the times I have to do business here.

When I get outside the suite, they are walking in. My stomach flips. Wes Petrov and his thugs each have a woman on their arm and are maneuvering them in. Aspen and her friends all look like the alcohol has hit them. I yell for them not to go in, but the music is loud. They don't hear me, or maybe they just aren't listening.

Filled with rage and worry, I pace until Maksim, Sergey, and Bogden arrive. Maksim barks, "How could you let this happen?"

"There are four Petrov thugs, plus a bodyguard and four women. I'm not Superman. I do have some limits," I seethe, pissed off his woman is causing me to be anywhere near a Petrov and boiling that Skylar's in there.

Sergey snorts. "You should have called for backup."

"It just happened. They've only been in there for two minutes."

Maksim steps closer to my face. "How did you let my woman get near a Petrov?"

"Your woman? She seems to think she's not," I point out.

Sergey steps between us. "This isn't the time for this conversation."

Maksim seems to realize Sergey is right. "Take the bodyguard, Adrian. Bogden, get your gun."

I release a big breath and open the door to the VIP room. As soon as I step in, I headlock Wes's bodyguard in one swift move.

The next few minutes are an intense exchange of threats, with knives and guns pulled. I try to contain the fury I'm feeling from everything regarding this situation. Watching Skylar sit on a Petrov thug's lap with his grimy hands all over her only adds to my anger.

Somehow, we get all four women out of the room until only Sergey and I remain. We each have a gun aimed at the Petrovs. I still have their bodyguard in a headlock.

Wes smirks. "I still think about Natalia. No one's ever sucked my cock as good as her."

Sergey steps closer to me and puts his arm on my biceps to stop me from flying at Wes. "Let's go."

"Ah. It's the boy who is branded with the devil but doesn't want to claim him," Wes taunts.

Sergey sniffs hard. "Your day is coming."

Wes laughs. "Is that a threat from an Ivanov?"

"Let's go," I tell Sergey. I push the bodyguard away from me, and Sergey and I keep our guns aimed in front of us. We leave the club as quickly as possible. Maksim and Aspen take off, and we get in the back with Kora, Hailee, and Skylar.

The alcohol seems to be in full effect. Kora is hitting on Sergey, but all I can concentrate on is Skylar. She's got her hands all over my body and even changes positions, so she's straddling me.

She was on a Petrov's lap.

She went into the room of her own free will.

She leans into my ear and whispers, "I think you should show me what you got, Mr. Bend Me Over."

Jesus.

Before I know it, she has half the buttons on my shirt undone. Her hands slide over my chest, and I grab her wrists. She's drunk, so I wouldn't have done anything with her tonight, but the fact she went into a Petrov suite and let one of them touch her ruins any possibility of us being together.

"Don't," I warn her.

She giggles and strokes my dick.

"Stop touching my cock," I tell her and hold her wrists again.

She kisses my neck and starts circling her hips on my hard erection.

For crying out loud.

When the car stops, I've never been so happy to drop a woman off. She stumbles out of the vehicle even though I help her out of it. I consider carrying her, but she straightens up, and we make it into her apartment.

How many shots did they each have?

I'm worried about her falling and hitting her head, so I take her to her bedroom. I put her on the bed, and she spins on her knees and throws her arms around my neck.

My heart beats faster. I wish I could turn off my attraction toward her, but there's something about her pulling me in.

"I thought you were going to kiss me earlier," she admits.

"When?"

"At the club."

"Before or after you decided to sit on a Petrov's lap?" I seethe.

A line creases between her eyebrows. "I didn't want to. He pulled me in and wouldn't let me go."

"Sure."

She tugs my head toward her. "Let's forget about it."

Her mouth brushes against mine. I put my fingers between our lips. "You lost your chance. I'll never be second to a Petrov."

"Adrian, I didn't—"

"You made your choice loud and clear. Have a nice life, Skylar." I step out of her grasp.

"Adrian!"

I ignore her attempts to convince me it was an innocent mistake. I hit the lock on her door and leave.

No matter how much I want her, it'll never be. She thought it would be fun to get attention from a Petrov.

If Aspen and her friends only knew what Petrovs do to women.

Wes's words about my sister Natalia burn me further. Her face plagues me. She was only sixteen when they took her. When I get in the car, I grab Sergey's bowl from him and take a hit. I don't usually smoke weed, but I need something to calm the rage I feel.

The Petrovs are the scum of the earth. Our Natalia is dead because of them. Zamir kidnapped her and gave her to Wes as a gift. She spent her last year of life in his whorehouse. They brutally defiled her, and we didn't know where she was until she passed. The Petrovs threw her body on our doorstep with a videotape of what they had done to her.

Hailee blurts out, "Sorry. Skylar drank a lot."

"I know. I was there," I bark.

"Easy," Sergey reprimands.

I sigh. "Sorry, Hailee."

I take another hit, trying to drown out the thoughts of Natalia and Skylar, with Petrov hands all over them, but nothing is strong enough to kill my ghosts.

One thing is sure. I was wrong about Skylar. I need to stay far away from her.

2

Skylar

Aspen, Kora, and Hailee are at my place. We're going to watch Boris fight and are having drinks first. Aspen just said Adrian's outside my front door.

Heat rises to my face. I pace the room. "Why didn't you tell me he's here?"

"What part of my bodyguard memo did you miss?" Aspen asks.

"So anytime we're with you, he's going to be by your side?"

"Unless Maksim is with me, then he might or might not be. Why does it matter?"

I walk to the door then come back. "It doesn't."

"You're such a bullshitter," Kora says.

"Why are you freaking out right now?" Hailee asks.

"I'm not." *I totally am.*

My friends all give me confused looks.

"I'll be right back." I panic and go into the bedroom. I don't know why I didn't expect to see Adrian. I cringe, thinking of the last time I saw him and how drunk I was.

He kept telling me to stop touching his cock.

I unbuttoned his shirt.

You lost your chance. I'll never be second to a Petrov. His voice and the loathing in his eyes have been on replay over the last week since I saw him. It's all I think about, and I can't seem to get past it. I didn't even want to be in the VIP room and definitely not on the lap of the thug who stuck his hand up my shirt when I tried to get off his lap.

I put my hands over my face. I'm not prepared to see Adrian yet. *Will I ever be?*

I ruined everything.

Why did I have to drink all those shots?

Aspen puts her hand on my shoulder. "Hey, you okay? I heard what happened."

"This is so embarrassing," I admit into my hands.

"Did you think you wouldn't see him again?" Kora asks.

I spin. "No. But I didn't expect to see him tonight. And I didn't want to go into the VIP room. You three convinced me and pulled me away from my conversation with him." I point to them, remembering how Adrian had me wrapped up in his body, trying to warn me about the dangers of the Cat's Meow. I thought he was going to kiss me.

"The night's still really fuzzy for me. I'm sorry," Aspen offers.

I shake my head. Nervous butterflies flutter quickly inside me. "It doesn't matter. I'm going to have to deal with it." I go to the mirror, smooth down my hair, then turn. "Do I look okay?"

"Yes. You look smoking hot, like you always do."

"Agreed," Kora says.

"Eat your heart out, Adrian!" Hailee chirps.

Aspen's phone rings. "It's Maksim." She hits the button. "Hi!"

She has a quick conversation with him and hangs up. "Maksim is in the lobby."

I attempt my bravest face. "I might as well face the music."

Aspen hugs me. "We were all drinking. I'm sure it wasn't as bad as you think."

"Mmmm...no, it was," Hailee says.

I groan, walking out of the bedroom. No doubt Hailee wasn't as intoxicated as the rest of us. She has a bigger brain, apparently, and can think while she drinks. I make a mental note to add "just say no" to my drinking phrases.

I take a deep breath, smile, and open the door. "Hi, Adrian."

There's a slight pause, and his eyes drift down my body and back to my eyes. My body buzzes, and heat flies to my face, but then his expression hardens. His icy-blue eyes get colder. In a deadpan voice, he says, "Skylar."

He hates me. My gut drops, but I raise my chin and step past him.

"Ladies. Are you going to behave tonight?" Adrian says.

"Yes, Dad," Kora jokes.

"Sorry about the other night," Hailee starts.

Adrian puts up his hand. "Let's not. Are you ready?"

"Jeez, Adrian. Way to forgive and forget," Aspen mutters.

He scowls. "You don't forget incidents with Petrovs. You should know that if you're going to be involved with someone in my family."

What does that mean exactly? What do the Ivanovs have to do with the Petrovs? I researched the Petrovs, and they are mob. It's not the first time I wondered this past week why there is bad blood between the two families.

Aspen straightens. "Point taken. Let's go."

He escorts us down the hall, staying by Aspen's side. We get in the elevator, and he gets in last and stands in front of the door.

I stare at the sleeve of tattoos on his arm until Kora drags her finger in the air from the top of his shoulders down to his ass. "Solid," she mouths.

My mind can only imagine what Adrian's ass looks like naked. I may have been drunk, but I was in awe of his ridiculously ripped torso when I tried to remove his shirt in the car. I cringe again, thinking about my drunk actions. My face heats with embarrassment.

Aspen slaps Kora's upper arm.

"Ouch," she blurts.

Adrian turns and raises his eyebrows.

"Sorry, neck cramp," Kora says.

He gives them a piercing glare, avoids me, then faces the door again as it opens.

He hates me.

I try to slow my rapidly beating heart, but every time I breathe deep, I inhale his sexy smell of peach blossom, Turkish rose, and amber. By the time we get to Maksim's car, my body is throbbing, and I can't think straight. I'm relieved when Adrian sits in the front and the divider window is up.

I barely hear the conversation on the way to the gym. When we get there, Maksim gives us strict instructions not to step out of the vehicle or building at any time without him or one of his guys. I glance out the window and, for the first time, notice the boarded-up windows and doors. It's rougher than the neighborhood where the Cat's Meow is located.

Adrian, Bogden, and Maksim form a wall around us and escort us quickly inside. The gym is an open space full of different kinds of punching and kicking bags. A ring sits in the middle with a black-and-white rope surrounding it. The dark mat in the ring has something written in Russian on it. Foreign words echo throughout the gym. I assume it's

Russian and Polish since Boris's opponent tonight is from Poland.

"What does that say?" I point to the ring.

"No past, no future," Adrian replies.

I look at him and quietly ask, "What does it mean?"

His eyes roam over my body again, as if I'm his prey and he hasn't eaten in days. When he pins his gaze on mine, his face hardens again.

He hates me.

Dmitri answers my question, and Adrian leaves. The conversation evolves when Anna and Nora join us, but I barely hear it. I see Adrian giving me a look of death through the office window.

He's never going to forgive me for going into a room I didn't want to go into. Never mind the fact I got fondled by a thug whose lap I didn't even want to sit on. I may have drank too much, but I remember trying to resist it all.

My embarrassment turns to anger.

Anna's voice cuts me out of my trance. "Was this the night of my rehearsal dinner? At the Cat's Meow?"

Aspen's face heats up. "Yes."

"We didn't know who they were," Hailee blurts out.

I can only imagine how scared Hailee was. She wasn't as drunk as the rest of us. I remember her trying to leave the room, but the thug picked her up and sat her on his lap.

"I didn't want to go into the room. They made me." My statement comes out as a joke, but I'm pissed about being looked down upon when I got manhandled.

Anna and Nora exchange a glance. I can't tell if they feel sorry for us or are upset.

Nora studies Aspen. "Why were you in a VIP room with a Petrov, or any man, if you're with Maksim?"

"Nora—"

"It's a fair question, Anna."

Anna sighs then gives Aspen a sympathetic look.

Oh no! These two bitches aren't going to guilt-trip Aspen or any of us.

I put my hand on my hip. "Before you judge Aspen, you should get your facts straight. Maksim dumped her."

"Skylar!" Aspen reprimands, and her face turns red.

Screw this. Someone needs to set the record straight. Maksim is the reason the entire night happened.

"No. They don't have a right to judge you. He broke up with you and went to the rehearsal dinner without you. We took Aspen out. And yes, we went to the Cat's Meow. Aspen didn't ask to go, but we weren't going to let her sit home and sulk. And we drank a lot. Way too much, okay? We all did stupid shit we regret. But we didn't know they were Petrovs or even what that meant. And none of us did anything with those men besides get manhandled on their laps, which wasn't fun, by the way," I seethe.

"Shh. Keep your voice down," Nora orders and gazes over her shoulder.

"Why? Is the Petrov name a secret around here?" I practically yell, pissed off about this entire conversation.

"She said to keep your voice down," Adrian growls.

I freeze then angrily spin. I point in Adrian's face. "You don't get to tell me what to do."

His arrogant scowl only makes me more upset. He orders, "Don't make a scene."

"Leave me alone, Adrian. You've made it clear what you think of me, so keep your opinion to yourself." I turn back to the women.

Adrian grabs my arm, spins me back to him, and in a low voice, says, "I need to talk to you."

My heart hammers harder.

"Let her go, Adrian," Aspen demands.

He snorts. "I'm off the clock. Stay out of it, Aspen." He maneuvers me several feet away into one of the offices and shuts the door. He pulls the shade down and spins on me. Blue fire burns in his eyes. "Let's get something straight since you don't seem to understand."

I glare and snottily reply, "What's that?"

"The Petrovs are dirt. Scum of the earth, and not to be mentioned in any Ivanov facility or around any of us."

I don't disagree with his theory on the Petrovs, but I yell out, "Why? What's the deal between your families?"

He steps closer. His scent overpowers me. "None of your business."

"Really? Since you're the one bringing it up, it seems like you want to talk about it."

His eyes widen. "I wasn't the one shouting their name in an Ivanov building."

"I'm tired of defending myself against a bunch of goons who held me against my will and shoved their hands up my shirt. I'm over this conversation." I step toward the door, and Adrian slams both his palms over my head.

I jump and spin. "Adrian, what the—"

"We're not done."

"Why? So you can run your mouth and make all your claims about the Petrovs?"

His face comes within an inch from mine. "Run my mouth?"

My eyes dart between his lush lips and steel-blue eyes swirling with fire and ice. He's a beautiful mix of anger and something I can't put my finger on. It becomes harder to breathe.

"Is there something you want to do with my mouth, printsessa?" He comes closer, tempting me, arching an eyebrow, as if in a challenge. "Hmm?"

Now I'm his printsessa again?

No. He didn't say my *printsessa, only printsessa.*

I attempt to speak, but nothing comes out. Blood pounds between my ears, and my insides quiver. I make the mistake of glancing at his mouth again.

He licks my lips, tasting them, before sliding his tongue against mine, moving it in and out with skilled speed and pressure. Then he stops and pins his sexy, emotion-filled eyes on me.

I'm still catching my breath when he flicks his tongue back in my mouth. He presses his hard flesh against mine. I reach for his neck, and he retreats, assesses me again, then resumes owning my mouth until my knees buckle and the only things holding me up are the door and his body.

Something about the way he keeps pushing his tongue in and out of my mouth then looking at me is dirty hot. It's as if he knows what he's doing to me. I'm not sure what to make of his expression. There's determination along with the disgust I saw earlier, but I don't have time to decipher any of it.

He spins me and splays his hand on my neck, forcing me over the desk. His hard body covers mine, and he says in my ear, "I think you need to learn the difference between a Petrov and Ivanov."

My voice cracks. "You don't listen."

Hot breath penetrates my skin.

His hands unfasten my pants as he speaks. "You wanted to be bent over. I'll show you what it's like when an Ivanov bends you over." He moves my hair to the side then presses his lips to the back of my neck.

Yes, please!

What the hell is wrong with me? He's being a dick.

Why does he feel so good?

Taking advantage of my backless shirt, he takes the flat part of the backside of his tongue and licks the length of my spine. Zings trail everywhere his tongue touches.

"Holy shit," I pant.

There's a loud clang on the floor. His palm splays on my back, and his mouth consumes my sex, just like how he did when he kissed me.

I squirm, pushing my lower body closer to him. Heat floods me, and he shoves his entire tongue in me, then sucks while continuing to flick. I grip the sides of the desk. "Adrian!"

Right before I come, he slides his tongue back up my spine. A condom wrapper lands on the floor to the right of the desk. He thrusts his cock in me.

"Oh God!" I cry out.

"You're coming with an Ivanov in you." His hand strums my marbled clit, he spouts off some Russian, then growls in English, "Look at me."

I turn my head.

Vicious words mix with savage kisses. "When you fuck a Petrov, remember what an Ivanov dick feels like."

"Wh—"

His mouth resumes diligently merging and unmerging with me at the same pace he's thrusting into my body. The circling of his hand matches, and every part of my body is in sync with his.

"I think you like Ivanov cock, don't you?" He refocuses on me.

Abhorrence fills me from his nasty comments. I can barely keep my eyes open. I've never felt so full of any man. Maybe he'll split me in two, but he's got my body sitting on the edge of a cliff, waiting to fall.

"Answer me," he barks.

"Yes," I pant.

He assaults my mouth again and thrusts harder and faster while increasing the speed of his fingers. Aggressive Russian gets added to his penetrating stare.

Sweat breaks out on my skin. My face burns, and I wish I could stop this. I wish I could tell him to get off me and shut up.

But I can't. Every part of me is putty in his hands. If it weren't for his cruel words and disgusted expressions, he would be perfect.

He's a sex god on steroids.

He's a dick.

At least he knows how to use it.

He—

"Oh God!" I scream as the most intense orgasm I've ever had rips through me.

He releases in me, growling out more Russian and the word printsessa, and dropping his head into the curve of my neck.

We don't move, breathing hard. For a split second, I forget about all the mean things he said. Then it all comes flooding back with his next statement.

He keeps his hand splayed on my back, reaches down, and pulls his pants up. When he removes his hand, I slowly turn over and drag my pants up. He holds my chin and leans down into my face. I think he's going to kiss me, but a new sense of loathing fills his eyes. "When you see a Petrov next, remember I was first."

Too shocked to respond, I watch him as he storms out of the office.

3

Adrian

SHE'S MAKING ME CRAZY.

How could she have associated with a Petrov?

Images of her on the thug's lap never seem to go away. All week, it haunts me. Then she brings their name into the gym—an Ivanov building.

The thought of her with any Petrov enrages me. I hate I'm still attracted to her. I'd give anything to go back and not do what I just did with her. Now I know what she tastes like and how she responds to me. It takes the notion of what I assumed she's like and blows it up. She's so much better than I expected.

Those goddamn lips.

She thinks it's okay to play with Petrovs.

VICIOUS PROTECTOR

I go into the bathroom and clean up. Maksim walks in. Things are still a bit off between us after the Cat's Meow debacle.

"You should tell your girlfriend to make sure her friends don't bring up Petrovs in our company."

Maksim's eyes turn to slits. "What are you referring to?"

"Ask your woman who sat on a Petrov lap."

Maksim reaches for my neck, and I reach for his.

"What the hell?" Obrecht yells when he steps inside and breaks us up.

"You better watch your mouth, Adrian," Maksim snarls.

"Petrovs," I seethe.

"We've gone over this. Aspen nor her friends knew who the Petrovs were. Stop blaming them. It was my fault Aspen was there. She didn't know," Maksim insists.

"That's funny. I don't recall you telling me to take them to the Cat's Meow and get so wasted they could hardly stand," I bite back.

Maksim angrily shakes his head. "Grow up, Adrian. It happened. It's over."

"This is only starting. Nothing is ever over with the Petrovs," I remind him.

He turns to Obrecht. "Talk some sense into your brother before he lets his anger get the best of him and he does something stupid." Maksim stomps out of the bathroom.

"What the hell is up your ass?" Obrecht asks.

"It's the Petrovs," I hiss. "Aspen and her friends were in a Petrov VIP room. On their laps."

Obrecht goes to the urinal and pees. He says, "Do you honestly think any of those women would knowingly get involved with a Petrov?"

"What if they are?"

He cocks his eyebrows. "What if they aren't?"

I shouldn't say it. It's below the belt, but I blurt out, "I think you, of all people, understand how the power of *what if* can destroy your life."

Obrecht's shoulders tighten. He finishes peeing, zips his pants, then turns. Scowling, he goes to the sink and washes his hands. "Since I'm in a good mood, let me teach you a lesson instead of slicing your tongue out of your mouth."

I snort. I would deserve it, bringing up Annika. She's the only woman he has ever loved. Obrecht may still love her for all I know. He wanted to marry her but found out the Petrovs planted her to spy on him and screw with his mind.

He turns the water off then pulls towels out of the machine. "When you let the past dictate the future, you let them win. You end up hurting people around you instead of the people who should receive your wrath." He tosses the towels and steps in front of me. "Those women out there don't know anything about our world or the Petrovs. So before you ignite a war with Maksim, try to remember Aspen's his woman. He's happy. I've never really seen him happy before. She's not the enemy, nor are her friends."

"You don't know if they are connected to the Petrovs or not."

Obrecht sniffs hard. "Of course I do. What do you think I did on Sunday, after Dmitri and Anna's wedding, when I found out what happened?"

Crap. I should have known. I stare at my reflection in the mirror, avoiding Obrecht's piercing blue eyes and clenching my jaw.

He holds my chin and turns my head toward him. "That's right, little brother. I researched every one of those women. Do you know the blonde is a kindergarten teacher in the ghetto? She's had numerous awards but refuses to take a position in a better district so she can keep helping kids who need her most?"

"Hailee's the innocent one," I mutter.

Obrecht tilts his head. "I've done my homework. I bet before the Cat's Meow they never heard the name Petrov. So why don't you take a breather and think about what a Petrov does to women."

"Don't ever act like I need a reminder," I seethe, anger bubbling again. The visual of Natalia's dead body fills my mind.

"You do. My guess is Aspen and her friends weren't in control in that room. And you know how the Petrovs take what they want."

Rage swirls so fast, my gut flips.

"Put yourself in their shoes before you do or say something you can't take back. And stop riling up Maksim. We're Ivanovs and on the same side." Obrecht pats me on the back and leaves.

I suddenly despise the reflection of the man staring back at me. Dread replaces my anger, and the color drains from my cheeks. Obrecht doesn't make mistakes. Since Annika betrayed him, he became the best tracker we have. He doesn't skip steps and wouldn't be confident if he had any doubts. Everything I just did, trying to prove a point to Skylar that I'm an Ivanov and not a piece of shit Petrov, makes my stomach curl.

What was I thinking?

She's going to hate me.

I hate me right now.

I leave the bathroom and go into the office instead of near the ring. The first round starts. I watch Aspen and her friends. Skylar doesn't have her normal glowing expression. She looks like she's going through the motions.

I'm such an asshole.

I debate about how to apologize and spend the entire match in the office, staring at her through the glass. When the fight ends, I attempt to approach her, but she steps between Aspen and Maksim and strikes up a conversation with him. As soon as it's time to go, I attempt to escort the women out of the gym with Maksim.

He turns and glares. "You're off the clock. My brothers and I will handle this."

Shit. He's still pissed.

I would be, too.

Skylar turns and practically runs down the stairs. I debate about following her, but it doesn't seem to be a good choice.

I go home, beat myself up all night, and decide I'll go to her apartment and apologize in the morning.

I don't sleep. The awful words I said to her play on repeat until the day's first light peeks through the window.

When I get to Skylar's building, she's jumping in a cab. I follow her to her office. She gets out, and I call after her.

"Skylar!"

She spins, furrowing her eyebrows. She realizes it's me and snaps, "What do you want, Adrian?"

I step toward her, and she retreats, so I stop. "I wanted to talk to you about last night. I—"

"I don't have time for your games." She takes several steps toward the entrance, and I reach for her biceps.

"Don't touch me!"

"Skylar—"

She pushes her magenta hair behind her ear. "I'm at work. Can you save whatever fucked-up speech you're going to give me when my boss isn't standing twenty feet away from me?"

I glance toward the building, and a man is scowling inside the lobby. He crosses his arms and appears to be waiting for Skylar.

"Tonight? Let me take you to dinner—"

She laughs. Her eyes glisten. "What is wrong with you? Jesus. Leave me alone. I'm not your toy." She turns and hurries inside.

"Fuck!" I cry out and go back to my car.

Not a minute passes when I don't think about what I did to hurt Skylar.

Why did it have to be while we were having sex?

What kind of monster am I?

Why do I still let the Petrovs get under my skin so much I can't think straight?

Nothing I contemplate seems to be a good idea to show Skylar how sorry I am. How does one make up for something like what I did?

No answer appears. Toward the end of the workday, I get a text.

Dmitri: *Meet us at the hospital. Aspen got bit by a poisonous snake.*

Me: *Is she okay?*

Dmitri: *Not sure what's going on right now. We just got here, and we aren't allowed back. She was unconscious when she arrived.*

I spend the quick car ride wondering how she managed to get bit by a poisonous snake in Chicago. When I get to the hospital, I learn Wes Petrov sent it to her. My hatred for the Petrovs sharpens once more.

Obrecht shakes his head. He mumbles, "You still think she and her friends are on his payroll?"

"I messed up. Last night, before I saw you in the bathroom," I blurt out, needing to talk to someone about my problem.

Obrecht's eyes turn to slits. "What did you do?"

"Something to Skylar."

"Like what?" he growls.

"I can't even say it. I got crazy with Petrov thoughts, and my mind wouldn't stop spinning."

He moves to the corner of the room. "You know you aren't supposed to be around people when you spiral."

I check no one is around us. "I was too far in. I didn't realize I was until it was over."

His face hardens. "Whatever you did, you better make it right. She's Aspen's friend. Maksim isn't letting Aspen go. She's here for the long term, which means her friends are going to be around. The last thing we need is any of Aspen's friends pissed off."

"I know. I'm not sure how to make it right."

"Get on your knees and grovel if you have to. Figure it out," Obrecht barks and joins Dmitri in his conversation.

The doctor comes into the waiting area and gives us an update. We slowly filter into Aspen's room. So far, Kora is here, but I haven't seen Hailee or Skylar.

Another doctor enters, and we all leave while he examines Aspen. Maksim finally comes out and tells us the update and to go home.

I walk down the hall, determined to go to Skylar's and tell her I'm sorry, when I see her, Sergey, Kora, and Hailee.

"How did—" Skylar sees me, and her cheeks heat. "I need to go to the restroom." She quickly turns and walks down the hall.

Great.

"Ladies. Aspen is passed out again. They expect her to sleep a long time because of her pain meds," I relay.

"What did the doctor say?" Hailee asks.

"The doctor said it was shallow and doesn't think she'll have any long-term issues. It's going to take a few weeks, possibly months, for her to be back to normal, or to know for sure," Sergey replies.

"Months!" Hailee shrieks.

I wince. "Easy there, killer. I'd like to keep my hearing."

"Sorry," Hailee mumbles.

I crack my neck. "Dmitri and Anna are staying with Maksim. He said to have the rest of us leave."

"I'll go get Skylar and tell her," Kora volunteers.

I walk past her. "No. I'll relay the message." I take long strides and am soon outside the women's restroom. I wait, hoping she didn't leave already.

Skylar steps out. Her eyes widen, and she turns and goes back inside.

I follow her.

"Adrian, leave me—"

I step forward, and she retreats until she's against the wall. Nothing I've done gives me a right to touch her, but I slide my hands over her cheeks.

She inhales sharply. Her bee-stung lips tremble. Anger and hurt morph into her eyes.

"I'm sorry, my printsessa."

She scoffs. "Now I'm your printsessa?"

I cringe. "I was an asshole to you. I'm sorry. The Petrovs—"

"Don't give you the right to treat me like a cheap whore."

I squeeze my eyes shut, loathing myself and what I did.

"Let me go, Adrian," she quietly says.

I step closer. "That wasn't my intention."

"No? What was?" She tilts her head, and tears fill her eyes.

"I was going crazy thinking of you with that thug."

"The one who wouldn't let me go and stuck his hand up my shirt?" she angrily says, blinking away a tear.

What did he do?

My chest tightens. I take my thumb and wipe at her tear. "What are you talking about, my printsessa?"

Her lip quivers harder. "Did you not hear a word I said last night?"

The thumping of my heart pounds into my chest cavity. I admit, "No. I'm sorry. I get in these...it doesn't matter. I'm an ass. The thug who did that to you, he will pay."

"You get in what?"

I focus on the white subway tile above her head. How do I even explain it?

She pushes my chest. "Take your silent self and—"

"They kidnapped, raped for over a year, and then killed my sister. I don't deal with Petrovs very well. I kept seeing you on that thug's lap, and it drove me crazy until I was spinning out and couldn't stop it," I blurt out.

She freezes.

Shit. Why did I just tell her that?

I step back. I take a big breath and release it. "I'm sorry, Skylar. You deserved better than what I did to you last night." I walk out of the bathroom and leave, wondering how I could have let the Petrovs get to me and screw up my chances with her. She's the only woman I've been interested in for a long time. I ruined us before we even started. The Petrovs once again destroyed my life, but this time, I let them.

4

Skylar

ADRIAN LEAVES ME STUNNED, WITH MY GUT TWISTING. AFTER our encounter last night, I went home and replayed it over and over, wondering if I missed something. Nothing made sense. Why would he treat me like that? Yes, he hates the Petrovs, but I told him I was held down and groped. He didn't seem to hear or care.

He hate fucked me.

Besides his nasty words, which echoed in my mind all night, I kept feeling his body all over mine. The way he took over and knew exactly how to touch me, left me wanting more. His kisses were the most animalistic experience of my life. He used his tongue as a weapon. Every touch proved he's a sinfully delicious, not afraid to be filthy, cocky stud who rarely exists.

He made me detest myself. All I want is more from him, and I shouldn't after what he said. I convinced myself I need to stay away from him. I'm not going to allow him to berate me. What he did was borderline abusive. My ex-fiancé from college was an expert at verbally ripping me to shreds. It took years of counseling to get to the place where I'm now at.

I know better.

During my morning workout, and while I got ready for work, I did my mental exercises my counselor taught me. I reinforced the things I love about myself and made a commitment to stay away from him. Adrian may be Aspen's bodyguard, but I won't be his punching bag or play toy to destroy. From here on out, he's just another guy for me to ignore when I have to be around him.

Seeing Adrian this morning tortured me. His apology brought up memories of my ex trying to convince me he won't ever bash me again. The biggest problem is my ex is nothing like Adrian. He wasn't nearly as sexy or cocky. His scent didn't intoxicate me. There was nothing in the bedroom my ex did to create the buzz in my veins that happens when Adrian just stands next to me.

They kidnapped, raped, and killed his sister.

He was spinning out. What does that mean exactly? Will he spin out again and take it out on me?

"Adrian," I call after him then step outside the bathroom. "Adrian!"

He freezes, takes a deep breath, and turns. Years of pain and regret swirl in his beautiful eyes. His chiseled features appear even sharper. Everything about him screams he's a breathtaking package of agony right now.

My heart bleeds for him. The memories of what he said to me last night disappear. However, I approach him cautiously. Something is telling me he's fragile. It's the opposite of everything he shows to the world, but I feel it. With every step I take, notes of peach blossom, Turkish rose, and amber get more robust. I attempt to calm my insides while figuring out what to say.

"I'm—" I stop. Is *I'm sorry for your loss* even adequate for this tragedy? How many times has he heard it? Words seem like a cop-out of some sort. Can anything comfort or bring peace to the situation? I highly doubt it. I'm not sure when this happened, but the pain seems fresh, and I'm not so naive to know that time doesn't heal all wounds.

He pins his steely gaze on me, waiting for me to say something, but I can't form a coherent sentence.

An entourage of medical professionals comes down the hall. Adrian reaches for me and protectively guides me closer to the wall. My flutters take off. I try to refocus on whatever it is I should say.

The crowd passes, and I glance up. I don't analyze it and reach for his cheek. "I'm trying to figure out the right words..."

His jaw clenches under my palm. "There aren't any. Last night is my fault. I—"

"I meant about your sister."

His head tilts up. His eyes dart to the wall above my head. In a deadpan voice, he claims, "It happened a long time ago."

"Adrian, what did you mean when you said you were spinning out?"

He grinds his molars then sniffs hard. "It doesn't matter."

"It does to me."

He slowly drills his tormented orbs back on mine. "I obsess about things until I feel like my skin is crawling. Then I take action, and it usually has me apologizing to someone after. My brother, Obrecht, made me realize I need to stay away from others when it consumes me." He briefly closes his eyes. "Sometimes, I'm too far in, like last night. All I saw was you on that thug's lap and his grimy hands on you. I couldn't handle it. A voice in my head said you knew the Petrovs before the Cat's Meow. It dug its claws into me."

"I didn't! I swear! Call me naive, but I never even heard of the Petrovs. I didn't want to be in there, and I tried to get away. I swear."

His expression darkens. "He will pay, my printsessa. He will never come near you or touch you again."

A chill runs down my spine. "What are you going to do?"

He stays quiet, scowling, making the anxiety in my chest grow thicker. I don't have any love for the Petrovs, but I don't want Adrian doing something stupid so he ends up behind bars, hurt, or killed.

"Let it go, Adrian. He's not worth it."

"Let it go?" he growls. "He put his dirty Petrov hands on you against your will. I won't sweep it under the rug. He'll get his moment of reckoning with me."

There's so much hatred in Adrian. I don't blame him. If someone bestowed the evil on my sister that the Petrovs did, I'm not sure how I would cope. Adrian only told me the quick facts. I don't even know the entire story. I assume the other details are gruesome and only drive his disdain for the Petrovs deeper. His voice is so sure, there's no room to argue with him. Anything I say to try and change his mind is a waste of my breath. I barely know anything about Adrian. The Cat's Meow incident, along with his job as Aspen's bodyguard, leaves no doubt he's a violent man at times. From the start, I should have shied away from him, but his magnetism wouldn't allow me. Every bone in my body has wanted him since I met him. After everything that happened, I still can't turn my attraction for him off.

Maybe I should give him another chance?

He verbally assaulted me. I can't fall back into old relationship patterns.

He's not Tim.

No. He's more dangerous than Tim could ever be. He'll swallow me whole, and I'll never come out.

His hatred turns to regret. "I'm sorry again about what I did to you. We should go. The others are waiting in the lobby." He doesn't give me time to reply and puts his hand on my back then guides me through the hospital.

I spend the time debating about what to say to Adrian. Do I want to give him a pass for what he did? Should I stick to what my counselor would have told me, which would be to run as far away from Adrian as possible? Can I ever be with him and not remember what he did the first time we were ever together?

Sergey, Kora, and Hailee sit on couches by the front doors. They rise, and Sergey says, "Kora and I have a dinner reservation. Can you take Hailee and Skylar home?"

"Yes."

"We can take a cab," Hailee says.

"No. You won't," Adrian replies, as if we have no choice in the matter.

Hailee raises her eyebrows and bites her lip. Kora smirks. Sergey puts his arm around Kora's waist and nods. "Great. Have a nice night."

We part ways and go to the parking garage. I assume Adrian has one of the black cars similar to what we rode in going home from the Cat's Meow, but he opens the back door to a Land Rover. "Hailee." He motions for her to get in, then he opens the passenger door for me.

Once we're all inside, he says, "Hailee, what's your address again?"

She rattles it off, and he pulls out of the space.

"Do you want mine?" I ask.

"No. I already know it." His eyes linger on my body before he refocuses on driving.

Flutters fill my stomach. If only last night had never happened.

It was so good.

Until he had to ruin it.

He apologized and seems sincere.

Tim always did, too. I've still got the mound of debt from the therapy bills.

I expect Adrian to drop me off first, since I live closer to the hospital than Hailee, but he drives to her place. No one speaks during the drive. I assume Hailee is worried about Aspen. I am, too, but my issues with Adrian consume me more.

When we get to Hailee's, he parks. I expect to stay in the car, but he opens my door.

"What's going on?"

"We're going to escort Hailee to her apartment."

"It's not necessary. I'm good from here. Thanks for the ride," Hailee replies.

Adrian snorts. He reaches in for my hand. "Come on, my printsessa."

Every time he calls me his printsessa, I feel giddy. No one's ever had a pet name for me before. It makes me feel like I'm his.

I can't be after what happened.

I should forgive and forget.

And I immediately return to all my old patterns.

My counselor's face pops into my mind. Her voice echoes, over and over. *"No man is worth your mental health."*

"I can't stay in the car?"

He raises his eyebrows and glances around. "In this neighborhood at night? No."

"Jeez. It isn't that bad," Hailee interjects.

"No offense, Hailee, but it worries me you live here," Adrian says.

"That's snobby," I blurt out.

A line furrows between his eyebrows. "I grew up two blocks from here. It has only gotten worse since I moved out. There's nothing pretentious about my statement. It's purely about safety."

My cheeks heat. "Oh. Sorry."

"It's not like I take strolls in the dark around here. I keep my apartment locked at all times, even during the day," Hailee states.

Adrian's face hardens. He leads us inside. When we get on the elevator, he asks, "Why are you and your friends so quick to dismiss your safety? Hmm?"

Hailee puts her hand on her hip. "I'm a teacher. I don't get paid a lot. There aren't a lot of options I can afford."

"You could get a roommate. Then you wouldn't have to live somewhere dangerous."

"Ever watch *Single White Female*? Not always the best idea. Plus, Hailee is the ideal candidate to have a roommate stalker," I tease.

"Why is that?" she asks.

"Blonde, blue-eyed, girl next door. Pretty and innocent—"

"Will everyone stop calling me innocent?" she barks.

I hold my hands up. "Jeez, Hailee. You don't have to get all bent out of shape."

She glares at Adrian. "I'm in my late thirties. I don't want a roommate. I have a job and can take care of myself, thank you very much. And while the neighborhood may not be the best, my apartment is very nice and clean!"

"Did I say anything about the inside or your cleanliness?" Adrian asks.

"Ugh. You're so rude and annoying."

"Because I think it's unsafe for a woman to live in this neighborhood on her own?"

Hailee shakes her head. "You're also a male chauvinist."

"No, I'm not."

The elevator opens, and she steps out. "You are." She stomps ahead of us.

Adrian mouths, "What's up her ass?"

I bite on my lip, keeping my mouth shut. Hailee's mom raised her and her sisters to be independent. She's never gone too deep discussing her father situation, but he wasn't around. Over the years, Hailee has helped Kora, Aspen, and me do more things than I ever thought possible. She has her own set of tools and can fix things, including minor electrical and plumbing issues. Her apartment is probably the nicest in the neighborhood because she's repaired and replaced everything wrong in it. Whenever there is an estate sale, or during the spring and summer months when there are garage sales in the suburbs, she'll go and find things for next to nothing. One time, she found a granite slab for pennies on the dollar.

She batted her eyes at the two guys selling it to her, and they installed it for free.

Hailee unlocks her door and steps inside. She spins. "Don't stand there. Come in."

Adrian motions for me to go first. He follows me inside and scans the unit. She recently repainted and changed everything to a blue theme. One accent wall is royal blue. Lighter coordinating blues add pops of color through vases, pillows, and pictures in the open floor plan space. Her cabinets are white. The countertop she got a deal on looks marbled. It's mostly white with some streaks of blue. Everything is cozy and looks new.

"You did a great job on those cabinets," I tell her. I haven't seen them since she painted them. "I'm glad your landlord gave you permission."

She nods.

"This is impressive, Hailee," Adrian says.

"See, I don't live in a dump."

"I never once said that. I discussed your safety. That's it. Don't add words to my statements."

"He's right, Hailee. You're taking this the wrong way."

She rolls her eyes.

I point to a large stack of construction paper. "What are you creating?"

"The umbrellas for the April Showers Bring May Flowers bulletin board. I need to cut out enough for my class and the other two classes."

"Why?"

"If I don't do it, the other kids won't have a bulletin board to decorate. The other teachers decided it was too much work. It's not fair to the kids. They like decorating things and seeing them on display."

Adrian walks over to the table and sits down.

"What are you doing?" Hailee asks.

He picks up scissors and a piece of red paper. His cocky expression appears. "Making some umbrellas."

"Seriously?" Hailee asks.

"Yep. You want to tell me what to do, or am I freestyling it?"

She scoffs. "You're going to cut out paper umbrellas?"

Adrian sets it down and crosses his arms. "Are you being sexist?"

"What? No!"

"Do you think I'm incapable?"

"Not sure. Are you?" Her lips twitch.

He pulls the chair out next to him. "Take a seat, my printsessa. My kindergarten teacher gave me an A-plus in my scissor work."

I laugh. "Your scissor work? Hailee, is that a subject I'm not aware of?"

She snorts.

Adrian smirks. It's arrogant and tugs at my heart. Some women may find it annoying, but Adrian's ego is panty-melting sexy to me. "I can even stay inside, on, or outside the lines."

"Wow. Impressive," I tease.

"Well, show us what you got then." Hailee sits across from us.

We spend the next few hours laughing and working. Hailee grabs another stack of construction paper, and we create the flowers to go with the umbrellas.

I'm happy to help Hailee. She's a teacher who could go to any district, have more resources, and make her life easier but won't. She wants to make an impact on less fortunate kids. Something about watching a man like Adrian help her with this task pulls at my heartstrings.

Adrian Ivanov has a heart beneath his cocky exterior.

It makes it almost impossible to ignore the voice in my head, saying to give him another chance.

5

Adrian

WHEN SKYLAR AND I LEAVE HAILEE'S, IT'S AFTER ELEVEN. As we step outside, a police siren fills the air, and I grow uncomfortable again thinking about Hailee living in this neighborhood. I quickly guide Skylar to my vehicle, open the door for her, and get into the driver's side, starting the car immediately.

"That was nice of you," she says.

"What?" I glance at her, trying not to focus on her lips. All night they've haunted me. Every time she smiled, laughed, or displayed her serious expression while concentrating, the ache in my gut exponentially expanded. I couldn't stop thinking about what it was like to kiss and lick her plump little lips.

She smirks. "I didn't take you as an arts and crafts kind of guy."

"A-plus," I tease and wink.

She smiles, lighting up against the darkness of the night. A soft laugh fills the car. She twists a lock of her magenta hair around her finger. The blue in her eyes deepens.

How could I have screwed this up so badly?

"Where do you live?" she asks.

"I just moved to one of the new buildings Maksim and his brothers built. It's called Skyline Estate."

She nods. "I heard about that building. It sold out in under an hour! I was going to look at it. The views are supposed to be amazing, even at night."

"They are. It's a clear night. Do you want to check it out?"

Silence fills the SUV. My stomach flips, and I curse myself for asking her. I'm about to retract my invitation when she says, "Sure."

My insides go giddy. I'm making more progress with her and don't have to drop her off. I attempt to play it cool. "You're in fashion?" I tear my gaze from hers, focusing on the road.

"Yep."

"You like it?"

"Most days. My boss is demanding. He's often an over-the-top twat. If he weren't so big in the industry, I'd find someone else to work for, but I don't have many choices in

Chicago. I suppose I should move to New York and take one of the jobs a few designers offered me."

Panic creeps into my belly. I just met her, but I don't want her anywhere except where I can see and touch her. "You would move?"

"Probably not. I love Chicago. Plus, my friends and family are here."

I try not to appear too happy about her statement. "You grew up here?"

"Yes, near Lincoln Park. I moved to San Francisco for fashion school then returned. I missed my mom and sisters, so it was good to be home."

"You moved back when you graduated?"

She doesn't answer right away and finally replies, "No. A few years after."

"What made you decide to come home?"

She taps her hands on her thigh and turns toward the window. Her voice lowers. "I needed to get away from someone."

The hairs on my arms rise. "Someone hurt you?"

She turns to me. Her forehead wrinkles. "Why did you ask me that?"

Blood races in my veins. I grip the steering wheel tighter, trying to contain my rage. "Who hurt you, my printsessa?"

"It was a long time ago. I'm over it. I blocked him, and he doesn't know where I live."

"He was your boyfriend?"

"No. Ex-fiancé."

Jealousy flares in my belly. She loved someone enough to want to marry them. I turn the blinker on and look in the rearview mirror. It's clear, so I veer into the other lane. I attempt to pry further. "What did he do to you?"

She hesitates, draws her bottom lip into her mouth, and bites on it. She twists her hands in her lap and studies them.

I put my hand over hers. "Did he hit you?"

"No."

"Cheat on you?"

"Not that I'm aware of."

There's a lump growing in my throat. I can't bring myself to ask her if it was sexual. Pictures of Natalia enter my mind, and I wince inside. My voice comes out hoarse. "Tell me."

"It's not what you're thinking. It wasn't physical." She avoids me but doesn't make me remove my hand.

I rack my brain, trying to figure out what it could be. Physical and sexual are out. No cheating. What is left? So much time passes, I urge, "Will you tell me?"

"Adrian..." She sighs. "It's better if we don't get into this."

"Why? I can handle it. I promise I won't go apeshit and find the guy and beat him to a bloody pulp. At least not tonight," I tease and wink but am also serious. I already want to kill the bastard for hurting her.

"I'm fine now. And I have lots of lingering therapy bills to prove it," she chirps.

"Okay, then tell me."

"Just drop it."

"Sorry, I can't."

"Adrian—"

"I need to know," I insist.

"No, you don't. It's not your business."

I try a different tactic. It's the truth, so I don't see anything wrong with using it. "If you don't tell me, I'm going to start spinning out about what he might have done to you. Then I'm going to dig into every part of your life until I find out who he is. When I find him, he'll have no choice but to admit whatever it is he did."

She closes her eyes. "Jeez. That's a bit extreme, don't you think?"

"I don't think anything is extreme where you're concerned," I admit.

She tilts her head. "I'm not sure if I should be impressed or scared by that statement."

My chest tightens. "You're scared of me, my printsessa?"

"No. Should I be though?"

"I will never hurt you."

Something passes in her expression. My gut drops. *I already have hurt her.*

I never will again. It's a promise I make to myself and plan on keeping. As much as I don't deserve for her to reveal anything to me, I can't forget about it. "What did your ex do?"

Her cheeks flush. "You just need to let it go."

"I can't. I told you how my mind works. Now, please, tell me."

She groans. "Fine. He used to say a lot of really nasty things to me. Now please drop it." She pulls her hand out from under mine. She crosses her arms over her chest.

Her words sink in, and my lungs constrict. The things I said to her the previous night while she was half naked and in a vulnerable position slap me in the face. I already regret my actions, but it caused way more damage than I could ever imagine. I didn't just hurt her. I did something to her she spent years trying to recover from. More guilt eats at me, gnawing in my gut. I feel sick. I admit, "Another apology for what I did to you seems pathetic right now." I pull into my parking garage and find a spot. Her quiet demeanor gives me the impression I can't do anything to ever make it right. I get out, cursing myself. I'm not used to screwing up with women. I usually take them out, have some fun, and nothing is stressful. Everything I want from Skylar seems impossible now. I walk around and open her door. I reach in and help her out.

She steps toward me. "Sincere apologies aren't pathetic, Adrian."

"I do mean it, but I'm not used to groveling. I don't know what I can do to make this right between us."

Her lips twitch. "This is you groveling?"

I arch my eyebrows. "Am I not doing a good job?"

She bites on her smile.

"Do you want me to do anything special so you'll forgive me?" I tease, taking advantage of her smile and tone.

"Hmm. Let me think about it. I'll take a rain check."

My hope flairs. "You will?"

Her face falls, and my gut drops. Then she answers, "No. I already forgave you. You can stop apologizing now."

I proceed with caution. "You did?"

She nods. "Mmhmm."

"When?"

"It might have been on your twentieth umbrella. Or maybe it was when you showed me your impressive rose drawing skills. Either way, I decided I won't pretend you don't exist when I'm with Aspen and have to see you."

"What if I want to see you without Aspen?" I blurt out. Blood slams between my ears, waiting for her to answer. It feels like forever passes before she speaks.

She opens her mouth several times. Nervousness fills her expression. My heart sinks when she talks. "I'm not sure if it's a good idea."

Not what I wanted to hear.

But she came to my house.

Minutes pass. She breaks our gaze, but I don't move. When she finally glances up, and her blue eyes peek out from under her long lashes, I see it. She still wants me. She's grappling with herself. I step forward, fist her hair, and palm her ass. I tug her as close to me as I can then lean so close my lips brush hers as I speak. "You said, not sure."

"Yeah." Her heart beats faster against my chest.

"There's room to change your mind, then." It's not a question. It's a fact, and I'm going to take advantage of the in she gave me.

A line forms between her eyes. She doesn't try to move. Her fists open, and she flattens them against my pecs. Her hot breath merges into mine. "Adrian, I..."

"I'm not him. I did the wrong thing, but I'm not him, my printsessa," I firmly state.

"I want to believe you."

"Good. Give me another chance, and I'll show you." I don't wait for her to answer. I use her admittance as permission to kiss her. Unlike the aggressive kisses I gave her the night before, I take my time exploring her mouth. The moment I slide my tongue inside her, she flicks back. I savor every part of her pretty pink mouth like it's my last meal, restraining the beast within me who's ready to ravish her. There's no room for mistakes. I'm not dumb enough to think her returning my kiss means she trusts me again.

The longer my mouth touches her sinful lips, the more desperate I am for her. My hunger grows. I pull back and study her eyes. They've turned heavy, and she breathes harder. It encourages me to take more. I dart my tongue in and out of her mouth faster, losing the ability to analyze what the right move is to regain her trust. Every breath, whimper, and return of my affection feeds something within me. I'm unsure what, but kissing Skylar stirs a part of me I didn't know existed.

"Tomorrow night," I mumble and attack her mouth once more.

"Hmm?" She slides her hands around my neck and lightly grazes her fingernails on my head. Her body trembles against mine.

A rumble builds in my chest. It escapes me, low, desperate for the rest of her. I'm ready to strip her naked and lick every inch of her porcelain skin. The memory of her body, clutching mine, quivering beneath my flesh, consumes me. I want her as mine. I *need* her as mine, but I still have damage to repair.

"I'll pick you up at six."

She freezes.

I scan her face. "I'm not him. I'll prove it to you." I kiss her again, aggressively using my tongue then studying her eyes. "Tell me yes."

She stays quiet, panting.

I repeat kissing her then looking at her, demanding she agrees to go out with me. Each time I retreat, she breathes harder. I tilt her head more then lick the midline of her neck.

A quiet yet ragged moan vibrates off her. Her nails dig into my scalp. She shudders hard against me.

My erection pulses into her stomach. I knead my hand over her ass cheek, restraining from sticking my palm in her pants. "We're good together," I murmur in her ear then resume tongue fucking her mouth.

Her knees give out. I don't stop, reach for her thighs, and pick her up, sandwiching her between the SUV and me. She wraps her legs around my waist. The heat from her sex penetrates my cock. She circles her hips at a torturous speed, grinding against my erection. I groan, tug her hair, then nibble on her ear before growling, "Admit you don't want me, and I'll stop."

She gasps when I drag my teeth over her beating pulse. "Tell me you don't wish to see me, and I'll take you home." I arch my eyebrow and pull back so she has to stare me in the eye and tell me. When she doesn't answer, I tease my lips against hers, retreating when her tongue swipes my bottom one. "Tomorrow night. Six o'clock."

She leans into my ear, grazing her teeth on my earlobe, continuing to terrorize my dick further. "Okay." The scent of salted caramel and pears tortures me more. Her breath skipping across my neck gives me tingles.

I step back, releasing her. I guide her to my penthouse, staying silent, keeping her back flush to the front of my body in the elevator. Every moment of the short journey to my unit is spent trying to put out the fire burning in my veins. I attempt to convince myself to show her the view and take her home so I don't ruin any progress I've made.

I open my front door and motion for her to pass. She steps inside, and I follow.

"This is beautiful. You had a good designer."

"Dmitri's wife, Anna, designed it," I admit.

"She did a great job. I love the way she mixed the metals with the wood. It's edgy but warm."

I nod, scanning the room.

"Wow. This truly is stunning," she states and goes to the window. Stars fill the sky over the darkness of the lake. Lights glow on buildings, outlining the city. The Ferris wheel on Navy Pier blinks in the distance. "Have you always lived in a penthouse?"

"No. I only bought this one because Maksim split it into fours. Otherwise, it would be too much space for only me." I pick up her hand. "Come. Let me show you something." I lead her through my bedroom and slide the glass wall open then flip the switch. Fire ignites on the glass wall of the balcony. A three-foot wooden ledge hangs a foot over it, as if it were a wide mantle. A pewter rail is on top of the wooden plank at the back edge.

"Wow!" she gapes.

"Anna had them add it last minute. It's what sold me on the place."

"It's incredible," she states and peers over the balcony wall. "Do you sleep with the wall opened up?"

"On a nice night, like tonight, yes. Summer depends on the weather."

She spins into me. "It's amazing, Adrian. I love it."

I don't reply. I stare at her. She's glowing, with all of Chicago lit up and the fire dancing around her. A gust of wind blows her hair. I step forward and push it off her face.

She inhales sharply and focuses on my chest. Her energy penetrates me, creating a buzz I've only felt around her. It happened when we first met. All night, it's been terrorizing my veins.

Her hair is pure silk. I twist it around my fist. Her breathing picks up. I gently tug her hair so she can't avoid me. She licks her lips, and my dick pulses into her stomach. A tiny whimper escapes her mouth. Anxiety and lust swirl in her expression. Her long lashes flick over her orbs several times.

My restraint is gone. She's in my home, standing outside my bedroom. All I want is to show her how good we can be together and prove to her I won't ever be the man I showed her the first time we were together.

"My printsessa."

"Hmm?" She arches an eyebrow.

"I'm not going to kiss you anymore tonight."

She swallows hard. "No?"

I shake my head. "If I kiss you, I'm taking you over to my bed, and you're not leaving all weekend."

A red flush crawls through her cheeks. It makes the blue in her eyes appear more prominent.

My pants become uncomfortable. I trace her cheekbone. "This sexy blush you have going on isn't helping me think decent thoughts right now." More heat scorches her cheeks. Her hot breath is torture. I want it all over my skin, and it pulls me in like a magnet. Instead of backing away, I lean closer, mumbling, "I should take you home."

She tears her eyes away from mine and focuses on my lips then gazes toward the bed. My heart races and my erection throbs. She slowly glances down between us then meets my eyes.

I don't move. If I do, I will have her, and I don't want her regretting me any more than she already does.

I'm a forty-year-old man. Show some restraint.

I'm a forty-year-old man who knows what I want.

Jesus. Why did I have to screw up? I shouldn't even be questioning this. If I hadn't messed up, I wouldn't be standing here with a hard-on. I'd be worshiping her in my bed.

She's not going to give me more chances. I've gotten farther than I thought I'd get tonight.

"I'll take you home." I force myself to step back, but she reaches for my biceps. Her fingers are electric, intensifying the buzz already annihilating my cells. I freeze.

I glance at her hand then into her big doe eyes.

"Earlier, you said, 'Tell me you don't wish to see me, and I'll take you home.'"

"Yes."

She takes a deep breath and cups my cheeks. "I never said I didn't want to see you anymore, so why are you taking me home?"

6

Skylar

NOTHING I'M DOING MAKES SENSE, AND I DON'T STAND A chance against Adrian. I woke up hating him this morning. Now, I can't seem to remember why I disliked him. It's as if my brain can't register to stay away from him when he's this close to me. He's the epitome of male sexual power, and his kisses earlier did nothing to satiate me. All he did was make me want him more.

Panic annihilates me when he says he's taking me home. I have no reason to feel it. It's a rational, safe course of action, but the only thing that feels right is staying with Adrian.

Words roll out of my mouth. "I never said I didn't want to see you anymore, so why are you taking me home?"

His jaw clenches under my fingers. I lower my hand over his heart. It pounds into my palm. I slide my other hand to the back of his head and step closer.

"Don't tease me, my printsessa," he firmly states.

I caress the back of his neck with my thumb. "One thing I've never been is a tease, Adrian."

He dips down so his mouth is an inch from mine. His icy-blue eyes pierce my gaze. He warns, "No? Then be careful of your next move. If you touch my lips, you're staying. If you pull away, I'm taking you home."

Blood pounds between my ears. His body heat penetrates through my dress and into my skin, in contrast with the cool night air. I inhale his scent, almost becoming dizzy from it. I barely have to move before my lips mold to his.

Our tongues slide against each other, and like every kiss Adrian's given me, it's carnal bliss with an underlying tone that nothing is off-limits. With every swipe of his tongue or press of his lips, it's as if he wants every part of me, and he'll stop at nothing to take it.

It turns me on. I've never felt so wanted or dominated by a man. Before I know what's happening, my dress pools at my feet. I stand on his balcony with labored breath and in nothing but my undergarments. A chill runs down my spine from the contrast of his warm hands and the cool night air.

He steps back, assessing me. The longer he stares with his sexy, arrogant expression, the harder it gets not to move. When he finally reaches for me, he picks me up and sets me on the dark ledge. It's about three feet wide. The wood is cold, but Adrian's dense frame is warm. He asks, "Are you afraid of heights?"

"No."

"Do you feel like you're on top of Chicago up here?" he asks.

I glance around. The other buildings are several floors lower. "Yes."

His lips twitch. "Enjoy the view, my printsessa." He inserts his tongue deep in my mouth while unhooking my bra then tosses it behind him. His warm mouth devours my breasts until I'm writhing against him and gripping his head.

"Oh God!"

"Lean back on your elbows," he instructs.

I obey. The back of my arm hits the metal rail. My head and shoulders are over it, making me slightly nervous. The night air cools my hot nipples quickly, keeping them puckered and hard.

Adrian places my hands so they grip the edge of the wood. "Hold on." He smirks then widens my legs. He drags his wet tongue from my cleavage through my belly button and down to my panties. His large hands slide over my outer thighs and around my ass. He takes a deep breath and mumbles, "Fuck. You're going to be the death of me." Instead of removing my panties, his mouth attacks them, slowly at first, as if it's a game to see how long he can terrorize me with a barrier between his mouth and my pulsating body.

The blinking lights of the city become fuzzy. Heat rolls through my body, competing with the springtime air. Zings ricochet in my cells. I move my hands from the wood to

Adrian's head. My voice comes out desperate and raspy. "Please."

He grunts then slides his tongue under my panties and rolls it on the edge of my hole. It's hot, slick, delicious torture. He pulls away and bites my clit through my panties.

"Adrian! Holy—"

He inhales again, as if my scent somehow gives him life. In a quick movement, he reaches for my damp panties and rips them off me. There's a slight sting, but I can't think about it for long. Adrian's entire tongue swipes my sex, over and over, the tip of it flicking on my clit every time he gets near it.

I rotate between glancing at Adrian and the city around me, no longer feeling the cold air. Sweat breaks out on my skin.

His tongue becomes a jackhammer, pounding deep into my sex, then coming out as fast as it went in. His fingers assault every part of me. My clit. My nipples. My mouth.

"Suck," he growls, inserting two of his fingers past my lips. "You're going to control my mouth now."

What does he mean?

He stops and arches his eyebrows, intently watching me suck his fingers. After several seconds, his expression becomes cockier. "Show me what you want, my printsessa." He places his mouth on my clit and sucks with the same intensity I am, flicking his tongue simultaneously.

My mouth forms an O, but he keeps his fingers lodged over my tongue. His mouth stops moving, and the arrogant expression of his grows. He taunts, "Can't handle it, my printsessa?"

Jesus.

My lips mold back over his fingers. I suck his digits like it's his dick, sliding the tip of my tongue along the length and applying pressure.

Everything I do, he replicates. I forget I'm sitting on the edge of a building, overlooking the Chicago skyline, naked and sweating on top of the cold plank. All I can focus on is Adrian's haughty, icy-blue eyes locked onto mine while he mimics every move my tongue and lips make.

My whimpers become louder. He has me on the cusp of flying, and I lean up. I slide my hands under the neck of his T-shirt and dig my nails into his back. He tugs my body closer to him so I'm barely on the ledge. My legs hang over his shoulders, and I grind my sex against his face. He inserts his fingers in and out of my mouth, as if it's his dick pushing into my body.

I'm desperate for it. Each time his fingers slide in my mouth, I hungrily attempt to suck them. "Please," I beg him every time he pulls out of my mouth, until I'm crying out into the night sky.

Like a wild animal who hasn't eaten in days, he savagely sucks me until an earthquake of endorphins destroys me.

"Adrian!" I scream as he continues to keep me high, buzzing, and so dizzy, I claw his back until he's groaning.

When the adrenaline fades, I'm still quivering and shiver as the cold night air hits my clammy skin.

VICIOUS PROTECTOR

He tilts his head up. The cockiest expression I've ever seen fills his face. He shimmies up my body, playing with my sensitive breasts, then taking ownership of my mouth with his.

He readjusts my legs, so they are around his waist, then picks me up and takes me into the bedroom. Every move he makes is fluid. There's no pausing or analyzing. Not one part of him lacks confidence in what he's doing. He lays me on the bed, steps back, and strips.

Oh. My. God.

How is this man with me right now?

I knew Adrian was a specimen of perfection, but seeing him naked and in the flesh is like seeing a masterpiece of art for the first time. There are so many places to look. My eyes dart from head to toe. Brilliant tattoos of crosses, snakes, skulls, and flowers adorn his arms and torso. His chest has a voracious lion with the letters L-E-V above it. Chiseled flesh lies under every inch of his skin.

He fists his erection, staring at me. I'm mesmerized, unable to tear my gaze away from his thick, long cock.

How did all of him fit in me the other night?

He reaches for his nightstand and pulls out a condom then slips it on. He lunges over me, propping himself up on his elbow, positioning his face over mine. His breath smells of my orgasms, and he pins his steel gaze on me. "You're mine, printsessa."

I reach for his face, but he holds his position steady.

"Do you understand?" he demands.

"Yes."

His eyes dart to my mouth, and he begins fucking me with his tongue until I'm moaning. He retreats, studying me, then returns to assaulting my mouth while grinding his shaft against my sensitive bundle of nerves.

"Oh God!" I scream, trembling hard against his muscular body.

"That's my girl," he growls in my ear. Then he quietly says something in Russian between kisses and stroking my head until I catch my breath.

"Please," I whisper, spreading my legs wider and bucking my hips.

"Please what, my printsessa? What do you want? Hmm?" He slides his tongue over my cheek.

Heat bubbles in my veins. I begin to sweat again. My voice cracks, "I want you, Adrian."

His mouth hangs an inch above mine. Blue flames burn into me. He shifts his hips and slowly enters my wet heat, groaning, as if in relief. He doesn't pull out but presses every last inch of his cock in me. I accept it all, as if God created Adrian's body exclusively for me.

Maybe he did. Every thrust he makes, I meet with eager perfection. Each kiss we have is fire. Any touch is an explosion of zings.

He uses every part of his body to ravish me, leaving nothing untouched. He gets on his knees, tugs me by my hips, then pushes my ankles to his chest. One of his arms holds my shins. The other hand dips to my sex. He pinches my clit, then rubs it with his thumb, then repeats it while slowly thrusting in me and watching my every reaction.

I cry out, and he smirks. He continues to do it until I'm shaking and my insides clench his shaft. He stops pinching me and only circles his thumb while pounding in me harder.

I dig my nails into his outer thighs and scream as adrenaline pummels me. I spasm on him, over and over, feeling a train of euphoria, unlike anything I've ever experienced before. It lasts and lasts until he growls out in Russian and spurts his hot seed deep within me.

His phone dings. He sucks on my big toe while running his fingers up and down my inner thigh.

Jesus. Does this man ever stop?

He releases me, grabs his phone out of his pants, then pulls the bedding back. "Slide under."

I do as he asks.

He sits on the edge of the bed, texts a few things, then groans.

I wince when I see the claw marks on his back. I must have done it when we were on the balcony. I reach out and trace the bloody trail. "Sorry."

He turns and grunts. He tosses the phone on the nightstand and slides under the covers. He cages his body over mine. "Don't say sorry to me after we have sex."

"I drew blood."

His smug expression fills his face. "As I recall, I was the reason you drew blood."

I bite down on my smile.

He kisses me. It's slow and gentle, unlike his other kisses. "Sergey is coming over."

"In the middle of the night? Did something happen?"

"I'm not sure what's going on, but everything is fine."

"Should I go?"

He scoffs. "No. You should stay in my bed. Do you have anything going on tomorrow morning?"

I rack my brain. "No. I have plans with the girls Sunday morning but nothing tomorrow."

He grins. "Good. Take a break. Rest up for later."

"Later?"

He traces my lips. "Sergey isn't staying long. When I come back, I'm waking you up."

7

Adrian

SERGEY DOESN'T STAY LONG AFTER HE REALIZES I HAVE company. When he leaves, I take some deep breaths. He told me he saw his ex, Eloise, with Wes Petrov at a private club. The uneasiness I feel whenever I hear the Petrov name crawls through my skin. I pace the penthouse. I can't go into the bedroom. I'm on the edge of spiraling, and I don't trust myself around Skylar right now.

I step out on the balcony from the other side of the house. I end up pacing, then staring out over the darkness of Lake Michigan.

Why was Eloise with Wes Petrov?

I can't wait to watch Wes take his last breath.

His thug that held my printsessa down will look into my eyes when he dies, too.

Skylar's arms circle around my waist, and her body wraps around my back.

I close my eyes, attempting to calm further, then put my hands over hers. I spin into her. She's naked, her teeth are chattering, and she's the most beautiful woman I've ever come across. I tug her into me. "You're freezing."

She looks up. Her magenta hair flies with the breeze, and her dark-blue eyes pin mine. She reaches for my cheek. "Adrian, is everything okay?"

I don't answer her. If I did, I would have to lie to her. I can't tell her what I will do to Wes or his thug who held her down against her will. I learned my lesson in the past about what happens when a woman learns about who you really are and what you are capable of doing. It doesn't matter if that woman loves you or not. The truth destroys everything. She must never see or learn about the monster within me. If she did, any positive feelings she has for me would vanish. And if she ever does grow to love me, it won't change reality, so I'll still have to keep it from her.

As much as I can't tell her the truth, I also don't want to lie to her. Instead of answering her, I dip down and lick her lips, then slowly work my way between the seam until she opens her mouth and grazes her tongue against mine.

I kiss her while moving her backward until we're in the bedroom. "Get under the covers, my printsessa."

"Are you coming to bed?"

"Yes. Let me close the doors."

"But it's nice."

I rub my hand over her cold ass cheeks. "Yes, but you're an icicle. And in a few hours, the sun is coming up, so let me open the blackout shades." I hold the blanket out, and she gets in. I tuck it around her, kiss her forehead, then shut the pane of glass and release the window treatments. When I turn back to her, her head sits propped on her fist, and she's smiling.

I drop my shorts, and she bites her lip. I say, "You look super happy right now."

"I am."

I slide under the sheet and tug her on top of me, palming her cold ass. "Are you always this happy in the middle of the night?"

Her grin gets bigger. "Maybe. I guess you'll have to test your theory on a different night."

There's a strange feeling in my chest. I'm not used to it and haven't felt it in over a decade. I try to ignore it and focus on Skylar. "Maybe you should stay all weekend."

She inhales a large breath and holds it. Time seems to stand still. I begin to wonder if I shouldn't have said it.

I'm not into playing games.

Maybe I freaked her out.

She slowly exhales and slides her hands over my shoulders between my back and the mattress. Her lips come near my ear. "If I stayed the weekend, will your back be able to handle it?"

"Sergey said you should put some antiseptic on them," I tease.

Her face turns crimson, and she buries her face in the pillow. She groans. "Oh no! I'm never going to be able to look at him again."

I softly chuckle and move her hair to the side. I kiss her shoulder, her neck, then move to her chin. "He doesn't know it was you."

She lifts her head. "No?"

"No."

"You...you didn't want him to know about us?"

I shake my head. "I didn't know if *you* wanted him to know. So no, I didn't tell him."

"Okay. Thank you. I don't care if he knows about us...assuming...um..."

"Assuming this isn't a one-off thing?" I finish for her. My gut flips at the thought. I already know I don't want a temporary thing with Skylar.

Her blush deepens. "Yes."

I kiss her, using every skill I have to steal all her breath until she's panting in my mouth. I tug her over me then murmur, "Does this feel like a one-off thing to you?"

She breathlessly admits, "No. God, no."

I pull her back on me. "Good. Now, can we return to my back?"

Her lips curve up. "You mean if you can handle me staying the weekend?"

I smirk. "I can be rather creative, my printsessa."

She traces my chin. "Like how?"

I murmur, "Oh, you naughty, naughty girl."

"How have I been naughty?"

I flip her on her stomach then cage my body around hers. I put my mouth on her cheek. "You haven't yet. But you're about to be." I trace my fingers over the curve of her waist, and she shivers. My head dips to her ass cheeks. I kiss each one then take the flat part of my tongue and drag it up her spine.

"Holy shit," she whispers.

I nuzzle the curve of her neck and murmur, "Turn over, my printsessa. Time to be naughty."

She softly laughs and turns so she's on her back. She tilts her head and smiles. "Like this?"

"Yep." I reach over and flip the switch for the fireplace. It's on the wall across from the bed. The room erupts in a warm glow. I tuck her hair behind her ear and give her a chaste kiss. She hungrily tries to lick me when I pull back. I'm only an inch from her lips, but I hold her down. "I want to watch."

She raises her eyebrows. "Watch?"

I purse my lips together and nod. "Yeah, my printsessa." I take her hands. I position one over her breast and the other over her pussy. "Show me what you do when no one is watching."

"Umm..."

I widen her legs then bend down and kiss her inner thigh. I put my hand on top of hers and manipulate it on her breast. After her nipple is hard, I move my hand to the one on her sex. I lock eyes with her and slide her fingers through her wet folds, noticing the way her chest rises and falls faster with every soft breath she takes.

I lick her thigh, right to the edge of her pussy. Inhaling deeply, I hold her scent in my lungs before releasing it. I lie on my shoulder, with my head between her legs, and stare at her fingers.

"Are you enjoying this?" she asks.

"Very much. Do you know how beautiful your pussy is?"

"No," she says, as if I'm joking.

I kiss her finger, which is circling her clit. "I don't lie, especially not about pussy." I hold her hand so she can't move it, flick the tip of my tongue, then lightly suck on her clit. She gasps, and I pull back. "Slow, my printsessa." I move her hand at the speed I want it. "Isn't that good?"

Her face flushes. "Yes."

I glide my finger into her, curling and swiping. "Good. I didn't say you could come yet. I only said to show me."

She looks at me confused, but it's short-lived. She whispers, "Oh God."

"Pull on your nipple."

She tugs lightly on it.

I slide my finger out of her then put it in front of her mouth. "Lick it and tug harder," I demand.

She obeys, desperately licking my finger and moaning.

"Good, my naughty little printsessa." I kneel on the mattress, sitting on my feet. I flip her on her stomach then pull her on me, with her ass against my erection. I hold her flush to my torso, move her hair to the side, and growl in her ear, "I didn't say stop touching yourself."

She turns her head. Her heavy eyes meet mine. I steal her lips and place my hand over hers. It's already working her clit, but I slow her down. I wet my finger in her juices then slide it back into her mouth.

"Show me how naughty you are, my printsessa."

She tries to slide on my cock, but I don't let her.

"Show me how you come." I take her free arm and bend it in the air then guide it around my shoulder so she's gripping my head. I watch everything from my angle behind her. The red in her cheeks grows. It makes the blue in her eyes pop. Her fingers expertly work the bundle of nerves between her legs. Her plump, juicy lips suck on my finger while her sinful tongue flicks against it.

"That's it, my printsessa."

Labored breaths, blinking long eyelashes, and dewy skin make my veins bubble with heat. I pull my finger out and kiss her, urgently circling my tongue in her mouth. She whimpers, and her body shakes.

I slide one arm over her chest, holding her shoulder. The other hand, I wrap around the front of her waist and clutch her hip. I thrust into her. "Fuuuuuck," I groan.

"Adrian...oh...oh God!" she cries out as her inner walls spasm on my shaft.

I slide my hand over hers. "Keep going. Don't stop."

"Oh...Adrian..." she cries out.

I grip her hips and guide her movements as she grinds on me, over and over. I kiss her trembling jaw while watching her eyes roll. "That's it, my printsessa. You're so beautiful, baby."

Her body collapses on mine. She becomes a rag doll, trembling in my arms. I suck on her chin, and when she can't pleasure herself anymore, she shoves her fingers in my face, and I suck on her juices.

She whimpers, with her mouth in an O. A bead of sweat rolls down her cheek. I thrust over and over until I finally slam her on me harder, and she spasms so violently on my cock, I detonate inside her. I grumble in Russian, "You're perfect, my printsessa."

In our aftermath, we don't move. My arms stay pretzeled around her. We try to catch our breath. I pull my head out of the crook of her neck to face her. "I love your lips," I admit and lick her bottom one.

She smiles and releases her arm, lowering it from my head.

I flip her on her back and pull the covers over her.

"Hey!" She laughs.

I slide next to her and tug her into my arms. "What's your natural hair color?"

She gasps as if shocked. "Are you trying to tell me you don't think pink is my normal color?"

I pull a lock of her hair in the air. "You can't tell. It's right up to your roots." I release it. "I like it, but what's your real color?"

"Blonde."

I chuckle. "A natural blonde wanting to color her hair. Imagine that."

She turns into me. "I know. I'm crazy, right?"

I peck her on the lips. "No. You're creative and unique. It's one of the reasons you intrigue me."

She raises an amused eyebrow. "I intrigue you?"

I trace my finger along her hairline. "Yes. Why do you seem surprised?"

She shrugs. "I'm pretty much 'what you see is what you get.'" She yawns.

I shake my head. "No. You're nothing of the sort, my printsessa." I kiss her. "Go to sleep."

She reaches for my face then bites her lip. Her eyes bore into mine.

"What is it?" I ask.

A small smile plays on her lips. "I'm glad I came home with you."

I can't stop the grin that overpowers my face. I kiss her again. "I'm beyond happy you came home with me. Now turn over and go to sleep."

She scoots onto her side and curls up to my body. I kiss her shoulder and tug her closer to me. As I fall asleep, the scent of salted caramel and pears flares in my nostrils.

Nothing has ever felt so perfect.

8

Skylar

BLACKNESS SLOWLY TURNS INTO A FAINT GRAY AS MY EYES adjust. The delicious scent of peach blossom, Turkish rose, and amber consumes me. *Adrian.* I curl into my pillow more, smiling.

I'm at Adrian's.

Visions of our bodies tangled together fill my mind. I roll over, but he's not next to me.

Where is he?

What time is it?

It could be nighttime for all I know. Since I got to Adrian's, it's been a rinse and repeat cycle of sex and sleep. The last time, I woke up to Adrian's head between my thighs. As soon as I came, he lunged up my body, kissed me in his dirty hot way, and tugged me back into his arms. His Russian accent was thicker, and he murmured, "Go back to sleep, my printsessa."

I put my hand over my lips then glance around the room. My neatly folded dress and undergarments are on the armchair. I go into Adrian's closet and grab the T-shirt he wore the night before. It's on the top of the laundry basket. I throw it over my body. It's soft and smells like him.

Did he leave?

I stroll out of the bedroom. My purse is on the table where I left it. I open it and remove my phone. The battery is almost dead. I have a missed call from Hailee. The time says it's one o'clock.

I call Maksim. He answers after one ring. "Skylar."

"How is Aspen? Does she want visitors today?"

"Not today. She's asleep. The doctor said she probably would be for the rest of the day. If she is up to it, I'll have her call you when she wakes up."

"Okay. Thanks." I hang up and get text messages from Hailee and Kora about our yoga/brunch date tomorrow. Kora says she can't go to the art exhibit tonight, which I forgot about.

The conversation ends and I get another text.

Hailee: *A teacher I work with wanted tickets to the show tonight. Her parents are in from out of town. Do you mind if we sell them to her? I wasn't overly excited about this the way Kora was, and I could use the extra money right now.*

Me: *Sure.*

Hailee: *Do you want to do something else tonight?*

I love Hailee, but the thought of another night with Adrian isn't something I can bring myself to pass up.

Me: *Would you mind if I pass? I have some things I need to take care of.*

Hailee: *Sure. No problem.*

I stare at my phone then glance around Adrian's penthouse. The views are incredible. It's a beautiful, sunny spring day, and the wind appears minimal, judging by Lake Michigan's gently lapping waves along the shoreline.

Is Adrian still here?

I would call him, but I don't have his phone number. *I agreed to stay with a man all weekend and don't have his phone number.*

This is a first.

Time to check this place out.

It makes me a tad uncomfortable, ambling through Adrian's penthouse, opening doors, but I'm not sure what else to do. If he left, he didn't leave a note, which isn't cool. My gut tells me he would leave me some sort of message. I plug my phone into the charger I pass then proceed throughout the entire unit. I get to the last door in the hallway and open it. Lyrics to Metallica's "Enter Sandman" blare out. Adrian's faced away from me, dripping with sweat, doing squat presses. The gym's entire wall is glass, overlooking Lake Michigan.

Holy shit. I put my hand over my stomach to steady myself. *How in the world is it possible for anyone to be that ripped?*

Jesus.

He's not wearing a shirt. The claw marks I gave him last night are faint but still visible. One cuts through his right shoulder, over the middle of his *Natalia* tattoo. It's the only tattoo on his back. Every muscle in his body flexes as he lifts what appears to be an absurd amount of weight. The sound of his grunt competes with the loud music.

I watch him, in a trance. When he puts the bar on the rack, he keeps his hands on it. His skull tattoo over his hand appears fiercer than it usually looks. He lowers himself so his knees are on the floor. He stretches his arms then puts his entire body on the floor and starts doing push-ups.

Real, beast-mode push-ups. Every movement up, he claps his hands. I stare in awe at his abilities and superhuman body.

After he does dozens of push-ups, he rolls over. The lion tattoo on his chest looks vicious. He does three sit-ups then notices me. He freezes near his knees. His eyes scan me, and I suddenly feel self-conscious.

I haven't even brushed my hair or teeth. He looks like he's ready to compete with Thor, and I'm a disheveled mess at one in the afternoon.

His lips curl. He jumps up and turns down the music. "You're awake."

I release a nervous breath. I'm unsure why I feel anxious. This man has more carnal knowledge of my body than my ex-fiancé, based on what we did last night and into the morning. "Sorry. I didn't mean to be a snoop or interrupt you. I wasn't sure if you left, and I don't have your phone number."

"You aren't interrupting. If I left, I would have left you a note. But we'll fix the phone situation, my printsessa." He winks at me.

If I had panties on, he could melt them.

I'm wearing nothing but his T-shirt.

I self-consciously glance down to see my nipples poking through the soft material. Heat burns my cheeks. I bite my lip and force myself to look at Adrian.

An expression mixed with amusement, lust, and arrogance faces me. If it was on anyone but Adrian, I'd want to slap that look off their face. Before he ever touched me, his cockiness drew me to him. It's as if I knew he could back it up. After last night, there's no question about his abilities. The blue flames in his eyes only create more flutters in my stomach. His twitching lips only remind me of how many things he did to me with them.

"By any chance, do you have a spare toothbrush?" I ask.

He shuts the music off, snatches a towel out of the cubbyhole, then wipes his face. He throws it over his shoulder and approaches me. The heat from his body forms an aura around him. It penetrates my skin and stirs my nerves again.

Even his sweat smells sexy.

He motions to the door. "Let me show you where I keep things."

"I don't want to interrupt your workout. If you want to tell me where it is, that works."

He shakes his head. "It's okay. I already finished my workout. I was just passing the time while you slept."

I gape at him. "That's what you do when you're bored?"

More arrogance infuses his features. "Yeah."

"Wow. Those push-ups were impressive, by the way. The squat thingys, too," I blurt out.

He raises his eyebrows and grins, as if I said something funny. "How long were you watching me?"

I shrug and fib. "Not long."

"Hmm." He grunts then puts his hand on my back, guiding me out of the gym. "Did you sleep well?"

"Yeah. Did you get any?"

"Some."

"Did I keep you awake?"

"No. I don't require a lot of sleep."

"Oh. Would not sleeping be part of your superhuman abilities?"

"Superhuman?"

"Yeah. I'm pretty sure anyone who can clap in the middle of a push-up and not fall on their face is superhuman."

He chuckles. "Is that all it takes?"

"You know that's almost impossible, right?"

He spins me so I'm against the wall, right outside his bedroom. His forearms press next to my head. The heat from his body assaults me. My heart races faster. He squeezes my biceps. His tone is playful. "I could teach you."

"Ha! Yeah, right."

He touches the fabric over my cleavage. "You don't have to wear my dirty shirts. Next time, pick a clean one."

I sniff the shoulder of his shirt. "I think the only thing dirty is me."

More amusement fills his face. He holds my chin and lowers his mouth inches from mine. "Do you like to watch or participate?"

A family of butterflies erupts in my gut. It's a feeling I can't seem to escape around Adrian. Something about him stirs every ounce of desire I have. "What do you mean?"

The corners of his lips turn up. His Russian accent comes out thicker. "I'm going to shower, my printsessa. Are you going to watch or join me?"

Fire burns my face. I open my mouth to speak, but nothing comes out.

He arches an eyebrow.

I still can't seem to form words. Both options don't seem to have any downsides.

"Hmm. Guess I'll let you think about it." He steps back then puts his arm on my back and leads me into the bathroom attached to his bedroom. He opens the drawer and pulls out a toothbrush in a box and toothpaste. "Feel free to use anything you want in here." He motions to the cabinet and drawers.

"Thanks."

He steps back, walks to the shower, then turns it on. I take the toothbrush out of the box, put the paste on it, then begin to brush my teeth. Through the mirror, I watch Adrian drop his shorts and step into the glass shower.

My heart hammers in my chest. Nothing about Adrian except the scratch marks on his back isn't pure perfection. The water rolls off his body, and I can't decide if he's sexier dry, sweating in the gym, or in the shower. Then he lathers liquid soap in his hands and rubs it over his bare flesh.

Good Lord.

I finish brushing my teeth, debating about whether I should join him or not. After searching for a hairbrush and finding none, I decide to keep watching. It makes sense he doesn't have a hairbrush since he keeps his hair almost shaved. I have one in my purse, but I don't want to miss the scene in front of me. I prop my bottom on the counter and cross my legs.

Adrian glances over and smirks. He finishes his shower and dries off then wraps a towel around his waist. He puts his hands on the counter near my bottom. "Did you enjoy the show?"

"Yep."

He pecks my lips. "I made a reservation at Sarcasm for seven."

"Wow! Impressive. I'm on the list for December. How did you get in?" I ask.

"I'm a silent investor. If you like it and want to move your reservation up, let me know."

I chirp, "Oh, the benefits of a date with Mr. Ivanov."

He licks his lips while his gaze drifts over my body. "Those aren't the benefits."

My flutters erupt. *I'm sure they don't even come close.*

I tease, "You're awfully sure of yourself."

"Only about things I know I can deliver on."

My lower body throbs. Heat flies to my cheeks. Images of waking up and glancing down to see Adrian pinning his gaze on me with his cocky smirk make me squirm on the quartz. The memory of his mouth all over my body intoxicates me. "I need to go home and get ready."

"Okay. Make sure you pack a bag." He steps back and goes into his closet. While he gets dressed, I go to the bedroom and put my clothes from yesterday on. He drives me to my place. When we get to my apartment, he drops me off at the door.

"You don't want to come in?"

"I have something I need to do first. I'll be back around six thirty."

"Okay."

He possessively tugs me into him, kisses me, and leaves me panting. I shut and lock the door. It's only three, so I decide I have time for a run. It's nice out, and I spend an hour jogging along the paved shoreline, thinking about Adrian and our night together. My counselor's voice pops into my head. *Go slow in your relationships.*

I ignore it. She definitely wouldn't approve of me spending the weekend with Adrian after what he initially did or since we just started seeing each other.

Adrian isn't Tim.

I'm not in my twenties anymore.

I push her voice out of my head and run faster. By the time I get to my apartment, I'm full of sweat and trying to catch my breath.

I go inside, take a shower, then fix my hair and makeup. When I'm satisfied with how I look, I go into the closet and assess my wardrobe. Sarcasm is a new five-star restaurant. It's been open since last fall, but the waitlist is insane.

I flick my wrists as I sort through my clothes hanging on the rack. I mumble, "No... Trying too hard... Not sexy enough... Yes!" I remove a new dress I bought a few months ago from a designer I met at a show. It's a purple bodycon dress with tiny black streaks throughout the abstract design. When I saw it, I had to have it. It costs more than I usually spend on clothes, and I haven't had the right occasion to wear it yet.

The pair of stilettos I bought from another local designer catches my eye. A student at the university designed them, and I picked the shoes up at an art fair. Purple and magenta swirl together on the canvas. I add a pair of black and silver dangly earrings and a watch I also got from an art fair.

For over an hour, I pace my apartment, staring at the buildings as the daytime light turns to dark.

Why am I so nervous? I date all the time and don't get anxious.

I've never had a man like Adrian coming to pick me up.

The door buzzer snaps me out of my thoughts, and my flutters increase when Adrian's deep voice and Russian accent hit my ears. "It's me, my printsessa."

I release the lock and wipe my sweaty palms on a dishtowel, then wash them with soap and dry them. Adrian knocks on the door, and I open it.

Oh, help me, Lord.

He's the hottest man on earth.

His black dress shirt has a few buttons unfastened. The letters L-E-V from his chest tattoo peek out. The line between his two pec muscles is well-defined, and Vs into his neck. He holds out a bouquet of Gerbera daisies. The skull tattoo covering his hand faces me. I'm unsure why I love it so much, since I'm not into skulls, but something about it always grabs my attention.

He's a bad boy who's too panty-melting.

Peach blossom, Turkish rose, and amber mix with the fresh flowers, creating an intoxicating scent. I take a deep breath as Adrian's eyes roam over me. He pierces me with his icy-blue orbs. "You look beautiful, my printsessa." He dips down and gives me a chaste kiss, which only leaves me wanting more.

"Thank you. You look nice, too. And I love Gerbera daisies. They are one of my favorite flowers."

"Took the chance you weren't into roses the way other women are."

"How did you know?" He's right. I think bringing a woman roses is nice but doesn't display a lot of creativity on a man's part.

His lips tick up. Blue flames travel over my body. It's as if his gaze alone is licking my skin with fire. A full-on arrogant expression fills his face. "There's nothing average about you or your flair."

The humming in my blood intensifies. I laugh to break up the butterflies dancing in my stomach. "I always think of the movie *Office Space* when I hear flair. Then I think of all the fifteen pieces they made Jennifer's character wear."

"*Office Space?*"

"Yeah. Have you not seen it?"

He shakes his head. "No."

"Oh, well, you should. It's a good movie."

He nods. "Put it on the list, my printsessa."

"The list?"

He shrugs. "Things to do on a lazy day. We should get going."

A lazy day with Adrian. Yes, please.

"Let me put these in water." I go into the kitchen. My apartment is an open concept, and Adrian strolls over to the window.

"You have a nice place," he says.

I remove a vase out of my cabinet. "Thanks. I've been here for about five years."

"I'm glad you live in a better neighborhood than Hailee or Aspen."

I glance toward him. He's got his hands in his pockets. His shirt stretches perfectly over his back. It Vs into his lower body and his tucked-in shirt displays his rock-hard ass.

Even Adonis, the god of beauty and desire, would be jealous of Adrian's body.

"They aren't the safest places, but it's what they can afford. I'm not sure what other choices they have, and I don't blame them for not wanting a roommate. The only way I would live with someone again was if I was in a serious relationship," I admit.

"Safety should come first," he insists.

I sigh. "It's not that simple."

Adrian spins. "Where's your overnight bag?"

My cheeks heat. I blurt out, "It's in my closet."

"Packed?"

"Yes."

"Do you want me to get it for you?"

"Sure."

I fill the vase, cut the stems, and put the flowers in it. "All done," I chirp when Adrian steps out of my bedroom with my bag. His signature cocky expression fills his face.

Why does that look turn me on so much?

I bet lots of women hate it. Maybe if his smirk regarded another woman, I would. Perhaps the idea I'm part of the reason he wears his arrogance makes my loins pulse.

He puts his hand on my back and guides me out the door and into the parking garage. When we get in his SUV, he veers through the structure, and we're soon on the road.

"Are you from Russia?" I ask.

He nods. "My mother made Obrecht, Natalia, and me immigrate. My father had already passed. I was sixteen."

"Was it hard?"

He shrugs. "Yes and no. Things in Russia had gotten dangerous. The first few years after we moved were challenging since we didn't know English, but we were happier." His voice fades, and his jaw clenches. He grips the wheel tighter.

I want to ask him about his sister, but I don't want to upset him. "Was it hard to learn English?"

"At first. It got easier." He puts on the blinker and turns. "What do you do? I know you work in fashion but not what you do all day."

I chirp, "Oh, I play dress-up. I try on outfits and give my opinions on clothes."

"Really?"

I snort. "No. I wish. Although it was my dream job when I was little."

"Does that position exist?"

"Not really. You're either a model who wears the clothes or the designer and buyers who have opinions about them." I turn in my seat.

"So you design?"

"Quite a bit, not that I get any credit for it."

"Why not?"

"Bowmen pays my salary. Everything I create he owns. I also pick out all the materials and order them. His last collection had twenty pieces. I designed sixteen of them and helped with the other four."

Adrian's eyes turn to slits. "That isn't right."

I shrug. "Is what it is."

"If you're doing all the designing, why don't you go out on your own? Start your own label?"

"Do you know how much money it costs to create a label?"

"No."

"A lot. Plus, I need my income to survive. At least Bowmen pays me a decent wage. For Chicago, my compensation is fair."

"Hmm."

"What's hmm, mean?"

"So you can sit down and design an entire outfit?"

"Sure."

"How long does it take?"

I shrug. "It depends on how intricate it is and how many items. It could range from an hour to several days."

"Did you design your dress?"

"No. I bought it at a show from a new designer I met. I don't design anything for myself anymore."

His eyes dart down my body, as if he's undressing me. He licks his lips then says, "It fits you perfectly, my printsessa. Why don't you make anything for yourself?"

Heat rushes to my cheeks from the way he's studying me. "By the time I get done with Bowmen's orders, I don't have energy left."

"Your boss sounds like a dick."

"I've called him worse," I admit. "So, are you or Obrecht older?"

"He's four years older."

"Really?"

"Why do you seem surprised?" He pulls into a lot and parks.

"I figured you were closer in age. How old are you?"

"Older than you."

"I don't remember telling you my age."

He checks me out again, and I try not to squirm. "You aren't forty."

I gape at him. "Obrecht is forty-four?"

"Yep."

"Wow. I would have thought you were both around thirty-eight."

Adrian unbuckles his belt and gets out. He comes over to my side and opens the door then reaches in to help me out. His strong arm cocoons around my body, and his palm grips my hip. "Your friends are all thirty-eight, but you're younger?"

"Did you research us?"

He snorts. "No. You don't look thirty-eight. My guess is you wouldn't be as close if you were in your twenties, so you're close to their age but a few years younger?"

"Thirty-six," I admit.

He opens the door and motions for me to go in. I step through. He encloses his arm around me again and leads me to the hostess stand. His body stiffens.

A beautiful woman with blonde hair pulled into a sleek French twist, a killer body, and perfectly manicured fingers bats her eyes. In a Russian accent, she coolly says, "Adrian." She quickly looks me over then refocuses on him.

Adrian's fingers grip my hips with more pressure. It's slight, but I notice it. In a voice colder than hers, he replies, "Dasha. I didn't know you were back in town."

"Two weeks. You know how much Yefim loves me. When he heard I was back in Chicago, he wanted me to work for him."

Adrian stays silent.

"I saw Ivanov on the list. I was hoping it was you." She scans his body, as if he's her man and I'm not standing attached to his hip. "You look well, Adrian. Time's been good to you."

His face hardens. "Is our table ready?"

Jealousy flares in my belly. I'm not naive enough to think Adrian doesn't have a past with other women, but Dasha looks like a model and has the sexy everything going on. Their exchange makes me believe she was something to him at one point or another.

"You aren't going to ask why I came back home?" She pouts.

"No. I don't care. Is our table ready?"

She softly laughs. Her voice oozes between sugar and ice. She coos, "Of course you do." She gives me another dismissive glance then leans closer to Adrian. "We'll talk later." She says something quickly in Russian while picking up our menus.

Adrian replies and scoffs. He guides me through the restaurant. The scent of her rose perfume floods my nostrils. They continue their conversation until we get to our table. I barely take in the sexy atmosphere while trying not to let Dasha see I'm affected by her.

She says in English, "I have the same phone number. Let's have coffee soon." She arrogantly stares at me while suggesting, "Or breakfast."

"That's enough, Dasha," Adrian reprimands.

My stomach flips. *Please tell me he doesn't want her anymore.*

How could he not?

They probably used to have hot sex.

Ugh. I don't want to think about it.

Great. Now all I can think of is her perfectly made-up face getting Os from Adrian.

Her smug exterior never waivers. "Have a great dinner. The food is excellent here." She leaves.

My insides shake with anger. *Is he still interested in her? Now that she's back from wherever she was, is he going to want to see her again?*

Adrian turns. "I'm sorry about that."

I force a smile. "It's okay. Who is she?"

Adrian glances at the ceiling then meets my gaze. "My ex-wife."

9

Adrian

NOTHING HAS CHANGED BETWEEN DASHA AND ME. SHE MAKES my blood boil as much as the day she left for Europe. I haven't seen her in years. She looks slightly older but not much. Time has done nothing to change my thoughts about her.

Skylar's eyes widen. "Your ex-wife?"

I sigh. "In the flesh."

"When did you get divorced?"

This isn't the conversation I want to have on my first date with Skylar, but I don't see how to get out of it. "We separated when I was twenty-seven, and our divorce was final five years ago."

She raises her eyebrows. "That's a long separation."

"It's complicated."

"How?"

"Do you really want to talk about this?" I drag my finger down the side of her throat. "I can think of much better topics."

She inhales slowly. "Maybe you should tell me now and then you don't have to tell me later."

"I'd rather talk about you, not her." It's true. There's nothing about my years or relationship with Dasha I want to revisit. My time with her was a product of our age, explosive chemistry, and my developing rage and pain over Natalia that made me into who I am today. Dasha didn't understand me then, and she sure wouldn't today. When things got rough, she bailed on me. I loved her, and she didn't love me enough to stay with me. It took a lot of time, but I don't have any feelings left for her.

Skylar tilts her head. "Adrian, you pried until I told you what you wanted to know last night. I think you owe me."

My pulse increases. Skylar still doesn't fully trust me. This is a perfect event to ruin the progress I've made. I cave. "What do you need to know, my printsessa?"

"She seemed interested in you."

I snort. Dasha made it clear she is, but I don't want any part of her. Anything with her would be purely physical, and I've done my rounds with her. I'm not the same guy who can't resist her advances. "There's nothing about her I miss or want to revisit."

Skylar doesn't look convinced.

"I'm divorced for a reason," I state.

"How long were you married?"

"I was twenty-three when we got married. We separated, and I haven't seen her since I was thirty-five."

"You tried to work on things for seven years?"

I shake my head. "No. She kept stalling. I had several investments Maksim had Obrecht and me make before I got married. They took off, and she wanted them. We finally agreed on a settlement."

"So you only stayed married that long because of financial reasons?"

And the fact Dasha knows I became a killer and kept coming back to me, declaring her love, then throwing me away again.

I choose my words carefully. Finances were the only reason we didn't split between those times. "That was what held it up, yes."

"Where did she go? She left Chicago?"

"The last time I saw her was when we signed divorce papers. It was five years ago. She said she was leaving for Europe. I assume that's where she went, but honestly, I don't know and don't care." It comes out harsher than needed. Dasha knows my secrets and all the mistakes I made. Maksim and his brothers had to help me clean messes up when I first sought out revenge for Natalia. Almost all the men who raped her, I killed. There are only two left I need to finish. Wes and Zamir Petrov will eventually have their day with my cousins, Obrecht, and me. It doesn't make me comfortable that Dasha is back in town.

She wants to reconnect, but I'm not falling for her trap this time.

"Why did you get divorced?"

She couldn't handle what I became. She didn't love me enough to stick by me.

"We were young. We shouldn't have gotten married. Can we change the subject? I didn't ask you out to talk about my ex-wife. She's not part of my life anymore and is never going to be again. I'd rather get to know you."

Skylar looks away.

My chest tightens. I put my arm around her and slide closer. "Is it a problem I'm divorced?"

She meets my eye. "No. But I don't like how she seemed interested in you. I'm not looking to get involved with someone who has something going on with their ex."

I have to give Skylar credit. I appreciate her honesty instead of going around her feelings. "She can be interested in me all she wants. It isn't going to change my mind about her." I lean closer to her lips. "There's only one woman who's gotten my attention in a long time, and I'm staring at her. She's the only one I'm interested in getting involved with."

Her cheeks flush.

"Good evening. I'm David. Can I get you something to drink? Perhaps a bottle of red from the chef's choice?" the server says.

"Do you drink wine?" I ask Skylar.

"Sure. That would be fine."

I nod to the server. "We'll take a bottle."

"Good choice, sir. The chef has prepared a five-course meal. It starts with a pesto and brie canape, followed by English pea soup and red snapper ceviche. The main course is lamb with minted asparagus. Dessert is strawberry shortcake with lemon cream. If you don't want the special, the menu has all our regular and seasonal items." He points to the papers in front of us. "I'll get your wine and give you a few minutes."

"Thank you," Skylar and I say at the same time, and he leaves.

I turn to her and rub my thumb over her hip. "What do you do for fun?"

"The girls and I do yoga together sometimes. I like art, especially the fairs where I can discover someone new. Of course, I love fashion shows. My taste in music is pretty diverse, so I'll pretty much go to any concert. If something big is happening in the city, I'll usually try to attend. I run on days I don't do yoga."

My eyes drift down her body. "Yoga and running look good on you, my printsessa."

She elbows me.

"Ouch! What's that for?"

"Your perverted stare is distracting me."

"Perverted?"

She smirks. "Are you claiming you don't have a perverted stare or know what I'm talking about?"

I take a sip of my water. "Perverted means two things."

"Oh?"

The waiter arrives with our bottle of wine. He opens it and hands me the tasting glass. I pass it to Skylar. "What do you think?"

She takes a sip then licks her sinful lips. "Delicious."

The waiter fills our goblets then we order the chef's special. When he's gone, I twist a lock of Skylar's hair around my finger. "Perverted is characterized by sexually abnormal and unacceptable practices or tendencies. There isn't anything abnormal I'm going to do to you that any man who looks at you wouldn't dream of doing."

Her face turns the color of our cabernet. "You said it has two meanings. What's the second?"

"Having been corrupted or distorted from its original course, meaning, or state." I move my thumb to her inner thigh so my entire palm is on her leg. "Sex is for pleasure. There isn't anything corrupt or distorted about it. Nothing has changed about what I want to do to you, and it doesn't involve hiding my intentions or pretending not to know what I want." I check her out again.

Her lips twitch. "You seem to be an expert on perversion. Is there a reason you know the definition? Too many women point out what I did?"

I grunt. "Nope. I learned it in school."

"Wow. Did you memorize all your vocabulary words?" she teases.

"Only the interesting ones." I take a sip of my wine. Blackberries and currents mix with a smoky flavor. I set the glass down and slowly swirl the liquid. "What's the strangest word you know the definition for inside and out?"

"Gobbledygook."

I snort. "Gobbledygook isn't a word."

"Yes, it is. It's in the Oxford dictionary, and the definition is meaningless language, made unintelligible by excessive use of abstruse technical terms, or in the simplest of terms, nonsense."

"Guess I learned something new," I admit. "When I first came to America, I felt everyone was speaking gobbledygook."

She lightly claps. "Bravo." She pouts her lips. "But I feel bad you had to go through that. I bet it was tough."

"I learned quick."

She smiles. "What's your strangest word?"

I drag my finger over her hand and up her arm. "Agastopia."

Amusement fills her face. "Aga-what?"

"Agastopia. Admiration of a particular part of someone's body. The visual enjoyment of the appearance of a specific physical aspect of another."

"This is in the dictionary?"

"Yep. The urban one, not sure about others."

She laughs. "Sounds like it could mix well with pervert in the same sentence." She straightens her back and holds out her chin. Her long lashes bat against her blue eyes, and my dick twitches. "My agastopia causes me to be a pervert."

I linger on each body part as I slowly reply, "My agastopia has me going crazy for your eyes, lips," I trace them then move my hand over her chest, "perfect breasts," I rest it on her lap, "and the most delicious piece of heaven I've ever tasted."

She holds her breath for a moment. Her voice cracks when she breathes out, "Well, nostrovia for agastopia." She takes a long sip of her wine and sets her glass down.

I lean in to her ear and take a nibble then say, "You know Russian, my printsessa?"

She turns her face so our eyes meet. "Only nostrovia."

"I like how it rolls out of your sexy little mouth." I steal her lips, which are sweet from the wine. Within seconds, her tongue plays with mine. She palms my head. Our kiss perfectly syncs. We're yin and yang, and not one part of our bodies doesn't fit together. It's another reminder of how good we are together. I've enjoyed many women over the years. No one has kissed me and made my veins pulse with fire until Skylar.

"Adrian."

"Yeah," I mumble and stick my tongue back in her mouth.

"Mmm." She kisses me back and murmurs, "Don't leave any tittynopes in your wineglass."

I freeze. "Titty-what?"

Her lips turn up. "Tittynopes."

"What are those?"

"The few drops remaining in the glass, or if you were eating, the crumbs that remain."

I return to her lips. "Impressive. I'm glad our date is going well, and I don't need to worry about my kakorrhaphiophobia."

She pulls out of our kiss. Her eyes light up. "What is that?"

"Fear of failure."

She bites on her lip then says, "I require a jentacular cup of coffee." Her hot mouth of perfection presses into mine, and my pants suddenly feel very restricted.

I ask, "Jentacular?"

She flicks her tongue inside me again, and I groan. She replies, "Anything breakfast related."

"I'll serve you any kind of coffee you want, my printsessa, as long as you're naked."

She softly laughs. "I like how you don't have typhlobasia."

"Now you're showing off. No clue what that means."

"It means you only kiss with your eyes closed."

"I'm multitalented," I claim, and between more kisses express, "I have to admit I'm relieved you love what my clatterdevengeance can do for you."

She retreats. "Your what?"

I suck on her lobe. In a low voice, I reply, "It means dick."

"I didn't know dinner was going to be so educational," she mumbles.

"I'm ready to teach you—"

"Pesto and brie canape," a server chirps out.

I release Skylar and turn to the server. "Thank you." He refills our wine and leaves. I pick up a canape and hold it to Skylar's mouth. "Try this."

She bites into it. "Mmm." She licks her lips then pats her napkin over them. After she swallows, she says, "I need to use the ladies' room."

I rise. "I'll show you where the restroom is."

She shakes her head and smiles. "It's okay. I saw where it was when we walked through the restaurant. I'll be right back." She leaves, and I sit back in the circular booth. Dasha strolls past our table with another couple, gets them situated, then slides next to me.

"What are you doing, Dasha?" I bark. Her rose perfume flares in my nostrils. I used to love it. Maybe it's another reason I can't stand the thought of giving Skylar roses and looked for something else. They always remind me of Dasha, and I don't care to think about her. The scent now annoys me.

She speaks in Russian. "Aren't you going to ask me why I'm back?"

I switch to Russian. "No. I don't care. Now get out of the booth."

She laughs and reaches for my cheek. I freeze. For years, I would have paid money to have her touch me. "So, you're still stubborn, huh?"

I jerk my face away from her and scoot to the edge of the booth. "I'm not interested in you or your games."

She smiles and moves closer. "I missed you, Adrian. I've had a lot of time to think about us."

"There is no us. You didn't want us, remember?"

"We were young."

I scoff. "We were thirty-five when we finally divorced. You strung me along for almost eight years."

"No, I didn't. I tried to make it work."

My heart thumps harder against my chest cavity. I wish Dasha still didn't get under my skin, but she does. I'm not sure what she's trying to achieve with this conversation. "Believe whatever you want, Dasha. I was there. You didn't like who I became, remember?"

She puts her hand around the back of my neck. "I can deal with it now. I'm a different person. Things...things have happened to make me look upon..." She picks up my glass of water and takes a sip. "I...something happened. It gave me a different perspective."

The hairs on my arms rise. I don't want Dasha anymore, but I don't wish harm on her. "What happened?"

Her face darkens. "Can we get together and talk? Please?" She leans closer, so her lips are next to mine. "We're good together, Adrian. We made a mistake, now let's fix it."

How many times have I heard that?

Nothing happened to her. It's all part of her game.

I take her hand and remove it from my neck. In a low voice, I reply, "We aren't good together. We didn't make a mistake. We won't be getting back together. I wish you well, Dasha, but don't come looking for me. You may be back in Chicago, but you didn't return for me. Don't make things up to try and pull me in. It isn't going to work this time."

She scrunches her face. "Something did happen." She traces the L-E-V letters on my chest, and my stomach painfully twists with my heart. "There isn't anyone else I could even talk to about it. You're the only one who would understand."

Is she telling the truth? What could have happened?

It doesn't matter. We aren't together anymore.

I rise and put my napkin on the table. I pull out my wallet then toss cash near the candle.

"Adrian, don't dismiss me. I'm your wife," she claims.

Anger bubbles inside me. I put both hands on the table and lean closer to her, so I don't make a scene. "You gave up the right to be Mrs. Adrian Ivanov. Remember? You didn't want any part of me. Stay away from me, Dasha. Nothing good can come from pursuing me. I'm not the man who wanted to keep you. He's gone. The one you're staring at doesn't want any part of whatever it is you're offering."

"Adrian?" Skylar's voice rings in my ear, and I don't miss the smug expression that crosses Dasha's face when she glances behind me.

I pick up Skylar's purse and put my hand around her waist. I switch to English. "We're going."

Skylar glances at Dasha.

"She doesn't even know Russian?" Dasha asks in our native tongue, as if it's a reason for me not to date Skylar. "You're trying to make something work with someone who can't handle you, Adrian. Look at her. She can't deal with the truth of who you are or what you do."

Unable to control my rage, I spit back in Russian, "Don't you ever talk about my woman or what I do again. And you better watch it, Dasha. You seem to have the impression I care about you or what happens to you. Let me reiterate. I don't. The next time you see me, walk the other way." I guide Skylar through the restaurant. When we get outside, I turn to her, with rage burning my bones. "I'm sorry, my printsessa. I didn't mean to ruin our dinner."

Skylar cups my cheeks. "You're upset. What did she want?"

I don't reply. I stare at her lips.

Something passes in her eyes. She softly asks, "She wants you back, doesn't she?"

I snort. "Just the typical Dasha game she plays."

Skylar bites her lip and looks away.

I turn her chin toward me and pin my eyes on her. "It's not happening. There isn't any part of me that wants her. I don't want you questioning this."

Skylar exhales. "Okay. Good to know."

I fist her hair and kiss her. "I'm sorry I messed up our dinner."

Her lips twitch. "I prefer taco cones to lamb."

"Taco cones?"

She points to a food truck. "We happen to be several feet away from the best taco cones on earth."

"I've never had one," I admit.

She gasps. "How have you survived?"

I chuckle. "I guess I'm going to find out."

We order taco cones and eat them on a bench overlooking Lake Michigan. It's night, so the water is dark, but the waves crashing along the shore are loud. I try to concentrate on Skylar and forget about Dasha, but a nagging feeling overpowers me.

I'm not sure what Dasha's ulterior motives are for coming back to Chicago, but I'm going to find out. Her claim to want me is only a smokescreen for whatever she has up her sleeve. It's her typical move. She's done it at least a dozen times, but I'm not the same man I used to be. This time, I'm not going to sit back and wait for her to show her cards.

10

Skylar

"Acnestis," Adrian blurts out. We finished our taco cones and are walking along the shore.

I wince. "Something to do with pimples?"

Adrian trails his finger down my spine. "The part of the back between the shoulder blades and the loins which an animal cannot reach to scratch." I shudder, and he takes his jacket off and puts it around me. He pulls both sides of the coat together. "The temperature is dropping. We should head back."

It's unfairly warm for this early in the spring. The wind coming off Lake Michigan is calmer than usual, but it still creates a chill on my skin. My lips slightly shake. I tilt my head up. "Biblioklept."

An amused grin lights up Adrian's face. The sun has set, and the only light is the streetlamps. His face seems sharper against the warm glow. "A bible thief?"

"Close. One who steals books."

He groans. "So close!"

"You almost had me. What's the score?" I ask.

"Five to five. I have to admit. I'm impressed with your vocabulary."

I bat my eyelashes. "Aren't all your dates as well versed as me?"

His cocky expression appears. He drags his eyes down my body and back up. "No. You're the only one with impressive skills." He slides his hand through my hair and leans down. "Besides the catastrophe in the restaurant, I had a good time. Thanks for not letting it ruin our night."

I can't stop the smile forming on my face. We ate taco cones, walked along the lake, and talked about random things while throwing out crazy words trying to stump the other person. It's the most fun I've had on a date in...well, forever. "I had a good time, too."

His icy-blue eyes pierce mine. "Sorry I didn't have coffee for you this morning. Tomorrow, I'll make you a raf in the morning."

"Well, I didn't wake up until one in the afternoon, but what is a raf?"

He jerks his head back and gasps. "It's a Russian coffee drink with espresso cream and vanilla sugar."

"Yummy. So it's like a latte?"

He furrows his eyebrows. "No. Lattes have milk. A raf is with cream."

"You seem very serious about this drink."

Arrogance appears on his face. "I promise it's better than any latte you've ever had."

I laugh. "That's a big statement to make."

More smugness erupts, which only makes my lower body throb. "I'll make you a deal."

"What kind of deal?"

"If it isn't better than any latte you've ever had, I'll scrub your kitchen floor naked."

The image of Adrian, on his hands and knees, cleaning my tile, wearing nothing fills my mind. I bite on my smile, reach up, and lace my fingers around his neck. "I might need to claim it's horrible just to see that."

His lips twitch. He brushes them against mine while he speaks. "I assure you, when I drop you off Sunday night, I won't be cleaning your floors. However, if you love it and I'm right, I get to teach you how to do a proper push-up."

"Do my arms need work?" I ask.

He palms my ass and tugs me so there's no room between us. "No. But you'll do it naked and keep going until I say stop."

I laugh. "Deal. Get ready to scrub floors."

Silence fills the air, and several moments pass. A firestorm of blue blazes in his orbs, taking my breath away. No man has ever indicated they wanted me with their eyes how Adrian does or displayed such a cocky expression about what he can deliver. It's electrifying and terrifying all at the same time. "We're good together," he finally murmurs then parts my lips with his tongue, kissing me with controlled speed, as if savoring every part of my mouth.

"I have brunch tomorrow with the girls," I mumble, suddenly remembering the text conversation I had with Hailee and Kora about meeting Kora's friend who wants to cook for us.

"Then I'll drop you off and pick you up. You can do your naked push-ups after."

I softly laugh, and he kisses me some more. "I can take a cab."

He snorts. "My woman isn't taking a cab."

His woman.

Is that what I am?

Have we already moved into me being his, or is it just a statement?

"Ready to go home, my printsessa?" He slides his tongue back in my mouth, and my knees go weak.

Home. He says it, as if it's where we both live.

"Mmhmm."

He pulls back. "Let's go." He guides me to the SUV and opens my door.

I slide in the seat.

"Adrian," Dasha's voice calls out then continues rattling off Russian.

I freeze, and my stomach flips. I watch Dasha trot through the parking garage like the building is on fire.

I need to learn Russian.

Why does she have to sound so sexy when she speaks?

Adrian's shoulders tense. He shuts the door and crosses his arms over his chest. He and Dasha have what appears to be a heated conversation, but since I don't understand a word they are saying, I can't be sure.

Dasha reaches for Adrian's arm, and he shrugs her off him. He angrily shakes his head and moves to the driver's side.

She keeps talking, follows him, and tugs on his shirt. Adrian spins. He lowers his voice. Even in the dimly lit garage, I can see his face turning red.

It seems to last forever. Dasha never appears to back down. She reaches for Adrian several times. Each time, he removes her hand or stops her from touching him. His actions should give me some comfort, but they don't. Dasha glows in the barely lit garage. She's like an angel of beautiful strength. I don't consider myself unattractive or weak, but I can't help comparing myself to the picture Dasha portrays. She and Adrian have a past and share the same culture. I don't even know my full heritage. Side by side, Adrian and Dasha are a stunning couple. I can visualize them together and Adrian looking at her the way he stares at me. I hear and see him saying "I do" while she wears a white wedding gown.

He points to the door she came through and says something. She replies then turns and goes in the direction he pointed. The entire time, he watches her until she disappears through the door, which only makes me more jealous.

Is he staring at her ass?

She has a nice one.

No, he's making sure she gets inside safely, that's it.

What if it isn't?

When she is no longer visible, he pulls out his phone and gets in the car. He turns on the engine and reverses out of the spot. "Obrecht," he growls, followed by more Russian. From time to time, I hear, "Dasha."

Why is he calling his brother about Dasha?

Adrian parks in the garage to his building and gets out. He comes around the front of the car toward my side, but I get out and meet him halfway. He puts his arm around me and tugs me into his body, as if I'm his possession. His lips brush my forehead before he hurls out more Russian. The conversation with Obrecht continues inside his penthouse. He paces in front of the glass. I perch on the edge of the couch, watching him, twisting my fingers, not sure what to do. His agitation only seems to grow. He slides his hand over his head and barks something out then hangs up.

Minutes pass. He doesn't move. I finally rise and cautiously approach him. I softly ask, "Adrian, is everything okay?"

His jaw stays clenched. He grinds his molars. "Yeah. I'm sorry, my printsessa. I don't mean to be rude."

"You weren't. It's okay. Umm...what's going on?"

"Nothing you need to worry about. Everything will be fine."

Will be. Not is fine. Will be fine.

"Adrian—"

He cuts me off with a kiss, savagely moving his tongue in and out of my mouth, as if I'm his lifeblood.

"Ad—"

His tongue shuts me up again, and he unzips my dress. Before I know it, I'm naked, facing the back of his couch on my knees, and he's licking my spine.

"Adrian," I whimper, still wanting to know what occurred between Dasha and him that required him to speak for over twenty minutes to his brother.

His lips brush my ear. He thrusts in me and growls, "We're not talking about it, my printsessa. She doesn't get our time. She's not the one I want." He drops his hand to my clit and manipulates my body further.

Blood, heat, and adrenaline mix into a potent concoction of chaos in my veins.

His lips travel across my jaw. "Look at me."

I turn my head, meeting his thrusts, short on breath.

His blue eyes are a mix of ice and flames piercing into mine. He doesn't speak until a domino effect of Os annihilates me. His intense gaze never falters. He mutters a mix of Russian and English against my cheek, but nothing seems to register as coherent.

The power of his body over mine is unlike anything I've ever experienced. When he finally releases, blackness flashes in my eyes. I go beyond any point I thought was possible. My nails dig into his leather couch, and my back arches into his dense torso.

He buries his face in the curve of my neck. His stomach muscles contract against my spine, sending fresh zings through my nerves. Several minutes pass before he pulls away from me and flips me over.

I reach for his face. "Adrian. What did she do?"

His face hardens again. "Nothing."

"Adrian, don't lie to me."

"It's taken care of, and we aren't talking about her, Skylar. Never. She doesn't get any piece of us."

I open my mouth, but nothing comes out. What Adrian is saying, I can't find fault in. I don't want her to have any piece of us.

But does she still have a piece of him?

She has to, or he wouldn't have had to call Obrecht.

Before I can speak, his tongue is in my mouth. He picks me up and carries me into the bedroom. For hours, we don't converse. He's an animal, focused only on me and how much pleasure he can create within my body.

The sounds and smell of us fornicating fill the air. Every time I think he's going to take a break, he pounces on me with more fervor. His face is between my thighs, I'm in the middle of an orgasm, and his phone rings.

He groans, finishes me off, then grabs the phone off his nightstand. He answers in Russian, sucks on my breast, then freezes with his tongue over my nipple.

He says more words I don't understand, rises, then hangs up. The hardness is back in his expression. His eyes turn dark. "I'm sorry, my printsessa. I have to go."

"What? It's the middle of the night."

"Yes. I'm sorry." He goes into his closet.

I get out of bed and follow him. "Adrian, what's going on?"

"I have to take care of something for work. I'm sorry. I'll have my driver take you home tomorrow."

The hairs on my arms rise. "You aren't coming back tonight?"

"No." He avoids looking at me, slides a pair of jeans over his legs, then reaches for a T-shirt.

"Adrian!"

He pulls his shirt over his head and sticks his feet in his shoes. He turns then kisses my forehead. "I'll call you in a few days." He passes me, leaving the closet.

"A few days? Adrian, please. Tell me where you're going." I reach for his arm.

He stops but doesn't turn. "Don't make this harder than it has to be, Skylar. I need to go. I'll talk to you soon." He continues through the penthouse and never looks back. When he leaves, I sit on the couch. My insides are shaking. I've never had any man leave in the middle of the night while with me. What could be so important, and why wouldn't he tell me what's going on?

Only one thought comes to mind.

He went to see her.

A chill consumes me. I pull the afghan over my body, realizing I'm still naked. No matter how much I try to convince myself that Adrian wouldn't go see Dasha in the middle of the night, and especially not when I'm in his bed, it's the only conclusion I have.

After so many minutes of sitting in terrorizing silence, I put my clothes on and grab my bag. When I get to the lobby, the security for the building orders a taxi. I avoid the curious gaze from the young man at the front desk. I shouldn't be bothered by it, but I feel like I'm back in college doing the walk of shame.

When I get into my apartment, it's after three in the morning. I attempt to go to sleep, but all I see is Dasha and Adrian. I finally let the tears fall.

How can anyone love so passionately like Adrian does but run to another woman the first chance he gets?

Because it's not love. It's sex.

I was in his bed. His mouth was on my body when he got that call.

He said it was for work.

He's Aspen's bodyguard. She's asleep, at home with Maksim.

I don't sleep. When the sun rises, I look at my phone, but I already know there's nothing there from Adrian. I curse myself for even expecting it.

Around eight, my phone dings with a message. My hope dissipates when I see it isn't from Adrian. I loathe how much I still want to hear from him.

Hailee: *I'm running late. I'll be there in ten.*

I almost tell Hailee I'm not going but then I decide I'm not going to let Adrian's dismissal of me stop me from hanging out with my friends.

Me: *Don't rush. I'm still getting ready.*

I throw on my yoga clothes and several layers over them. I put eye drops in to try and get the red out of my eyes. When Hailee's Uber pulls up, I'm already in the lobby.

She assesses me. "Skylar, what's wrong?"

The truth of my night is too embarrassing to talk about, even with my closest friends. I force a smile. "Nothing. Tell me what you know about Kora's friend we're meeting."

11

Adrian

WHOEVER SAID AN EYE FOR AN EYE, A TOOTH FOR A TOOTH, didn't understand reality. Once an injustice occurs, there's nothing that can even the score. Any repercussion possible won't undo the harm or destruction. The blink of satisfaction you feel while avenging whoever wronged you only lasts a split second. Eventually, it's over. There's no more pain to inflict upon your enemy. The emptiness and hole in your heart are still there when it's over. Wes Petrov's last few days with us are no different.

For fifteen years, Obrecht and I patiently waited for this day. It's no different than Maksim, Dmitri, Boris, or Sergey. The crimes Wes and his father bestowed upon our family are beyond hideous. Each one molded us into who we are today and took people we loved and destroyed them. My aunt, their mother. Our sister, their cousin. My wife, their friend.

Deep scars are dangerous. They have time to fester. Plans surrounding your moment of reckoning develop. Every idea has time to simmer then get sharpened to perfection.

Fresh wounds have more emotion to them. There isn't enough time for strategy. Take an old scab and add a new one, and you've got the most intense situations possible.

It's the catalyst for what is happening now. Wes and his three thugs hang upside down in the garage. My eyes zero in on him and the man who put his grimy hands on my printsessa. However, the choice of who to spend my time on is chosen for me. It's not often the six of us Ivanovs are at the garage together, but we don't usually have Petrovs here.

All of us have the same and also different reasons for wanting Wes dead. His latest stunt, sending the poisonous snake to Aspen, almost killed her. It gives Maksim first dibs. I spend those hours evoking fear, more than pain, into the thug who held Skylar down against her will. Since that's what she felt, it's only appropriate he experiences it. I'll inflict his pain after I get my shot at Wes.

Hours pass. I don't know what time or day it is. The garage is the one place I'm allowed to act while I'm spinning out. If I had to guess, I'd say all of us go into some zone. I don't know how we would do the things we're capable of and move about everyday life if we didn't. The biggest struggle for me is pulling out of the trance. Others have the same issues.

Maksim finally steps back and allows Sergey to have his turn. Obrecht, Boris, Dmitri, and I take part. When Sergey is through, there's hardly any life left in Wes. I see a peace briefly enter Sergey's eyes, but it's short-lived. The devil within him comes back.

VICIOUS PROTECTOR

By some miracle, Wes is still conscious. My brother and I do exactly what we promised him we'd do. Then I return to my original victim and make sure he'll never lay eyes on my printsessa again.

The calm I saw in Sergey's eyes, I never get. Half of my vengeance for Natalia is over. Zamir is the only one still alive. The thug who represented a threat for my printsessa is no more than a pile of ashes sinking in Lake Michigan.

Why don't I feel any satisfaction?

Everyone except Obrecht has left the garage when Sergey and I return from disposing of the remains. Sergey goes to shower, and I sit across from Obrecht. He's rolling a joint on the desk. Neither of us smokes a lot, but Obrecht always does after every kill. He says it allows him to stop spinning. I get mixed reactions, so I only smoke it after if I don't need a clear head. Today isn't a time for me to get lax. I have another situation to figure out.

I drink a sip of water. "Dasha's showed her cards too many times. It's her typical game. She isn't in Chicago for me. So why is she here and trying to get me back?"

Obrecht licks the rolling paper, seals up the joint, and lights it. He takes a deep inhale, holds it in his lungs, then slowly releases it. "She needs money?"

"She's working, so she can't be rolling in it."

Obrecht grunts. "We know how much she loves to work."

Once Dasha and I got married, she decided she didn't need to keep her job. Since I worked, she thought it was best to stay home. I wasn't happy she quit her job without talking to me, especially after we had just signed a lease for a new luxury apartment. Shortly after Dasha told me what she did, Natalia disappeared. We never talked about Dasha's job again.

Obrecht is right.

"Agreed. She wouldn't be working if she had any other choice," I add.

"She didn't reveal anything in your conversation about what she's after?" Obrecht takes another hit.

I replay our conversation in the garage. "No. She kept trying to convince me she missed me. She kept claiming we made a mistake and we needed to fix it."

He scoffs. "After five years?"

"Right?" I nod, surprised when I still feel the sting. I don't love Dasha anymore, but it still hurts when I think about how she threw me away over and over.

I kept taking her back.

At least I won't this time.

Sergey steps out of the bathroom with wet hair. Obrecht hands him the joint and states, "The balance is off. Rossis will have more power now."

My mind immediately switches to the war we started between the two most powerful crime families, the Rossis and Petrovs. The goal is to have them kill each other off until nothing remains of either of them, but for total destruction, we have to monitor the war and take guys out on either side when the power shifts too much to one family.

Sergey takes a hit and leans forward. "I told Boris we need to bleed Zamir out. Slowly kill him, find out about every part of his operation, and take it over. If we run it, we can slowly destroy it all. If we only kill Zamir, it won't ever fully die."

"Boris go crazy on you?" Obrecht asks.

He shrugs. "He didn't like it."

"What did Maksim say?"

Sergey snorts. "Boris didn't tell him. You know what Maksim and Dmitri would both say. I thought Boris would have my back so we could approach them together, but he didn't."

"That's because you're talking crazy. We let this Rossi/Petrov war play out. One by one, each side gets smaller. Then we kill Zamir. Nothing will be left at that point," I insist. The last thing we need is Sergey trying to infiltrate Zamir's organization.

"It sounds too easy to me," Sergey claims.

"I hope it is." Obrecht rises. "Let's get out of here."

We step outside. Obrecht's driver pulls up. I get into the backseat. My brother hits the button, and the divider window closes.

"I thought I'd feel better," Obrecht quietly admits.

"No matter what we do, nothing will bring Natalia back or take away what those bastards did to her." I sniff hard and grind my molars. "Watching Wes choke on his dick gave me a small moment of satisfaction."

Obrecht's jaw clenches. He stays quiet, staring out the window. "Mom called."

I groan. "More guilt about not having grandbabies for her?"

"Yep."

A twinge of pain races up my chest. It's been fourteen years since Dasha and I lost our baby. The doctors said it was stress and to try again. Dasha never said it, but I know she blames me. Hell, I blame me.

Six months into her pregnancy, Dasha found out I was on a killing spree. Any man who I discovered raped my sister, I hunted and filleted. The twelfth man I killed created a trance I couldn't escape. I was spinning, obsessing over what I had done, who I had become, and what kind of father I could be now that I was this new man. Then I fixated on how many more men I needed to destroy.

I told Dasha every detail, but I don't recall any of it. She remembered every single thing I said. When she couldn't pull me out of it, she called Obrecht. He stayed for a week until I snapped out of it. By then, Dasha couldn't sleep. Within a few days, I noticed she was barely eating and practically had to force-feed her. Later that week, we woke up in the middle of the night with blood-soaked sheets. Nothing was ever the same between Dasha and me again. When she wanted a divorce the first time, I angrily threw our wedding vows in her face. "Until death do us part."

She held her chin higher in the air. In Russian, she coldly stated, "The Adrian Ivanov I married died."

She was right. I couldn't deny it. The day Natalia got kidnapped, I started withering away. The boundaries I had about what I would or wouldn't do as a man toppled over. It affected everything about me, right down to how I fuck. I felt the shift the night it occurred. Dasha sure as hell experienced it, too.

I had played by the rules. Too many of them seemed not to matter anymore. It included fucking my wife how I wanted to, instead of the prim and proper way she insisted upon.

"Tell me you love to be fucked like this, instead of how we used to," I growled, determined to find one thing better about me, which in turn was better for her.

Every obscenity of pleasure would come out of her mouth. Not once did she ever admit it though. She couldn't give me one thing.

She despised the new me.

If she wasn't addicted to our new type of sex, our divorce would have happened sooner. I loved her. I had since we were kids in school. Too many times, she kept coming back, leaving me, then returning with a new claim to accept and love every dark piece of my soul. My tattered heart clung to every empty promise she'd make me.

Obrecht's voice jolts me out of my journey down memory lane. "Eloise shows up with Wes. Dasha's back in town, coming on to you. Aspen got—"

"What does Dasha have to do with Wes?"

Obrecht taps his thigh. "Nothing, why?"

"You made it sound like you think her moving back to Chicago has to do with the Petrovs."

"I didn't—"

"Dasha's a lot of things, but she would never turn on us like that," I growl.

Obrecht holds his hands up. "If you let me finish my sentence, I was going to say our lives were a lot simpler before these women showed up. Mom doesn't ever consider the details of her getting what she wants. The details, of course, meaning *pain in our ass* women problems."

The thought of falling asleep with my body wrapped around Skylar's consumes me. I admit, "If it's between having the naked woman of my choice in my bed every morning and dealing with extra problems, versus no woman but no problems, I'm picking the woman every time."

I need to make sure she never finds out what I do or am capable of.

"Spoken like a man with a dick," Obrecht says.

"Maybe you should use yours more before you get too old to get it up," I suggest.

"My dick gets plenty of action, don't you worry," Obrecht claims. "Hey, did you make things right with Aspen's friend?"

Guilt fills me. "She was in my bed when you called."

Obrecht raises his eyebrows. He whines, "Oh, come on, brother."

"What? She's a fucking hundred on a scale of one to ten."

He shakes his head. "Getting involved with Aspen's friends is a recipe for disaster."

"Why? What does Aspen have to do with it?"

"If it doesn't work out, Aspen's going to be upset. That means Maksim—"

"Can kiss my ass. I'm head of the security team. I guarded Aspen as a favor to him. He knows it, and I know it. And what I do in my personal time has nothing to do with Aspen."

"Suit yourself." The car stops in front of my building. Obrecht puts his hand over the door. "Mom wants us to come over for dinner tomorrow night. It's been a long time. I told her we'd go."

I sigh. "All right. What time?"

"She said seven."

I nod. "Okay. See you later."

"Take care, brother."

I fist-bump him and get out. For the first time since I left, I turn my phone on.

Tuesday, one-fifteen.

When did I leave?

Early Sunday morning...three days. Shit.

A replay of how I left Skylar is like a movie reel. My gut sinks further. I pull up Skylar's cell and hit the button. It gets sent to voicemail.

It's the middle of the workday. She could be busy. Don't freak.

I pace the sidewalk and text her.

Me: *I'm back. Can I see you when you get out of work?*

She never responds.

My phone rings. Thinking it's Skylar, I answer it without looking at the screen. "Printsessa."

"Aww. You never called me printsessa before." Dasha's voice hits my ear.

Fuck.

I focus on the traffic. "Dasha, why are you calling me?"

"You didn't return my calls. Actually, your phone has been off. What happened, Adrian?" She lowers her voice. "Who was it?"

Rage and surprise crawl up my spine. Dasha knows better than to discuss anything that may have to do with me killing anyone. The fact she has any idea what I might have been doing irritates me. "I don't know what you're talking about," I sternly claim then slowly demand again, "Why are you calling me?"

"Aidy, let's have coffee. Please."

I ignore her using the nickname she created for me. I always thought of it as her way to claim me as hers, since no one else in the world called me it. During our separation, I realized she used it when she wanted to get her way—using it now, after everything we've experienced together, seems manipulative. "Damn it, Dasha. We went through this the other night. Not happening."

"I got in trouble, Aidy!" she cries out.

My pulse pounds in my veins. I step closer to a light pole, stepping out of the way of the pedestrians and bicyclists. "What are you involved in?" I grit out, trying to stay calm.

"I can't talk about this on the phone."

I crack my neck and stare at the blue, cloudless sky. "I won't be played by you, Dasha."

"I'm not. I swear. Please. Can we meet? I don't know what to do."

I scrub my hand over my face. No part of me wants to have anything to do with Dasha.

Emotions fill her voice. It drops lower. "I'm the mother of your child."

Our son may have died, but he fit in the palm of my hand when he was born. I only got to hold him for several minutes, but if I try hard enough, I can feel him lying on my fingers. I snort hard. "Fine. Coffee and that's it, Dasha."

"Okay. Thank you, Aidy."

I hang up, walk down the stairs, and focus on the water rushing down the river. My stomach pitches. What did Dasha get herself into? I glance at my phone and pull up Skylar's contact info. I try to call her, but it goes to voicemail again. Her face when I left pops into my mind again.

By the time I get to my penthouse, I'm spiraling. I need to see my printsessa. I try to convince myself I should stay away from her until I'm in a better mental state. Then I walk into the bedroom and smell her scent on my pillows. A pair of her panties twist around the sheets. I sniff them. It creates a mixture of polarity, both calming and full of energy.

I don't think. I go straight to her apartment, jimmy the lock, and sit on her couch, waiting for her to arrive home.

It may be inappropriate, but if I don't see her, I'm going to crawl out of my skin. I text her.

Me: *Heads up. When you come home, I'm here, so don't freak.*

Skylar: *Did you break into my house?*

Me: *Yes.*

Skylar: *You're admitting it?*

Me: *Yes. Come home.*

Skylar: *Are you crazy?*

Me: *Probably. Now come home.*

Skylar: *Get out, Adrian.*

Me: *No. We need to talk.*

Skylar: *I have nothing to say to you.*

Me: *Yes, you do.*

Skylar: *Leave, Adrian.*

Me: *Come home. I miss you.*

Dots pop up on the screen then disappear. It happens several times.

Skylar: *Go back to your wife, Adrian.*

My chest tightens. Dasha's only been back a short time, and she's already affecting my life.

Me: *EX-wife. EX being the key word.*

Skylar: *Don't be there when I get home, Adrian.*

Me: *Sorry, but I'm not leaving until we talk.*

My phone rings once, and I answer it. "I missed you, my printsessa."

"This isn't a game, Adrian," she seethes.

"I know. I just got back. I'm sorry—"

"You left me naked in your penthouse."

"Yeah," I humbly admit.

"Get out of my apartment," she demands.

"No. And you need a better lock. I ordered you one. I'll install it tomorrow when it comes."

"What? Adrian, have you lost your mind?" she cries out.

I smile. "Maybe. Hurry up and come home."

"You don't have a right—"

"Call the cops if you don't want to see me. Otherwise, get your sexy-self home. I'm hanging up now."

"Adrian, don't you dare—"

"Come home, my printsessa. Yell at me in person instead of over the phone. You'll feel better."

"You're the most annoying—"

"You're wasting time. Come home." I hang up and walk to the window. My stomach fills with nerves. I'm not sure how I'm going to get through this one.

12

Skylar

Kora is busy with work. Aspen is still recovering. Hailee agrees to meet me at the bar. We choose one between our two apartments. Part of me is glad it's just Hailee and me. The fewer people who know about Adrian, me, and his middle of the night disappearing act, the better. I don't know what to make of it and my friends won't, either. The last few days, I've tried to convince myself he wouldn't have left me to see Dasha, but the more I analyze it, the crazier I feel.

Hailee leans forward with her drink. "What's going on? Are you okay?"

"Adrian is in my apartment." I take a long sip of my martini. "Right now."

Hailee scrunches her face. "And this is bad because?"

"For starters, he broke in."

"Like a thief would?"

I shrug. "Hopefully, he's more skilled than that, and nothing is broken. Oh! But get this! He has the nerve to order me a new door lock and says he's installing it tomorrow."

Hailee rolls her eyes. "He needs to chill over his safety obsession. But can we back up a minute? Why would he break into your house and then call you? I'm confused."

"Ha!" I take another long drink and put my glass down. "You and me both. Especially after we ran into his ex-wife, who happens to be sexy, super gorgeous, and made it clear she wants him back."

Hailee winces. "Ouch. Does he want her back?"

"He says no. But then, in the middle of the night, he got a call and left me naked in his penthouse. Three days later, he contacts me and informs me he's in my apartment."

"Psycho," Hailee says and stirs the straw in her drink.

"He won't leave, either."

"Call the cops. They'll make him leave."

"That's what he said to do."

She groans. "He's so cocky."

My insides pulse. "Yeah. Why am I so attracted to it?"

A thick line forms between Hailee's eyebrows. She shakes her head. "No idea, but what a weirdo. Then again, the hot ones always turn out to be. Did you call the police?"

"No."

She arches an eyebrow. "Don't tell me you're going to let him get away with that? Kora would file a restraining order against him if you told her what you just said."

"I know," I admit.

Hailee studies me then annoyingly sighs. "You like him, don't you?"

"Of course I do. I slept with him. Did you miss the naked part?" My cheeks heat, thinking of all the things we did before he disappeared into thin air.

"I didn't miss the part where you claim he left you for his ex-wife in the middle of the night."

My pulse quickens. "He said it was for work."

She scrunches her face. "Doing what? He's Aspen's bodyguard."

"Exactly." I finish my drink and let the cold gin slide down my throat.

"Why are you contemplating this? Run as fast as you can. You aren't the type to stick with a cheater."

My heart pounds faster. "I don't know he's a cheater. Adrian and his ex-wife were arguing. I don't know Russian, but he was angry. He was insistent he didn't want any part of her. Then he got the phone call."

"She was on the other line?"

"I don't know. I assumed it was her, but I don't know."

Hailee takes a deep breath. "If you want to stick with Mr. Cocky Break-In Boy, then you need to know for sure. Have him show you his phone. It'll show who called. If it wasn't her, then maybe he's telling the truth about work."

"What would he be doing?" I motion for the server to bring another round of drinks.

"You're asking the wrong person."

Hailee and I finish another drink. My stomach stops flipping, and I attempt to order another, but Hailee stops me. "If you're going to see Adrian, no more drinks."

I take a deep breath and bite my lip. I'm already slightly buzzed, and another drink will send me over the edge. "You're right. I need to have all my decision-making abilities available."

"Are you able to stay strong around him?" Hailee says in a doubtful tone.

"Yes. I'm not going to roll over and ignore what happened."

"Good. Don't let Mr. Cocky Break-In Boy get in your pants and convince you he's innocent."

"Jeez, have some faith in me."

Hailee smirks. "I'll have more faith if you don't have another one. And if he did leave you in the middle of the night for his ex-wife, then you better not stay with him."

"Of course I wouldn't!"

She looks at me like she doesn't believe me.

"Stop doubting me."

She takes the last sip of her drink. "Besides his killer body, what do you like about him?"

"Jeez. He spent hours helping you with your project," I remind her.

"I didn't say he doesn't have any redeeming qualities. But he's super arrogant and seems like a player."

"Tell me what you really think," I mumble and finish my drink.

She cringes. "Sorry."

My heart races, thinking about Adrian. "He's more than a hot body, Hailee. He does have an ego, but he's sweet and makes me laugh. We... I thought we clicked."

Hailee smiles. "Okay. That's good. I just don't want you to be his doormat."

"Adrian isn't like that," I insist.

"If he's leaving you in the middle of the night for another woman—"

"Then I'm not sticking around." I slap cash down on the table and slide out of the booth. "I've got this. Thanks for meeting up with me."

She rises and hugs me. "Are you going to be able to resist him if he doesn't give you answers?"

"Yes," I say confidently, but my insides quiver.

"Look at his phone. It'll give you all the answers you need."

I give her a tiny salute, and we share an Uber. The driver drops me off first. I take a deep breath and enter my building. I step on the elevator. My phone dings.

Adrian: *Are you avoiding me, my printsessa?*

I don't reply.

Adrian: *Come home. I miss you.*

Flutters take off in my stomach. I remind myself not to get my panties in a twist like when Adrian left me naked in his bed to go off to God knows where.

Who was he with?

He broke into my home.

Why am I not pissed?

I seriously have issues.

I stand outside my door, giving myself a pep talk.

I need to see his phone.

Taking a deep, anxiety-filled breath, I take my key out but pause. *He's inside.* I reach for the knob and open it. Adrian stands at the window with his hands in his pockets. His tucked-in, gray, fitted T-shirt stretches across his shoulders, V'ing into his jeans. He turns, checking me out with his icy-blue flames, and my heart stammers.

Jesus. Why does he have to be so sexy?

He left me in the middle of the night while I was naked.

I stand straighter. "Adrian, this isn't appropriate. You can't just disappear for days then break into my apartment."

His jaw clenches. He lurches toward me. Every step across my small family room makes my pulse beat faster. I shouldn't let him touch me, but I can't seem to move.

He cups my cheeks and tilts up my head. His laser stare fixates on me. "I missed you, my printsessa."

My chest tightens. I inhale his intoxicating scent and swallow the lump in my throat. My voice comes out weak. "Did you not hear what I just said?"

"I had to leave for work. I'm sorry it took days. And you didn't answer my calls," he states, as if it makes it okay.

"I have a job," I fire back.

"Yes. So do I."

"Mine doesn't have me leaving you naked in my bedroom at three in the morning."

He briefly shuts his eyes and sighs. His Russian accent comes out thicker. "I am sorry. I wouldn't have gone if it wasn't important."

I attempt to look away.

He holds my cheeks firmly. "Do you think it was easy to leave you in my bed, my printsessa?"

"What was so urgent?"

His face darkens. "I cannot discuss my work."

My voice shakes. "You're Aspen's bodyguard. She's still recovering. Don't lie to me, Adrian. You went to see Dasha, didn't you?"

He grunts, and his face falls further. "I'm the head of Ivanov security. I manage dozens of men. Aspen means everything to Maksim. I am the best. It's why he had me guard her." It could be a cocky statement, but I don't hear the ego Adrian typically displays, only confidence.

"Why do the Ivanovs need security?" I blurt out.

"You're asking questions I cannot answer, my printsessa. My work is confidential."

"In the middle of the night?"

"Sometimes. Yes."

A wave of emotion hits me. I try to look away again, but he won't let me. I blink hard, but a tear falls. What he says could be the truth, or I could be a fool. "Is your ex-wife someone you have to attend to for work?"

His thumb wipes my tear. "I have not seen Dasha since the parking garage when I was with you. What part of I don't want her do you not understand?"

My lip quivers.

His face moves closer to mine. Every chiseled feature appears more prominent. "We can't do this, my printsessa."

Panic engulfs me. I don't breathe, dying inside, not wanting him to tell me we're through even though I'm not convinced he wasn't with Dasha, or maybe even some other woman. *What the heck is wrong with me?*

"We can't be together if you don't trust me."

I close my eyes, needing to avoid his piercing gaze. There's hurt in it. I admit, "I want to trust you, Adrian."

"Then stop doubting me."

I open my eyes. "I think if my ex showed up in Chicago after being gone for years and declared he wanted me back, then I got a call in the middle of the night and left you, naked in my bed, you would struggle, too."

He firmly states. "I wasn't with Dasha. She did not call me that night. What is it going to take for you to believe me, my printsessa?"

I feel guilty asking, but I hold out my hand. "Show me your phone. If she didn't call you, then show me who did."

He assesses me for a moment. I almost think he might attempt to avoid showing me. He draws in a deep, controlled breath. "Obrecht called me. I'm going to show you it was him. Once I do, are you able to get past this?"

My chest tightens. "Are you going to leave me in the middle of the night again?"

"Possibly. I don't always get to pick and choose when I'm needed." He brushes his lips against mine as he talks. "If you believe any part of me wants to tear myself away from you when you're naked or clothed, then I've done a poor job demonstrating my intentions with you."

"What are your intentions?" I ask as my eyes drift from his to his lips.

He releases me and steps back. "They don't involve you not trusting me or thinking I want any part of my ex-wife." He takes his phone out of his pocket, unlocks the screen, and pulls up the call log. "Here."

I hesitate.

"Take it," he insists.

The feeling I'm about to have to eat crow fills me. I should be happy to see proof, but I suddenly feel foolish. I glance at the screen. All the names are men. Sergey is on it as well as Obrecht. Between the phone call he got before he left me, it appears as if his phone has been off for several days. There are only two names on the call log between that night and today. I wince and attempt to joke, "Sorry. Hopefully, you and Snake had a nice conversation?"

His face hardens. "No. I didn't. Snake is Dasha."

I put my hand over my gut. "You just told me she didn't call you."

He shakes his head. "I said she didn't that night. You didn't ask about today."

"Am I supposed to ask you every day if she called?" I angrily snap.

He tilts his head and scowls. "Don't be dramatic. I've not lied to you. I told you Obrecht called and I had to work. I didn't have to tell you Snake is Dasha. Give me some credit. Or do you not want this to work between us?"

Blood pounds between my ears. I hand him his phone. "I don't want to be made into a fool, Adrian."

"You think that's my intention?"

"No. But why is your ex-wife calling you? And you talked to her. It didn't go to voicemail. Next, you'll be telling me you're meeting up, and I'm supposed to just look the other way."

He focuses on the ceiling, and guilt erupts in his expression.

Anger and jealousy explode so powerfully, I lose my cool and raise my voice. "You're going to meet up with her?"

He glances down at me. "Yes. There's something she insists she needs to discuss with me. I'm not going to get back together with her. She knows where I stand, and I'm not bending."

I turn, crossing my arms and looking away.

"What do you want me to do, Skylar? Lie or tell the truth? I'm beginning to feel like I'm damned if I do and damned if I don't."

I spin on him. "What would you think if I met up with my ex-husband?"

He arches his eyebrow in amusement. "You have one?"

"Not funny."

His face falls. "I wouldn't like it. But I would trust you to meet in a public place, have a conversation, and return home to me."

"Why do you have to meet her?"

"I already answered this."

"You can't let her go, can you?"

"Jesus. What part of, I don't want her and want you, do you not understand?" he barks.

I bite on my lip. I want to believe him, but I keep seeing Dasha's perfectly made-up face.

Adrian's cheeks turn red. He nods in disgust and angrily spouts, "Tell you what, my printsessa, when you can trust me, come find me. I'm not going to apologize for having a very public cup of coffee with the mother of my child."

"You have a child?" I blurt out.

His face falls, and he sniffs hard. He quietly says, "No. He died."

My stomach twists. I reach for his arm. "Adrian, I'm—"

He shrugs his arm away from my hand. "I don't need your pity, Skylar. I haven't lied to you, and I'm tired of trying to prove to you something you don't want to see for what it is."

I open my mouth to speak, but nothing comes out.

With a piercing glare, he scoffs, "You're a smart woman. Why don't you ask me why I have her listed as Snake in my phone instead of Dasha?"

I stay silent, with my insides shaking. My lack of words only seems to upset Adrian more. He grunts, and I watch him walk out of my apartment.

Nothing he said I can rationally argue. My heart hurts, wondering what happened to his child. Guilt eats at me because I selfishly think, *he has even more reasons to still be or fall back in love with Dasha.*

All night and into the next day, the pit in my stomach grows. He proved to me he was at work. He didn't lie about talking to Dasha. Adrian isn't the one in the wrong. I am. The more time that passes, the harder it gets to figure out how to make things right between us.

13

Adrian

NOTHING WORKS TO STOP MY MIND FROM SPINNING. SKYLAR'S inability to trust me mixes with everything I feel toward Dasha. It creates a bigger web than I anticipate, and all night, it's as if spiders are crawling under my skin.

Everything about Dasha reminds me I used to be a different man. I assume the man she married, the one she wanted, is the same man who would have made Skylar happy. If I could find a way to take the scarring secrets that at one point didn't exist in my life, and tell Skylar about them, I would.

I can't. Not only would it put her in danger, but she'd also never be able to look at me again.

I try not to think about how life was before I changed, or how Dasha could barely tolerate looking at me when I first told her who I had become. The same hunger I see in Skylar's eyes used to be in Dasha's. Then everything changed. Every ounce of affection Dasha had for me was lost. It was another cruel slap in the face. My baby sister was dead. Pieces of my mother, Obrecht, and me were destroyed. There was no way to put us back together, and the only option was to become someone new.

It's taken years to figure out the parts of me I still value. I've spent too many hours coming to terms with the skills I possess and rationalizing how what I do may morally be wrong, but is the only choice I have to rid the world of more sorrow.

Skylar deserves no part of my demonized reality. I've compartmentalized my life over the years. I'm finally at the point where I'm confident I can keep my two universes separate. And I'll do everything to protect them so I never have to see the light in Skylar's eyes dim the way I caused it to in Dasha's.

If she doesn't trust me, it'll never work.

We're good together.

Jesus, so fucking good.

Why did I leave her and not try harder to convince her?

I pace most of the night, inside and on the balcony. I can hardly look at my bed. The rumpled sheets still smell like her. Visions of her all over my place haunt me. Her laugh and voice crying out my name feel like a scab being ripped open.

The next day, her new lock arrives. Since I'm still spinning out, my decision comes fast and without any analysis about whether it's the right move or not.

I go to her apartment and pick her lock again. A panic-filled annoyance claws at my chest. I don't like that Skylar doesn't have security. All guests have to do is push the buzzer until someone lets them. It's a busy building, so my guess is it never is long between tenants and guests coming and going, eliminating the need to even use the buzzer. Anyone could have broken in. I push the thoughts of Natalia that creep into my mind away and focus on the door.

The commercial lock I bought also has double dead bolts. I use my drill and add the second hole. I'm cleaning up the sawdust when Skylar walks in.

"Adrian," she says in surprise.

Her voice makes the hairs on my neck rise. My blood pumps harder. Her navy shift dress hits mid-thigh, showcasing her silky skin. Each of her pouty lips appear fuller, making my pants feel tighter. Her contoured cheekbones are perfection, showcased by her sleek ponytail. More stunning than anything are her eyes. And the thing that worried me the most, that fear I had lost her and she was at the point where she doesn't want me anymore, doesn't exist. All I see is the way she's staring at me. Hope swirls with the same look she's always given me. A part of her still wants me. She's not at the quitting point yet.

I can still save us.

Still, I proceed with caution. "Hi."

"What are you doing here?" It's soft and non-accusing.

I dump the sawdust in the garbage then put the broom and dustpan away. We both step toward the other. "I changed the locks." I hold the two keys out to her.

She glances at them. "Are you able to pick the new locks?"

"Yes. They aren't a guarantee against anyone getting in, but it's the best you can have on these doors." The sweet scent of salted caramel and pears drifts to my nose, and I groan inside.

She drags her finger over my palm and picks up one key, holding it in front of my face. "So you don't need this to get in?"

"No."

Her brows furrow. "But it's easier if you have the key, right?"

"Yes."

"Is it safe to say you might try to break in again?" She bites on her lip and steps closer.

I stay silent with my heart hammering in my chest. I've already crossed the line by picking her lock twice. My actions are on the verge of stalker psychotic, but this is the problem when I spin out. I don't think rationally. I allow my emotions to lead me. It usually takes the form of things that could land me in jail. But I won't lie and can't guarantee her I won't ever do it again if I feel the need.

She tightly smiles. "Thank you for switching my locks. I didn't realize there was a problem."

Instinct takes over. I reach up and cup her cheek while stroking my thumb across her jaw. "I'd feel better if you had real security in your lobby."

She smirks. "Well, I don't." She puts the key on the counter and closes my fist over the spare. "Maybe it's safer if you have this one and don't pick my locks anymore."

The air becomes thicker. "What does this mean, my printsessa?"

She opens her mouth and scrunches her face. Her cheeks redden. She closes her mouth and stares at me.

I drag my finger over her lips. "I'm not into games."

"I-I don't want to be made into a fool, Adrian."

"You aren't. I wouldn't do that to you."

"I'm not normally a jealous person, but..." She looks away.

I turn her chin to me. "But what?"

"I hate she's trying to get you back, and you have a history together."

"The thing about history is it's in the past. It isn't the future."

"She's made it clear she doesn't want it to be in the past."

I nod. There isn't any point denying it. "You're right. But there's always an ulterior motive for Dasha. It's why she's in my phone as Snake. So I'm going to tell you this again, and I need you to believe me."

Skylar takes a deep breath. "Okay."

I lean down to her lips. "I don't want her. I want you. Whatever she has up her sleeve will eventually come out. When it does, there still isn't going to be any part of me that wants her."

"Okay."

Relief fills me, but Dasha is only part of our problems. I hold her face closer to mine. "What about my work? You understand I can't talk about it, and there are going to be times I need to leave?"

Her eyes widen. "Are you involved in something bad, Adrian?"

I grind my molars but don't break our gaze. I fill my lungs with air. "Bad is subjective. But I would have to answer yes since I don't want you subjected to any part of it. If we're going to be together, you need to be okay not knowing details of my work."

A line forms between her eyebrows. She bites on her lip.

Shit. I'm losing her.

There's no other way. She won't want me if she knows.

"My printsessa—"

"Okay. I will deal with not knowing."

I freeze. "You will?"

She nods and puts her hands behind my head. "I-I missed you. A lot."

Happiness curls in my chest. "I missed you, too."

She lightly drags her nails over my neck. "What are you doing tonight?"

"Noth—" My mother's face pops into my mind. *I forgot.* I quietly mumble, "Crap."

"What's wrong?"

If I take her, my mother is going to have a field day with fifty thousand questions.

If I don't take her, I don't get to spend time with her tonight.

"Adrian?"

"How much do you like mothers?"

She smiles. "I have a mother whom I love very much. Why do you ask?"

My heart races. I've not had anyone meet my mother since my divorce. "I have dinner with Obrecht and my mom tonight. Do you want to be put under the microscope and get barraged with questions while eating whatever Russian meal my mom's cooked?"

Her grin fills her face. "You make it sound so exciting."

I shrug. "Just being honest."

"Hmmm."

My gut flips. "Is that a no hmmm or a yes hmmm?"

She brings her lips to mine. "Is dessert at your mom's or your place?"

I slide my hands over her ass and palm her cheeks. "Both. If you don't eat my mother's medovik, her feelings will be hurt."

She softly laughs. "What is medovik?"

"You'll see." I kiss her, unable to stare any longer at her sinful lips. The moment we connect, fire burns in my veins, mixing with sweet relief. My printsessa is once again mine. I order, "Pack a bag."

She doesn't let go of me. "What should I wear?"

"To my mother's or my house?"

She puts her finger on her chin and pretends to think. "Let's start with your mother's."

I glance at my attire. "This is what I'm wearing. Put on something comfortable."

"How much time do we have before we need to leave?"

I glance at my watch and groan. "If we're going to be on time, ten minutes. If we're late, I'll hear about it from my mother all night."

Her eyes widen. "I guess I better hurry, then."

"One other thing."

"What's that?"

"My mother has a really thick accent. If you don't understand what she's saying, just let me know. She tries, but a lot of Americans have a hard time understanding her."

"That must be challenging for her."

I shrug. "She's used to it."

A kind smile fills my printsessa's face. "Maybe you should teach me a few words on the way over so I can say the basics."

I raise an amused eyebrow. "You want to learn Russian?"

"Is it hard?"

"Some people think so. Dmitri's wife, Anna, caught on quickly."

"Good. You can teach me some words on the way to dinner. I need to get ready. I'll be right back." She starts to walk away, but I pull her back into me.

I kiss her, fucking her with my tongue like I'm starving and haven't eaten in days. When I finally pull away, she breathlessly asks, "What was that for?"

"In case you forgot how good we are together."

She beams. "Maybe you should show me again?"

I shake my head. "Nope. Go pack."

"Aye, aye, sir." She leaves the room.

I text Obrecht.

Me: *Are you with Mom already?*

Obrecht: *Yes. Please tell me you aren't going to be late. I'm dying over here. I need Mom to focus on someone besides me.*

Me: *I'll be there soon. Can you do me a favor?*

Obrecht: *What?*

Me: *I'm bringing Skylar. Can you tell Mom to go easy?*

Obrecht: *Is this a joke, or are you really bringing her?*

Me: *No joke. She'll be with me.*

Obrecht: *Brave man.*

Me: *Not funny.*

Obrecht: *Who said anything about funny? But maybe she'll put all her energy into you now.*

I groan.

Me: *Are you going to help me?*

Obrecht: *I'll see what I can do, but you know Mom.*

Me: *That's what I'm afraid of.*

Obrecht: *So don't bring her. Kind of early for that anyway, isn't it?*

Me: *Just talk to Mom. Please.*

Obrecht: *On it, but it's your funeral, little brother.*

"Ready?" Skylar says, coming into the room. She's wearing skinny jeans, an off-the-shoulder fitted sweater, and ankle boots.

This woman can wear anything.

"You look hot, my sexy little printsessa." I take her bag. "Come on. Let's get this over with."

She scoffs. "Don't sound so excited."

"Sorry. I don't bring women home. I apologize for my mother ahead of time."

She freezes and tilts her head. "Never?"

"No."

"So...what's your mom going to do?"

I shake my head. "No idea, but if she gets any wedding magazines out, don't be surprised."

Skylar's face blushes. "Really?"

I sigh. "I hope not, but she did it to Obrecht's date once."

Skylar bites on her smile but a laugh escapes. She puts her hand over her mouth. "Thanks for the warning."

What am I thinking, taking her with me?

I kiss her again then murmur, "Promise me something."

"What?"

"Don't hold my mother against me."

She snickers. "Promise."

I exhale and hand Skylar her key so she doesn't forget it. I put her spare in my pocket. I place my hand on her back and guide her out of the building. All I can think about is my mom and her bridal magazines. I tug Skylar closer to me and kiss her on the head before stepping out into the fresh air.

As I start the engine of my SUV, my nerves dance in my stomach. I can only hope Obrecht convinced my mom to be on her best behavior.

14

Skylar

Adrian teaches me a few Russian words like hello, nice to meet you, and goodbye on the way to his mother's. "Are you okay to walk a few blocks in those shoes?"

"Yes, why?"

"It's a nice night. My mom lives between Obrecht and me. Are you up for a stroll?"

"Sure."

Adrian pulls into the parking garage, and we get out. He takes my hand and guides me to the outside. It's a beautiful spring night. The fierce wind from the day prior is gone. There are lots of pedestrians on the streets. It's still reasonably early. The sky has a pink hue, and the darkness hasn't set in yet.

"How was work today?" Adrian asks.

"I designed an awesome jacket. Actually, it would look good on you."

He wiggles his eyebrows. "With or without clothes underneath it?"

My face flushes. "Ha! Anyway, Bowmen wants to use it as an anchor piece in the next show."

Adrian's face falls. "I don't understand something."

"What's that?"

"Why does he get to take all the credit for your work?"

"I told you, I'm his employee. It's how it works."

Adrian motions for me to turn right at the corner. "He should give you some credit."

"No. It's normal. You don't know who designed those pair of jeans you're wearing. Or your shirt. You buy a label. An employee designed it. It's how it works," I insist.

"If you're designing most of the pieces, you need your own label, my printsessa." He pulls my hand up to his mouth and kisses it.

"It's too much money."

"How much?"

I snort. "Way more than I have. Plus, I wouldn't be able to survive without my salary."

"Forget about survival for a minute. What would it take to start?"

I shake my head. "Honestly, I don't know. I researched it a few years ago, and after I crossed the six-figure mark, I stopped. It's too big of a risk for me. I'm grateful I have my job. Chicago isn't New York, Paris, or Milan. The opportunities are limited."

"You have your job because you're talented."

"You haven't seen my work."

He grunts. "I don't need to see it to know this. You're designing most of his pieces. He's riding your coattails."

Everything Adrian is saying I've thought at one time or another, but it's dangerous for me to think those thoughts. "I understand your position on this, but getting upset won't change anything. It's how the system works. I have enough to support myself, and I get to do what I love. If I spend my time focused on the parts of my job I don't like, it won't change it. Nothing is perfect. So I choose to focus on the things that make me happy."

Adrian slides his arm around my shoulder and tugs me closer to him. He kisses the top of my head. "You have a good attitude, but answer this. If money weren't an issue, would you start a label? Would you want to have your own company?"

There's a mix of emotions in me. It was my dream to create a label, but over the years, I came to accept it's not in the cards for me. "I think a lot of people would do a lot of things if money weren't an issue."

He stops and faces me. "I'm not asking about other people. I'm asking about you."

I sigh. "It's a loaded question."

"How?"

My stomach churns. "I don't have the option to leave Bowmen."

Adrian's eyes turn to slits. "What are you talking about?"

"Bowmen made me sign a new contract with him. If I leave, I have to pay him a substantial amount of money for his 'training.'" I put my fingers in quotations.

Adrian scowls and seethes, "What training? You said you've worked for him for years."

"Calm down."

"Skylar, what are you talking about?"

Embarrassed, I look away. "I've always had a contract with Bowmen. When I got my last promotion, he made me sign a new one. I didn't think it was any different. I assumed it was the same, but it wasn't. It's my fault. I didn't read the fine print." Heat rushes to my face. I'm still kicking myself over how stupid I was to sign something without reading it first. All I could think about was the excitement of being promoted and the raise he was offering me.

Adrian turns my chin so I have to face him. His icy-blue eyes are so cold, fog could be coming off them. His Russian accent gets thicker. "What's in the fine print?"

"If I leave Bowmen, I have to pay him fifty thousand dollars."

"That's absurd."

I shrug. "I signed it."

"How is it even legal? What did Kora say?"

"I've not shown her. She said she thought it wouldn't hold up in court and would find me an employment attorney, but I don't see the point. If I leave Bowmen, I'll have to move to New York or another city with bigger opportunities. The last thing I want to do is rock the boat. Bowmen would fire me."

Anger flares in Adrian's expression. "You're designing all his pieces. I doubt he'll fire you. And you shouldn't feel chained to him. Tell Kora to give you the name of the top employment attorney in Chicago."

Anxiety fills my lungs. "No. I'm not pissing Bowmen off."

"It's not going to hurt—"

"Do you want me to have to move, Adrian?"

His eyes widen. "Absolutely not. But it's not going to hurt—"

"Yes, it will. You don't know him or the industry I'm in. Word travels fast, and other designers will blackball me. Bowmen will make sure of it. I've seen him do it to several other designers who stood up to him."

Adrian's face darkens. A look so vicious it gives me the chills appears. His accent becomes thicker. "If he tries to fuck with you, he'll have me to reckon with. In fact, he already crossed the line with this contract he manipulated you into signing."

Fear crawls through my body. "Adrian, he isn't. This is my work."

"And he's trapped you into staying with him."

"No, he hasn't," I try to say confidently, but it comes out weaker than I want. Adrian's right, but the situation is what it is. I may have been drunk at the Cat's Meow, but I remember how Adrian held Wes Petrov's bodyguard in a choke hold. Even intoxicated, I saw how he could have snapped his neck in an instant. The Petrovs aren't the same situation as Bowmen.

"I think it's time your boss and I had a little chat."

My voice comes back, and I firmly reply, "Adrian, this is my job. You don't want me to interfere or know anything about yours, so don't you dare get involved with mine."

"It's not the same thing."

I put my hand on my hip. "No? Tell me about what you spend your nights doing when you get those calls."

His jaw clenches. "We've gone over this."

I nod. "Yes. We did. I agreed to stay in the dark. When you lift that restriction, then we can discuss you interfering in my job. Until then, don't."

He grinds his molars. "He's taking advantage of you."

"I'm a big girl. My choices are my choices. This is the line I draw. Don't do something that puts my career in jeopardy."

He stays silent.

"You don't have to like it, but you have to agree. Just like I don't like what you made me agree to."

He huffs out a big breath of air. He grumbles, "Fine."

Relief fills me. He may not disclose the details of his job, but I'm not naive. Adrian is a violent man when necessary. However, my world and his aren't the same. Whatever he is involved in doesn't compare to my boss headaches. I reach up and put my arms around his neck. "Are we close to your mother's?"

"Next building."

"Then kiss me before we get there and help me reduce my collywobbles."

He raises his eyebrows. "Collywobbles?"

"It's the weird feeling in your stomach or an overall bellyache. In my case, it's nerves."

His lips twitch. "Don't be nervous. I'm the one who should have the collywobbles, not you."

"Why would you?"

"My mother is a loose cannon."

"What does that mean?"

"Oh, you'll see."

"Should I be scared?"

He scoffs. "No. I probably should be though."

"Now I'm intrigued, and my collywobbles are intensifying," I tease, but it's also an admittance.

He leans to my mouth. "So you want me to kiss your collywobbles out of you?"

"Mmhmm."

He guides me closer to the building and out of the path of pedestrians. He fists my hair and tugs my head back. Blue flames study my face, causing me to hold my breath in anticipation. He comes closer but doesn't kiss me. His tongue flicks my ear, and he murmurs, "When we get home tonight, I'm going to wabbit you."

"Rabbit me?"

"Not rabbit. Wabbit with a w."

"What does that mean?"

"It's a Scottish term for being exhausted."

"Nice one."

"Scores even again." He kisses my neck then moves on to my jaw.

"So competitive," I tease as tingles erupt down my spine.

He slowly moves his tongue over my lips. I open my mouth, and he slides it inside, working my mouth like a popsicle, then pulling back to stare at me before coming back for more. He groans in my mouth when my knees give out, pulling me tighter to his frame of muscle. He kisses me more then mumbles, "Collywobbles gone?"

"No. You gave me different ones."

His lips twitch. "We're going to be late."

"We should go then," I say, not moving.

"Yep." He sticks his tongue back in my mouth for several moments then pulls back. He gives me a chaste kiss then guides me into his mother's building. We get through security and onto the elevator. He pushes the button for the tenth floor.

My stomach flips. I haven't met anyone's mother in a long time. Adrian's description of her doesn't do anything to calm my nerves. I concentrate on inhaling the scent of his skin.

"Ready?" he asks when we get to the front of her door.

"How do I say hello again?"

He pecks me on the lips. "Just speak English. No one expects you to know Russian."

"I know. But tell me again?"

"Zdravstvuyte."

"Zdravstvuyte," I repeat.

"Excellent," he beams.

"And how do I say, thank you for having me?"

"Spasibo, chto priglasili menya."

"Spasi...what is it?"

He chuckles. "Stick with zdravstvuyte for tonight. We'll work on phrases in the future."

"But—"

The door opens. A striking woman with blonde hair to her shoulders, the same icy-blue eyes as Adrian and Obrecht, and a bright smile on her face says something in Russian while glancing between Adrian and me.

Adrian guides me inside and shuts the door. He replies in Russian, kisses his mother on the cheek, then steps back. "Mom, this is Skylar."

"Zdravstvuyte," I say.

Her smile grows. "Zdravstvuyte." She kisses my cheeks then takes both my hands and studies me. She turns to Adrian and says something in Russian. A faint blush crosses his cheeks. He replies in Russian then says in English, "My mother thinks you're beautiful."

"She is," his mother says in English with a thick Russian accent. I understand what Adrian meant. I have to listen closely when she speaks, but it isn't so thick I don't know what she says.

"Thank you, Mrs. Ivanov."

She swings her finger through the air, and her eyes brighten. "No. You call me Svetlana."

"Okay."

Obrecht clears his throat. He steps in and kisses my cheek. "Skylar. How are you?"

"I'm good. You?"

He smirks. "Living the dream."

Svetlana takes my hand. "Come. My sons never bring women to me."

Adrian and Obrecht both groan.

"Here we go," Obrecht mutters.

Svetlana spins and says something in Russian then faces me again. She motions to the couch. "Sit, please. Can I get you a drink?"

"I'm okay right now." I sit, and Svetlana takes the seat near me. Adrian and Obrecht sit in chairs across from us.

Svetlana starts an onslaught of questions about how Adrian and I met, how long we've dated, and about my background. Adrian keeps trying to get her to stop asking questions, but I don't mind. She's just interested in who her son is seeing. I can't blame her. I instantly like her. Adrian appears normal except for how he keeps tapping his fingers on his thigh, which I find amusing. Adrian Ivanov is one man I don't expect to ever get nervous.

"Skylar, do you have any children?" Svetlana asks.

"No."

She tilts her head. "But you like children?"

"Yes."

Adrian groans. "Mom—"

"What? You two would make beautiful babies."

Well, Adrian did warn me she's a loose cannon.

We would have adorable babies. The vision of little Adrians running around fills my mind.

Adrian closes his eyes and shakes his head.

Obrecht rises. "Time for a drink. Let's go."

Adrian stands and holds his hand out to me.

"You go ahead. I'm good with your mom."

Adrian looks at me like I'm crazy. To screw with him, I turn to Svetlana. "Speaking of babies, do you have any pictures of Adrian when he was a baby?"

Svetlana jumps up, beaming. "I do! Let me get the book."

Adrian's eyes widen. He mouths, "Don't encourage her."

I wink. "Go, have your drink."

Mischief fills Obrecht's eyes. "Mom, do you still keep them by your bridal magazines?"

"I'm going to kill you," Adrian mutters to Obrecht.

I bite my smile.

"I'll be in the kitchen," Adrian says.

"I'll be here," I chirp.

His mom shows me baby pictures, which also include Obrecht and their sister, Natalia.

"She was beautiful."

A sad smile crosses his mom's face. Her eyes glisten. "She was."

I put my hand over hers, unsure what to say. Once again, *sorry for your loss*, doesn't seem to be powerful enough.

She puts on a brave face and shuts the book. "I think dinner is almost ready. Can you excuse me? I'll be back in a moment."

"Sure."

I get up and go into the kitchen just as Obrecht says, "When is she going to stop nagging us about marriage and kids?"

Adrian groans. "Mom needs to stop living in la-la land, thinking that scenario is for either of us." He takes a sip of his beer.

My heart stops. I haven't dated Adrian long enough even to have the marriage and kids' conversation. I've often wondered if kids are in the equation for me, since I'm already thirty-six. I've never been married, but I eventually would like to find my forever person. Something about not even having the option with Adrian stings.

His mom walks into the room as the oven timer rings in the air. I jump, and Adrian spins on his barstool. "Come sit." He pats the one next to him.

We spend the rest of the night eating and laughing. I do my best to push what I heard Adrian say out of my head, but it never entirely vanishes. If he doesn't want kids or marriage, is it something I'm willing to accept?

What makes it harder is Adrian's been married before. He had a child. I don't know the details about it or how his son died. I assumed Adrian would tell me more when he was ready, but it hurts he wanted it at one point with Dasha.

We've not dated long enough to make a lifelong commitment, but I can't help but think I'm right in front of him, and he already knows he doesn't want it with me. When we get to his place, it's on the tip of my tongue to ask him if he's serious about never wanting kids or getting married again, but the moment we step into his penthouse, his hands, lips, tongue, and teeth are all over me. I momentarily forget about what he said and spend the rest of the night tangled in his body.

15

Adrian

Three Weeks Later

OBRECHT KNOCKS ON MY OFFICE DOOR.

"You're back earlier than I thought," I say.

He rolls his shoulder and cracks his neck. "Dead end. Zamir really is a ghost. Lost him in Detroit."

My stomach lurches like it does every time I hear or think about Zamir. I attempt to ignore it. "Detroit?"

"Yep. Another special night at Secrets Lounge. Guess who showed up to the club."

"Who?"

Obrecht's face darkens. "Mack Bailey."

A chill runs down my spine. The Baileys are a prominent crime family who's always been at war with the O'Malleys. Now that Boris is marrying Nora and she's having his baby, it links the Ivanovs to the O'Malleys. "What's the son of the Bailey clan doing in a Russian strip joint?"

Obrecht scowls. "Having a good time with Ludis Petrov."

My gut drops. Ludis is Zamir's son who handles his operation from Michigan to the East Coast. "Maksim know?"

"Not yet."

"Shit."

"Yep. The Petrovs have made some sort of alliance with the Baileys."

"Fuck." I scrub my face. "This never ends, does it?"

"Nope. We need to find out what kind of alliance they have. It could throw the Petrov/Rossi balance off without us knowing it."

I sigh and glance up at the ceiling. "I thought we were making progress."

"We are," Obrecht insists. "We knew the war wasn't going to be short term. Darragh will be more than happy to take out some Baileys if it comes down to it."

Darragh is Nora's uncle and head of the O'Malley clan. His son, Liam, just got paroled a year early from prison and is next to take over. It doesn't instill a lot of confidence in us, since Liam hasn't always made the best choices.

"I'll let you know when I find out more about whatever is going on with the Petrovs and Baileys. Bogden said to give this to you." Obrecht slaps down a four-inch-thick yellow envelope on my desk.

Finally, something I can give to Sergey to get him off my back for a few minutes.

"This should be fun," I mumble and pull out the photos.

"That Kora?" Obrecht asks.

I snort. "Nope. That would be her sister."

Obrecht sits back in the chair and crosses his arms. "How does Kora share blood with this woman?"

"You're asking the wrong person. Talk to Sergey. I've got other dickheads to follow," I grumble.

"Who?"

"Some cocksucker. He's part of a divorce case Kora's involved in. I already had a run-in with him and Kora in the street, which ended with her telling me off. I had to add others to tail him. He's lucky I didn't kill him in the street."

"Who is it?"

"Jack Christian is his name."

Obrecht's forehead creases. "Christian?"

I lean closer. "Yeah. You know him?"

"He's taking his company public in the next few months. It's been all over my investment sites."

"Yeah, I know."

Obrecht scratches his chin and sits back.

"What?"

"Men like that almost always have vices."

"Do you want to tell me something I don't know?"

He motions to my folder. "What do you have so far?"

I grunt. "Nothing leading to anything to use against him." I shove the folder at Obrecht.

Obrecht fills my desk surface with pictures and notes then carefully reviews each item. He picks up the 8x10 photo of Jack at an upscale bar. He's drinking Scotch with the mayor. "You have other photos to go with this one?"

"What's the date?"

He glances at the photo. "The seventh."

I open my desk drawer, pull out another folder dated for that time frame, and plop it on the desk. "Don't fall asleep. So far, Jack Christian is a typical rich guy who hobnobs with politicians and other entrepreneurs."

Obrecht points at me. "Which is exactly why he has demons in his closet."

"Yeah, well, he hides them pretty well."

We study the photos. After several minutes, Obrecht points to a man. He's in a black leather jacket. His hand tattoo looks like his bones with a serpent wrapped between them. He's sitting several seats away from Jack. "Who's this?"

"Random."

Obrecht shakes his head. "In three places?"

"What are you talking about?"

Obrecht points to three pictures taken on different days, in different bars. In two of them, he's barely noticeable. I take a closer look. In one image, you can only see the back of him, but his hand tattoo makes it impossible for it to be anyone else.

I look closer.

How did I miss this?

"Who do you have on him?" Obrecht asks.

"Pavel, Vadim, and Cezar. He's covered at all times."

Obrecht taps the mystery man. "Find out who this guy is to Jack. My gut says he's following him or has something underhanded going on with him." Obrecht rises. "You need to look closer. The answers are always in front of you with these types of people. I'm using your shower. Mom's got her friends over for her weekly card game. I can't handle having to listen again to all of them discuss which of their daughters they want to hook me up with."

"Having fun at Mom's?" I smirk.

"I was never so happy to leave town for the week. Maksim better get my place finished. I had everything timed perfectly."

"Yeah, well, it's better they found the electrical issue instead of it burning down. That would be a great headline. *The state-of-the-art Ivanov complex, Serenity Plaza, burned to the ground due to faulty wiring in the penthouse.*"

Obrecht grinds his molars. "Doesn't make living with Mom any better."

"It's only for another week. I told you to crash with me."

"Thanks, but I'm sure Skylar wouldn't want me hanging around."

"She wouldn't care, but she doesn't live here."

Obrecht raises his eyebrows. "When's the last time she stayed at her place?"

I try to remember, but I'm too obsessed with her to not have her in my bed every night. I finally admit, "I don't know."

"Mom said you all had a lovely lunch." He smirks.

I groan. "Mom cornered Skylar and me. I couldn't get out of it. Mom brought the Spring *Vogue* Wedding Edition, claiming she was sharing her love of fashion with Skylar."

"Jesus. The woman never stops. What bathroom should I use?"

"Don't care. You know where the towels are."

He leaves, and I study the photos closer. "Jackie boy, what are you hiding?"

"Adrian," Skylar calls out.

"In the office." I stuff everything back in the folders and put them in my drawer. I meet Skylar in the hallway. "My printsessa, what are you doing home so early?"

An annoyed smile appears on her face. "I needed to get out of the office, or I was going to kill Bowmen. But I have ten minutes before I have to return."

"Why?"

"He decided to add six more pieces to the show. Guess who gets to work all night?"

"Your show's next week."

"Yep."

"He can't keep you all night."

"Oh, but he can. Anyway, I came to put something comfortable on, and I think I left my favorite pair of yoga pants and sweatshirt here. They weren't at my place."

"I'm pretty sure you did, and I washed them today."

Her eyes widen. "You did my laundry?"

"Yep. But don't worry, I read the tags to make sure they could go in the washer and dryer." I grab her hand and steer her into the bedroom closet. I open a drawer. "I put everything here except your dresses, which are hanging up drying in the laundry room. Are these the pants you want?" I remove the black pants from the drawer and hand them to her.

She bites her smile, glances at the pants, then back at me.

"Did I do something wrong?"

"Nope. I didn't expect you to do my laundry, much less look at my tags. Thank you." She pulls my head toward hers and kisses me.

"Does this mean I should cancel our reservation tonight?"

She winces. "Sorry."

"It's okay. You want me to bring you dinner later?"

"Thanks, but Bowmen will order food so no one has any excuse to leave. He'll have our office on lockdown so visitors can't disturb our workflow."

"Your boss is a dick."

She snorts. "Don't need a reminder. I get to experience it every day."

"You should let me have a little chat with him."

"Not funny, Adrian."

"I'm not joking."

"Yes, I understand that." She gives me a peck on the lips. "I have to go. I'll see you tomorrow for Nora's reopening."

"You aren't coming home tonight?"

"It's going to be late when I get done. I'll probably get a few hours of sleep then it'll be time to go back to the office. I assumed I would go to my place. If you're smart, you'll be asleep when I get out of work."

I palm her ass and tug her into me. "Call me when you finish. I'll come get you and bring you back to my warm bed."

She furrows her eyebrows. "It might be three in the morning."

"So? Another reason you should call me. I don't want you running around at that time in the morning."

She scoffs. "Wouldn't call it running around."

"You know what I mean."

"It's not the first time I've had to work late like this. I don't want to keep you awake all night."

I push her magenta hair off her neck and kiss her collarbone. "Until I know you're safe and not out and about in the Chicago streets, I won't sleep. We can go to your place for the night if you prefer."

She pulls away. "The Chicago streets?"

"It's not safe for you to be by yourself."

"In a taxi? Going straight to my apartment?"

"Do you not want to see me tonight?"

"Mmm...did I ever say that?"

"Good. It's settled, then. Call me when you finish working."

She cups my cheeks. "Or..."

"Or?"

"I could hop in an Uber, get dropped off here, and sneak into your bed so I don't wake you up." She beams, as if it's a brilliant idea.

"You aren't taking a cab or Uber."

"Why do you always act like something is wrong with public transportation?"

A stinging sensation surrounds my heart, and my pulse pounds against my neck. I walk out of the closet and into the bedroom. "It's not safe."

"Millions of people a day use public transportation," she claims, following me.

VICIOUS PROTECTOR

"Yep. And you don't have to. Call me when you finish tonight. Let me grab my keys. I'll take you back to work." I stroll out to the kitchen.

She follows me. "Adrian, I don't need you to drive me to work or pick me up. I'm more than capable of getting back and forth. I appreciate the offer but—"

I spin on her. "Your safety isn't up for debate."

"You're overreacting. A taxi is perfectly safe—"

"No, it's not," I firmly state, quickly losing my patience with this conversation. Skylar is constantly fighting me about using public transportation. It makes my blood boil.

She laughs. "I've lasted thirty-six years riding around in taxis and Ubers. You're acting like I'm going to get kidnapped by a harmless driver, which isn't fair for the poor drivers—"

I lose my cool and bark out, "When you get kidnapped by a taxi driver, taken to a whorehouse to be broken in, and—"

"That's enough, Adrian!" Obrecht's voice cuts through the air.

Great. I sniff hard and stare at the ceiling.

"Where's your office?" Obrecht asks Skylar.

She quietly says, "Five blocks from here."

"My driver is downstairs. I'll meet you in the lobby and drop you off." He glances at me, pats my back, then quietly leaves.

I slowly look at Skylar.

Her eyes are wide. She's clenching her yoga pants and sweatshirt. She swallows hard and quietly asks, "Adrian, is that what happened to Natalia?"

I don't reply. I can't. My chest is too tight. Rage and sorrow claw at my lungs. It's been over fifteen years, and it still hurts like it happened yesterday. I avoid Skylar's pity-filled eyes.

She reaches for my bicep. "Adrian—"

"I don't want to discuss this."

"I...um..."

I kiss her on the forehead. "Get dressed, or you'll be late. Call me when you finish working."

I try to step back, but she reaches up and clasps her hand around my neck. "I'm sorry. I—"

"You didn't do anything wrong, my printsessa. I'm sorry I yelled. Go change."

She hesitates.

"Go."

She slowly obeys and goes into the bedroom. I turn and put my hands over my face. All I see is Natalia's cold, dead body on our doorstep. My mother's face and voice scream in agony as she held her. Tears streamed down Obrecht's face as he tried to drag my mother away from Natalia.

Pull it together.

Zamir is still alive. Over fifteen years, and he's still breathing.

Skylar's arms slide around my waist. I press my arm and hand over hers, take a deep breath, and spin. I avoid her eyes as much as I can and give her a chaste kiss. "Obrecht's waiting for you downstairs. I'll walk you out."

"Adrian—"

"Come on." I guide her to the elevator. We get in, and I push the lobby button. I wish I could get my insides to stop shaking, but they only seem to quiver harder.

The elevator passes the sixth floor, and Skylar hits the stop button. "Adrian—"

"I can't talk about this. Not right now."

She reaches up and cups my cheeks. I close my eyes, wishing I weren't so weak. Every time I think I have a handle on Natalia's death, it sneaks up on me.

Skylar nods. "Okay. Umm... I-I—"

I pull her into me and put my lips on the top of her head while speaking. "I don't want you in cabs or Ubers alone. I know you do it during the day, and I don't like it. Nighttime is even more dangerous. Promise me you aren't going to put yourself in that situation anymore."

She looks up. "Okay. I promise. No more nighttime rides alone."

I release a deep breath. "Good." I peck her on the lips then hit the button for the elevator to move again. The doors open quickly, and Obrecht and I exchange a glance.

"Ready?" he asks Skylar.

"Yes."

I kiss her again then watch her disappear through the doors with Obrecht. I pull my phone out of my pocket.

The phone rings twice. Maksim answers, "Adrian. What's going on?"

"I need a trailer, and you can take it out of my wages."

"For who?"

"Skylar."

He lowers his voice. "Is she all right?"

"Yes, and I need to make sure it stays that way."

16

Skylar

OBRECHT LEADS ME TO THE CAR, AND WE GET IN. FOR SEVERAL minutes, we don't speak. When the driver stops outside my work building, Obrecht unrolls the divider window. "Give us a minute."

"Sure," the driver says, and the window closes.

Obrecht gives me a small smile. "My brother likes you."

"Is this where you tell me you don't?" I nervously ask.

He jerks his head back. "No. Not at all. Why would you think that?"

"I was being sarcastic."

"Oh. Gotcha."

I clear my throat. "Sorry. You were saying?"

He pins his icy-blue eyes on me. They're replicas of Adrian's and Svetlana's, but something about Obrecht's is different. There's a warmth in them Adrian doesn't possess, as if he's your friend. I noticed it the first time I ever laid eyes on him. He restates, "Adrian likes you."

"I like him, too."

He nods. "My mother likes you."

"I like her, too," I repeat like a broken record. It's the truth though. Adrian made Svetlana sound like a basket case, but all I see is a strong woman who is also sweet as sugar. In many ways, she reminds me of Adrian.

"You can add me to the I-like-you-too list," he says then winks.

"Umm...thanks." *Where is he going with this?* My stomach swarms with jitters.

His face turns serious. His Russian accent becomes thicker. "You and your friends need to consider your safety a little better."

"I know, I'm sorry—"

He holds up his hand. "I'm not judging or trying to talk down to you, but there's a lot of bad people out there."

"I know."

He shifts in his seat and leans forward. "No. You don't know, and I hope you never do. *My* family, we know this too well. So if an Ivanov says to do something for your safety, it's best not to fight it. There's a reason for everything we do. Nothing is ever by chance."

"I didn't know," I admit, feeling guilty about how I fought Adrian over not taking public transportation in the middle of the night by myself. It seemed extreme at the time, but now all I can think about is how stupid I was for arguing with Adrian about it. After all, I know he's overly cautious.

Obrecht's jaw clenches. "You couldn't have."

There's a knock on the window, and my gut drops when I turn toward it. Through clenched teeth, I ask, "What is she doing here?"

Dasha's long blonde hair is blowing in the wind. She has silver mirrored sunglasses, red lips, and perfectly manicured fingers. A red minidress fits her curves perfectly.

"I can't discuss it."

I gape at Obrecht as horror fills me. "Are you...oh my God!"

A confused expression fills his face. "What?"

"You're dating Adrian's ex-wife?" I whisper so Dasha can't hear.

"Fuck no!" he says in an insulted tone.

She knocks again. In her thick Russian accent, she demands, "Let me in."

I glance at her then back at Obrecht. I continue to whisper, "She looks dressed for a date. You look dressed for a date..." I point to his suit.

"Skylar, if anyone hates Dasha more than Adrian, it's me. Whatever you think, I can assure you is not happening."

"Obrecht! Open up!" Dasha says and tries to open the door.

"Then why is she here?" I harshly whisper.

"Adrian knows. If he wants to tell you, that's his choice."

"Seriously?" I spout.

"Yes. And I didn't know you would see her, so I'm sorry."

"You're outside my office building. You were meeting her here?"

"No." He points to the tower next door. "She lives there."

My stomach flips. Dasha lives next to my work. *Ugh. Can she just go away and leave us alone?* "The windows are blacked out."

"She knows my car and driver."

"But you're not dating?" I ask, suspicious again.

"Have I not said fuck no loud enough?" he asks in a pissed and annoyed tone.

"She wants Adrian back. Why are you meeting her?"

He avoids my question. "Yes. I knew she would eventually return."

My entire body tightens. "Because she loves Adrian?"

He scoffs and looks out the window at her. "No. She's never really loved Adrian. He thinks she did, but she didn't."

Anger and sadness consume me. There are so many things about Adrian to fall in love with. He deserved to have a wife who loved him. I despise thinking about what I assume his past life with Dasha was like and guess it's all I can do, since Adrian and I don't talk about her. Even though I can't stand the thought of Dasha with Adrian, I would rather she did love him during their marriage than not.

"Because she loves you?" I ask.

He groans. "Skylar, I like you, but you need to listen better. I wouldn't let Dasha anywhere near my dick. Can you get past whatever scenario you're playing out in your head?"

I sigh. "Okay. Sorry. But if she never loved him, then why would she come back?"

"Why does anyone go to anyone? Protection. Love. Money. Sex. Power. I suspect her motives are a combination of all those things. And in her warped mind, she thinks she loved Adrian."

"Obrecht!" She knocks again.

He cracks the window and speaks to her in Russian. She says something, and he softens his voice. She rattles something else off then sighs and steps back.

He closes the glass and pins me with his gaze. "No one wants to see you get hurt, Skylar. Listen to Adrian when he tries to keep you safe. We don't do it to play games."

Guilt rears its ugly head, mixing with my annoyance and jealousy that Dasha is standing outside the car. "I need to go."

"Hold on." He rolls the divider window down and instructs his driver, "Watch Dasha. I'll be back."

Obrecht gets out and reaches in for me. When I step out of the car, Dasha purses her lips. Staring me down in her six-inch heels, she speaks Russian. The only word I recognize is Adrian.

"Don't speak his name," I sneer at her.

She steps forward. Her rose scent makes me nauseous.

"Dasha," Obrecht warns.

A smile curves her mouth. She firmly says, "Mrs. Adrian Ivanov. My name, not yours."

"No. You don't own Adrian's name anymore," I tell her then step closer. "You never deserved it."

She condescendingly says, "No? My name is Ivanov. Yours—"

"That's enough, Dasha," Obrecht reprimands then speaks aggressively in Russian. He points to the car, and the driver opens the door.

Obrecht says something else I don't understand, and Dasha glares and gets in the car. Obrecht puts his hand on my back and escorts me into the building. "I apologize you had to see her and... Jesus, just because she's her."

I stop next to the security desk. "You aren't acting. You honestly don't like her, do you?"

He shakes his head. "No. I don't. I do, however, like you. You seem good for Adrian even though you're Aspen's friend."

"What's wrong with Aspen?"

"She's engaged to Maksim."

"Is there something about Maksim I should know?"

"No. Just...it doesn't matter. The point I'm trying to make is we all like you better, so make sure you stay safe, okay?"

How many times is he going to warn me about safety? "Yes. I think you've been extremely clear."

"Great. I have to go deal with the snake in a dress. Call Adrian when you get off work." He turns, but I reach for his arm.

"Wait!"

Obrecht spins and raises his eyebrows.

"Um...is Adrian..." I take a deep breath. "Is he okay right now? He spins out at times and—"

"He told you?"

"Yes."

He studies my face and cautiously replies, "He'll be fine. It's good you have work so he has a few hours by himself. He needs to stay away from people when he goes down the rabbit hole."

"But you don't?"

Obrecht's face hardens.

"Sorry. I don't mean to pry, but you're brothers, and I'm sure it was just as tragic for you." I bite on my lip, not sure why I'm asking Obrecht a question so personal. "Sorry, you don't have to answer if you don't want. It isn't my business."

"I cope in other ways."

"Skylar! Everyone is upstairs. You're holding up our progress," my boss's voice rings in my ears.

I close my eyes. *Yep, because I'll be the one directing and designing everything.* I open my eyes. Obrecht's are in slits and directed at Bowmen. I mumble, "I have to go."

"Skylar!" Bowmen barks.

Obrecht steps forward, but I move in front of him. I quietly say, "It's my boss. Don't." I'm not sure what he'll do, but I don't need any altercations with Bowmen. I have to pick and choose my battles, and this isn't one of them.

A low growl comes out of Obrecht. He tears his glare away from Bowmen. "Have a good night."

"Thanks." I quickly spin and join my boss.

Bowmen's face is red. He shakes his head at me and runs his hand through his bright-blue hair, which is his color of the week. "What are you doing down here? I've been looking everywhere for you."

I force a smile and put on my most cheerful voice. "I'm here."

He pushes the elevator button and glances toward the door where Obrecht is still standing, scowling. "Who is that? New boyfriend?"

None of your business. "Nope." The doors open, and I step into the elevator. "So what do you think we need for the new pieces?"

Bowmen stands next to me, and I press the button for the fourteenth floor. The doors shut, and he replies, "Let's make this into a training session. What do you think the collection is lacking?"

My insides twist, and I count to ten. This is Bowmen's way of trying to make me think he has all the ideas, and he's adding value to my skills. In reality, it means he has no plan. This entire addition is on a whim because something happened that caused his confidence to shake. Now, the entire office will have to pump him back up so we can leave. Even though I created almost the entire collection, I know what Bowmen needs to hear.

Best to give him credit and mad props.

I swallow my pride and think of my paycheck. "I think the line you created is the best work you've done. The statement pieces are edgy and trendy. I wouldn't want any distraction."

"You don't think we need more?"

"We have five more items than normal. Are you trying to trick me?" I ask in a teasing tone, hoping he'll forget about this idea and let everyone go home. Adrian and Obrecht may claim I need to stay away from Adrian when he spins out, but I'm worried about him and don't want him by himself, even if it means I stay in a different room until he snaps out of it.

"No, I'm not. So tell me what you believe is lacking."

Crap. There's no getting out of it. I'm going to be here all night.

The elevator opens. As we make our way through the hall and into our office suite, I cringe. Adding anything to the collection could destroy the value and demand for it. Too much isn't always better. We also only have a week, so this is nearly impossible. Anything we add has to align with fabrics and other material we already have. Against my better judgment, I tell Bowmen the truth. "I don't see what would enhance what we have. I'm sorry, but I think we should stick with what we've done and not add anything."

The doors open, and he snaps, "Wrong answer!"

Awesome. Ugh.

I shouldn't push Bowmen's buttons. He doesn't have any ideas for this unnecessary project, but there is nothing I can think of that won't harm the collection. If I had a brilliant idea, it would be his. I've never created anything for him that wasn't a winner, but I know the first time I do, he'll fire me. I'm not going to be held accountable for this insane knee-jerk move of his. "You're right. This is a great time to teach me. Please give me instruction."

Now we're never going home.

Bowmen scowls then glances over my shoulder. He claps his hands and orders, "Everyone, meeting room, now." He shakes his head at me. "I expect you to get your creative brain working." He passes me and stomps into the conference room.

Dread fills me. It's three-forty-five in the morning when Bowmen finally lets us leave. The extra pieces he decided on, I advised against, but Bowmen doesn't listen. Each new item makes the collection I designed now look cluttered and tacky.

Why do I work for this idiot?

I have no other options unless I move.

Maybe I should.

No, I'm talking from emotion, not reality.

Everyone leaves, including Bowmen. I can't seem to tear my eyes off the destruction. I spent months perfecting this. It was my best work ever. The additions changed it from an edgy masterpiece into a resemblance of last year's trends.

My eyes can't seem to move off the jacket I designed. It's the one I told Adrian he would look hot wearing. Several gaudy patches now fill the sleeves and back. Bowmen had one of his interns create them in under an hour. I've never felt so connected to a piece I designed.

Adrian would never wear this.

I wouldn't want him to. It's no longer worthy of his body.

It hits me. I designed this jacket with Adrian in mind.

I go into my office and double-check I have the design I created on my cloud. I work from home a lot. Bowmen's never had a problem with me keeping my work on my personal cloud. He has no access to it, but as long as I keep designing his lines and keep the media buzzing about his label, he doesn't care.

I turn off my computer, fish my phone out of my purse, and unlock my screen.

Adrian: *Something came up. Bogden is waiting in the lobby for you and will bring you home.*

He sent the message around midnight.

Surely Bogden isn't still in the lobby?

I call Adrian, but it doesn't ring and goes straight to voicemail, so I hurry downstairs. When I step off the elevator, the janitor is cleaning the floor, the night guards nod to me, and Bogden is sitting on the couch. As soon as he sees me, he rises.

"I'm sorry. I didn't know you were here. I just pulled out my phone."

Bogden smiles and a dimple appears. I assume he is in his early thirties. He brushes his brown hair off his forehead. His brown eyes are cold like most of the Ivanov men. His accent is thick Russian. "It's not a problem. Are you ready to go home?"

"Yes."

He guides me to the car. When he gets in, I lower the divider window. "Have you heard from Adrian?"

"No, ma'am."

I assume he's taking me to my place, but he parks in the garage for Adrian's building. "Oh. I thought you were taking me home?"

"Adrian instructed me to bring you here. Do you want me to take you to your apartment?"

Maybe Adrian is here and his phone is off.

I shake my head. "No. I can stay here."

Bogden turns off the car and escorts me into the penthouse. When he leaves, I search for Adrian, but he's nowhere. I undress and slide into bed, but I can't sleep.

Where is he?

Did he meet up with Obrecht and Dasha? Is he still with her?

Why am I thinking this way? He said he doesn't want her.

Obrecht said Adrian knew he was meeting Dasha.

What if he's avoiding me because of what happened?

I toss and turn all night, inhaling the scent of Adrian on the pillows, wishing he were with me. The sun rises quickly. I shower and try to call Adrian again, but it's the same as before. I text him.

Me: *I hope you're okay. Can you call me when you get this? I'm worried about you.*

I get ready for work and leave. When I get in the lobby, Bogden is waiting. "Ready for work?"

Confused, I say, "Have you not gone home?"

"No, ma'am. Are you heading to work or somewhere else?"

"Work. But I can—" I take a deep breath. "Adrian told you to be my driver?"

"Yes, ma'am."

This is extreme. It's daytime.

Obrecht's voice erupts in my mind. *"If an Ivanov says to do something for your safety, it's best not to fight it. There's a reason for everything we do. Nothing is ever by chance."*

"Have you heard from Adrian?"

"No, ma'am."

The anxiety in my chest tightens. *What is he doing? Where is he? Is he okay?*

"Should I take you to work or somewhere else?"

I sigh. There's nothing I can do right now. "Please take me to work."

17

Adrian

BEFORE NATALIA'S DEATH, I NEVER KNEW ANXIETY. YOU could say I was fearless. Now, all I worry about is something happening to Skylar. We've only been together for a month, but every night, she's in my bed. I'm obsessed with her. I can't be away from her. No matter what, I need to keep her safe.

Her lax attitude toward her safety disturbs me. I watch her walk out of the door with my brother, cursing myself for letting my emotions get the best of me. There are better ways to handle things than yelling at her, and I detest myself for not controlling my reactions.

I return to my penthouse. I walk around, spinning out more and more. I try to work out, but nothing works. Natalia's dead body, my family's pain, and my printsessa's beautiful face all mix with an image of Zamir.

He's still alive. It's been over fifteen years. And that bastard is still alive.

As long as he's breathing, he's a risk to Skylar's safety.

I don't know how much time passes, but the sunlight of afternoon turns into darkness. I find myself staring out into the Chicago skyline. The buildings are all lit up. I can't see the lake anymore. It's too dark. I turn on the fireplace on my balcony and step outside. My phone rings.

"Obrecht."

"You need to come to Dasha's."

My stomach twists. "Why?"

"Come now."

The uneasiness I feel whenever I think about Dasha ignites. I told her I would meet with her. But then, after talking to Obrecht, he convinced me to let him speak with her instead. So I did.

"All right. I'm on my way."

I get in my SUV and drive over to the address Obrecht sends me. My gut drops.

She lives next to the building Skylar works at?

When I step into Dasha's apartment, the sight of her alone makes my skin crawl.

She looks like she's ready to hit the town. She's in a form-fitting red dress. Her makeup looks flawless like always, and her long hair has perfect curls. Her fake eyelashes and nails serve as a reminder that nothing is ever completely true with Dasha.

She steps up and comes towards me. "Adrian. It's good to see you." She embraces me and kisses my cheek, but I retreat.

"Don't," I warn her. My mind is still off, and I don't trust what I might say. I turn to Obrecht. "What's going on?"

Obrecht scowls. "Seems your ex-wife has made a deal with the Poles."

The pit in my stomach grows. I snap, "What kind of deal?"

"The kind you make with a Zielinski," Obrecht seethes.

I spin on Dasha. "Are you insane?"

Dasha's eyes fill with regret and fear. But she's a sly woman. She knows how to manipulate and act. Toward the end of our marriage, I finally wised up. I learned to take anything she says with a grain of salt. Her face falls. "I didn't know, Adrian. I swear I didn't know until it was too late."

I take two large strides and put my face in front of hers. "Dasha. What did you do?"

"It was a mistake. I swear it was a mistake, Adrian. I just needed some money and...well, I did what I had to do," she insists with tears in her eyes.

"What exactly would that be, Dasha? You don't just accidentally get into bed with the Polish mob," I growl.

Dasha's eyes flash with guilt, and I feel sick.

She slept with one of those bastards.

She puts her hand on my arm, and I shrug it off. Her voice would make any man feel sorry for her, but I know better. "I took a trip. I was in Italy. I met Bruno's son. I didn't know it was him. I swear I didn't know!"

Fierce rage hits me. I take every ounce of anger and put it in the delivery of my words. "How would you not know, Dasha? You know Zielinskis are mafia."

"Well, I don't exactly hang out with mob people, Adrian."

"Really? It seems to me you do."

"Zielinski is a common name. I didn't put two and two together," she snaps.

"How fucking irresponsible can you be?" I accuse.

"Oh, and you're perfect, right, Adrian?"

Full of disgust, I seethe, "Who did you sleep with? Which one?"

She stays silent, glaring at me.

"Jesus. Don't tell me you slept with Bruno. He's our parents' age."

She wrinkles her nose. In an insulted voice, she says, "Of course not."

"Then, who?"

"I met Kacper, and we hit it off."

I spin toward Obrecht. "Am I seriously listening to this right now?"

He grunts. "Your ex-wife, not mine."

"Thanks for the reminder."

"Excuse me, I'm in the room," Dasha complains.

I point at her. "You have two seconds to tell me what you've done, Dasha."

Her lips tremble. It only makes me angrier. My years of Dasha playing me are over, but the problem is I never know if her actions are real or fake. "I-I met Kacper in Italy."

"Bruno's son?"

"Y-yes. We..." She swallows hard. "We got along really well."

"You mean you fucked him?" I seethe, pissed she'd do something so stupid.

She stands straighter and sticks her chin out. "We had a relationship, yes."

I turned to Obrecht. "Can you tell me the important parts of what she did?"

Obrecht's jaw clenches. His scowl intensifies. "She ran drugs for the Zielinskis."

I spin back to Dasha. "What in God's name were you thinking?"

"I needed money. Kacper said I was only transporting items for him since he didn't have time. I didn't know there were drugs inside the suitcases. And now, if I don't keep doing it, they're going to kill me." Her tears fall down her cheeks.

For years, Dasha's known how to crawl under my skin. I fought to keep her for so many years. Now I look at her and wonder why I ever tried to save our marriage. How could I have ever loved this woman? She knows everything about Natalia's death. There's no way I buy she didn't know what she was getting involved in. "You're on your own, Dasha. This doesn't have anything to do with me. If you don't remember, we're divorced. You didn't want any part of me. Whatever trouble you're in, I really don't care."

She gapes at me. "Adrian, how can you—"

"God, I can't believe you would do something this stupid."

"I didn't know," she protests again.

"Doesn't matter. I don't owe you anything. Stay away from me." I motion to Obrecht. "Are you ready to go?"

He shakes his head. "She didn't tell you why she's in Chicago."

More dread fills me. Blood pounds in my ears. I resist the urge to look at Dasha.

Obrecht glares over my shoulder at Dasha then pins his steely gaze on mine. "Bruno wants her to transport heroin over the border into Canada. Since she's still an Ivanov, he wants her to do it with our trucks."

A chill runs down my spine. Over the years, we've invested in a lot of companies with Maksim and his brothers. One of our investments we made before Dasha and I got married is a trucking company. She fought hard to get it in our divorce but finally agreed to let it go and take cash. While we are silent investors on most of our investments, Obrecht and I oversee this company's management. Heat floods my cheeks. I bark at Dasha, "How would he even know we own it? It's not a publicly traded company. It has layers of organizations around it."

She turns to the window. Her hands shake.

I lunge in front of her. "You told him?"

She doesn't deny or admit it.

In a low voice, I growl, "How could you?" I don't remember ever feeling so betrayed.

She puts her hands on my chest. "Adrian, I'm sorry. I—"

I hold her wrists. "Do not touch me ever again." I release her and spin to Obrecht. "And she is not an Ivanov anymore. This is not our problem."

"She didn't change her last name."

More surprise shocks me. "You said you couldn't wait to no longer be an Ivanov. You were embarrassed to hold my name after what I became. Why are you still using it?"

Tears rapidly fall down her cheeks. "I still love you, Adrian. I always have. We made a mistake. I see that now. I was wrong not to embrace who you became. I'm sorry. Please. I want to make things right. I'm the mother—"

"Stop using our dead son as leverage," I yell at her, losing any control I have. I ball my hand into a fist, feeling the outline of his body in my palm. "You don't get to do that."

She puts her hand over her mouth and cries harder.

I wonder if I'm the most heartless man on earth. There's no pity left for Dasha. I always feel guilty our son died and it was my fault. But I can't do anything about my actions and the role I played in her miscarriage. Now, Dasha's time is up. I will no longer allow her to use him as a chess piece in our relationship.

Her face crumples. "They will kill me, Adrian. Do you understand? I will be dead?"

"That's your fault, Dasha. You aren't a stupid woman. I don't believe you didn't know who you were fucking. You're too smart not to ask what you would be transporting. They only have information about our company because you told them."

"I didn't tell them intentionally. It just came out. Honestly, Adrian, I wouldn't do that to you. No matter what's happened to us, I still love you. I'm not lying," she claims while wiping her face.

Obrecht crosses his arms. "They're expecting her to use our trucks."

"Well, tough shit, they aren't," I snap.

"You know it's not that easy, Adrian. We're going to have to meet with Zielinski."

"There's no way in hell our trucks are delivering heroin anywhere."

"No, but we're going to have to pay Zielinski something. He's not going to let this go." Obrecht shoots Dasha daggers.

I spin back to Dasha and hold her chin so she hears my message loud and clear.

She holds her breath and gives me big doe eyes. I used to fall for them but not this time.

In anger, I bark, "It's a good thing I don't love you anymore. It makes this a lot easier. We aren't meeting any Zielinskis. You aren't using our trucks. Whatever happens to you,

Dasha, I don't care. This is beyond anything I ever thought you would do."

She throws her arms around me and buries her face in the curve of my neck. "Adrian, I'm sorry. I didn't know. I swear. Please believe me. I would never intentionally hurt you or your family." She picks her head up. "I know I've made mistakes, but do you really want me dead?"

My conscience takes over. I soften. "No. I don't want you to die, but I don't understand how you could do this."

More tears fall, and something in Dasha's eyes makes me cave more. "I got reckless. There was so much pain about...everything we went through. You know what Natalia meant to me. She was the only sister I ever knew. I-I could barely cope when it happened. And I was pregnant—"

"Stop using—"

"I'm not! You want honesty. I'm giving it to you. I didn't know how to deal with any of it. You didn't, either. We were young, and it was tragic. And then our son died."

I grind my molars, trying to keep my emotions from escaping.

Her voice cracks. "There was so much grief. Neither of us knew how to handle it. When we finally split, I-I just didn't want to feel anymore. I wanted to be someone else. And you did that, didn't you? You transformed and did what you had to, but I didn't know what to do with my pain. When I got to Europe, all the years of trying to cope hit me. And I was alone. I didn't have you to call. Everything you used to do to give me a brief moment of relief from it all, I couldn't find again. No one, and nothing, could give it to me. And the more I tried to find it, the worse things got."

My heart cracks all over. I wish it didn't, but it becomes a shattered piece of glass. Against my desire to not allow Dasha to get to me, she has. I don't know if she's playing me, but it's the most sincere I've seen her since before Natalia died. As much as I don't want to care about her, I still do. I don't want to get back with her, but no matter how much I wish I could erase our past, I can't. And I had a role in her demise. I know I'm not innocent. If I were the husband she had needed, she wouldn't have ever gone to Europe.

Her face twists. She asks again, "Do you really want me dead?"

I reassure her again, "No. Of course I don't."

She falls apart again in my neck, and I put my arms around her to comfort her. "Please, Adrian. I swear I didn't know. I would never hurt you or your family intentionally."

I blink hard, staring out the window at the building next door. Suspicion creeps back up. I release Dasha. "Why do you live next to Skylar's office?"

Her eyes widen. She shakes her head. "I didn't know. I swear. If I hadn't seen her tonight—"

"You saw her?" I growl.

She holds her hands out. "With Obrecht. If I hadn't planned on meeting him, I wouldn't have known."

I study her, trying to decide if she's telling me the truth or lying. I can't be sure, but my gut tells me she's not fibbing.

Regardless, I look at her and say, "If you go near her, I will make sure the Zielinskis aren't your only problem."

Hurt crosses her face. "I won't. I promise."

I lower my voice. "Dasha, what did you think was going to happen? Did you believe we would give you our trucks to transport drugs?"

"No. I thought you would help me."

"How?"

She looks out the window and bites her lip. I wait, knowing she has some idea in her head, and I want to know what it is. She finally locks eyes with me. "I-I thought you could kill him."

"Jesus fucking Christ, Dasha," I mutter. There's already been enough pain today, but I dig the spear deeper. "You hated me for who I became. Now you're okay with it?"

"I was wrong, Adrian. I'm not sure how to get you to see how much I regret everything I did to you," she cries out.

"You're asking us to put a target on our backs," Obrecht points out. "Oh, wait, you already put one on it."

She glares at him. "There's no other way to get me out of this. They aren't any better than the Petrovs."

"You should have thought about that before you slept with one and transported their drugs."

"I already explained this!"

"Whatever."

Dasha turns back to me and grasps my cheeks. "Please, Adrian. Help me."

My stomach twists. "Fine. I need time to figure this out. But you stay away from Skylar. If you go near her, I'll hand you over to Zielinski myself."

"I already promised I'll leave her alone."

"Good. There's one more thing."

"What?"

"You and I are over. We are never getting back together. I don't love you anymore, and there isn't anything you can do to change it."

Betrayal and surprise fill her expression. Either Dasha is even better at acting than I thought, or she finally understands I don't want her anymore. Part of me feels bad, but I remind myself Dasha isn't someone who easily quits. I need to make it crystal clear with her she can't manipulate me like she used to.

"Tell me you understand."

She wipes her face. "Okay."

I go toward the door.

She grabs my arm. "Adrian."

"What?"

"Thank you. And I'm sorry...about everything."

I nod, fighting emotions lodged in my chest. I open the door and leave.

Obrecht follows but says nothing until we are alone in my car. "That was intense. You all right?"

I avoid his gaze. "Dasha's done a lot of things, but I never expected something like this."

"Yeah. How could she not have known?"

I scrub my face. "I don't know."

"But you believe her?"

I pin my eyes on his. "Do you?"

"You were married to her, not me."

I scoff. "Does it even matter if she knew? I can't throw her to the wolves and let her die."

"Speak for yourself."

"Obrecht!"

He groans. "Fine. Rafi will be at the Cat's Meow. Let's pay him a visit and see what he knows."

I pull out my phone and call Bogden.

"Adrian," he answers.

"I need you to go to Skylar's work. I'll send you the address. You wait for her and take her to my place. In the morning, take her to work. Don't let her out of your sight."

"Got it."

I toss my phone in the cupholder. I hate the Cat's Meow, but if anyone can get us info, it's Rafi. "How much cash do you have on you?"

Obrecht pulls out his billfold. "Few thousand. You?"

"Same. We'll stop at my house and pull more from my safe."

"I told you she'd come back someday and try to destroy you again."

I turn on the engine and reverse out of the space. "Really? You're going to rub this in my face?"

"No, brother. I'm going to remind you Dasha is a snake."

"I already know that."

"Do you?"

"What does that mean?" I snap.

"She put on a good show, complete with a new plate of tears. She divorced you, but now she wants you. So convenient."

I inhale the air slowly. "Yeah, well, I don't want her."

"God, I hope you don't change your mind. She's destroyed you enough."

"I'm not innocent in the demise of our marriage, you know."

Obrecht points at me. "That, right there, is what's going to get you in trouble. Dasha filed for divorce. She strung you along for years. Don't forget it."

"I won't. I meant what I said. I don't love her anymore."

"Good. I'd hate to see you mess things up with Skylar. This is a typical Dasha move. Swoop in the moment you have someone new in your life. Don't let her mess with your head again."

"I'm not."

"Good, but be careful. History tends to repeat itself," Obrecht warns.

History can't repeat itself. Dasha may have screwed up several of my past relationships, but I wasn't dating any woman who was anything like Skylar. The only person who can destroy my relationship is me.

I need to keep Skylar safe.

She can never find out about the monster who lives inside me.

However we decide to get Dasha out of this situation and off the Zielinski's radar, it needs to stay in my vault of secrets. Tonight's conversation with Dasha only solidifies it more. Skylar only needs to know me as the man she does. The other part of me isn't worthy of her love. And I've never craved anyone's love as much as I want hers.

18

Skylar

It's near five when I get a message.

Adrian: *I'm not in a situation to talk right now. Can you go to Nora's reopening with your friends? I'll try to meet you there, but I can't guarantee I'll make it.*

Me: *You won't be back tonight?*

Adrian: *Something else came up. I'm doing my best. How did work go last night?*

Me: *Don't ask. Are you somewhere safe right now?*

Adrian: *Sorry to hear that. Don't worry, my printsessa. I'm safe, but I have to go. Bogden will take you wherever you want.*

Me: *Okay. I hope I see you tonight.*

Adrian: *Me, too. I miss you.*

My heart skips a beat.

Me: *I miss you, too.*

Relieved Adrian is safe, I sit back in my chair, staring out into the Chicago skyline. There's a peek of Lake Michigan between two buildings, and I can faintly see a few boats. I wish Adrian would tell me where he went and who he was with, but I remind myself I agreed to his terms.

I text Kora and Hailee.

Me: *Change of plans. Okay if I go with you to Nora's tonight?*

Kora: *Yep.*

There's no answer from Hailee, but she stays late and helps tutor the older kids often.

Me: *Adrian is making Bogden drive me around. I'll swing by and pick you both up.*

Kora: *Sounds good. I need to finish this draft first. See you tonight.*

There's a knock on my office door. "Come in."

My friend, Fiona, steps in and shuts the door. I've worked with her for the last six years. Her sentiments regarding Bowmen mirror mine. She plops into the seat across my desk and rolls her eyes.

"Oh, no. What's going on?" I ask.

"Bowmen wants me to create a headband for the collection."

"A headband?"

She slowly says, "Yeah."

My heart sinks further. I force a smile. "This is one instance I'm happy only his name is on the collection."

She snorts. "It's like he's trying to commit fashion suicide. I don't understand why he's taking your brilliant designs and screwing them up."

I shrug. "Nothing we can do about it." I turn off my computer and stack my papers into a neat pile. "I have plans tonight, or I'd help you create"—I glance at the piece of fabric in Fiona's hand and cringe—"your headband."

She rises. "Have fun. Bowmen just got on the phone with New York, so I'd leave now if I were you."

"Thanks for the heads-up." I sling my bag over my shoulder and manage to escape an encounter with Bowmen. The last thing I want is any more interaction with him. Several times today, he made snide remarks about my inability to be creative, since I don't have any fabulous ideas for him. I almost threw some out to appease him, but anything I would have suggested wouldn't have been something to make the collection better. It would just be another thing to destroy it further, and Bowmen's already done enough damage.

I text Bogden when I get in the elevator. By the time I get to the lobby, he's pulled up to the curb. He's standing next to the back door and nods to me as I approach.

"Ma'am."

"Bogden, you can call me Skylar."

He smiles and opens the door. "Okay. Where would you like to go?"

I debate about my place or Adrian's. The outfit I want to wear is at the penthouse. "Adrian's, please."

"Sure thing."

It doesn't take long until I'm standing inside Adrian's. He must have been home because my laundry he did the day before is no longer hanging up. The shirt he wore the day prior is flat on the counter. A large, damp circle is on the chest area. I lean closer, and the smell of stain remover and some floral scent flares in my nostrils. I pick it up and study the stain.

Is that foundation?

I sniff harder. *Roses.*

Dasha always smells like roses.

Obrecht was with Dasha, not Adrian.

Am I going crazy?

Why would her makeup and scent be on Adrian's shirt?

I put the shirt back on the counter then hold it, steadying myself.

Could the foundation be from me?

Adrian did pull me into his chest yesterday when we were in the elevator.

Mine doesn't usually rub off.

Or does it?

There's only one way to find out.

I go into the bedroom closet. My clothes hang neatly on the rack. The first two drawers of Adrian's have my things in them.

He cleared his drawers out for me.

My heart soars like it did when he told me he did my laundry, but it's bittersweet.

I take my yoga T-shirt and stare at it. My stomach quivers. I rub the shirt on my cheek then pull it away from me.

Brown streaks stain the white material. I sigh in relief. It doesn't explain the rose scent, but that could be part of the stain remover. I return to the laundry room and find the stain remover. It reads, floral garden scent.

I open the cap and sniff it then Adrian's shirt. I can't tell the difference, but my sense of smell might be overwhelmed at this point. I flatten my shirt next to Adrian's and pour the stain remover over the makeup I rubbed on it.

After several minutes of staring at our two shirts, I go back into the closet. I sit in the middle of the small room. Adrian may have issues with his mind spinning, but I've officially gone into *what-if* mode. Time passes until my phone snaps me out of my thoughts.

Hailee: *Got it. Leaving school now. Can you pick Kora up first so I can change?*

Me: *Sure.*

I rise, throw my hair in a claw clip, then shower quickly. I refresh my makeup and put on a pair of skinny jeans and a purple crocheted top.

What if he spent the night with Dasha?

He wouldn't do that to me. He doesn't want her.

What if he's lying?

He doesn't love her anymore.

What if he does?

My phone alarm rings. I take a deep breath and try to avoid the shaking in my gut. When I get to the lobby, Bogden is waiting for me.

We pick up Kora then Hailee. When we get to the pub, Aspen arrives with Maksim. I glance around the bar for Adrian, but I don't see him anywhere. We find an empty circular booth and sit in it.

My phone vibrates. I pull it out of my purse.

Adrian: *I'm on my way. Is everyone there?*

Me: *Yes.*

Adrian: *I have something I need to do when I get there. It's work related. As soon as I finish, I'll find you.*

Me: *Okay.*

Relief Adrian is okay mixes with the anxiety from my unanswered questions. *The makeup could be mine. Roses are in the stain remover he uses. I don't want to accuse him of something, but if he was with her—*

"Earth to Skylar," Hailee teases and waves her hands in front of my face.

"Oh, sorry!"

"What do you want to drink?" Hailee motions to the server.

"Gimlet, please."

"Gin or Vodka?" she asks.

"Gin, please."

She leaves, and Hailee announces, "So I met a new loser online."

Aspen leans in and rubs her hands together. "Oh. Do tell!"

"I think we should wait for drinks first."

"Don't be a tease, Hailee!" Kora says.

"I'm starting to get a complex. It's like I'm a magnet for the weirdos. Why can't I find a nice guy?"

Kora snickers. "That's the wrong statement to make."

Hailee's eyebrows furrow. "How so?"

"You've met plenty of nice guys. They bore you to death, you don't connect, and the sex is blah. Maybe you should accept the fact you're nice enough for both of you and go out with the weirdo for once."

Hailee shakes her head. "He said he wanted to lick my furry pussy."

"Well, guess I arrived at the right time," Sergey says and slides into the booth.

Hailee's cheeks turn crimson, and we get into a conversation about all the crazy things guys have said to us over the years. It makes me appreciate Adrian more.

I need to talk to him.

Sergey leaves, and I glance around the pub. I still don't see Adrian. Nora pulls a chair next to our table and sits. Anna joins us, too.

"There's the superstar!" Aspen beams.

"Anna's the one who designed it. She gets the credit, not me. She even came over and made my brothers redo things she didn't think were perfect," Nora replies.

"You all did great," I assure them. I never saw the pub before the renovation, but it's beautiful.

"Did you see Killian?" Nora asks Hailee.

Aspen shakes her head, and her eyes widen.

"What?" Nora turns to where she's staring. Some girl is playing tongue tag with Killian.

Nora scowls. "What's that slag doing here? I didn't have her on the list. He's not that into her... God, he can't be..." Nora glances behind her, shooting them another dirty look, then focuses on Hailee again. "He probably didn't know you would be here—"

"It's fine, Nora. We've only spoken a few times."

"Well, don't look now, but Mr. Melt Your Wet Panties is checking you out, Hailee," Kora claims.

She blushes and sits up straighter. "Who?"

We all glance at the sexy bad boy who's intensely focusing on Hailee. After teasing Hailee some more, Nora turns, and her face falls. "Yeah, who..."

Anna says in a bubbly voice, "It's Nora's cousin, Liam."

"How do you know him?" Kora asks.

"Nora and I had lunch with him. He's super charismatic and nice. He's funny, too."

"You've been holding out on us, Nora," I tease.

She doesn't reply and looks slightly uncomfortable.

The man approaches our table. While staring at Hailee, he says, "Nora, are you going to introduce me to your friends? All stunning lasses, by the way."

"Umm..." Nora picks up a glass of water and takes a long sip.

Hailee's cheeks turn as red as Nora's hair.

Anna steps in and makes introductions.

The server, Darcey, comes over. "Nora, I don't mean to interrupt, but Darragh said to come get you. He's talking to Boris near the back."

"Oh. Okay. Thanks." Nora leaves, and Liam takes her seat, focusing all his attention on Hailee. Kora, Aspen, Anna, and I all eye each other. Hailee's face stays red the entire time. Kora excuses herself for the bathroom, and Adrian steps inside.

More relief fills me. He's told me twice today he's fine but seeing him seems to make it real. He surveys the bar and motions to Boris. They speak briefly. He scans the pub again, catches my eyes, and winks before motioning to Maksim and his brothers. He disappears into the back of the restaurant.

Flutters erupt in my stomach. I engage in more conversation with the girls and Liam, trying to pay attention.

"I missed you," Adrian's deep voice rings in my ear. Tingles form where his lips brush against my neck. Peach blossom, Turkish rose, and amber float in the air.

I turn my head. My smile hurts my cheeks. "Hey."

He kisses me on the lips. "Almost done. I need a few more minutes, okay?"

"Sure."

His icy-blue flames stay fixed on me for a moment. Heat races to my cheeks. He leans into my ear. "Stunning like always, my printsessa." He kisses my cheek and stands straight. "Liam, you're needed."

Liam stays focused on Hailee. "I'll be right back. Don't go anywhere."

Her face turns maroon.

Adrian squeezes my shoulder and leaves with Liam.

"Spill it," Hailee says, looking at me.

"Me? What about you and Mr. Melt Your Wet Panties?"

Hailee scoffs. "You were present. I think we need the scoop on Mr. Bend Me Over."

"Don't call him that," I say.

Kora returns and slides into the booth. "Why not?"

"Do you want me to still call Sergey Mr. Russian Cubby?"

"No, it's Mr. Glue Sniffer," Hailee comments.

Aspen scrunches her face. "Eww. He sniffs glue?"

Kora throws Hailee a dirty look. "No. He does not sniff glue."

"Not anymore. He used to," Hailee adds.

"Stop trying to change the topic. What happened between you and Mr. Melt Your Wet Panties while I was gone?"

"Nothing," she claims, her face turning red again.

I lean into the table. "Anna, what do you know about Mr. Melt Your Wet Panties?"

She shrugs. "I only met him once. He's a nice guy. It seemed like Nora, Killian, and he are super close. You should ask Nora about him. I don't know much."

"Are you going to chicken out or date him, Hailee?" I ask.

"He hasn't asked me out."

"Not yet. He will," Aspen assures her.

"Yep. You should get rid of the voice in your head telling you to run and say yes," Kora adds.

Hailee tilts her head. "I didn't say I had a voice in my head."

We all give her a knowing look.

"What?"

"He's a bad boy," Kora teases.

"In a give-me-some-major-Os way," I follow.

Aspen smirks. "Maybe you shouldn't wear panties on your date."

"Stop it!" Hailee covers her face with her hands.

Anna laughs then rises. "My brother Chase, and sister-in-law Vivian, just got here. I'll see you later."

We all say our farewells, and she leaves.

"So what's up with you and Adrian?" Aspen asks.

I shrug.

She raises her eyebrows. "He just kissed you."

"Yeah."

"Is it serious?"

"It's new," I say. Every bone in my body wants Adrian to be the one. I think he's serious about me, but the vision of our shirts lying in his laundry room fills my mind. If he spent the night with Dasha or some other woman, my heart is going to break.

"That's vague," Aspen replies.

"What's vague," Adrian asks as he approaches. He slides next to me and tugs me into his chest then pecks me on the lips.

My cheeks heat. "Nothing. Are you done now?"

His cocky expression fills my face. He locks eyes with me. "Yeah."

"Do you want a drink, or do you want to go?"

His lips twitch. His eyes twinkle. He picks up my drink and takes a big mouthful. "I'm ready if you are."

We say our goodbyes. I ignore the smirks on my friends' faces. We step outside, and I ask, "Did you drive?"

"No. I dropped my SUV off earlier. Obrecht and I came in his car. Let me text Bogden." He pulls out his phone and hits some buttons then places his hands over my cheeks. The moment his lips meet mine, I melt into him, wanting more than anything to be his and his alone.

He retreats. "Do we need to stop at your place for anything?"

His closet, with my clothes hanging in it, pops into my mind. "No. I have enough at your place, but I have to talk to you about something."

"Why do I get the feeling I'm in trouble?"

Please tell me you weren't with her or anyone else last night.

Bogden pulls up to the curb.

Adrian studies my face then releases me. He opens the door, and we get in. He instructs Bogden to go to his place and pulls me on his lap. "What's on your mind, my printsessa?" His fingers stroke my cheek.

I struggle with what to ask him. I don't want to accuse him of something he hasn't done. I'm not the type of woman who needs her man to reassure her how much he wants her every minute of the day. When I'm with Adrian, all I feel is how much he desires me. On the other hand, I don't want to be a fool and stay with a man who sleeps with other women.

"Skylar? What is it?"

The air in my lungs restricts. Fear of what he may say, regret for what my question might do to our relationship, shame that I may look extra needy to him paralyze me.

"My printsessa, if you don't tell me what's wrong, I can't fix it."

"You won't lie to me? No matter what?" I blurt out.

He studies my eyes, and his forehead wrinkles. "No. Is this about Dasha?"

My gut drops, and I put my hand over it.

Did he sleep with her?

"Obrecht told me she was outside of your work."

Oh. Thank God.

I take a deep breath. "Ummm...yes. That wasn't what I was referring to. Well, not that incident."

"Incident?"

"I... I saw your shirt. In the laundry room."

The line deepens between his eyebrows. "Okay. What about it?"

"Did you sleep with her? Or someone else last night?"

His face falls. "Of course not. I told you I had work to take care of."

My insides quiver. I blurt out, "Was it my makeup or Dasha's on your shirt?"

He shifts in the seat, licks his lips, and clenches his jaw.

I swallow the lump in my throat. "Please don't lie to me."

"I won't lie to you. I never have. Every time I told you I don't want her anymore and I want you was the truth. It still is.

And everything I'm going to say to you, Obrecht will confirm if you don't believe me."

A bit of worry leaves me but not all of it. "Okay."

"I don't know if it's yours or Dasha's. But it doesn't matter—"

I gasp, and a tear falls down my cheek. "You slept with her?"

"Jesus, Skylar, no. How many times do I need to tell you I don't want her?"

"But you just told me—"

"You didn't let me finish." He wipes my tear with his thumb.

I stay quiet.

"Can I finish?"

I nod and sniffle. My heart pounds in my throat.

"Sometime around eleven last night, Obrecht called me and told me to meet him at Dasha's. She did some stupid shit, and now Obrecht and I need to handle it."

"What do you mean? What did she do? Why would you have to take care of her mess?"

"I can't tell you what she did. It's too dangerous. She got involved with some bad people."

"Then why are you getting involved?" I cry out.

"There's no choice."

"There's always a choice."

"Not on this one."

"Why?"

He sighs. "Because she's an Ivanov."

His words are a stinging slap on the face. Through clenched teeth, I seethe, "You're divorced."

"I know, but she still uses Ivanov. The deal she made is in our name. So we're going to take care of it, and then she's on her own."

I turn toward the window, still reeling in pain from his words and the truth. She was his. She continues to show the world she is his.

He turns me toward him. "I'm not lying to you. You can ask Obrecht."

"You were with her all night?"

"No. We were only in her place for a short time...under an hour."

"But it could be her makeup?"

"Yes. She got upset and was crying really bad."

"And?"

"She threw herself at me, and I hugged her. That's it."

Jealousy flares through me. I hate the thought of him comforting her. "Am I supposed to feel sorry for her now?"

He snorts. "No. You should feel sorry for Obrecht and me. We had to deal with her."

"This isn't funny."

His face falls. "No, it's not. Obrecht and I were working all night to figure out this issue with Dasha so it can be over.

When we got done, another issue happened that Obrecht and I had to deal with."

"Another Dasha issue?"

"No. It was an Ivanov issue."

"What does that mean?" I ask.

Adrian hesitates.

"Let me guess. Something else I can't know," I say in frustration.

He sighs. "This needs to stay between us."

He's going to tell me?

"Okay."

"I mean it. You can't discuss it with your friends or anyone."

"I won't."

"Human bones were found on one of the new Ivanov building sites. Not just one. A lot of bones. And someone stole pallets of steel from a site several lots over. Obrecht and I were dealing with those issues all day. So these are the answers to your question in no particular order. I was with Dasha for less than an hour. Nope. I still don't want her. I didn't sleep with her, nor will I ever again. The only woman I want to sleep with is you. And yes, I would have rather been with you last night."

"Ad—"

He puts his fingers over my mouth. "I understand why you have the questions you do, but I need you to tell me what I need to do for you to trust me."

Blood pumps hard between my ears. He's not hiding he saw Dasha. I don't like it, but he didn't lie to me. "Tell me what Dasha did."

He tilts his head. His eyes get smaller. "You know I can't do that, my printsessa. I already told you it was dangerous. One thing I will never do is put your safety at risk. You know this about me."

"If you have to worry about my safety, then how can I not worry about yours?" I say.

"I am not an average man. I understand how to take care of myself. You should never worry about my safety."

"That's a cocky statement, Adrian."

"It is true." Hurt fills his eyes. "Tell me. Is my honesty with you not enough for me to earn your trust? It would have been easier for me not to tell you anything about Dasha last night. It hurts me to look at your eyes when I tell you something that I know will upset you. But I do, so I'm not lying to you. And it doesn't seem to earn your trust."

Guilt fills me. "I do trust you, Adrian."

"Those questions don't scream trust, Skylar."

I shut my eyes and take a few deep inhales. When I open them, Adrian still has his gaze pinned on mine, intensely waiting for me to respond to him. "You told me when you spin out that you obsess about things until you feel like your skin is crawling, right?"

"Yes."

"That's how I feel about Dasha."

19

Adrian

DISGUST TAKES HOLD OF ME. IT'S NOT A SECRET SKYLAR ISN'T comfortable with my interactions with Dasha. It's why I had Obrecht meet with her. I pushed her off for almost a month, and I finally figured out Obrecht could eliminate my problem. I didn't expect to have to meet her or that she would have gotten her or us involved in something so dangerous.

I cup Skylar's cheeks. "Don't give her power."

"I don't want to, but I can't help it. When I saw her yesterday..." Skylar's face scrunches. "She still claims she's Mrs. Adrian Ivanov."

I snort. "She's not, and I have the divorce papers to prove it."

"I know. But she was at some point, and she's so sure of herself when it comes to you."

"Listen to me. She can say what she wants. We're through. I also warned her to stay away from you. If she comes near you, I want to know."

Skylar focuses on the ceiling. "So, how many nights are you going to have to be gone to solve her problem?"

My heart beats faster. Somehow, a miracle occurred. Darragh's contact planted evidence on both of Bruno Zielinski's sons, Kacper and Franciszek, for the bones found on the city lot. Right before Obrecht and I arrived at the pub, the police arrested them. In the meeting we had in the back alley, Darragh and Liam informed us Bruno created an alliance with Giovanni Rossi, the head of the Italian mob. Darragh assured us they would arrange for Kacper's and Franciszek's murder in prison.

But it's also clear Bruno is coming after the Ivanovs. Darragh believes it's due to Maksim and his brothers giving too many jobs to Polish workers. When men are employed, they don't need to succumb to men like Bruno or Zamir. I didn't ask Obrecht in the meeting. His eyes told me he wondered the same thing as me. *Are we being targeted because of Dasha?*

I push a lock of Skylar's hair behind her ear. "Dasha's issue is handled for now. There's no reason for me to see or talk to her. Obrecht will deal with her if needed. I know it bugs you. It's why I pushed off my meeting with her until tonight. If Obrecht didn't need me there, he wouldn't have called me over."

She bites hard on her bottom lip.

Anxiety fills my chest. I know what it's like to spin out. My printsessa having to deal with what I experience over my ex-wife makes me feel ill. "It kills me she's affecting you like this. What can I do so you believe me?"

She pins her gaze on mine. "I do believe you. It's what's so scary, Adrian. When you tell me you don't want her, and you only want me, I believe you."

"I do only want you. It's why you're in my bed every night. I can't stay away from you. You know I'm crazy about you, don't you?" I stroke her cheek. Blood pounds hard between my ears.

A tiny smile plays on her lips. "Ninety-nine percent of the time, yes."

Not the answer I wanted to hear.

My stomach twists. "That's not good enough, my printsessa. What is causing you to doubt my feelings for you?"

"Only when you disappear. It's..." Her lip trembles and tears slide down her cheeks. "I worry about you. I don't know where you go or who you're spending the night with. It..." She squeezes her eyes shut.

I hate myself for putting her through this.

I should let her go and lead a normal life.

I'm a selfish bastard. I can't.

"Look at me."

She opens her pain-filled eyes.

"I'm not sleeping with anyone else. If I could tell you everything, I would. I shouldn't have even discussed the things I told you tonight. I'm sorry about who I am and what I do. If I could escape it all, I would. But I can't."

Her voice lowers. "What do you mean by escape it?"

Crap. Why did I say that?

"Adrian, I don't know what the Ivanovs are involved in, but I know it's not all properties. You can trust me—"

"I do trust you. Do not question my faith in you," I sternly insist.

"I'm not like other women."

"Yes. I know. You're special and—"

"That's not what I mean, Adrian. Whatever you're involved in, I'll be okay with it. Just tell me."

Dasha said that.

I will not lose my printsessa.

"I can't," I insist.

"How can you say you trust me if you don't let me into your world?"

"We've been over this, my printsessa. Every move I make is with your safety in mind. I will never involve you in my other world. You don't belong there."

"Shouldn't I get the choice?"

"No. I will never subject you to it," I state and mean it. Skylar doesn't need to be tainted. And I don't want to change the way she sees me. I brush my lips to hers as I speak. "Are we going to let my job come between us?"

"I don't want it to."

"Okay. Good. Me, either. What can I do so you don't feel this way?"

"Tell me everything."

"You know I can't do that. So what else can I do?"

"I don't know. I...can you call me or at least text when you're gone?"

"I did. Last night before I left and as soon as I turned my phone on. Even if you hadn't sent me a text, I would have messaged you. All I could think of was you. I was worried about what was happening at your work and if you got home at a decent hour to sleep. And I sure as hell didn't want to be anywhere besides next to you."

The car stops in front of my building.

"Could you keep your phone on? Maybe text me a bit more when you're gone so I don't worry?"

Oh, my printsessa. I'm in a trance with blood all over me most of my nights away from you.

"Most of the time, I cannot have my phone on. But I promise you, I will text or call as soon as possible." I hold my breath, waiting for her to give me some indication she can accept our situation and still wants me.

She stays silent.

I fist her hair. "I cleaned my closet out so you have room. I've not done that for anyone."

She smiles. "I saw that. I would clean a part of mine out for you, but we never stay at my place."

"Do you want to? We can."

"No. I love your place."

I move my face next to hers. "Good. I love my place more when you're there."

"You do?"

"Yes. And you know what I think?"

"What?"

I steal a few quick kisses then reply, "Besides these two times I had to be gone for work, I think we're pretty happy together. What's your viewpoint?"

Her eyes brighten, and she nods. "Yes. We are."

"So we've been together for about a month, right?"

"Yes."

I wrap her hair around my fist. "If we've had four days apart because of my work, that means we have at least twenty-six days together. I don't remember any of those twenty-six days being bad, do you?"

"No."

"Okay. So if the majority of the time things are great, does that make the few times I'm away worth it?" My heart races as I wait for her to answer.

What if she says it isn't worth it?

She presses her lips to mine. I hold her to my mouth and part her lips with my tongue. She tastes good. So fucking good. No matter how many times I kiss her, she only gets sweeter. The craving I have for her only intensifies.

"We're good together, my printsessa," I mumble against her lips.

"I know." She rearranges her body so she's straddling me. I wrap my arms around her and end our kisses. "If you don't get your sexy little ass out of the car, I'm going to fuck you so hard, you'll never be able to look Bogden in the eyes again." I lean in and lick behind her lobe. "I don't want you in the car. I want you in my bed. You know why?"

She shakes her head. "No. Why?"

I pin my gaze on hers. "Because it's where you belong."

A tiny smile forms on her lips.

"I've not touched any woman since I've met you. Not even before the Cat's Meow."

"No?"

"No. And I've not brought anyone around my mother, or given them access to my penthouse, or wanted to see them every day."

"You haven't?"

"Nope. You know why?"

She stays silent.

"They aren't you. And I wish this wasn't between us. It causes you to doubt my feelings and who we are together. I understand I'm asking a lot from you, but I'm going to ask you to somehow find peace with this arrangement we have. I don't want to lose you, and I can't just do my life over again."

She rubs her thumb over my jaw. "Would you? If you could?"

I take a moment to consider how to answer her question. The truth of my world I can't disclose to her, but I tiptoe close to the edge. "I don't like to live in regret or think about the past. I can't change it. I am who I am. But every day, there's one thing I did I can't hide from. No matter what happens, I think about it. So if there was one thing I could do over, I know what it would be."

"What?"

I swallow the lump in my throat. "I would never have put Natalia in that cab."

The color drains from her face. She opens her mouth then closes it. Her eyes fill with tears again.

It becomes harder to breathe, and I have to look away. I've never said that statement out loud before. Now Skylar knows my sister's last year on earth she spent in hell because of me.

My printsessa turns my face toward hers. "That's not your fault, Adrian."

I inhale and release the air slowly. "I didn't tell you for you to try and convince me it's not. I know what my role played in her demise, but you asked me, and I won't ever lie to you."

She kisses me. It's sweet and full of everything too good for me. Like every moment we spend together, I feel it all. She deserves better than a man who does what I do. Yet, I can't seem to allow myself to let her go. She's mine, and I will do everything in my power to keep her.

I retreat from her lips and swing open the door. "Come on, my printsessa. Let's go home instead of sitting in this car."

We get out, and I guide her into the penthouse. All night, we stay engrossed in each other. The next few days, everything is back to normal, until Skylar doesn't come home after Nora's dress fitting, so I text her.

Me: *Sergey said you had his driver drop you off at your place? Are you coming home? Should I come there?*

She doesn't respond, so I call, but it goes straight to voicemail. Any bad vibe I could have annihilates me.

Obrecht walks into my penthouse as I'm putting on my shoes.

"Make it fast. I need to leave," I tell him.

He says in Russian, "I know where he is."

The blood in my veins chills. *He* is Zamir.

"Tonight?"

"No. Soon."

I should be disappointed. All I've obsessed over for fifteen years was getting my day with Zamir. Instead, relief mixes with my desire to make him pay for his sins. My gut is telling me something is wrong with Skylar. She never has her phone off.

"Good. I look forward to it." I step into the elevator, and Obrecht follows.

"Where are you going?"

"Skylar's. She isn't answering her phone. Igor dropped her off over an hour ago. Hagen said she hasn't left."

Obrecht arches an eyebrow. "Hagen?"

Shit. I forgot no one knows about my tail besides Maksim.

"Yeah."

"Why is Hagen on Skylar?"

"So nothing happens to her. You know how she and her friends are. They don't think about their safety. And now that the Zielinskis have us on their radar, I can't be too cautious."

Obrecht bobs his head as if debating. "Does she know?"

"No. And it's going to stay that way. I'm not giving her any reason to worry or ask questions. Plus, I don't want to spend any more of my time discussing Dasha."

"What does Skylar think you do when you disappear?"

My stomach twists. "I don't know. She worries and hates it."

"What did you tell her?"

"That I can't discuss anything."

Obrecht stays quiet, but I feel his disapproval.

"Do you have any better ideas? I'm not going to lie to her. And you know she can't ever find out who I really am. She'll run faster than Dasha did."

"That's not true."

I grunt. "Of course it is. She's a much better person than Dasha could ever be."

The door opens, and we step into the lobby. Obrecht grunts. "I won't argue that. However, I don't think you can keep her in the dark forever, little brother. Eventually, it's going to have to come out."

"No, it won't," I firmly insist. "We have an understanding."

"This is why I don't get serious with anyone. Keep it light, you don't have to deal with the drama."

"My printsessa isn't someone to casually date," I seethe, pissed at the very notion of the idea.

Obrecht stops walking. "Shit."

I spin on him. "What?"

"You have it bad, don't you?"

I stay silent.

"Jesus. What is it with Aspen's friends and all of you?"

"What does that mean?"

"Sergey. You. If anything goes wrong, you and Sergey are still going to have to see these women."

He has a point, and it's moot. I don't need to talk to Sergey. I know him, and he's in as deep as I am. I tease, "I don't think Hailee's taken if you want a date."

"The kindergarten teacher?"

"Yep."

Obrecht's eyes turn to slits. "I'm not stupid enough to go down that road, but you should rephrase your statement. She's not with an Ivanov."

A chill moves down my spine. "What are you talking about?"

"Did you not notice Liam at the pub?"

My pulse ticks faster in my neck. "What about Liam?"

"He's into Hailee."

"Shit. Tell me she isn't into him?"

Obrecht shrugs his shoulders. "My guess is she likes him."

"She's a kindergarten teacher, for God's sake. She's the innocent one."

Obrecht snorts. "Yep. And Liam O'Malley has his eyes set on her."

"Jesus. Fuck. I should warn her—"

"Really? You're going to let Skylar sit in the dark but go tell her friend to stay away from Liam?" Obrecht glances between us and steps closer. He lowers his voice. "We're no different from him, except he's murdered one man. How many have we tortured and killed?"

"Point taken, but it's Liam O'Malley. Hailee's a nice girl. She's trying to make the world a better place."

"Still not your place to interfere. And if you do, I suspect you're asking for issues with Skylar."

I scrub my hands over my face and groan. "You're right. I need to go. Drop me off at Skylar's?"

"Sure."

Within minutes, I'm standing outside Skylar's apartment. I don't knock and use the key she gave me. When I walk in, she's not in the main room. I go into the bedroom.

The shades make the room dark. It takes a moment for my eyes to adjust, but she's curled into a ball on the bed. She has her face smashed into the pillow. Faint sobs fill the air.

My heart races faster, and I lunge across the room. I pull her into my arms. "My printsessa, what happened?"

She jumps from surprise then hides her face in my chest. Her body shakes against mine.

I hold her tighter to me. Rage bubbles inside me, but I'm not sure where to direct it. "Please tell me what has you upset."

"I can't."

"Why not?"

"I-I tried to convince myself it's not important, but it is. I-I don't know how to make it not be," she mumbles so quietly, I struggle to hear her.

My stomach drops like I'm going down the first big hill of a roller coaster. I push my hands in her hair and make her look at me.

Is this the point where she tells me she can no longer deal with my secrets?

My mouth goes dry. I force myself to find out. "What isn't important?"

Her face turns red. She tries to turn from me, but I don't let her. Her mouth opens then shuts. More tears pool in her deep-blue eyes.

"Tell me."

She wipes her face. "I tell myself it doesn't matter. The only thing important is being with you and how happy we are together. I tried to forget about it, but seeing Nora today just..."

Nora?

"What did Nora do?"

"Nothing! I-I saw her in her dress. And she's having a baby. I've never focused on getting married or having kids. I'm not the girl who obsesses about it, but I do want it. So it hit me that if I stay with you, I'm giving it up."

If she stays with me. If *being the keyword.*

She's contemplating leaving me.

Nausea slams into my gut. "Because of who I am?"

Her eyes widen. "No. I heard you and Obrecht talking."

I scan my memory but don't know what she's referring to. "When?"

"At your mom's. Obrecht commented on your mom nagging you about marriage and kids. You said, 'Mom needs to stop living in la-la land, thinking that scenario is for either of us.'"

My heart drops. *I'm such an idiot.* "My printsessa, I—"

"You don't have to apologize for what you want. And we've not been together that long. It's not something I sit around thinking about, but I couldn't stop looking at Nora in her dress, with her baby bump, and thinking I'll never have it." She looks away and bites on her lip while more tears drip off her chin.

"It's something I don't think about when Obrecht and I talk about my mom. She..." I stop, blinking hard, trying to keep my emotions in check. "Dasha doesn't have family. She and my mom were close until..." I don't know why I can't talk about this without getting choked up. So much time has passed, yet the wound feels fresh. "We lost Natalia. Several months later, Dasha miscarried. She was six months pregnant. Our son died during labor. I held him in the palm of my hand. He was so tiny, but he..." I clear my throat. "He was beautiful."

Skylar turns into me. "What was his name?"

I smile and blink harder, staring at the ceiling. "Lev. It means lion in Russian. He would have been fourteen this year."

Her hand traces the L-E-V tattoo on my chest. I close my eyes. I don't like talking about any of this, but my words created damage. I'm not going to lose her over this.

She quietly asks, "And that's why you don't want kids or to get remarried? It's too painful?"

I shake my head. "No."

She scrunches her face. "Then what—"

"It's hard to think you'll have something again when it's ripped away from you. It's easier not to expect it or pretend you don't want it. Do I want anything resembling what Dasha and I had? No. Even our first few years, before they kidnapped Natalia..." I blow out a big breath. "I look back and see how wrong we were for each other. But it doesn't mean I would never get married again. And I'm forty, so my window for kids is running out. It's not that I don't want them, but even when you're young, they aren't guaranteed."

She places a knee on either side of my hips. "Adrian, I never know what to say to you. Anything I can think to say to try and offer some comfort sounds wrong. You've experienced so much loss, and nothing seems to feel right."

I slide my hands in her hair. "There isn't anything to say. I know you feel bad about it, and it's genuine."

"I know, but—"

I kiss her. It's heaven mixed with hell. I've hurt my printsessa. She's debating about giving up what she wants for her life for me. I don't want her to give up anything. The fact she's contemplating it pains me. I pull out of the kiss. "If I ever get married again, it's going to be with a woman like you. And I'm open to having kids if you want them, but I can't guarantee it. If I could control it, I would. I'd give you everything you want, but life isn't always fair."

She sniffles. "No, it's not."

"I'm sorry you heard my conversation with Obrecht. It was a stupid thing to say. And it doesn't apply to you."

A line forms between her eyes. "So it's not off the table with you? I'm not saying right now, but—"

I put my fingers over her lips. I tell her what I refused to say to several other women whom I dated since divorcing Dasha. I couldn't give them what they wanted, since it wasn't true for them. "No, my printsessa. Nothing is off the table with you."

20

Skylar

PEACH BLOSSOM, TURKISH ROSE, AND AMBER DELICIOUSLY tease my nostrils. Tingles ignite on my hip where Adrian's dragging his fingers. I open my eyes and turn over to face him. His cocky expression is a laser going straight to my core, heating everything in its path.

"Morning, my printsessa." He cages his body over me and brings his lips to mine, pausing next to them. "We have fifteen minutes before the alarm goes off."

I can't control the smile forming on my face. I tease, "Should I try to get some more sleep?"

He slides his hand between my thighs then grunts. He mumbles, "I don't think your pussy wants to rest."

I squirm against his hand.

He arrogantly raises his eyebrows, drilling his icy-blue orbs into mine. He gives me little chaste kisses while gliding his fingers in me and murmuring, "Wet, sexy pussys need love, not sleep."

I laugh. "Is that so?"

"Mmhmm." His tongue attacks mine and a wave of flutters rolls through my veins. "Pussys that are ready for me get rewarded." His fingers move in and out of my sex while the heel of his palm circles my clit.

I close my eyes as the sensations build, desperately returning his kisses while whimpering into his mouth.

His hot breath hits my neck. "You know what I thought when I woke up this morning?" He flicks his tongue on the spot behind my ear that always creates an intense buzz on my skin while increasing the pressure on the bundle of nerves between my legs.

"No...oh God!" My toes curl and tremors ignite in my body.

His lips brush against my ear. "I love you, my printsessa."

My heart skips a beat. I freeze, but he doesn't and continues to manipulate my body. "Adrian!" I cry out as I spiral into bliss.

Like everything he does, he intensifies the moment. His fingers slide out of me, and his cock takes their place, thrusting against my spasming walls in one fluid motion. He moves his face in front of mine, studying me with his piercing blue flames. "I love you."

Before I can respond, he plunges his tongue back in my mouth, controlling my ability to do anything except return his affection.

He's so good. Everything about him is always so damn good. I can hardly speak or form a coherent thought as he professes his love for me, speaking as his lips press on my neck.

He growls, "I love everything about you."

My arms grip his shoulders. I dig my nails into his back, and a groan vibrates in his chest. He brings his lips an inch from mine.

"I love you, too," I breathe. More heat floods my body, and pellets of sweat break out on my skin, merging with Adrian's.

His mouth curls up. "Yeah?"

"So much," I admit.

He moves hair off my face. "I cleaned more of my closet out." He dips to my neck and sucks on my pulse while thrusting harder in me.

"Thanks...that's...oh God! Adrian! Oh...oh God!" I scream as everything turns white, endorphins explode in my cells, and I quiver hard into his muscular frame.

He studies me in his signature way. It makes me feel as if I'm the only person in the world he cherishes. His cocky confidence also reflects in his orbs. When my orgasm slows, his face turns stern. "Move in with me."

"Move in?" I manage to get out, breathing hard.

He licks my lip. "Yeah."

I don't contemplate anything about it. I only know I want to be with Adrian. "Okay."

A smile erupts on his face. "Good answer." He kisses me while thrusting harder. He growls something Russian in my ear then pulls out and removes the condom. He ties it up and tosses it on the floor. I reach for him. "Adrian—"

He lunges back over my frame, kisses me, then smirks. "I'm not done yet. We have a few more minutes." In a graceful swoop, his face is between my thighs, and he's paying homage to my sensitive, swollen sex.

"Jesus," I pant, gripping his head.

He tugs on my hips, and I ricochet from one high to the next until my alarm goes off. I grab my phone off the nightstand and hit the *off* button. He kisses my clit then moves up my torso, spends some time licking and sucking my breasts before sliding his arms under my body and ravaging my mouth once more.

My second alarm goes off, and I groan.

He rolls off me and turns it off. "I'll contact the movers."

I laugh, and the surge of happiness I feel with him and no one else fills my chest. "Just like that?"

His cocky expression reappears. "I want you in my bed every night."

More flutters take off in my belly. "I am in your bed every night."

"Yeah, but I don't want to wonder if you will be."

"Aww. Does Adrian Ivanov stress about whether he's going to get laid or not?" I tease.

His face falls. "It's not about that, my printsessa. I love you. I don't throw that word out there without thought and absolute certainty."

My heart swells again. I get on my knees and straddle him. "I love you, too. And I wouldn't say it just to say it."

He traces my lips. "So I'll schedule the movers?"

"I have a lease for another nine months. And I don't think there's any point in bringing my furniture here. Maybe I can find someone to sublet? I need to see if my lease allows it, but maybe I could rent it furnished."

He squeezes my ass cheek and pecks me on the lips. "Bring whatever you want. We'll figure out what to do with the rest of your stuff. You better get ready, or you're going to be late for work."

I rise and pick my phone up off the nightstand.

Fiona: *Did you see the reviews?*

The fashion show was yesterday. Initial social media posts weren't great. Adrian came to the show. He whisked me away when some newer designers were kissing Bowmen's ass. I stopped looking at the comments online within a few minutes of getting in the car with Adrian. Then I turned my phone to silent to avoid calls from Bowmen. Once he saw the reviews, he would no doubt freak out. I would hear it from Bowmen at work today, so I decided I wasn't going to give him the power to ruin my evening.

I click on the link Fiona sent and groan. "He had to ruin my masterpiece." As expected, the major critics didn't like the line. They use words like "last season," "cluttered," and "trying too hard."

"You should start your own label," Adrian says for the hundredth time.

"We've gone over this." I walk into the bathroom, and he follows me.

"Yeah. It's not impossible. Once we sort out what to do with your apartment, what bills will you have?"

I turn on the shower. Panic takes hold. I didn't think about money when I told Adrian I'd move in. "I don't know. What is my half of the bills for this place?"

He snorts. "Nothing."

I tilt my head. "I can't just mooch off you."

Amusement crosses his face. "Mooch off me?"

"Yeah."

"You aren't, and I have plenty for both of us. We should look at what it would take for you to go out on your own."

"I can't. I would have to pay Bowmen to leave."

"Ask Kora whom we should see to review your contract."

My stomach flips. "It's too risky."

"Why?"

I step into the shower and Adrian follows. "I would be without a paycheck. It's expensive to create a label. Plus,

Bowmen is going to blackball me if I leave."

"So what? You don't need to work. I have money. We can put a business plan together. It would include a budget. Once we know the numbers, we can figure out if we should get a business loan or use cash."

"Cash?" I laugh nervously. "I think you're under the impression you're dating some other woman. I don't have tons of cash. I have my retirement account I add to and a small slush fund."

"I have money," he states again.

I let the water soak my hair then grab the shampoo. I give Adrian a quick peck on the lips. "You're really sweet, but I can't take your money and have you supporting me."

'Why not?"

"I...well, because it's yours. It's not mine."

"It's mine to use for what I want," he insists.

"Yes, but what if we break up?"

"Why are you discussing us breaking up? I just told you I loved you and asked you to move in. We aren't breaking up," he adamantly states.

Panic seizes me. I've not lived with anyone since my ex-fiancé, which was over ten years ago. I didn't think about anything when he asked me to move in. "What happens if we do break up and I'm living here?"

He swipes the shampoo off my hand and rubs his palms together. "Spin."

I obey.

He massages my scalp and leans into my ear. "We aren't breaking up. Stop worrying. If we did, it's not like I'm going to kick you out so you're homeless."

"You're such a great guy," I tease but shouldn't. He hit my fear straight on.

"I am. And I would never do anything to hurt you. Close your eyes." He takes the sprayer and rinses the shampoo out of my hair.

I turn to him and lace my fingers around his head. "I know you wouldn't."

"Then don't second-guess moving in."

"I'm not. I want to move in with you, but I need to be realistic."

"We aren't breaking up, and once you move in, you aren't moving out, my printsessa. You'll break my heart if you do." His eyes tell me he isn't joking. If something did happen to us, he would be in pain.

I wrap my arms around him tighter and kiss him. "I'd break mine, too."

"Good. No more break up talk," he says.

We finish our shower, I get ready for work, and Adrian drops me off. "Can you pick me up at four so I can get ready for the rehearsal dinner tonight?"

"Sure. If anything pops up, I'll send a driver, but as of now, I don't have anything pressing going on." He gives me a toe-curling kiss, and I debate about calling off work and spending the day with Adrian, but Bowmen will go nuts if I do. I pull myself away from Adrian and joyously stroll into the building.

I internally groan when I get to the elevator and Bowmen is there. He scowls. "Why didn't you answer my calls?"

I force myself to smile. "I had plans last night."

The elevator opens, and we step in, along with several other people. I stay quiet while my insides quiver. As soon as we get inside our office suite, Bowmen turns to me. "This is your fault."

"Excuse me?"

His angry expression turns darker. "You didn't bring any ideas to the table. What am I paying you for?"

My mouth hangs open. Millions of responses, including that he can take his job and shove it up his ass, fly into my mind, but I don't respond. He continues accusing me of destroying his collection, in front of the entire staff.

I avoid the sympathetic stares from everyone, except for Kevin. He's the one person who has an amused expression on his face. He's always wanted my position and is jealous of my role. He's the one person on the team who would backstab me to get my job.

"You aren't an intern, are you, Skylar?" Bowmen seethes.

My insides quiver harder. I take a deep breath to find the confidence in my voice. "No, I'm not."

This is abusive. Why am I taking this?

What am I supposed to do?

I can't get fired.

He continues assaulting me verbally then excuses everyone. All day, I pay for Bowmen's bad reviews. He slams more work on my desk around three. "Don't leave until you finish this."

I go through the pile then text Adrian.

Me: *I need to meet you at the rehearsal dinner.*

Adrian: *Why? What's wrong? What did that dick say to you?*

I can't tell Adrian what's happening. He'll strangle Bowmen with his bare hands. I hate lying to Adrian, but I don't see any other choice.

Me: *All's good. I have work to finish. I'll meet you there.*

Adrian: *I'll pick you up on my way.*

Me: *No. I don't want you to be late. I'll meet you.*

Adrian: *I'll send Bogden, then.*

Me: *Okay.*

Adrian: *If you get done early, let me know.*

Me: *I will.*

Adrian: *Are you okay?*

Me: *Yes. I'll see you tonight.*

Adrian: *Love you.*

Me: *Love you, too.*

I spend the next few hours finishing Bowmen's pointless tasks, which he designed to punish me. Bogden picks me up and drops me off at the restaurant. Kora is the first person I see, and I beeline toward her. "Hey. Have you seen Adrian? Bowmen was on one of his kicks and kept me late."

"You need a different boss, but they just left."

My heart pounds harder. "What do you mean, left?"

She shakes her head. "Boris walked in and they all just left. Sergey said if he's not back, to meet him at the church tomorrow."

My stomach flips. I pull out my phone. As I read Adrian's message, I mumble, "Something came up. I'll meet you at the wedding tomorrow." Panic fills me. I glance at Nora. She's alone and looks as if she might cry. *They left Boris's rehearsal dinner. What could be so important they would need to leave Nora on her own? Why won't Adrian be back until tomorrow?*

I demand to know. "What is going on, Kora?"

"I honestly don't know."

Aspen joins us. "Skylar, you look beautiful."

"Where did they go?" I ask. Something terrible is about to happen. I can feel it.

Aspen shakes her head. "I don't know."

"Please tell me. I can't handle not knowing anymore."

"We honestly don't know, Skylar," Kora says.

"Is this normal for you? Always being in the dark?" I snap.

Aspen's eyes widen. "No. It's not an everyday occurrence. And Maksim doesn't keep me in the dark. He tells me what I need to know. The things he deems dangerous for me to know, he doesn't."

"And you're okay with it?" I ask, upset she at least gets told something, but I'm always in the dark.

When will the day come that Adrian realizes whatever secrets he holds, I will handle and still love him?

Aspen sticks her chin out. "Yes. He would die for me. All he thinks about is how to protect and love me. So while I worry about his safety and don't enjoy him not being here with me, I know he wouldn't have left if it weren't important. And when he returns, whatever is safe to tell me, he will."

Well, that's more than I get.

Adrian only thinks about loving and protecting me, too. Is this so bad if that's what I get in return for him keeping his secrets?

I turn to Kora. "And you? You feel the same?"

She nods. "Yes. I don't like it, but there isn't any other choice, except not to be with Sergey. I won't choose that option."

I close my eyes. *If you're going to play in their sandbox, don't pretend you don't understand what they are capable of and use it as an excuse to run down the road,* Nora's warning to Kora and me during her dress fitting keeps playing in my head. I mutter, "What have we all gotten involved in?"

Aspen nervously glances at Kora. She softly asks, "Have you talked to Adrian about this?"

I sarcastically laugh then turn away and cover my face. The tears well and I do everything in my power not to let them fall.

Kora pulls me into her. "Hey."

"I need to go."

"Okay, let's go," she says.

I shake my head. "No, you stay."

"Aspen, you're staying with Nora tonight?" Kora asks.

"Yes, that's always been the plan."

"Okay. We'll see you tomorrow. Skylar, you come stay with me at Sergey's tonight."

"No, really—"

"It's not up for discussion. Let's go."

We hug Aspen, sneak out the side door, and hop in a cab. We say nothing until we get inside Sergey's. The entire ride, my mind floats between Nora's statement and the fear, frustration, and nagging voice in my head, saying Adrian can't continue to keep me in the dark while reminding me I agreed to his terms.

We spend the rest of the night watching rom-coms, ignoring the elephant in the room, and glancing at our phones for unsent messages. I try not to go down the *what-if* road, but I'm dying inside, worrying about where Adrian is and what he's doing. I'm not ignorant. Something dangerous is taking place.

I finally speak up. "I'm so worried. I hate not knowing what's going on."

Kora's hazel eyes glisten. "I know. It's not ideal, but it also isn't anything we can stop. They have their situations that pop up."

"What are those situations?" I attempt again to get any insight into what the Ivanovs are really involved in.

A sympathetic smile appears on her face. "I'm sorry. I don't know what Adrian's story is. I only know Sergey and his brothers. I can't break Sergey's trust in me, and I don't want to tell you something about Sergey that may not be true for Adrian. You have to talk to him."

"He won't tell me," I claim, swallowing the lump of emotions growing in my throat.

She furrows her eyebrows. "Maybe he just needs more time."

"Sergey told you. We all started dating around the same time." Hurt fills my voice.

Kora grabs my hand. "Sweetie, talk to him some more."

"I promised him I wouldn't. He said I have to be okay not talking about his work. I agreed to it." I wipe the tear off my cheek. "I'm worried about him. What are they doing?"

"I honestly don't know. But, Skylar, if you can't deal with not knowing what Adrian does, then you need to tell him."

More tears drip down my face. "I love him. I don't want to lose him."

Kora strokes my hair. "I know you do. But is love enough if you're in the dark?"

"I want to think it is. I told myself it was. The thought of not being with Adrian is so painful, I get heart palpitations thinking about it," I admit.

Kora sighs. "I know the feeling."

The room falls silent for several moments.

Kora asks, "I've known you a long time, right?"

"Yes."

"I think I know you better than anyone else," she adds.

"I agree."

"Okay. I can't tell you for sure what Adrian's story is, but my assumption is it is just as gruesome as Sergey's but maybe in a different way. If I told you that knowing what I know about you, if his story is anything like Sergey's and he's doing anything Sergey is, that I believe you would accept it and still love him, would that give you any comfort?"

"I already know I'll still love him. I just want him to tell me the truth."

She takes a deep breath. "Sergey wouldn't have told me if something hadn't happened. I honestly think if you give Adrian a bit more time, it'll eventually come out. If it's like Sergey's truth, it's not going to be easy for him to tell you. And from what I can gather, all the Ivanovs detest themselves in many ways over who they are. And Sergey's pain is deep. If Adrian's is anything like his, my advice is to love him and wait. But that's me. I can't tell you what to do, but no matter what, I'll support you."

I sigh. "You aren't making my curiosity any less."

She winces. "I'm sorry. I thought it might help you."

I think for several minutes. Her words do give me some comfort. "No, it did. Thank you. I hope you're right. Maybe I do need to give Adrian more time to understand how much I love him and will stick by him."

She hugs me. "I'm sorry I can't give you more. I wish I could. I hate you're going through this, but I also see how much you love Adrian."

"I do." I rise. "Let's go to bed. Tomorrow can't come soon enough."

"Agreed." She follows me down the hall and we go into our rooms.

The next morning, we get ready for the wedding. Adrian still hasn't messaged me, and Sergey hasn't contacted Kora. When we get to the church, Nora is stressing, and her auntie is giving her grief about her dress. We get her auntie out of the room and Darragh comes up and pulls her away.

"Thank God. That woman is a nightmare," I mutter.

"That's an understatement. Hailee better think twice about getting with Liam. His murder rap is nothing compared to her," Kora quietly adds.

I snicker.

Kora grabs my arm. I turn to see Adrian, Obrecht, and Dmitri through the window. I sigh in relief then feel Kora's nails dig into my arm.

Where are Sergey and Boris?

I put my arm around her waist. "Come on."

Her voice cracks. "Where is he?"

"Let's go find out."

I try to stop my tears from falling when I step in front of Adrian. He's in his tux, looking gorgeous as ever, but something is in his eyes. I don't know what to make of it.

"Where is he?" Kora asks, interrupting the conversation the Ivanovs are having in aggressive Russian.

Maksim hesitates.

"Tell me where he is," she demands.

Dmitri leads her to the side door and inside.

Adrian pulls me away from the others.

I cup his cheeks. "I've been so worried. Why didn't you text or call me?"

"I'm sorry. Our phones are dead. I'm fine. You look beautiful." He kisses me.

"What happened?"

"You know I won't answer your questions, my printsessa. It's too dangerous for you to know. Let's forget about this and celebrate good things today." His eyes plead with me to drop it.

Give him more time. He will eventually tell me.

Nora's voice also fills my head again. *If you're going to play in their sandbox, don't pretend you don't understand what they are capable of and use it as an excuse to run down the road.*

I take a deep breath and smile at Adrian. "Okay. But give me another kiss."

21

Adrian

Three Weeks Later

Zamir is dead. No one is left. Every man who ever touched Natalia is now dust. I've felt off since we left Boris's rehearsal dinner to kill him.

Why don't I feel better?

It's still not over.

Kacper and Franciszek Zielinski aren't dead yet.

"The O'Malleys haven't finished the job. The longer this goes, the higher our risk," I state to Obrecht.

He gives me his *no shit* expression. "Liam will be here any minute. You want something to drink?"

"Sure." I walk out to the balcony. It's a beautiful spring day. Lake Michigan sparkles, creating a blinding glare. The waves are gently lapping against the shore, and the sidewalks below are full of pedestrians. "Your place turned out nice." Obrecht finally moved in a few days ago. He was out of town, but the movers handled everything.

He joins me on the balcony and hands me a bottle of water. "Yeah. Anna did a good job."

The buzzer goes off, and Obrecht releases the lock. Liam joins us on the balcony. "Nice view."

Obrecht nods then hands him a water. He motions to the chairs. "Have a seat."

"I know what you're going to ask, and the answer is not yet," Liam says then takes a swig of his water.

"It needs to be taken care of," Obrecht insists. "Every day they stay alive is another day Boris is at risk. We need the bones case closed."

Liam puts his bottle down and taps the pads of his fingertips together. It reminds me of Darragh. I'm not sure if it should comfort or scare me. There's no getting around reality. Liam is going to be the leader of the O'Malley clan. "Can we cut the bullshit?"

The hairs on my arms rise. "What do you mean?"

Liam's gaze darts between Obrecht and me. It feels like forever before he announces, "I know why Dasha is here."

My gut drops. "And what reason would that be?"

Liam leans closer. "I tried to warn you about Dasha. Do you remember that?"

My stomach churns. Time passed and life took all of us on different paths. But at one point, Liam and I were close. We did everything together. The moment I met Dasha, he told me she was trouble. I didn't listen. It eventually drove a wedge between us. Dasha and I got serious. Liam stepped into his O'Malley shoes. Neither of us agreed with how the other was running their life. Eventually, Liam ended up in prison, and I was married to Dasha.

I spout, "What's your point, Liam? Do you want me to say you were right? Will that make you feel good?"

Liam scowls. "No, Adrian, it won't. But I know Dasha is running drugs for Zielinski."

My skin crawls. I glance at Obrecht.

His jaw clenches. "How do you know?"

Liam sits back in his chair. "You two seem to underestimate me and the O'Malleys. We keep our enemies close. Now that Nora is an Ivanov, I have no choice but to watch Ivanov alliances, too."

"The Ivanovs are not aligned with the Zielinskis. Nor are we enemies. You know this," Obrecht seethes.

"Dasha Ivanov made a deal with those bastards. It is Ivanov business whether you want it to be or not."

"What are you accusing us of?" I snap.

Liam scoffs. "Nothing. But your ex is putting our families at risk. A threat against an Ivanov is now a threat against the

O'Malleys. It is not in any of our best interest Kacper and Franciszek live."

"Then why haven't your men killed him yet?" I accuse.

Liam's eyes turn to slits. "While I understand your eagerness to eliminate our problem, there are logistics to handle. One of the biggest ones is to pin this on the Rossis, or did you forget our war?"

"Don't insult us," Obrecht growls.

Liam drinks the rest of his water. "It's happening soon. My guys will line up everything and strike when the time is right. We can't afford any mistakes."

"So you came here to give us no answers," Obrecht mutters.

"No, dickhead. I came here to tell Adrian to watch his wife."

"Ex," I bark.

"Your ex-wife is a snake. You know this. She's in bed with Zielinski. I don't buy she isn't setting you up. As long as she's using the Ivanov name, she better watch her back. We won't sit back and allow her to put targets on either of our families."

I wish I could stick up for Dasha, but I can't. I'm still trying to wrap my head around how she could ever get into a situation where she's sleeping then working, for a Zielinski, but I don't believe she would ever intentionally hurt my family or me.

"Dasha's been handled. Have your boys take care of those two thugs as you stated they would, and our issues go away," Obrecht demands.

Liam rises. "See, that's the problem. I don't have a good feeling about Dasha. It's the same feeling I've always had about her. There's just something about her. My gut says she's only starting whatever she has up her sleeve. So control your wife."

"Stop calling her my wife," I scoff.

"She's still using your name," Liam points out.

Time to change the subject.

"Yeah, well she's been told to stop. But by the way, I'm glad you're here. I wanted to talk to you."

"About what?" Liam asks.

"Hailee."

Liam's face turns suspicious. In a firm voice, he asks, "What about Hailee?"

"She's a good person."

"Yeah, she is." He pierces his eyes into mine.

I narrow my eyes on him. "She's a bit innocent to get involved in your world, don't you think?"

He glares. His voice turns to ice. "Don't get involved in my business."

"Hailee's your business now?" My gut twists at the thought. I can't see Liam being anything but trouble for Hailee.

Liam's eyes intensify. "Yeah. She is."

"Shit, Liam. She's a kindergarten teacher," Obrecht mumbles.

"Yeah, she is—an amazing one. You can keep your nose out of it as well. Besides, I don't see you living a happy relationship life."

"Relationship?" I blurt out.

Liam's face drops. "God, you're such fucking hypocrites."

"Why is that?" I ask.

He crosses his arms over his chest. "You two sit on your high horses, judging me. I've grown up, but I've also served my time. How much have you served for your sins?"

The truth hangs in the air. I hate myself for it. Liam is right. Obrecht and I guiltily exchange glances.

"Thought so. I'll let you know when my guys take care of things." He spins to leave, but I follow him to the elevator.

"Liam."

He turns, his face hardened. "Don't talk to me about Hailee. I like her. I'm not going to forget about her."

My pulse increases. "Okay. What else do you know about Dasha?"

"Just what you do. If I find out more, you'll be my first call."

"Thanks. Why don't we grab a beer sometime?"

"Why? Are we going to go back to pre-Dasha days?" He raises his eyebrows. The last time we ever hung out, he kept insisting Dasha was terrible news and I needed to break it off with her.

When I first came to America, I barely spoke English. Boris was already best friends with Killian when I met Liam. For some reason, we just gelled. "Probably not. I was thinking post-Dasha. That way, we aren't young, dumb idiots."

Liam takes a deep breath and nods. "Got me there."

My guilty conscience takes over. It hits me that Liam was there for me when I immigrated and had no friends. He's always had my back, even now. Coming out of prison can't be easy, and the penitentiary they had him in is one of the worst places on earth.

"I'm sorry if I'm a dick sometimes. And I guess I just lied. I would like to get back to where we were pre-Dasha...minus the young, dumb idiots part."

He chuckles. "Young is taken care of. I think the other part we'll have to make sure we don't fall into again."

"Agreed."

"Sounds good." We slap hands, he leaves, and I rejoin Obrecht on the balcony.

"If Liam knows about Dasha, who else knows?" Obrecht asks.

I sigh and glance across Chicago. "Dasha is a lot of things, but she wouldn't intentionally hurt us."

Obrecht's phone rings, and he holds up his hand. "Tell me what you got."

A set of fire truck sirens blare through the air, and I watch them maneuver through traffic, along the river, then down Michigan Avenue.

"Do you know what the connection is?" Obrecht's voice pulls me out of my trance. He shakes his head at me while listening then asks, "You're sure he's an O'Malley?"

My gut drops.

"Okay. Thanks for the update." Obrecht hangs up and says, "Your hand tattoo guy who's following Jack Christian around is an O'Malley."

A chill runs down my spine. "Why is an O'Malley following him?"

Obrecht calls Liam and puts it on speaker. "We've got an issue we need clarification on."

"What's that?" Liam asks.

"Not over the phone. Where are you?"

"A few blocks. I can turn around. Meet me when I pull up. I don't have a lot of extra time," he demands.

"Fine." Obrecht hits the button and puts his phone in his pocket. We leave his penthouse and meet Liam as his car pulls up.

As soon as we're in, Obrecht asks, "Why is one of your guys following Jack Christian?"

Liam's eyes turn to slits. "What business do you have with Jack Christian?"

"We've been trying to find dirt on him. You?" I reply.

Liam's voice is deadpan. "Figuring out how to take him down once his company goes public and gets listed on the stock exchange."

"Why?"

"That's O'Malley business. Why do you need info on him?"

"He's in the middle of a divorce. Kora's representing his wife. He threatened both of them. I'm pretty sure his wife has already seen his wrath."

Liam's face hardens. "You need enough leverage for him to finish the divorce?"

"That's my guess, but Sergey wasn't specific."

"Are you willing to share your intel with me? After you get what you need?"

I shrug. "Sure. I don't mind seeing the bastard further destroyed."

Liam scratches his chin and thinks for a few moments. "You need to become a member."

"Of what?" Obrecht's eyes turn into his distrusting glare.

"There's a private club. It moves locations and events are pop-up style. Jack never misses. My guy can't get in because of his record. Neither can I, plus, I'm an O'Malley. They don't let anyone linked to crime families inside. It's mostly politicians and businessmen. But you two, well, you would be their ideal candidates. You've got money, and your name isn't associated with anything bad. Plus, it's easier to hide in a group than by yourself if you're trying to get proof of things while you're there."

"So it's a sex club?" I ask, my gut twisting. I went to one with Sergey and wasn't impressed. It's not the only one I've had to experience. It's not my thing. Sergey and Obrecht are the only Ivanovs I'm aware of who are into those places. While they are each into different things, I have zero desire to hang out in one. My guess is if Jack is involved, the females aren't members, unlike the clubs Sergey and Obrecht belong to.

Strippers and prostitutes are something I stay away from. All they do is remind me of what the Petrovs did to Natalia. I know many aren't forced like Natalia was, but I still don't like it.

"Yeah. You get a notification an hour before your entrance time. If you don't arrive at the exact time, you don't get in. There's no other warning. Once you're inside, anything goes. You two up for it? I guarantee you'll get everything we both need on Jack."

Obrecht grunts. "Why do I have to get pulled into this? It's Adrian's assignment."

"There's another man I need dirt on, too," Liam admits. "As I said, a group is less noticeable than a lone wolf in these types of situations. Once you pound the hammer down on Jack, you won't get back in."

"So now I'm doing O'Malley jobs?" Obrecht grumbles.

Liam shakes his head. "No. We're exchanging favors. You got a problem with that?"

"What do we need to do to get a membership? Sergey's all over my ass, and I'm tired of my guys following this dickhead," I admit.

Liam raises his eyebrows at Obrecht.

Obrecht scowls. "Fine. Don't get used to me working for you. Who do you need dirt on?"

"Judge Peterson."

"Who's the guy with the hand tattoo?" I ask.

"Finn O'Malley."

"Who is he?"

"My cousin. He went inside the year you immigrated. He got out a few months after I did."

"What was he in for?" Obrecht asks.

Liam's face hardens. "Murder. You want me to set up your membership or what? The woman who runs it will allow me to vouch for you."

"But she won't let you in?" I suspiciously ask.

"My record doesn't allow me entry for a lot of places. Doesn't mean she's not in my pocket."

"Fine. Do what you have to do. Get us in. We'll get your info for you, but I don't work for you, Liam. Neither does Adrian," Obrecht states.

"Yeah, I'm clear on what this is."

Obrecht nods, and we get out. Liam drives off, and I turn to my brother. "I don't like exchanging favors with Liam, either."

"Yep, but you've had surveillance on Jack and are coming up with nothing. Do you have a better plan?"

"No."

"Then let's get in and get out."

"Fine. I need to go. I'm going to be late for my lunch with Skylar." I leave and walk several blocks to Skylar's office building. I'm almost there when I hear, "Adrian."

My skin crawls. I spin. Dasha's dressed like she's heading out on a date to a nightclub. She's wearing a short pink dress and stilettos. It strikes me as odd in the middle of the afternoon.

She tries to pull me into a hug, but I step out of it. "What do you want, Dasha?"

"Jeez, you don't have to be rude when we see each other." She pouts.

"Is there something you need?"

"I-I haven't heard from you. Obrecht keeps—"

"Yes, Obrecht is who you will deal with, not me," I bark in frustration.

"I-I got a call." She glances around us and lowers her voice. "Kacper called me from prison. H-he's still expecting me to go through with it."

"Yes, Obrecht told me. You need to stick with what we told you to say. You're working on getting access to our trucks and are close."

"Adrian, I-I'm scared. He sounded angrier than normal. Maybe we should go ahead and do one of the deliveries—"

"Have you lost your mind?" I shout.

"Shh. Keep your voice down."

I place my hand on Dasha's elbow and move her away from the sidewalk. "You need to stick with the story and do what we instruct you. Do you understand me?"

She scrunches her face and reaches for me. "Aidy, I'm trying—"

"Try harder." I shrug out of her grasp and turn. The first person I see is Skylar staring at us.

Great.

I meet her in front of her building, dip down, and kiss her. "My printsessa, how's your day going?"

She glares toward Dasha. "What does she want?"

"To annoy me." I put my arm around Skylar's back and guide her down the street. "Tell me how your day was going before you had to see Dasha."

She snorts. "Dasha's the icing on the cake."

I stop walking. "Oh?"

Skylar sighs, and stress fills her face. "He's never going to stop blaming me for the flop."

"When are you going to let me help you get out of this? You're talented. You don't need to put up with this," I insist.

"Forget I said anything. I shouldn't complain. Where are you taking me for lunch?" She smiles.

"Why do you do that?"

"Do what?"

I cup her cheeks. "Act like how your boss is treating you is okay. It's not. We both know it. Let's talk to the attorney. I asked Kora who we should talk to—"

"You did what?"

"I got a name—"

"I'll be blackballed from the industry. You don't understand how this works," she frets.

"It isn't going to hurt to have them review your contract—"

"No."

"He's taking advantage of you."

"It's not your business. This is where we draw the line, remember?"

Blood pounds between my ears. "It's not the same thing."

She scoffs. "Tell me what Dasha is involved in or where you went the night of Boris and Nora's rehearsal dinner. Give me one thing, Adrian, and then you can involve yourself in my career. Until then, stay out of it."

"I can help you."

She pins her deep-blue eyes on mine. Her voice softens. "I know you want to help. This isn't black and white. Let's change the subject."

I reluctantly agree, and we continue down the street. "Should we take the weekend and go through your apartment? I can schedule the movers." The last few weeks, our schedules haven't been clear for us to focus on Skylar's apartment. Her lease allows her to sublet, and she wants to decide what to move, toss out, donate, or keep for the renter.

She groans. "Bowmen's threatening to make us work. Can we tentatively plan?"

The nagging feeling in my gut grows. Every time we discuss moving Skylar's things into my place, there's some reason we can't. All of them are legitimate reasons, but I'm ready for her things to be at my place and it to be a done deal. "Sure."

We spend lunch in our usual banter. We each throw a few new words out the other has never heard. When I drop her off at work, everything is good between us, like it usually is.

The next few weeks, things are busy, but we carve out time to go through Skylar's apartment. When we finish, I survey the small pile of boxes. "I'll supervise the movers tomorrow when you're at work."

She smiles. "There's no going back now. I guess you're stuck with me."

I chuckle and pull her into me. "I was getting worried you didn't want to do this."

"Why?"

"It's been six weeks since I asked you to move in."

Her eyes widen. "We've both been swamped."

"I know. I still had to shut the voice up in my head."

She strokes my cheek. "I'm sorry. You should have told me. I could have done it after work or something."

I kiss her then admit, "Yeah, but then I wouldn't have had as much time with you in my bed."

She drags her fingers over my cock. "Would have been a tragedy."

"Agreed." I kiss her again. "Let's go home. I'll take care of the rest of this tomorrow. Then you can work on the subletter."

"Thanks."

I walk over to a box and pull out a La Perla outfit made of mesh. It's the color of Skylar's hair. "I don't recall seeing you in this."

She arches an eyebrow. "It's new."

I study the material and then check out Skylar. Her cheeks are maroon by the time I meet her eyes. "Maybe we should break this outfit in to celebrate you moving in."

Her lips curve. "Maybe we will."

I grunt and put it back in the box. The next day, I have the movers help me unpack everything. When they leave, I put the outfit on the bed. I have a few errands I need to take care of around town. Skylar won't be home for a few hours. I leave the penthouse and am just finishing up when Obrecht sends me a message.

Obrecht: *Come over.*

My gut flips. I head over to his penthouse. As soon as I get inside, I seethe. Dasha is pacing his family room.

"What's going on?" I ask.

"That's what I'm trying to find out." Obrecht scowls at Dasha.

"What did you do, Dasha?" I bark.

"Nothing!"

"Visiting Kacper in prison isn't nothing," Obrecht barks.

I step closer to Dasha. My anger ratchets up, and I ball my hands into fists at the side of my legs. "What did you do?"

"He told me I needed to come. What was I supposed to do?"

"And you didn't bother to inform us?"

"I didn't know what he wanted. I didn't want to bother you," Dasha cries out.

"You're on your own, Dasha," Obrecht claims.

She gapes between us. "I haven't done—"

"Haven't you? You slept with a Zielinski. You ran drugs for them. You told them about our trucks. Now you're going behind our backs and visiting him in prison? Do you think Adrian and I are stupid?" Obrecht growls.

"No! I—"

"What did he want, Dasha?" I ask.

"He...reiterated he loves me. He wanted to know when I was going to deliver on my promise."

I swallow the bile rising in my throat. He loves her? I doubt he knows what love is or gives a rat's ass about Dasha past what she can do for him, but they had that kind of relationship?

It goes deeper than I thought.

"What did you tell him?"

"I stuck with our story. I told him I was working on getting access to the trucks. I didn't tell him anything else, I swear!" Dasha cries out. "Adrian, you have to believe me."

My phone rings. I glance at it. "Get her out of here," I say to Obrecht, disgusted we're trying to keep Dasha alive, and she's making stupid decisions that could jeopardize everything.

Liam needs to come through for us. Until he's dead, Dasha's a bigger liability for us, too.

How did I ever trust her?

I step out on the balcony and answer my phone. "I'll be home soon, my printsessa."

"You weren't joking about supervising the movers. I expected to come home and have to unpack."

"If they put anything somewhere you don't want it, go ahead and move it," I reply.

"Everything is great, Adrian. So... I thought I'd make dinner? You'll be home?"

"Yes. Soon."

"Okay. Maybe I'll change into something a bit more comfortable since there's an outfit sitting innocently on the bed," she teases.

My dick perks up, imagining her in the magenta outfit. "Sounds good. I'll be home soon. Love you."

"Love you, too. Bye."

I go back into Obrecht's. Dasha is gone. He shakes his head, scowling. "What's Dasha up to? There's no reason for her to have visited him and not disclosed it to us."

"I'd say Dasha is a stupid woman, but you and I both know she's not," I add. A bad feeling claws in my chest.

"At least we were smart enough to put a tracker on her," Obrecht points out as his phone buzzes. He glances at it then me. "Club night."

My stomach drops. "I just made plans with Skylar."

Obrecht strolls to his bedroom door. "Cancel them. You know it's now or never. I need to change."

I groan then shoot her a text.

Me: *I'm sorry, my printsessa. Something came up for work. I'm not sure what time I'll be home tonight.*

Skylar: *You'll be gone days or just late tonight?*

Me: *Should be late tonight.*

Skylar: *Okay. Be careful.*

Me: *Will do. Love you.*

Skylar: *Love you, too.*

Obrecht comes out. "Ready?"

"I hate these places," I grumble.

"Tough shit."

"Easy for you to say. You frequent these places."

He slaps me across the head. "Where we are going is full of prostitutes. I don't go to those places. My clubs are all consensual, and you know that."

"Great. I'm going to hate it even more," I grumble.

"We don't have a choice. Let's go."

We have Obrecht's driver drop us off at the underground club. It's in a residential neighborhood. We pass the security guard, get let into the penthouse, and my skin crawls further.

The entire floor is full of debauchery. Strippers, dressed in skimpy outfits, also serve as prostitutes. We stay at the bar, ignoring their advances, and waiting for the judge and Jack to appear.

For several hours, they don't. When they finally arrive, neither takes notice. Jack comes in first. To get the pictures I need, it requires me to leave the bar area and go into the room Jack is in. He's so high on coke, he doesn't recognize me from our run-in on the street or even attempt to ask who I am. He and the judge are friends, partaking in activities in the same room. Obrecht and I play the part, stuffing dollar bills down strippers' pants but not letting things cross that line. The entire time, I feel suffocated. I attempt to not think about Natalia or Skylar, but all I feel is guilt. Are these women forced into being here like Natalia was, or is this their choice?

Throughout the evening, Jack and the judge each dig their graves deeper. When Obrecht and I finally have enough on each man, we leave the club. It's turning light outside.

I go to Obrecht's and print off the photos I took. He goes into his room to sleep, and I text Sergey to meet me at my place. When I step inside my penthouse, Skylar jumps off the couch.

"Adrian, are you—"

She freezes. The color drains from her face.

"I'm sorry things took longer than I anticipated. I—"

"Why do you smell like perfume?" she demands.

My stomach flips. "I was working. I told you—"

Her lips tremble. "Your work involves lipstick marks?"

What is she talking about?

I glance in the mirror and cringe. Red and pink marks are on my neck. I pushed strippers off me all night as best as I could without blowing my cover.

"You've kept me waiting here all night, and now you have perfume and lipstick on you?" Her voice is full of betrayal.

"It's not what you think!" I growl.

"You must take me for a fool, Adrian!"

"You aren't."

She looks away then quietly says, "Who is she? Or they, since you seem to have had multiple lips on you."

"How many times do I have to tell you I'm not seeing anyone else and I don't want to?" I don't mean for it to come out defensive, but it does.

She pins her hurt eyes on me. "Then tell me where you were."

"I told you, I was working."

"Where? Doing what?"

Silence.

"Goddammit, Adrian!"

I try to embrace her. "Skylar—"

"No! Let me go!" She grabs her purse.

"Don't leave like this."

"Then don't tell me to wait in your bed all night and arrive smelling like a whorehouse!" she yells.

"Skylar!" I attempt to pull her into me again.

She pushes away from me. "No. Don't try to kiss me smelling like whoever you just fucked all night."

"I did not fuck anyone."

"Goodbye, Adrian." She trots to the door that opens into the hallway with the elevator.

"Skylar, don't—"

She opens the door, and Sergey is there. He winces. "Morning?"

She pushes past him and leaves.

"Skylar!"

She gets in the elevator, and I slam my hand against the wall. "Shit."

Sergey steps toward me. "I'd ask how you're doing, but..."

I stomp back into the main room, shaking my head.

In Russian, Sergey says, "She's right. You reek."

"Thanks to your little assignment." I toss the envelope at him.

"What do you mean?" he asks.

My skin crawls for the hundredth time in the last twenty-four hours. "I had to spend the night in an underground strip club slash whorehouse, telling multiple women to stop grinding on my cock, to get that." I point to the package.

He cocks an eyebrow. "Why don't you just tell Skylar?"

"That I was at an underground club getting lap dances all night all in the name of Ivanov business? Yeah, that would go over really well."

"It might be better than her thinking you were screwing around on her."

And now I'm fucked. She's going to leave me for good. No matter what I do, I can't escape the filth of this life. "I need a shower. I'm going to burn these pants. Your evidence is self-explanatory. Give me something better next time. Let me break someone's neck or some other assignment that doesn't involve pussy juice on my new slacks." I leave Sergey, slamming my hand on the wall, and going into my bedroom.

When I throw my clothes in the laundry basket, the first thing I notice is the magenta mesh on top of the dirty clothes. My heart sinks further. I step into the hot shower and scrub my skin until it's red. When I get out, I'm no closer to figuring out how to make things right between Skylar and me. The only thing to my advantage is she lives here now. She can't avoid me forever. After work, she'll eventually have to come home. My only hope is I figure out how to make this right between now and then.

22

Skylar

HEAVY FLORAL PERFUME AND THE SCENT OF SEX NEVER LEAVES me. All day, no matter what I work on, I can't escape the smell. Every time my tears flow, I quickly pull my emotions together.

He didn't smell like Dasha. Unless she has a new perfume, it wasn't her typical rose one.

Who was he with?

There were different lip marks on his neck.

Damn, Adrian!

I ignore Adrian's text messages and phone calls. I delete the voice messages he leaves before listening to them.

All my stuff is now at his place.

We didn't even make it an entire day.

Go to Adrian's, pack a bag, order movers tomorrow.

At least I still have my apartment and furniture.

By five, I'm still a wreck but am adamant about sticking to my plan. I'm not going to be with someone who cheats on me. When I step off the elevator in the lobby, I freeze.

Sergey waves, and I cautiously approach him.

"What are you doing here?" Heat fills my cheeks, embarrassed from earlier this morning when he heard Adrian's and my fight.

"Sticking my nose where I shouldn't." Sergey holds out a four-inch thick, yellow envelope.

I glance at the package. "What is that?"

Sergey shifts on his feet. "I'd appreciate it if this stays between us. If Kora finds out I did this, she's going to be angry with me."

Very slowly, I enunciate, "Okay..." My eyes dart between his face and the package. "Then why are you telling me? You do realize she's my best friend, right?"

He nods. "Yep. But it's my fault Adrian wasn't home last night. Kora has a client whose husband has threatened both her and Kora. He's not a good man. I asked Adrian for help. This is what Adrian got for me last night. He only went into this environment to help me. Obrecht was with him. He didn't cheat on you, but he had to play the part with the strippers. But it wasn't anything more than what you would have experienced with the strippers at the Cat's Meow."

"Are you throwing that night in my face? I was single—"

Sergey holds his hands in the air. "No, not at all. I'm putting last night into perspective. The truth is, Adrian can't stand strip clubs or anything that passes that boundary. It reminds him of what they forced Natalia to do. He was only there to help me get what I needed to protect Kora."

"He had lipstick marks from at least two different women on his neck," I blurt out.

Sergey nods. "Yeah. That's what strippers who also are prostitutes do. I'm sure they tried to lure him into more all night."

"Prostitutes," I repeat, but my voice cracks. My lungs tighten.

Sergey firmly states, "He didn't do anything with them. He wouldn't."

I focus on the brick wall, not knowing what to make of this conversation.

Sergey pushes the envelope in my face again. "This is what he needed to get for me. He didn't cheat on you. Adrian wouldn't do that to you."

"Where else does he go? The night of the rehearsal dinner—where did you all disappear to?"

Sergey's eyes darken. "I can't tell you. But there sure as hell weren't any women with us. Now look at what's inside, please. I can't leave these with you, so you get one look."

Part of me wants to rip the envelope up. The other half is too curious. I want to know what Adrian was doing. Why was he with strippers and then hiding it? "I consider myself pretty open-minded. If he wanted to go to a strip joint, I'd go with him," I blurt out.

Sergey's mouth twitches. "Yes, I'm sure you would. However, if you look at the contents, I am fairly certain things will become clear why Adrian didn't invite you."

I cave and pull a stack of photos out of the envelope. My mouth turns dry. "Holy...is that...is that Jack Christian?"

Sergey glances around us and pulls me to the corner of the room. "You know him?"

"When we were at Selena's, his picture popped up on TV about the merger. We were trying to figure out how to work the remote when the news came on. Selena started shaking. She and Kora only discussed a little bit about her situation, but he sounds like a nightmare."

Sergey's eyes swirl with anger. "Jack is bad news. How do you know Selena?"

"Kora arranged for us to go to her apartment after yoga a while back. She made us brunch. I only met her once. She seems super nice."

"She is. So, hopefully, you can understand why this divorce needs to get finalized for both her and Kora's sake?"

I study the lewd pictures of Jack doing everything under the sun with several women and lines of coke. The time and date stamps are on each photo. I pin my gaze on Sergey's. "Is this what Adrian does for you? Hangs out at strip clubs?"

"No. Not usually. But in this case, yes. I'm sorry, but Jack would have recognized me. I needed Adrian to handle this."

"So you're going to blackmail Jack into divorcing Selena?"

Sergey's voice is deadpan. "Yes. Men like this aren't used to losing. The only way they do is by legitimate threats."

I sort through the photos again then put them into the envelope. I hand it to Sergey. "Why can't Adrian tell me this?"

Sergey tilts his head. "Would you have listened to him this morning?"

"If Kora came home smelling like cologne, cigars, and sex, would you have reacted any different?" I snap.

"I'm not judging you, Skylar. But put yourself in Adrian's shoes for a minute. I don't need to inform you of the legalities of this situation. I just put you in danger, and when Adrian finds out, I'm going to get an earful. No matter what, he's always going to do what he sees is the best thing for your safety."

"Then why are you telling me?"

Sergey studies me for several moments.

"What?" I uncomfortably ask.

"Adrian's never loved anyone besides Dasha."

"I'm so sick of Dasha being part of the conversation," I admit.

Sergey snorts. "All of us are. She's still using our name. Trust me. No one is a fan of hers. My point is, he loves you. I don't want the reason you break up to be due to the job I needed him to do. He didn't cheat on you. If you don't believe me, talk to Obrecht. He was with him the entire night. Neither are a fan of places with prostitutes, so the only reason they were there was to help me nail this guy."

I study Sergey's face, not sure what to say.

"Do you think I would show you these pictures if it weren't true?"

Sergey is right. It's not information Adrian would ever share with me due to the risk of me knowing. And Kora will be upset if she knows Sergey interfered with a divorce case. "No, he wouldn't show me."

"So if he was at a strip club all night getting lap dances from strippers to get me the leverage I need to protect Kora, is that a reason you would break up with him?"

My insides quiver. I think about his question. I can't say I would. I don't have a problem with strip clubs or lap dances. "No. But if he would tell me things, I wouldn't have to worry all night or feel like he's cheating on me."

Sergey sighs and shakes the envelope. "As you can see, it's not a black-and-white situation. I just admitted to you what I did behind Kora's back. If she finds out, I'm in the doghouse. But I'm doing what I think is best to keep Kora safe. I guarantee you Adrian is putting you first in his decisions about what he feels is safe for you to know."

"Why does it—"

"Sergey, what are you doing here?" Adrian's voice cuts me off.

I jump and spin.

Adrian's icy-blue eyes are lasers, focusing on the package in Sergey's hands.

"What are you doing here?" I throw back at him.

"You haven't answered my messages or calls. It's after five. I waited outside for you but thought maybe you were still upstairs." He glances between Sergey and me then scowls at him. "Not sure what is going on here, but if that's what I think it is—"

"It is. I showed her."

He steps in front of Sergey. "Are you stupid?"

"Adrian!" I scold.

He spins. "You don't have any business knowing about what he showed you."

"So it's better for me to assume you had an orgy with several women?"

Adrian's face hardens.

"Why can't you trust me enough to let me in a bit? I could have handled this if—"

"This is not something you should have any knowledge of," he says in a low tone then turns to Sergey. "You had no right to put her in this position."

"Sometimes you're too stubborn, Adrian. This is one of those times. Nothing good happens from her not knowing the truth. Have a good night." Sergey walks away, and we watch him until he disappears out the door.

My heart beats hard in my chest. I quietly ask, "What were you going to tell me?"

Adrian turns and slides his hands on my cheeks. "That I love you, and I'd never touch another woman."

"How were you going to explain last night?"

He slowly inhales. "I don't know. But you have to believe me—"

"Jesus, Adrian. That's the problem. You expect me to have blind faith in everything you do. You don't give me anything. Sergey trusts me more than you do—"

Adrian angrily shakes his head. "I do trust you. This isn't about trust, and I've told you that several times. You just saw one aspect of my job. Now do you understand why I don't want to put you in any positions where you could get hurt?"

"Your lack of disclosure is hurting us, Adrian."

He dips down to my face. "Please listen to me. I will never put you in a position that could harm you. Sergey should not—"

"I was coming home to pack a bag. If Sergey didn't show me those pictures, I would have left you. Do you not understand this?"

He clenches his jaw and pins his steel-blue eyes on me. Hurt fills his expression. "How could you believe I would betray you with another woman?"

"If you were in my shoes, you wouldn't be asking me that."

"So is this how it's going to be? Every time I have to work, you're going to assume I'm cheating on you?" Pain is all over his face.

"I didn't think that until you came home with lipstick marks and smelling like a whorehouse."

"And I hated every minute of it."

Sergey's admission pops into my mind. I soften my voice. "Yes, Sergey told me you have a hard time with strippers and prostitutes."

He blows out a breath of frustrated air. "What else did Sergey tell you?"

I place my palm over his racing heart. "Adrian, I don't want to know these things from Sergey. I want you to tell me them."

He stares at the ceiling and blinks hard.

"Adrian, look at me." Sad eyes meet mine. It makes my heart break. He holds so much pain inside. "I need you to let me in."

"What do you want from me? I professed my love for you. I moved you into my house so I can spend every free moment with you. I won't ever lie to you. I'll die protecting you. So please tell me what else you want from me. Besides telling you about my work, which I can't for reasons we've already discussed. Tell me what I'm supposed to do that I'm not."

I shake my head. "I don't know. Everything we struggle with seems to be surrounding your work and lack of disclosure."

Adrian closes his eyes tightly then drills them into mine. "Are you breaking up with me?"

Before I can even think about it, I reply, "No. I love you. But I want you to let me in. If your work involves you at a strip club all night, just be honest and tell me. I'm not going to freak. I actually do trust you. I don't get bent out of shape over strippers if I'm with a man who can keep it at a lap dance and not cross the line."

"I don't even like strip clubs."

"Yes, Sergey just informed me. I also was with you at the Cat's Meow," I remind him.

He scoffs. "How do we get past this? Tell me so we can go home."

I swallow the lump in my throat. I'm not sure what I'm fighting about anymore now that I know the truth about where he was and what he was doing.

He places his forehead on mine. "Don't throw us out, my printsessa."

My mind screams for me not to run from him. I love him. I want us. "I'm not. But, Adrian, I feel like there are layers upon layers of who you are, but you don't want me to know the real you."

"You know me. I've let you in more than I've let any woman in since my divorce. Anything I don't tell you is to keep you safe."

"Because you're a man who does bad things?" Nervousness flutters in my belly.

He glances behind his shoulder. I think he's going to deny it, but he strokes my cheek. "At times, yes. Please don't ask me more about it tonight."

I lace my fingers around his head. It's a bigger admission than I've gotten before. "Okay. Thank you for admitting that."

He says against my lips, "I love you. Please, let's go home."

When I nod, he kisses me, controlling and owning my mouth until I can hardly breathe. In his embrace, I feel everything I always do with him—safety, love, and that I'm his.

The desperation I usually have around him intensifies. Relief he didn't cheat on me mixes with my desire to know the things he doesn't tell me. My addiction for him only gets worse. No matter what happened this morning, he is the only thing I want. He's the oxygen I need to breathe. I have to believe whatever our issues are, we'll get through them. If I just give him more time, he'll eventually tell me everything.

23

Adrian

Several Weeks Later

BORIS COMES INTO THE GARAGE. "LIAM CAME THROUGH. HE eliminated your problem, but I wouldn't take your eyes off Dasha yet."

Kacper and Franciszek Zielinski are dead.

The sense of relief I thought I would feel is nowhere. Maybe it's because my feelings mirror Boris's. I want to believe it's over now, that Dasha isn't so far into the mob other Zielinskis will come after her, but I can't be certain. I'm still uneasy about how she got on the Zielinski radar, and I don't trust her. "Our tracker is staying on her."

Boris nods then points to the back room. "Who's in there?"

I sarcastically reply, "Two Polish fucks involved in our stolen steel."

Boris pulls out his blade and opens it. He presses on the tip then plops down on the desk chair. "My blade's a bit dull." He pulls the drawer open and removes the flint then sharpens the steel blade.

"How's married life?" I ask him.

He grins. "Perfect. My wife is pregnant and can't get enough of me. I'm a happy man. You and Skylar doing okay?"

"She's not happy I had to cancel our dinner plans. I'm hoping when I get home, I can skip the back and forth over where I've been and why she can't know."

Boris furrows his eyebrows. "She doesn't know anything?"

I shake my head. "No."

"I thought you were serious about her? Didn't she move in?"

"Of course I'm serious about her."

Boris stops scraping his knife on the flint. "Then you need to tell her."

"Not you, too," I groan. Obrecht and Sergey both won't get off my ass about telling Skylar. I keep reminding them I've been down this road before. I'm not going to lose her over what I do for my work.

"Once I told Nora—"

"Nora's an O'Malley. She has this life ingrained in her. Skylar won't be able to handle it," I claim.

"Why not? She doesn't seem super sheltered."

"Neither was Dasha."

"Dasha's a selfish snake," Boris seethes.

"Which is my point. If she can't handle it, a good woman like Skylar isn't going to. Next topic." I change into a new set of clothes. No matter what angle I look at everything, my conclusion is always the same. I'll do everything in my power to hold on to Skylar. Confessing I'm a murderer who could have a degree in torture isn't going to make her want to stay with me.

We go into the back room. Two men have their ankles and wrists bound so they can't stretch any farther. They are naked and stand on the tips of their toes. Their bodies shake from the amount of time they've hung in our garage and the fear I'm assuming is annihilating them.

They shout out in Polish. I pretend I don't understand their language, hoping to get more information than they might willingly give me, but I'm fluent.

Boris puts the flat edge of his blade on the man we suspect is in charge. "Let's discuss our steel."

The man's eyes widen, and he blinks hard, darting his eyes between Boris and me. "I don't know anything about steel."

I tsk several times and slide the point of my blade gently down his torso, stopping above his dick. A thin line of blood pops out on his skin. "Liars have consequences they typically don't like."

He shouts out his denial about knowing anything. When Boris moves the point of his knife to his eyeball, he screams, "Okay! Don't! Please!"

The man hanging next to him shakes harder and pisses himself. I step forward when he finishes. "Do you have something you want to say?"

The two men speak in Polish with each other. It's desperate, fear-filled, and angry. It gets louder as the conversation progresses. The man who pissed yells, "I told you she was bad news."

"She set us up. How was I to know?" the other man replies.

She? Who is she?

"The trucks should have been there. Where were they? This is your fault. I told you to stay away from all of them, but you couldn't, could you?"

"Shut up. You wanted the money as much as I did," the man barks out.

My skin turns clammy. *She? Trucks? Tell me I'm jumping to conclusions.* "What trucks?" I growl.

The men look at me, surprised I know Polish and followed their conversation. They go quiet, and I hold the knife to the mouth of the man who pissed himself. In Polish, I threaten, "If you don't tell me everything you know, I'm chopping off your toes, then your fingers, then your tongue. I'll stop the bleeding, so you have to hang here and feel the pain for days. Right before you beg to die, I'll release the hungry rats on you. Do you understand me?"

It doesn't take long before the men confess to everything. I spend the time holding it together as they tell us more and more.

Dasha constructed the entire plan to steal Ivanov materials. She was going to use our trucks to get the steel to off-market sellers. Millions of dollars she stole from us, but she took something else from me. The very last piece of humanity I have toward her.

There's no more giving her the benefit of the doubt. She was the mastermind behind the entire plan. Her ties to Zielinski are deeper than we anticipated. She betrayed all of us.

She played me again.

I may not have gotten back together with her, but she wanted Kacper dead for a reason. *She had us do her dirty work. She stole from my family.*

When the men finish confessing, and I'm confident they don't know anything else, we kill them, incinerate their bodies until they are nothing but ashes, then dump the remains in Lake Michigan.

"You going to say anything?" Boris asks when we get into the car. It's the first words he's spoken since the Polish men told us their truth.

I can barely look at him. The lump in my throat feels enormous. I swallow hard and admit, "I thought Dasha couldn't hurt me anymore. She couldn't handle who I became, but what has she become? How did this happen? Did I miss it when we were married?"

Boris stares out the window. "Dasha's always wanted money, but I didn't expect her to ever do anything like this."

"You think this is only about money?" I ask.

Boris scans my face. "What else would it be about?"

I tap the wheel and shake my head. "I'm not sure. I couldn't figure out how she could have accidentally gotten into a relationship with a Zielinski to start with."

Boris cracks his neck. "I don't know, Adrian. Dasha's always been out for Dasha. Let's go talk to her."

I drive to Dasha's building. It's past midnight. When we get to her front door, I knock, and it opens. Boris and I step in. He flips the switch, and the light turns on.

My stomach drops. The color drains from Boris's cheeks. The entire apartment is empty.

"She left," I blurt out.

"She knew we had them," Boris states.

I take out my phone and call Makar, the tracker I assigned to Dasha. A ring blares in the direction of the closet. Boris crosses the room and opens the door. Makar's body is stuffed in the closet. His head is bleeding, and he's unconscious.

"Call an ambulance!" Boris shouts, and I hit 9-1-1.

What the fuck did you do, Dasha?

Hours pass before the hospital staff declares Makar is stable. They tell us we won't be able to go into his room until the next day. When I get home, it's almost morning. I forgot about Makar's blood on my clothes. I take a hot shower and stare at my reflection in the mirror. I've never felt so confused.

How could Dasha have done this?

How did I never see what she was capable of?

Where is she? What is she planning next?

Did I turn her into this person she's become?

I'm spinning out, stuck in my thoughts when Skylar puts her arms around me and presses her warm body to my back. "Adrian, are you okay?"

How do I tell her about Dasha?

I would have to explain the Polish mob, and that's going to lead to everything else.

I need to increase security on my printsessa. Who knows what Dasha is up to?

I turn and slide my hands through Skylar's hair, tilting her head up. Concern fills her deep-blue eyes. Her bee-stung lips slightly part, and I press my mouth to hers, opening her lips farther with my tongue.

There's nothing slow or gentle about my kiss. Her sweetness mixes with every messed-up, hurtful thing I'm feeling. It all but destroys me.

I let the devil into my life.

Then I let her in again.

She could have harmed my printsessa.

Everything about my actions becomes selfish. I take every morsel of affection Skylar gives me and demand more. I don't answer her questions when she barely gets them in. I use my tongue, and the rest of my body, to take us to the place where only we exist.

For a short moment in time, I forget about Dasha's betrayal, Natalia's hell on earth, and all the men I've tortured and killed. The only thing that exists is my printsessa. "More," I demand, pulling away from her lips and locking my gaze on hers. She barely inhales new air before my tongue is back in her mouth.

"Missed you," she gets out then moans as I lick her teeth.

"Need all of you," I mumble and spin her around. I slide my arm under her waist, splay my hand on her back so she's leaning over the counter, and tug her ass toward me, sinking into her wet heat and groaning in relief.

She whimpers then turns her head. I lean over her and tug her lip between my teeth then demand, "Don't stop being you."

She sticks her tongue into my mouth, and I thrust harder. "Adrian!" she cries out, drilling her eyes into mine in the mirror.

"I mean it," I tell her. "I love you. Everything about you. Don't change."

"I'm not. I won't," she whispers. A slight tremor rolls through her, and her mouth forms an O. Her eyes become heavy, and she shuts them briefly.

"Look at me," I demand.

Her lids fly open.

"I don't want you to be someone else."

She squeezes her eyebrows. "I'm not."

I thrust harder, move my hand to her clit, and bury my face into the crook of her neck. "I love you, my printsessa. Exactly how you are. Don't change."

She keeps repeating she won't, and I keep telling her not to change. We come together, and when I finally lift my head out of her neck, I realize I'm spinning out. I pull away from her, and she quickly turns into me, circling her arms around my torso.

"Adrian, what happened?"

I look away and blink hard. I wish I could tell her everything, but anything I could say leads to Skylar finding out I'm a killer. Instead of answering her, I lead her to the bed and hold the covers up for her to get in. I scoot next to her and tug her into my body. "We have a few hours until the alarm rings. Let's try to get some sleep."

"Adri—"

"Shh. Sleep, my printsessa. We need sleep." I kiss her on the forehead and pull the blankets around us. I avoid her eyes.

"I'm worried about you, Adrian," she softly says then rolls into me, cupping my cheek.

"Everything is fine. As long as I have you."

"You do have me," she reassures me.

I kiss her again. "Good. Don't let me go."

"I won't."

I slide my tongue back in her mouth. After several minutes, I flip her so I'm spooning her. "Go to sleep, my printsessa."

I listen to her calm breathing for hours, holding her tight, trying to figure out what Dasha's next move could be. The problem is, I don't know what her end game is.

One thing is certain. I'll never fall for her story again. The next time we meet, she better be ready. Dasha's days of manipulating me are over.

24

Skylar

SOMETHING IS GOING ON WITH ADRIAN, BUT HE WON'T TELL me. It's been weeks since he came home in the middle of the night with blood on his clothes. I found them in the laundry basket the next day. When I asked him what happened, he said someone at work got hurt, and he took them to the hospital. He won't tell me anything else.

Every time we go somewhere, Adrian has a driver and an extra man with us. Sometimes, it's Bogden. Other times, it's someone I've never met. The man always escorts us in and out of places, sticking close to me.

"Why do we have a bodyguard with us?" I asked the first night when Bogden escorted us inside.

Adrian shrugged and replied, "I'm extra cautious; that's all."

"About what?" I asked.

Of course he wouldn't tell me and insisted it was too dangerous for me to know. After that, Bogden has escorted me anywhere Adrian can't.

A few weeks pass. I notice a man following me. At first, I think I might be going crazy. But every day, I start to spot him. I even see him waiting on a bench below my office building during the day. He has never approached me, but I wouldn't want to be in a dark alley with him. He screams danger. It freaks me out, so I pull out my phone, zoom in, and snap a photo. I send it to Adrian with a text.

Me: *I think this man is following me.*

Adrian calls me.

I answer. "Hey. I don't know if I'm overreacting, but—"

"It's my guy, Hagen," Adrian says.

The hairs on my arms rise. "Hagen? Who is that? Why is he following me?"

"Let's talk about it tonight."

"Adrian, tell me right now why you have someone following me," I demand.

"Not over the phone, Skylar."

Frustrated, I hang up. I finish work then go home. I start dinner and get a message.

Adrian: *I'm going to be a few more hours.*

Me: *I'll turn the stove off.*

Adrian: *Okay. Sorry. I'm rushing.*

Me: *You'll be home tonight though?*

Adrian: *Yes, it's normal stuff.*

What does normal stuff mean in Adrian's world?

I try not to think about the secrets Adrian keeps from me. Besides a few times a month when he doesn't come home, everything is perfect between us. We have fun together. He supports everything I do. I feel loved by him. But those nights he's gone tear me up. I rarely sleep. The gnawing in my stomach has gotten worse during these times.

I wish he would tell me what he does or where he goes. He has demons from these nights. I see them. When we have sex when he returns, I feel them. And something is eating at Adrian. I've seen it since the night he came in with blood on his clothes.

I change my clothes and pass the time working out in Adrian's gym. I'm on the elliptical, listening to my music with my headphones in my ears, when Adrian pinches my ass.

I jump and screech, pulling my headphones out of my ears.

Adrian's cocky grin is on his face. "Should have let you keep going. I had a good view."

"Ha! Funny!" I step off the machine.

Adrian dips down and kisses me. "We should go to the hospital."

"Why? Is something wrong?"

He grins. "Nope. Nora had the baby. Boris said everyone can come visit now."

"What did she have?"

"A girl. Here, Boris sent a picture." Adrian taps the screen of his phone then hands it to me.

A tiny baby with hair red like Nora's is sleeping. "Aww. She's adorable!"

Adrian tugs me into him and kisses my head. "Go get ready. Why don't we grab dinner out after?"

"Okay."

He pats my ass. "I'm going to make some phone calls."

"I won't take long." I peck him on the lips, go into our bedroom, then hop in the shower. I don't take long and quickly rinse off. Within ten minutes, I'm in clean clothes and putting fresh makeup on. I go out to the family room. Adrian is pacing, having a conversation in aggressive Russian. My ears perk up, and my heart races when I hear Adrian say, "Dasha," several times.

He sees me, hangs up, and smiles. "Ready?"

"What's going on with Dasha now?"

He shakes his head. "Nothing."

"Then why did you just say her name?"

He grunts. "Because she's a pain in the ass that needs to be dealt with."

"What does that mean?"

"Nothing. Let's go see the baby." He guides me to the elevator.

"Sometimes you make me feel like a foolish woman," I blurt out.

He jerks his head back and freezes.

The elevator opens, but neither of us move. He finally says, "What am I doing to make you feel less than what you are?"

"So many secrets, Adrian. When I first met you, everything about you was mysterious. I won't lie and say it didn't make you more attractive. But at this stage, shouldn't the enigma be diminishing?"

He steps forward, fists my hair, and puts his other hand on my ass, tugging me into his dense frame. "We're happy, my printsessa, aren't we?"

"Yes, we are."

"My work is not part of us."

"Then why do you have a man following me around?" I put my hand over his racing heart. "If I didn't know you and what's in here, I would think you're a man I should stay away from. It's not normal for a boyfriend to have his employee follow his girlfriend around."

"It's for your protection."

"So you say. Against what or who?"

Adrian's face hardens. "There are threats I need to protect you from. Bogden and Hagen, they are there for when I can't be. An extra bodyguard is with us when we are together in case I go down."

My pulse increases. "You go down? Adrian, what are you talking about?"

He shakes his head. "It's just a precaution. Maksim does the same with Aspen at times. She's okay with it. You can ask her about it."

I scoff. "I suppose I could. However, Maksim talks to Aspen. She knows what's happening. I don't."

He takes a deep breath, holds me tighter, and aggressively kisses me until I'm returning his enthusiasm and my knees weaken.

"You feel this between us," he murmurs against my lips.

"Yes. Always. Our love is not in question," I state.

Flames dance in his icy-blue eyes. "This doesn't happen to people. What we have isn't worth letting anything come between it. My role in our relationship is to keep you safe, and I will. No matter what, I will do whatever I have to for you to never experience anything traumatic. I will throw everyone to the wolves and watch them get torn to pieces before I let anyone harm you. And I won't taint what we have by telling you details that can only serve to put you in danger."

My heart soars and hurts in a conflicted battle. Adrian's gone through so much trauma. I know he means every word he said, and it's because he loves me. But before him, I never had to worry about my safety. I don't understand why I need to now. If being in danger is a by-product of loving Adrian, then it's a price I'm willing to pay to keep him. Yet I know nothing about what I could be in danger from. The secrets Adrian keeps from me only get bigger, along with my frustration.

"We are what matters, nothing else," he reminds me, kissing me again. He retreats and guides me into the elevator. "Let's go see the baby."

I stay locked in Adrian's arms, sinking into his body, not wanting to be anywhere, except with him. I don't fight him anymore about his secrets. He changes the subject, and we go to the hospital and see the baby.

All the Ivanovs and O'Malleys are there. I finally get to hold Shannon. My heart melts. She's precious. I glance at Adrian and wonder if someday we'll have this moment for ourselves, but I don't miss his slightly sad smile or the emotion that fills his glistening eyes.

The image of a younger Adrian holding a baby smaller than Shannon chokes me up.

When we leave the hospital, he slides his arm around my shoulder and leans into my ear. "You'd make a good mom."

"Yeah? How do you know?"

"You're a natural." He kisses the top of my head, and we don't say anything else until we get to dinner. The rest of the night, we fall into our natural state of who we are as a couple. I try to push the nagging voice out of my head to ask Adrian more questions about why he had a man following me around in addition to a bodyguard. It seems extreme, especially when I don't know what or who he's trying to protect me from.

When we get home, I need him to tell me. If I'm in danger, I have the right to know. This isn't just his work anymore if I'm involved.

After dinner, we make out in the car. By the time we get into the penthouse, Adrian has my clothes shed before I step into the family room. All night, he's an insatiable animal. The moment he comes, he's lurching over some other part of my body, doing something to me that gets me off and makes him hard again.

Morning comes, and I remind myself I need to find out what's going on. Adrian isn't in the bedroom, so I shower, then wrap a towel around my hair. I think I hear Kora, so I step out into the main room. Her face scrunches, and I'm immediately concerned. "What's wrong?"

She puts her hands over her face, inhaling deeply.

"Holy...what are you wearing?" I ask.

She glances at her jeans and baggy sweatshirt. "What?"

I jump up and grab her hand. She has a brilliant pink diamond on. "When did you get this?"

She stares at it, as if in shock.

I tug on her hand. "That's from Harry Winston."

"It is?" she asks.

"Yeah. It's from their summer collection. Bowmen lashed out at me last week when the manager called and said we couldn't use it in our upcoming shoot. He said the purchaser paid twenty percent more so he didn't have to wait to get it. It was a showcase item. It's super rare."

Kora's lips turn up.

I pull at her hand again. "Can I see it? Please!"

I slide it off her finger and hold it to the light. "Wow. This is incredible." I spin it then look closer. "What does this say?"

"What?" Kora asks.

"There's something engraved, but I think it's in Russian," I mutter, looking closer.

She peeks at the ring. "I don't know. Sergey didn't show me or tell me about it. He slid it on my finger. This is the first time I've taken it off."

"Adrian, come read this and tell us what it says."

She grabs the ring from me. "No, it's okay. I'll ask Sergey." She slides it back on her finger.

"Okay. Well, it's beautiful," I tell her, trying to swallow down my jealousy. I don't need a fancy ring. I love hers, but I wonder how Adrian and I will ever get there when he can't even tell me why he has extra bodyguards following me.

"Thank you," Kora says.

"When are we going dress shopping?" I ask.

She laughs. "I'm not even sure when the wedding is."

I hug her. "I'm happy for you."

"Thank you."

"So...why are you here? And where is Sergey?" I ask, glancing around the room, looking for him.

Kora gazes at Adrian just as his phone rings.

He holds his finger in the air. "Yes. I'll tell her. See you soon." He shuts his phone. "Sergey said to make a list of what you want from his penthouse or your place. Until further notice, you're staying somewhere else."

"Where?" Kora asks.

"Not sure, but it's best if he doesn't say anything over the phone. He'll be over once he picks your stuff up."

I smile. "Is someone going to tell me what's going on?"

Adrian's face hardens.

You have to be kidding me.

So Kora gets to know things, but I'm the idiot who gets to stay in the dark again?

I glare at Adrian. "Again?"

He clenches his jaw and focuses on the ceiling.

I turn to Kora. "You're going to keep me in the dark, too?"

"Skylar—"

"We're supposed to be best friends."

"We are."

"Not if you're going to lie to me," I assure her.

"Skylar, I've not lied to you. Things are complicated."

I scowl at Adrian. "So Kora can know, and I'm assuming Aspen will know, but I'm not trustworthy enough to tell?"

"I never said that," Adrian replies. His Russian accent sounds thicker. He pins his blue eyes on me. "I've told you this isn't about trust."

I blink hard, willing myself not to cry.

How can I want to marry a man who won't tell me anything?

It's always going to be like this.

He's never going to let me in.

I swallow the lump in my throat. My hands shake. In a soft voice, I say, "I'm done, Adrian."

His eyes harden further. "Stop this foolishness. We've gone through this."

"Yeah. You obviously don't listen." I spin toward Kora. "I expected more from you, Kora."

"Skylar," Adrian bellows out.

"Don't, Adrian!" I open the bedroom door and slam it. I freeze, scanning the master suite until nothing registers through the blur of my tears.

Am I really going to leave him?

Yes. This isn't how a relationship is supposed to work. He will never trust me.

I go into the closet and pack a bag. After I get dressed, I walk out of the bedroom.

Adrian steps in front of me. "What are you doing?"

"I said I'm done."

"You can't leave right now," he firmly states.

I sarcastically laugh. "You don't own me, Adrian. And you can't keep me here against my will."

"You aren't leaving this place until I tell you it's safe," he barks.

I huff and move toward the door.

Adrian steps in front of it. He growls, "Don't ignore me, Skylar."

"That's rich coming from you."

"I don't ignore you," he states, his eyes full of hurt.

"Move, Adrian."

"This isn't up for debate. It's not safe for you to leave, and you aren't going anywhere until I say," he reiterates.

"Skylar, you need to stay," Kora blurts out.

I spin on her. "Why, Kora? Tell me why."

"I got attacked this morning," she admits.

My pulse pounds harder. "What?"

"Someone entered Sergey's penthouse and attacked me in the kitchen. Adrian is right. Until he says it's safe, you can't leave."

My heart races. "Why would I be in danger if you got attacked?"

She looks at Adrian, and I turn to him, too.

He stares straight ahead, avoiding my eyes, his chiseled face emotionless.

I demand, "Tell me, Adrian."

He stays quiet and doesn't move.

"If my safety is at risk, I deserve to know what's going on. Look at me," I order.

He doesn't.

I reach up and smack him. A red mark appears on his face. As soon as I do it, I feel horrible but also want to do it again, until he tells me what is going on.

He blinks hard then slowly puts his hand over his cheek. He glances down at me with the same emotionless expression, which only hurts me more.

"I hate you," I whisper, turn, and ignore Kora. I trot past her into the bedroom, with more tears falling down my face. I don't hate Adrian. I love him. But I hate how he can't let me in.

Several minutes pass. There's a knock on the door. "Skylar."

"Leave me alone, Kora," I yell out, wiping my tears on the pillow. I bury my head in it, wanting some other reality to be mine—one where Adrian tells me things and trusts me. But that isn't our life. He isn't capable of letting me in.

At some point, Adrian comes in. He cages his body over me. "I'm sorry this is hard for you."

"I'm done, Adrian," I manage to get out.

"Don't say that. You're upset and—"

"No!" I roll over. "I'm not doing this anymore. I can't."

The color drains from his face. "Skylar—"

"Tell me everything right now, or I'm leaving. I mean it, Adrian. I can't stay in the dark anymore."

He closes his eyes. When he opens them, he rolls off me. "Don't do this."

"I'm sorry. I love you so much," I confess through tears. "But I can't be with someone who won't show me who they are and tell me what is going on."

He says nothing.

I stand in front of him and hold his cheeks. "What is so dangerous or bad, you can't tell me?"

"You'll hate me," he quietly says.

"No. I will never hate you. And I'm sorry I said that out there. I love you—more than anything. Please, tell me. I don't want to leave you."

He opens his mouth then shuts it. He turns his face toward the wall.

My heart has never hurt so much. We've come to the end, and there's no turning back.

25

Adrian

Every fear I had has come true. My printsessa left me. I'm pacing the penthouse, trying to figure out how to get her back, when Maksim calls. "Sergey and Kora are at the hospital. Kora is unconscious. Boyra is dead. Igor is, too. He was working for him."

Chills course through me. Igor has been a part of our family forever. He's been Sergey's driver and trusted ally. *How could we not have seen it?*

First Dasha, now Igor. Who else is against us?

When I get to the hospital, Skylar is there. She's sitting on a chair with her hands over her face. I sit next to her and pull her into me.

She sobs hard. "What happened to her?"

"I don't know yet. How did you find out?"

"I'm her emergency contact. The hospital called."

Skylar slowly picks her head out of my chest. "Who hurt them?"

My heart beats faster. If I tell her it's Boyra, she's going to want to know more. I tighten my arms around her and kiss her forehead. "Everything will be okay."

She freezes then pushes away from me. Anger emanates off her. "You're going to keep me in the dark? My best friend is lying in a hospital bed, and you're going to continue this charade of silence?"

I stare at the ceiling, avoiding her eyes.

Her voice turns cold. She quietly says, "Damn you, Adrian."

The next few hours consist of Skylar avoiding me, a mix of hospital workers and Ivanovs coming and going, and lots of private conversations that exclude Skylar and the other women. Kora wakes up. The doctor tells us she will be okay, but it's past visiting hours, and no one is allowed back. We eventually all leave.

I don't even make it through the night. At three a.m., I use the key she gave me to her apartment and sneak into her bedroom. My heart breaks further when I hear her sobbing into her pillow. I slide into bed next to her and draw her into my arms. "Don't throw us away."

She tilts her head up. "Wh-what are you doing here?"

I stroke her cheek with the back of my knuckles. "I love you. You love me. We're meant to be together."

"Then tell me who you are and where you go."

My stomach twists. "You know I can't. We've been through this. Until Kora came over—"

"Jesus, Adrian! Don't you dare blame this on Kora! Have you not been listening to a word I've said? How many times have I asked you to tell me—"

"And how many times have I told you it's dangerous?"

She slides up on her knees. "You make me into a fool, Adrian."

"How? Because I want to protect you and us?"

Her voice shakes. "You think this is protecting us?"

I turn away from her, unable to stare at the pain in her eyes. I won't do to her what I did to Dasha. All I've thought about since seeing Dasha's empty apartment and learning she's farther into Zielinski's web than I ever thought possible is that I did that to her. I made her change because she isn't the woman I married. Looking back, I can't see anything except how I was the catalyst to make Dasha into whatever she is now. I don't excuse what Dasha is doing or whatever she's involved in, but I won't make the same mistake with Skylar. No matter what, I'll protect her from others and all the possible ramifications that comes from knowing my truth.

I grasp her cheeks and choose my words carefully. "I know it's protecting us. You don't know what can happen. I've seen it—"

"With Dasha?" Betrayal weaves into her tear-filled expression. Her lips tremble, and a clawing sensation tears at my gut.

"You know I don't love her anymore. There's nothing Dasha—"

"You don't get it, Adrian!"

"What don't I get? I'm in love with you. I want to spend my life with you, not her."

"She got all of you, Adrian. Every piece of you, she got—the good, the bad, the ugly. But you expect me to sit blindly next to you, only getting what you determine to show me. That isn't a relationship. I don't hide my faults from you, yet you seem to think I can only handle the good in you."

The air in my chest becomes thick and stale, but nothing entering my lungs seems fresh. I quietly admit, "My truth turned Dasha into a monster."

"I'm not her, Adrian. I can handle it. Whatever it is, tell me."

I almost cave, but the image of Dasha not getting out of bed for days when I told her I had killed Natalia's rapists pops into my mind. Lev, lying in my palm, cold from death, reminds me how much destruction my truth causes. "No, you're better than her. Every part of you is beautiful light and goodness. I won't destroy you because that's what it'll do. It'll turn everything we have into sad memories. In the end, you won't remember there's anything else to me, except what I tell you."

She moves her knees to the headboard, so there is no room between us. Her heavenly hands cup my cheeks. "No one is perfect, Adrian. I already know you're capable of bad things. I still love you. There isn't anything you can tell me that will change it."

"If nothing will change it, then it shouldn't matter what you know. Why do you want to take what we have and taint it?"

"I cannot stay in the dark, Adrian."

"You aren't in the dark. You're in the light, and I won't do anything to take you out of it."

Neither of us moves for several moments. Her hot breath merges into mine. I almost think she's going to let it go when she releases me, jumps off the bed, and points to the door. "I need you to leave."

My heart sinks. "My printsessa—"

A fresh wave of tears fall. "Don't come back until you're ready to tell me everything. I won't continue to be blind."

I step in front of her. "You told me you understood my work was confidential—"

"For crying out loud, Adrian," she blares out. "You have men following me. Your work is part of who you are. I should have never agreed to it."

"Then why did you?" I angrily ask.

She yells, "Because I was stupid, okay? I thought we could separate it, but we can't. And no matter how much time we spend together, you don't trust me."

"I do trust you. I keep telling you this, but you don't believe me."

The expression on her face changes, and it crushes me. It's pain, as if I've somehow betrayed her. "If you trusted me, you would know I could handle your truth. You would tell me everything and have faith that I would still be here. When you got done telling me, I would still be in love with you. All of you, Adrian, even the pieces you think aren't lovable."

In a last ditch move to convince her to drop this, I tug her close to me. Reality and perception are two different things, and I know it too well. She can't ever know, but I don't want to lose her. She's my life. I blink hard, try to stop the quivering in my gut, and put all my cards on the table. It's not how I wanted her to find out, but it's the truth. "Come home. I bought you a ring. I've been planning out how to ask you to marry me. We belong together."

Her mouth opens and then shuts. Glistening streams of tears fall down her porcelain cheeks. She swallows hard then whispers, "Tell me everything, Adrian, then ask me. My answer will be the same, no matter what. But I cannot marry you if I don't know who I'm marrying."

"You know me. The man I have shown you is who you deserve. I will not give you anything but him," I insist.

Her face crumples. She puts her hand over her eyes. "You don't get it."

"My printsessa—"

"You need to leave, Adrian."

"Don't do—"

Her voice shakes, and she straightens her shoulders. "Now. Until you can let me in, there is no us."

Blood pounds between my ears. I stare at her, willing her to change her mind so we can go back to us, but she doesn't. "When you realize you're making a mistake, I'll be waiting for you."

She closes her eyes and turns away from me.

A knife slices through my heart. I leave and use the key to lock the door behind me. When I get in my car, numbness replaces the pain.

We have it all, together. Why can't she get past this issue?

She promised she would keep my work separate.

I go home, alone, wondering how we got to this point. I know she loves me, but why can't she keep her end of our agreement? She thinks she needs to know everything, but she doesn't know what she'd be allowing into her life.

For weeks, I can barely eat. I text her the same thing every morning and night, except when I have to go to the garage.

Me: *I love you. Please come home.*

I never hear anything back. Sometimes I see the dots appear on the screen, as if she's about to send me a message, but they always disappear. I keep Hagen on her. There's no way I'm taking any chances and leaving her unprotected. As much as I try to figure out where Dasha went and what she has up her sleeve, her disappearance makes me anxious.

Several weeks pass. I spend a few days at the garage with Obrecht, Maksim, and Dmitri, torturing two Polish men and three of Rossi's guys. No matter who we pick up, no one knows where Dasha is. We don't find out anything else about her possible motives.

"Maybe she's gone and is never coming back," Dmitri states when we finish with the men and Obrecht turns the incinerator on.

"No. She'll be back. I feel it in my gut," I insist and turn on my phone. When I see I have a voice message from my printsessa, false hope fills me, along with a twisting of my gut. She left it two days ago.

The sound of her voice alone tears at my heart. Her message only serves to break it further. "Adrian, um..." She takes a deep breath. "It's me. I..." She clears her throat. "Bogden can't continue to drive me everywhere. Please don't have him waiting for me anymore. I-I hope you're doing okay." The line goes dead. I relisten to it several times, rotating between anger and devastation. I'm pissed she's doing this to us. I stare at the garage walls, full of rage over who I am and that it even needs to be an issue in our relationship. The feeling I'm losing her for good, and she's never going to change her mind and come home, rips through me. I listen to her message again and pound on the wall. "Fuck."

"Whoa! What's wrong?" Obrecht asks, stepping out of the bathroom with a towel around his waist, fresh from a shower.

"Skylar wants me to remove Bogden as her driver."

He raises his eyebrows. "Did you think she'd allow you to keep tabs on her forever?"

"It's not about that. It's about her safety, and you know this," I claim. "Just because she needs time to come to her senses doesn't mean I'm going to put her in danger."

Obrecht huffs. "She isn't going to change her mind. You don't listen, Adrian. Tell her or move on. She isn't going to cave on this."

"Why aren't you telling her, Adrian? If you love her, you need to tell her," Maksim insists.

Dmitri nods. "I thought Anna would leave me, but she didn't. If she loves you—"

"Jesus. When is everyone going to understand this? I've been down this road before. I turned Dasha into a—"

"Dasha's made her own bed. That isn't on you," Obrecht seethes.

I shake my head and point at my brother then Maksim and Dmitri. "We aren't like them."

"Meaning?" Maksim growls.

"Your story isn't ours. Zamir didn't turn us into torturous murderers. We voluntarily went into this."

"Because he kidnapped and raped your sister," Dmitri barks. "He is to blame."

"It's not the same," I insist.

Maksim strips so he can shower. "Skylar's mad at Aspen and Kora."

"Here we go," Obrecht mutters under his breath.

Maksim scowls at him. "Have something you want to say?"

Obrecht releases his towel and steps into fresh clothes. "I warned Adrian it was a bad idea to get involved with Aspen's friend. Now we're going to hear about it forever."

"Shut up, Obrecht," I growl. "Why is she mad at them?"

Maksim sighs. "They know about us and aren't in the dark. She wants them to tell her, but they won't. You need to."

I groan. This conversation is getting old. "Not happening. Get in the shower, or I am."

Maksim pierces me with his icy-blue eyes and tosses his shirt in the burn barrel. "Sometimes you're a fool, Adrian. This is one of them."

"Everyone mind your own business," I grumble.

Maksim grunts and steps into the bathroom. I go outside and call Skylar, but it goes to her voicemail. I text her.

Me: *I just got your voicemail. Please call me.*

Skylar: *Let me guess. You can't tell me why it's taken you two days to respond?*

I attempt to call her again, but she doesn't answer.

Me: *Can you please answer? This is childish.*

Skylar: *No, I can't. I'm at work. I'll be taking a taxi or Uber home tonight. I've not decided which, but it isn't your business anymore. You made your choice, Adrian. Let me move on.*

The hairs on my neck rise. Panic sets in. *Move on.*

Me: *Why are you doing this to us?*

Skylar: *I have to go. I can't afford to get fired. Take care, Adrian.*

"Shit," I call out and slam my hand on the building as Obrecht walks out and his driver pulls up.

"I gotta go. Stop being stupid and talk to Skylar, or move on."

Move on is quickly becoming one of my most dreaded phrases. I open my mouth to say something nasty to Obrecht when the phone rings. My stomach twists, and I hold my fingers in the air to Obrecht. I growl out, "Dasha, where the fuck are you?"

"Adrian, I need you to sign the trucking company over to me."

"Are you out of your mind?" I bark and put it on speaker.

Her voice is firm with a hint of fear. "This isn't a request, Adrian. You have to sign it over to me, or-or there will be consequences."

I put my hand over Obrecht's mouth. "Like what, Dasha? Are those fucks you're in bed with going to hurt you?"

Her next statement sends chills down my spine. I've never heard her voice so cold. "No, Adrian. I won't be the one receiving the consequences. You will."

Obrecht moves away from my hand. "Dasha, whatever you're—"

"You've been spending a lot of time with unit two A, haven't you?" Her voice is sweet and friendly. To a passerby it would sound like an innocent question.

The color drains from Obrecht's face.

"She's pretty. A bit naive, though, don't you think? Although I have to hand it to you, she's a lot younger than you. Then again, she likes them older, doesn't she?"

Obrecht's face turns red with anger. I'm not sure who Dasha is referring to, but Obrecht loses his normal calm composure. "If you come near her, or anyone I care about, I will—"

"You'll what? Don't make empty threats. You're an Ivanov. Women and children are off-limits," she taunts.

"Snakes aren't," he hisses.

I sternly say, "Dasha—"

"I'll give you a week to get the paperwork in order. All cash in the bank accounts is to transfer into my name as well. Add another five million in it before you re-register the account. Don't piss me off." She hangs up.

"That fucking—"

I don't hear the rest of Obrecht's rant. I call Bogden.

"Adrian—"

"Where's Skylar?"

"In her office. She hasn't left the building."

"She goes nowhere without you or one of our other guys. I'm doubling up her security. If you see Dasha anywhere, call me immediately."

"Got it."

I hang up and turn to Obrecht. "Who was Dasha talking about?"

"A woman in my building named Selena."

"How does she know about her?"

"How the hell do I know?" He sneers as he walks to his car. "I have to make sure Selena is okay. Shower and get your ass to my place. We need to figure this mess out. Tell Maksim and Dmitri what your ex-wife is doing. Have them call Boris and Sergey." He puts his phone to his ear and gets in the car.

I send a message to Skylar.

Me: *Something just happened. I can't pull Bogden off you. Do NOT go anywhere without him. This isn't a request.*

I slam my hand against the building again and walk in. Dmitri steps out of the bathroom. I shake my head, full of rage. "We've got a problem."

26

Skylar

Adrian's text message infuriates me. I don't reply since Bowmen's on a roll, giving everyone unnecessary work. He's still livid about the collection flop. I'm his main target to take it out on. When I finally leave the office, it's after seven. I step off the elevator. Bogden is waiting and quickly approaches me.

"I made it clear to Adrian—"

Bogden's eyes appear colder than usual. "There's a legitimate threat. You cannot go in any car, except with me."

I haughtily laugh. "If Adrian thinks—"

"This isn't a ploy of some kind. You must take your safety seriously."

I stop walking and spin on him. "What does legitimate threat even mean, Bogden?"

His jaw clenches. "You'll need to speak to Adrian about it."

"Oh, that's convenient for him, isn't it?"

Bogden lowers his voice. "Can you please not fight me? I promise you, Adrian doesn't have me with you for no reason."

"Do you understand how annoying it is for me to have you driving me places when I don't even know what I'm supposed to be worried about?" I admit to him.

He solemnly nods. "I'm assuming it's not easy."

"Then please tell me what the threat is."

Bogden's eyes turn to slits. "If I could, I would. You need to speak with Adrian."

I laugh again, but my vision becomes blurred.

Bogden puts his hand on my back and leads me to the car. I don't fight him. I'm confused over so many things. I don't know what I'm supposed to exercise caution over. The voice in my head says Adrian is trying to keep tabs on me. The other voice says I don't want anything to happen to me. Like always, I have no answers. I contemplate calling Adrian, but I already know he won't give them to me.

My alarm beeps. I glance down then groan. I forgot I agreed to go out with a guy I met online. It happened quickly, in my moment of trying to figure out how to get over Adrian. I roll the divider window down. Bogden is in the front seat next to the driver. I say, "I forgot I have..."

What do I say to Bogden?

Do I want Adrian to know I'm going on a date?

No. He'll flip.

It doesn't matter. He made his choice.

I need to move past him. He and I are never going to be.

I clear my throat. "I have a date. Please drop me off at Stratosphere. And you aren't escorting me around, Bogden."

"I cannot leave you unattended."

"You are not—"

"I'll stay out of the way, but I will be there, watching over you. Do not take this threat lightly."

"Once again, if I knew what it was, I might take it seriously," I snap then roll up the divider.

It doesn't take long to get to Stratosphere. Bogden stays several feet behind me, and when I see the man I agreed to meet, my stomach flips.

What am I doing?

I need to get over Adrian Ivanov.

The man is everything Adrian isn't. He's one hundred percent all-American—a straitlaced corporate guy in a suit. Any woman would be thrilled to get a date with him. He's polite, probably makes a ton of money, and dresses nicely. His brown eyes and hair probably put most girls' panties in a twist. All he does for me is make me miss Adrian more.

Our date doesn't last long. I can't seem to get past the first twenty minutes. I excuse myself and leave. When I get in the car, I curse myself for ever falling for Adrian Ivanov. I laugh at the irony. I'm trying to escape him while riding in his car with his bodyguard.

I pick up my phone to call Kora but stop. The last conversation I had was with her and Aspen. I begged them to tell me what they knew about the Ivanovs and Adrian, but they wouldn't. They kept saying Adrian needed to tell me. She wouldn't even tell me what happened that landed her in the hospital. I almost call Hailee but don't.

I want to talk to Kora. She's my best friend. It's what makes it hurt even worse.

As if she knows I'm thinking about her, my phone rings.

I answer, "Did my bodyguard message you to call me or something?" It's semi-snotty, and I cringe after it comes out.

"I'm outside your place. Are you home soon?"

The car turns the corner. "Two seconds, and I'm pulling up." I hang up, and Adrian's driver parks behind a similar vehicle.

Kora and I both hop out. Bogden and another man I've not seen before do as well. Kora embraces me, and all the emotions I've been holding in threaten to come out.

I pull away. "Let's go inside."

Bogden and the other man follow us to my apartment. Kora and I say nothing until we're inside by ourselves.

"You can't stay mad at me forever," she claims.

"Can't I?"

She tilts her head. "No. You can't. I'm not Adrian."

"No, but you know whatever it is he's hiding and won't tell me."

She sighs. "I don't know everything about Adrian. Sergey told me very little, except for what happened to his sister. He said it's not his place to talk about Adrian."

I push my knee to the back of the couch and turn to her more. "You know what the Ivanovs are into."

She closes her eyes. "This is hard for me, Skylar. You have to understand how much this is killing me."

"You? You get to go home to the man you love every night. I'm dying. I even tried to date someone else tonight to forget about Adrian, but I can't."

"Then talk to him again."

"He's never going to tell me. Why can't you?"

"I cannot betray Sergey's trust. What he told me, I won't ever repeat. I promised him. You know how I am about confidentiality."

"This isn't one of your clients," I bark back.

"No. It's not. It's my future husband. That makes it more important I don't betray his trust in me."

Everything about her statement stabs me in the heart. My insides quiver and my lips tremble. I wipe my wet cheeks. "Adrian bought a ring. He..." I can't finish and cover my face while sobbing.

Kora slides over and embraces me. "Shh. Maybe he needs some more time."

I shake my head. "No, he's never going to tell me. And then he sent this text he won't take Bogden off me because of some threat."

Kora's body stiffens.

I retreat from her arms. "What do you know about this?"

She holds up her hands. "Nothing. But if he says there is a threat, you need to take it seriously."

"Who am I supposed to be scared of, Kora?"

Her face falls. "I don't know. Honestly, I don't."

"Why won't you tell me what happened that landed you in the hospital?" I ask her for the hundredth time.

She sighs. "We've gone over this."

"I'm your best friend. Give me something."

She gets up and walks to the window. She scratches her neck and studies the building across from mine.

I join her. "Please. Tell me what happened and why it's so hush-hush. You were hurt and unconscious. Put yourself in my shoes. The hospital called me, and when I got there, they gave me zero information on what happened to you. I'm your emergency contact, and I got nothing. Why is that? What are you protecting the Ivanovs for when you ended up unconscious in a hospital bed?"

She squeezes her eyes. In a low voice, she replies, "Did you ever think they're protecting me?"

A cold, deep chill races down my spine. "From what?"

She opens her eyes, takes a controlled breath, and furrows her eyebrows. "You can't ever repeat what I'm going to tell you."

"Okay. I won't. I promise."

Several moments pass. She finally speaks. "I won't tell you who, or why, or where. The only reason I'm telling you this is because you are my best friend. I don't want to live with secrets between us, Skylar. You have to know how much I don't want it, but things aren't black and white. There are reasons you can't know things. So if I tell you, will you promise not to hate me more when I don't answer any of the questions you're sure to have?"

"I don't hate you," I assure her. "It's what's so hard about this."

She nods. "Yes. I know."

"Okay. Then please tell me."

Her voice falters. "I-I..." She clears her throat. "I killed two men. One of them fell on me and knocked me unconscious."

I gape at her, processing what she admitted. "Are you in trouble? With the police?"

She shakes her head. "No. Darragh took care of it."

Chills and surprise consume me. "Darragh? Liam's father?"

"Yes. So you understand why I can't discuss this further or ever again?"

I hug her. "Are you okay?"

She squeezes and releases me. "Yes and no."

"No?"

"I don't regret killing those men. I do worry about the truth coming out and there being ramifications. However, the thing I'm not okay with is what this is doing to you or us. I want to tell you everything I know, but I can't. I see how much you and Adrian are hurting. I wish I could take it away, but if I betray Sergey and you learn things about Adrian from me and not him, it's not going to save your relationship."

Her words cut me because they're true. Whatever Adrian's secrets are, I need to find out from him.

He's never going to tell me.

Kora's eyes fill with tears. "I don't want this between us. I'm caught in the middle, and I'm not sure what to do. You're my maid of honor. You've been my best friend for as long as I can remember. I-I don't have a family anymore and..." She turns away. Fresh tears drip off her chin, and my eyes fill as well. Kora just lost her mother and sister. "Even when they were alive, you were my family."

My heart hurts. I've already lost Adrian. I don't want to lose my friends, too. And it's not their fault Adrian won't tell me. I can't blame Kora for not disclosing whatever it is Sergey told her. If Adrian made me promise not to tell anyone something, I wouldn't.

I hug Kora tightly. "We are family. This is a happy time. I'm going to stop asking you about Ivanov secrets."

"You are?"

"Yes. I don't like it, but you're right not to break Sergey's trust in you."

She swallows hard. "If I could tell you, I would."

I sigh. There's never going to be a happy solution to this issue. Whatever I do, I can't lose my friendships over Adrian's inability to open up and let me in. "I know you would."

I change the subject to her wedding, and we spend the rest of the night talking about other things. When she leaves, a part of me is relieved. I don't want any anger or hostility between us.

The next few months leading up to the wedding, I spend dating, trying to find someone to take as my plus one. I can't get through any of them. Bogden inconspicuously follows me everywhere I go, and I once again wonder what the threat is, or if this is Adrian's way of keeping me under his thumb.

He wasn't a controlling dick when we were together.

I was in his bed every night. He didn't need to be.

Almost every night and morning, I get the same text.

Adrian: *I love you. Please come home.*

Sometimes a few days pass, and I always wonder where he is and what he's doing. I don't respond. The few times I almost do, I delete the message I wrote.

When it's time for the rehearsal dinner, I avoid Adrian like the plague. All night, my heart hurts. He looks as sexy as ever. His ice-blue gaze is on me whenever I glance his way, but I also see the sadness in his eyes.

Once again, I don't know why the universe has to be so cruel. I need to get through the wedding and move on with my life.

Without truth, Adrian and I can never exist as a couple. It's clear he's never going to change his mind.

Within minutes of stepping into my apartment, I get a text.

Adrian: *I love you. Please come home.*

I cry myself to sleep for what feels like the millionth time since leaving him.

27

Adrian

FOR MONTHS, I'VE PATIENTLY WAITED FOR MY PRINTSESSA TO come home to me. Unless I'm at the garage or taking care of some other Ivanov issue, I know her every move as it's happening. I tell myself it's for her safety. Dasha hasn't popped up anywhere. No matter how hard we search for her, nothing turns up. She could be in my backyard or across the world. Our lack of intel on Dasha makes me nervous. We didn't meet her demands, and we've not heard from her since.

I hate that Skylar is seeing other men. Each date she goes on never lasts long, nor does she get past the first one. It still doesn't bring me any relief. Every time she meets a new man, I refrain from showing up and trying to convince her to come home. I keep telling myself she'll eventually realize what we have together isn't replaceable. She won't find it anywhere else, and I need to give her time to come to terms with our situation while reminding her how much I love her.

As Sergey and Kora's wedding gets closer, I become antsier. It will be the first time we've spoken since our exchange about Bogden, and that wasn't really a conversation. Every text message I send Skylar gets no reply. By the time evening comes, I've convinced myself once we're in the same room, my printsessa will remember how much we belong to one another.

I'm one of the first people to arrive at the rehearsal dinner. Skylar arrives fashionably late. The room is full of guests, but everyone seems to disappear, except her. Our eyes lock from across the room. She blinks hard then turns away from me.

Not the best reaction to seeing me, but what did I expect?

She only gets more beautiful.

God, I miss her.

My pulse beats hard in my neck. I give her space, and when she leaves to go to the restroom, I make my move. Instead of trying to convince her to come home, a bomb hits me. I turn the corner and freeze.

"Are you moving to New York?" Selena asks Skylar.

I take a step back so they can't see me, but I can still hear.

"I have till Monday morning to give Marcus an answer."

Who the fuck is Marcus?

Has Bogden not given me the correct information? Did one of these guys from her dates pan out?

Panic fills my soul.

"And he's creating the position specifically for you?" Selena asks.

"Yeah. It's an amazing offer."

"Congratulations. I'm happy for you, but I'm also sad you'll be so far away."

Skylar's voice cracks. "Thanks." She clears her throat. "It's strange thinking about New York as home. I'm sure the girls will visit me, and I'd love for you to come with them."

Home? New York isn't home.

She belongs with me.

She's moving.

"Sure! I don't know a lot about New York. Jack took me once, but I ended up staying in the hotel most of the time. He was in business meetings and didn't want me wandering around the city by myself."

"God, he's a dick," Skylar says.

Selena cheerfully says, "Yep. I'm so grateful he's out of my life."

"Me, too! When you come to New York, I can be your tour guide."

Why does she sound like she's already made this decision?

"Count me in," Selena chirps.

"Do me a favor?"

"What's that?"

Skylar lowers her voice. "Don't tell the girls yet. Until I know what I'm doing, I don't want them to know. As happy as they will be for me, they will also be sad I'm moving."

"I won't say anything. Do you know a lot of people in New York?"

"No one, really."

"You're brave. I only moved to Chicago because of Jack. I would never be able to do something like that all on my own. Plus, Chicago is home to me now. I'd miss it."

"I will miss it, but..."

I lean closer as silence fills the air.

"You okay?" Selena asks.

"Yes, no, I don't know." Her voice shakes. "Sorry. I thought I could get through this...but... I keep telling myself New York will be good for a fresh start."

I close my eyes and try to regulate my breathing.

She cannot move. Not unless it's somewhere with me.

"There isn't any way to work it out between you and Adrian?" Selena softly asks.

"No. The ball is in his court. I..." Skylar sniffles. "It's taken a few months, but I finally realized something."

"What?"

"Adrian doesn't love me. He only thinks he does. If he did, he would see how he's killing me. He would trust in my love for him. But he doesn't. Instead, he assumes I'm like his ex-wife."

"What do you mean?"

"He thinks whatever he tells me that I'll react to it how she did. You know what hurts the most about that?"

I peek around the corner.

Selena has her arm around Skylar. "What?"

"His ex-wife is a snake. She's selfish, and while I don't know all the details about what happened in their marriage, what I do know is snakes don't love. They aren't loyal. They aren't trustworthy. Even Adrian insists she's one. He won't let me in because of how a snake reacted. So what does that make me in his eyes?"

My heart drops. I hide behind the wall again.

"Okay, enough about all this. I'm sorry. I didn't mean to get into this. This weekend isn't about Adrian and me. It's about Kora and Sergey."

"Don't apologize. I'm always here if you need to talk," Selena states.

"Thanks."

They go into the women's room. My brain says to go into the bathroom and talk to Skylar, but I can't seem to move. *She thinks I don't love her.*

Obrecht approaches me. "Have you seen Selena?"

I point to the hall.

He studies me. "What's going on? You look pale."

"I think Skylar is moving to New York. I overheard her telling Selena." My gut flips so fast, I think I might get sick.

Obrecht shakes his head. "Stop playing the village idiot, Adrian. If you want her, tell her. Months have passed. She hasn't once wavered in what she needs from you."

I don't reply. I walk away from Obrecht with my mind spinning and insides full of rage. Two thoughts won't leave me the entire night.

She's moving to New York.

She thinks I don't love her.

Our seats are on opposite sides of the room. My guess is Kora intentionally designed it that way. I spend the rehearsal dinner hardly listening to any conversation. I can't even hide my obsession with Skylar. Obrecht kicks me under the table.

I scowl at him.

"You're staring at her," he mutters.

"Mind your own fucking business," I grumble.

"Don't know why I bother wasting my breath."

"Me, either." I refocus on Skylar. As if she can feel me staring at her, she blushes and glances at me, then turns away.

Toward the end of the night, I'm spinning out. She's going to put hundreds of miles between us, and I need to stop her, but I can't figure out how.

At the end of the night, she leaves. I go to follow her, and Obrecht steps in front of me. "Not tonight, Adrian. You're spinning out."

"Stay out of this."

"What happened the last time you went around her like this?"

I freeze, and my gut flips, thinking about what I did to her the first time we were together.

"Go home, Adrian. Get some sleep. There's no other option. Either decide to tell her or let her go," Obrecht insists.

"I'm not letting her go," I sneer.

"Then tell her."

Selena approaches us and assesses me. "Adrian, are you okay?"

"Yeah. I'll see you tomorrow." I spin and leave. I tell my driver to go to the hotel Skylar and the other girls in the wedding party are staying at. It's off Michigan Avenue not far from the River. Bogden confirms they are in their suite, and I sit outside the building for hours, debating what to do. My car door opens and snaps me out of my thoughts.

Dasha slides in, and my rage intensifies. Her overpowering rose perfume flares in my nostrils. I instantly feel nauseated.

Why is she outside my printsessa's hotel?

Where has she been?

What does she have up her sleeve?

"Dasha, what the fuck are you doing here?"

She reaches for my cheek. Her voice is cold like her hand. In Russian, she says, "Adrian, you intentionally ignored my directions."

I shirk out of her grasp and pull the gun out from under my seat. I point it at her. "You don't call the shots, Dasha. Now tell me what you've done."

She laughs and strokes my thigh. "You think I believe for one second you'll kill me? I'm a woman. Or have you crossed that boundary, too?"

I hate that she knows my limits and is right. "You're one to talk about crossing boundaries, Dasha."

She scoffs. "If you kill me, or this car moves an inch with me inside it, the two dozen men I have surrounding us will make sure you die along with me."

The pit in my stomach widens. "Why, Dasha? What made you turn to the Zielinskis?"

"Jesus, Adrian. You think you're the only person who should make a living?"

"Are you kidding me? You've really done all this just for money?" I seethe.

Her eyes turn to slits. "What else is there?"

A storm festers in the pit of my stomach. "Why us, Dasha? You could take from anyone in the world. Why target the Ivanovs?"

She throws her head back and laughs, as if I just asked her a ridiculous question. "You have what I want, Adrian. I held out for eight years to get what was owed to me."

"What in God's name—"

"The trucking company should have been mine!"

"I bought it before we were married!" I hurl back.

"And why do you think I married you?"

The air in my lungs thickens with my shock. My veins pulse with rage.

"That's right, Adrian. The moment the Ivanovs tried to build their empire, I was sent in."

"By Zielinski?"

A sinister smile forms on her face. "Zamir Petrov had an alliance with him. My mother is a Petrov. My father was a worthless no-name, not worthy or able to keep her in the life she was accustomed to. When I found out who we were, I went to Zamir. My mother was his third cousin. He promised me if I left you penniless, I could have it all. But then you had to go screw me over, didn't you?"

"I gave you sixty percent of our assets in cash," I bark out then clench my jaw, trying to control my urge to put my hand around Dasha's neck and never stop squeezing. She told me she was an orphan. My entire marriage to her was a sick game for Zamir to screw with another Ivanov.

She's a Petrov.

I loved a Petrov.

"So you're working for the Petrovs, and the Zielinskis were just a ploy in your game?" I spit out.

Her lips curl up. "Zamir disappeared. No one knew about our little deal. I met Kacper and everything fell into place." She leans closer and her rose perfume suffocates me. "By the way, thanks for killing him for me. No one knew about us, except his closest men. And they're now under my control."

Nausea fills me and I swallow the bile climbing in my throat.

Keep her talking. I need to find out everything.

"How many men, Dasha?"

Her face turns serious. "Adrian, it's over. You have until tomorrow at noon to transfer the company and bank accounts. And your delay has cost you. It's not an extra five million. Make sure you add ten."

I slide closer to her and put the gun under her chin. "You think you know me, Dasha. I can assure you, any notion you have of who I am or what I will do, you're underestimating."

She never flinches and smiles. Reaching up, she drags her finger from the side of my forehead down my cheek. "Do you know what I told myself when Lev died?"

Every ounce of willpower I have not to shoot her, I evoke. I keep the gun positioned under her chin, and in a deadpan voice, I ask, "What would that be?"

"I'm no longer stuck with you."

My chest tightens as potent anger swirls in my veins.

She leans closer. "You know what I'd let you do? For old times' sake?"

I stay quiet, grinding my molars.

She moves her hand to my crotch. "I'd let you fuck me one last time." She leans closer to my ear. "We always had a good time fucking your anger out of you, didn't we?"

My heart doesn't seem to beat correctly. I don't know who this woman is. I'm not sure how I spent so many years in love with her. How can the mother of my only child be so opposite of who I thought she was?

I hold her wrist in the air. "Don't ever touch me again."

"Or what? What will you do to me, Adrian?" she asks with wide eyes before a sinister smirk appears on her face.

Every limit I have, she's pushing. I'm already spinning, and if she doesn't get out of my face, I'm going to do something I'll never forgive myself for, since she's a woman.

Ivanovs don't kill women or children. It's one of the issues we've gone round and round about regarding Dasha. If she had a dick, I'd have my driver take us directly to the garage.

But she's a Petrov.

She's still a woman.

Dasha's admission that her relationship with Kacper Zielinski was on the down-low makes sense. He was married. Enough time has passed without anything happening after we didn't give her what she wanted last time. Now that Kacper is dead, we need to find out if she really has his men under her control or if she's lying. If they are, how many are there and who are they? No intel Obrecht or anyone else found on Dasha points to her having ties with anyone besides Kacper.

I release her wrist and lean over and open the door. "Get out. And if I ever see you around here again, there won't be any boundaries left for me. Are we clear?"

She pouts then glances at the hotel. "Oh. She still doesn't want you, does she? She couldn't handle who you are, could she?"

She's pushed all my buttons. I don't trust myself any longer. I roll down the divider window. "Seb, drag Dasha out of the car if you have to." I sit back and keep the gun aimed toward her.

She haughtily laughs. "If he touches me, you'll have dozens of bullets shot in here faster than you can duck. Noon, Adrian. Tomorrow. There will be no more warnings."

I grab her chin and push it up so she's staring at the ceiling. She gasps, and I slide closer. I press the barrel of the gun to her cheek. "The next time you threaten me, I will show you consequences. And don't think because you're a woman I won't treat you like a man. The thing about snakes, Dasha, is I don't give a fuck what sex they are. The only thing I do with someone like you is torture and kill them. I suggest you think real hard before you make your next move." I release her and kick the door open. "Get the fuck out of my car."

She takes a deep breath to recompose herself and gives me a final glare. She slides out. "Noon. Tomorrow. Don't disregard me, Adrian." She shuts the door, and I call Bogden.

"Boss," he answers.

"Where is Skylar?"

"In the hotel."

I already knew that, but I sigh in relief. "I want you stationed outside her hotel all night. If Dasha comes anywhere close, don't hesitate to do whatever is needed to protect my printsessa."

Bogden is silent for a moment.

"Do you understand me?" I firmly ask.

"Yes. Protect at all costs."

"Yes."

I message the trackers we have who are all searching for Dasha.

Me: *She's in Chicago. I'm outside of the hotel the wedding party is staying at and Dasha says she has a dozen men watching us. I don't know if she's bluffing or not. Follow her, but make sure no one sees you.*

I text Obrecht, Maksim, and his brothers.

Me: *Dasha showed up. She's demanding 10 million and the company by noon tomorrow.*

Maksim: *Where is she?*

I get another text from our tracker.

Vlad: *I'm on her.*

Me: *Good, don't lose her.*

Vlad: *I won't.*

I return to the group text.

Me: *Vlad's on her.*

Obrecht: *Dasha came to your place?*

Me: *No, I'm outside the hotel. She jumped in my car.*

Sergey: *Did you talk to Skylar?*

Me: *No.*

Sergey: *You need to talk to her.*

Me: *You need to mind your own business.*

Sergey: *You're an idiot.*

Boris: *Lay off. She's not the one. If she were, he'd have told her by now.*

Me: *Shut the fuck up. Everyone. One more thing. Dasha pulled an Annika on me. It was all for money.*

Obrecht calls.

"What?" I answer, annoyed and staring out the window at my printsessa's hotel. My heart's beating so fast, I put my palm over it.

"You okay?"

I snap, "If she comes near me again, I won't keep in mind she's a woman. And God help her if she lays a finger on my printsessa."

"Do you want to come over?"

"No. I need to go." I hang up and put my phone in my pocket. I instruct my driver to park the car across the street where I have a better view of the hotel entrance. All night, I watch for anyone suspicious looking walking into the building. My mind spins further and further into my obsession with Skylar, her possible move to New York, and my altercation with Dasha. Besides the disgust I feel over Dasha revealing she's a Petrov and all that means about my life with her, the thing I can't stop hearing Dasha say is, *"She still doesn't want you, does she? She couldn't handle who you are, could she?"*

When the sun rises, I reconfirm the men I have stationed around Skylar and meet the guys at the gym. I confirm all the security with Maksim and we go through possible scenarios with Dasha.

Noon comes and goes. Dasha's never left her hotel room, according to Vlad. When it gets closer to the wedding, my skin is crawling. I take a quick shower and leave. When I see Skylar, I can't handle it anymore. My spiraling thoughts include the engagement ring I bought her, her impending move to New York, and all the months I've spent obsessed over her feel suffocating.

My printsessa tries not to glance at me, but I don't give her much choice. I never take my eyes off her. She's mine. I've tried to be patient and let her come back to me, but it finally hits me. She's never going to, and I'm about to lose her.

There are no other options. I have to tell her and take the risk she won't want me.

If Dasha was always a Petrov, then did I really change her into the monster she is?

Did she ever love me? Did she ever love Lev or want him?

Everything I've tried to protect my printsessa from becomes cloudy. Dasha and my marriage were a sham. Was anything real?

I don't have time to dwell on what Dasha did to me. Every excruciating second staring at my stunning printsessa creates a deeper anxiety in my chest.

I'm going to lose her.

I can't.

The moment the photographer releases the wedding party, Skylar hightails it to the restroom. I follow her and wait for her to come out. My heart slams against my chest cavity.

She steps out, and her voice cracks. "Hi."

I don't think. I put my hand on her spine and steer her down the hall.

"Adrian, what are you—"

"Quiet, my printsessa."

God, I missed how good she smells.

She relaxes and melts into my body.

I lead her into an empty room and spin her into the wall. I cage my body around her. She gasps and stares at my chest with her lips shaking.

"Look at me, Skylar," I demand.

She swallows hard and slowly lifts her head. She tries to stop her tears.

"Stop ignoring me, my printsessa."

"What do you want me to do, Adrian?"

I brush my knuckles over her cheek. "I want you to come home."

She scoffs. "Home?"

Not in New York.

"Yeah. You belong with me."

Her eyes fill with tears. "In a house of lies?"

"I've never lied to you."

"No. You leave me in the dark. It's the same argument we had when we broke up. So unless you changed—"

I press my mouth to hers, no longer able to hold myself back. She's mine, and she needs a reminder who she belongs to. I fist her hair and tug her head up.

"We can't—"

I don't let her speak any more. I fuck her mouth with my tongue, not letting up. I thought I remembered how good she tasted, but my memory was nothing compared to now. I groan and pull her dress over her hips, quickly slide my fingers in her sex, and push my palm to her clit. She freezes, but I don't, continuing to manipulate her body with my mouth and hand. Within seconds, she whimpers and submits to me the way she always does. It only happens because we are meant to be together. Her flesh trembles against my frame and it about sends me over the edge.

So many things I missed about her.

I move my lips to her ear and command, "Unzip my pants."

She doesn't, so I push my tongue back in her mouth and grab her wrists, positioning her on my groin. "You're going to show me you still want me, my printsessa." I suck on her lip.

She unbuckles my belt and unfastens my pants.

Within seconds, I have her panties to the side. Using my fingers, I V her sex. Then I rub my erection against her clit.

Her mouth forms an O, and I shove my fingers I had in her pussy in her mouth. "Suck," I command and move my hips faster against her until she's moaning, sucking my fingers hard.

I watch her face, studying her every reaction until her eyes roll and her body shatters against mine.

Fuck, I love it when she comes.

"Good girl," I growl and reach for the back of her thighs. I wrap them around me as I thrust into her, wanting to detonate inside her tight, wet cunt that I've been dreaming about for months.

"Adrian!" she cries out.

I pet the side of her head, never taking my eyes off her, and murmur, "I've missed you. Tell me you've missed me."

"You know I have," she whispers.

Good. I haven't lost her yet.

I nod. "Agree you won't stay away from me anymore."

She closes her eyes, as if grappling with herself.

"Tell me, my printsessa," I growl, staying steady with my thrusts.

"Give me something. Anything to show me you'll let me in," she begs.

I slide my tongue down her neck until it hits her collarbone. She shudders.

"We'll talk tomorrow when we wake up," I mumble into her shoulder and thrust harder, not sure how much longer I can last.

She freezes.

I pick up my head and pin my gaze on hers.

"You're going to tell me things?" she asks.

I cock an eyebrow and nod. "Some. Not everything. Can you live with that?"

"What does that mean?" A tear escapes her eye.

I lick it, squeeze her hips, and move her faster with my thrusts. "I need you home, my printsessa."

"Adrian, what—"

"It means you'll know everything important. More than anyone knows about me or what I do."

She nods and whispers, "Okay."

I return to kissing her mouth, aggressively whipping my tongue around her at the pace of our thrusts.

Her whimpers get louder until she's limp in my arms and shaking. I grunt, bury my head in the curve of her neck, and fire my hot seed deep within her. My body shudders against hers.

Neither of us moves, trying to regain our breath. I finally pull out, release her legs, and take my handkerchief out of my tux. I clean her up then reposition her panties and dress.

She reaches for my cheeks. "Adrian, you promise you will tell me?"

"I don't lie to you, my printsessa. Tomorrow, we will talk. Not tonight. This is not the place to do it."

She hesitates but finally agrees. "All right. I can live with that."

I put her hand to my lips and kiss it. "Tonight, we have fun." I lean closer. "Don't ever forget you're mine, Skylar."

She tugs me to her lips. Our kiss is soft and slow, unlike the urgent hungriness of our other kisses. When she retreats, she admits, "It hurt so bad, being away from you."

"Then stop running from me."

"I need you to let me in, Adrian."

I clench my jaw. I gave her my word I would tell her, so I will, but I still don't like the idea. I'm still worried she won't be able to handle it. "You may not like what you see."

She cups my cheeks. "You don't need to worry about that. I promise."

I don't reply. I guide her out to the reception. The rest of the night, we're glued to each other's side, unable to keep our hands to ourselves.

During the bouquet toss, my mother comes up to me. She laces her hand around my biceps and puts her head on my arm. She tilts her head up and drills her icy-blue eyes on me. "It's nice to see you happy, Adrian."

"We'll see if she stays or runs after tomorrow."

My mother's forehead creases. "What happens tomorrow?"

"I have to tell her everything. I have no other options. But we both know what I did to Dasha when I told her."

My mother huffs. She releases my arm. "You didn't do anything to that snake." My mother knows what I've done to try and avenge Natalia's death. Dasha told her. I never planned on her learning about it, but Dasha didn't spare her from any detail.

"You know I did," I insist.

"No, Adrian. You don't become a snake. You're born one. We're the ones who were fooled by her." She glances at Skylar, who is next to Hailee on the dance floor, waiting for the tossing of the bouquet. "Skylar loves you. I saw it the first time I met her. Don't confuse what you thought you had with Dasha with Skylar. She won't react how Dasha did."

My mother's words give me more hope that my printsessa won't run from me when I tell her. I tug my mom in for a hug and kiss her on the forehead. "Don't get excited. I still have to ask her. But I bought a ring."

I don't remember the last time I saw my mother look so happy. "I'll be your first phone call, right?"

"No. I'll bring her over, and we'll tell you in person."

My mom's grin widens. "Even better. I get my bridal magazines out."

I chuckle then spend the rest of the night dancing with Skylar. Kora and Sergey leave, and I turn to my printsessa. "Ready to go home?"

She gives me a chaste kiss. "Yes."

I tug her back to my lips and kiss her until her knees wobble. I murmur in her ear, "When we get home, I'm using my teeth to undress you. And my tongue is going to get reacquainted with that throbbing little pussy of yours."

She takes a deep breath.

I cockily grunt. "It's throbbing right now, isn't it?"

"Yes," she whispers.

"You're already wet for me, aren't you, my printsessa?" I flick my tongue several times on her earlobe, and she whimpers.

"You're so fucking wet. I know you are." I suck on her lobe.

"Mmhmm."

"I'm going to let you ride my cock in the car while I watch you touch yourself. Do you want that, my printsessa?"

"Yes," she breathes and squirms against my erection.

I squeeze her ass and give her a peck on the lips. "Let's go home. Where you belong."

Worry enters her heavy eyes. "Tomorrow—"

"I will tell you everything you want to know." I firmly hold her face to mine. "Tell me again you'll still love me."

"I will always love you, Adrian. Nothing will change it. No matter how dark or evil your secrets are, it won't break us."

I take a deep breath.

Her eyes are full of so much love. It pains me to think of losing her again. She says, "Let's go home. I'll stay tonight. Tomorrow, after you tell me, you will still find me in your bed. And the night after that, I will still be with you."

I can't speak. She's so confident in her declaration. I put my hand on her back and lead her outside, not thinking about security or looming threats.

My driver pulls up, and we're almost to the car when bullets ring through the air, pain sears into my lower back, and I fall over. All I hear is Skylar screaming as everything turns black.

28

Skylar

THE BULLETS SEEM TO FIRE FROM NOWHERE, AND BEFORE I CAN jump, Adrian slumps to the ground. His bodyweight pushes me with him, and he falls over me. Blood pools all around him. I scream while trying to find the bullet hole and how to stop him from bleeding out, but he's too heavy for me to lift him.

Obrecht and the Ivanov brothers come racing over at some point, but I barely notice. All I see is Adrian, pale, with blood seeping out of him. Everything seems like it moves in slow motion. When we get to the hospital, a nurse takes us aside.

"Mr. Ivanov is in surgery. He's lost a lot of blood. We're doing the best we can, but if you have family that needs to be here, I would call them now."

"You have to save him," I cry out.

Aspen tugs me closer to her.

"I'm sorry, ma'am, we're doing the best we can," the nurse repeats then leaves.

I look at Aspen for answers, but her face is void of them. I search everyone's, but all I see is uncertainty and fear.

"Obrecht," I whisper.

He blinks his icy-blue orbs hard and walks away. Selena takes off down the hall behind him.

Dmitri comes over to me. "Skylar, let's sit. There isn't anything we can do right now."

I sit, not sure what else to do, dizzy and feeling nauseous. *Why did I not see who gunned him down?*

"Dmitri, who shot him?"

His face hardens. "One of Bruno Zielinski's guys."

My gut churns. I put my hand over my stomach. "Why would the Polish mob want to hurt Adrian?"

Dmitri swallows hard. "I can't discuss this with you."

"He got shot," I cry out.

"I'm sorry, I—"

"Get away from me."

Dmitri's eyes widen.

"Move!" I scream, unable to control my ongoing rage. I'm sick of never knowing anything, and I've never been so afraid.

Dmitri moves across the room. Hailee takes his spot. I sit stunned as tears pool in my eyes. There's so much I don't know about Adrian. So many things he's hidden from me.

None of it matters. The only thing important is that he lives.

The nurse comes back out. "We need blood. Whoever can donate, please do so, quickly."

The vision of Adrian bleeding to death on a cold, metal table fills my mind, and I break down. I wasted so much time staying away from him. I just got him back. He was finally going to let me in.

Hailee embraces me tighter.

"He can't die," I whisper. But the fear in her face and everyone else's does nothing to comfort me.

Bogden escorts Adrian's mother into the waiting room. I lock gazes with her, and all I see is Adrian's icy-blue eyes. Svetlana's register fear and sorrow.

I go over to her. She's shaking, so I put my arm around her and lead her to the seats. "Come sit with me."

More worry fills her expression. "Where's Obrecht?"

Maksim replies, "He needed a walk. I'll go find him."

"No. Let him be," she states.

Maksim pats her on the shoulder and sits across from us next to Aspen.

"Any news?" she asks.

"Can you donate blood? The hospital has asked us all to do so. The others went but most of us have been drinking so I'm not sure what the rules are," Maksim replies.

Svetlana nods and wipes her face. "I didn't drink tonight. I didn't know why, but something inside me felt like it was a bad idea."

I reach for her hand. "I had a few glasses of wine. I don't think they'll let me donate, but I'll go with you."

Svetlana squeezes my hand and doesn't let go of it. She donates blood, and the hours seem to drag on. No one says much. From time to time, the Ivanov brothers and Obrecht huddle in the corner with Bogden, who keeps coming in and out of the room.

Each time, Svetlana tenses and closely watches them. Obrecht keeps looking at her and shaking his head, then walking down the hall. Selena sometimes follows him, sometimes stays in the seat next to Svetlana, who keeps an intent watch over the men.

She knows what's going on.

I turn to her. "Do you know what's going on?"

Her eyes tell me she does. Mixed in is betrayal and hatred. They fill with tears again. One drips down her cheek as she says, "He loves you."

"I know."

"He was going to tell you everything."

I turn more to face her, surprised she might know Adrian's secrets. "You know?"

Her face hardens. "Let's go for a walk."

My heart pounds in my chest cavity. Svetlana leads me down the hall and into the chapel. She glances around. No one here, and she points to seats. "Let's sit."

My insides shake. For so long, I've wanted to know what Adrian is involved in and why he thinks I won't be able to keep loving him. And the Ivanovs have information on whoever shot Adrian on lockdown.

"You know why the Polish mob shot Adrian?" I ask.

Svetlana's gaze pierces mine. Once again, they remind me of Adrian's eyes, and I have to work hard to keep it together. "My sons don't tell me everything. Certain things are for my protection, and I trust whatever they don't tell me is for my safety. What I do know is Dasha is involved."

The hairs on my arms rise. "Dasha? His ex-wife did this?"

Svetlana's eyes turn to slits. "Yes. I don't know how or why she got involved with a Zielinski. She knows they are mafia. But she slept with Bruno's oldest son. He's now dead."

Chills consume me. I can hardly speak. "Adrian killed him? For Dasha?"

Svetlana's eyes widen. "Adrian did not kill him. But you know what my son is capable of?"

I open my mouth to speak then shut it. So many things crossed my mind about what Adrian could be hiding from me. I never said it out loud, but ever since the Cat's Meow, when he put a headlock on Wes Petrov's bodyguard in one swift move, I knew what he was capable of doing. I carefully choose my words. "Deep down, I knew before I ever kissed

Adrian that he could kill someone with his bare hands if he wanted to."

She takes a deep breath. "This did not stop you from dating my son?"

I shake my head. "No."

"But he does not know what you told me?"

More regret fills me. Adrian and I wasted so much time over his secrets. Maybe if I had asked him outright, we could have gotten past it, and I wouldn't have had to stay away for months. "No."

"It does not bother you?"

Does it bother me?

Adrian is a killer.

"I...umm..." I clear my throat. "I love Adrian. I knew he was different when I first laid eyes on him. I don't know who he's killed or why he does what he does, but I have to believe there's a reason for what he does."

She sighs, and her eyes fill with more tears. "Yes."

"Will you please tell me?"

She takes my hand. "After the Petrovs defiled and killed our Natalia, he and Obrecht hunted down every Petrov and any other man they could who harmed her." She looks at the candles burning several feet in front of us and lifts her chin. "They didn't just kill them. They tortured them for days, finding out anything they could about the Petrov whorehouse and what happened to Natalia."

My insides shake harder. Not because I'm scared of Adrian or think less of him. I don't know what I would do if someone harmed my sister the way Natalia was. I tremble, thinking about Adrian and what that had to have done to him as a person.

"Adrian and Obrecht both dealt with things differently. Obrecht, well, he's more like his father. He can stay calmer and takes a walk. I'm not sure exactly how he gets through things.

"Adrian deals with things the way I do—bringing the situation inside himself and giving it free rein. He started spinning out. He always could get lost in his mind, even as a boy. But this was different. At one point, Obrecht had to stay with him and Dasha for a week to get him sorted."

My heart hurts more. I imagine a younger Adrian in a deep trance, trying to deal with the pain of his sister's brutal ending to life and what he had done to avenge it. "Obrecht told you what they did?"

She shakes her head. "No. Dasha did. She told me every sordid detail Adrian disclosed to her while he was spinning out. She was pregnant at the time. The only thing she could think of was herself. She kept crying about how she was married to someone else, and it wasn't fair. There was no sympathy for Adrian or what he was going through. When she told me, I was trying to process everything. My sons were both torturers and killers. It's not something I thought they could ever be. But I also never thought my Natalia would go through what she did. I couldn't be upset with them. I was happy those monsters paid for what they did in their final breaths. All I kept hearing was Dasha go on and on about how Adrian trapped her into marrying him." Svetlana laughs. It's sad and full of pain. "She married him before they kidnapped Natalia. My Adrian wasn't a murderer when they got married. He didn't trap her into anything. She hinted for two years about getting married before he asked her."

My hatred for Dasha grows.

"When they lost the baby, she blamed Adrian. He did, too. But it wasn't his fault. Dasha stopped eating. She would barely drink water. He tried to get her to eat and even forced her to go to the hospital and get IVs several times. Looking back, I don't think she ever wanted the baby."

My pulse pounds harder. "Why?"

Svetlana's tears fall. "It was the first good thing that happened since Natalia died. We were all still raw from it. But I remember how she looked. I didn't think anything about it at the time, but Adrian was so happy and excited about becoming a father. Dasha barely smiled. Her entire pregnancy, she kept talking about gaining weight. Over the years, I've had time to distance myself from her comments. I didn't want to think anything bad about her when she was Adrian's wife. But I always had a nagging feeling about her. I could never put my finger on it. Obrecht never cared for her, but he couldn't tell me why, so I told him to behave. Adrian loved her, and I didn't want our family to cause him any unhappiness."

"Adrian said you and Dasha were close?"

Svetlana shrugs. "She was my daughter-in-law. I wanted a relationship with her. I tried to see the good in her and dismissed the nagging voice in my head."

We sit in silence for a few moments. "Svetlana, Adrian said he changed Dasha. He said he destroyed her."

She huffs. "I'm not a mother who thinks her children are perfect. I know their faults. I see their imperfections. Adrian is no saint, but he did not destroy her. She is a snake."

I snort. "Seems to be the general consensus."

Svetlana's eyes chill me further. "She is. Do you know about snakes?"

My blood turns cold. I shake my head.

"Snakes lie quietly, waiting to strike their unsuspecting prey. They are hunters and easily irritated. They act rashly, biting anything in their way. Dasha's always exhibited those traits. Even before they got married, she'd do things to Adrian."

"Like what?"

"Little verbal cuts, but then she'd act like it was a joke. Over the years, it got worse, even before Natalia got kidnapped."

Every part of me wants to strangle Dasha. If she was in the room, I don't doubt I would. "Why would Dasha want Adrian killed?"

"She demanded he sign their trucking company over to her, along with ten million dollars."

I gape at Svetlana. I knew Adrian did well, but her admission is a reminder I don't know anything about Adrian and his business.

Svetlana's voice turns to steel. "I don't know anything more. What I do know is my sons have a line. Women and children are off-limits. If I see her, she better run and hide. There will be no hesitation or boundary to cross."

Kora clears her throat. Svetlana and I turn. Neither of us realized she had entered the room. She changed out of her wedding dress. "Sorry to interrupt."

"It's okay. I think Skylar knows what she needs to at this point?" Svetlana raises her eyebrows at me in question.

I give her a small smile. "Yes. Thank you."

She squeezes my hand, pats my leg, then rises.

Kora informs us, "Adrian is out of surgery."

I put my hand over my heart. "He's okay?"

"The doctor said he lost a lot of blood and had to have several transfusions. The bullet got lodged in his lower back muscle. They wanted to eliminate any damage possible, and that's why it took so much time to remove it."

"Can we see him?"

"Not yet."

Svetlana puts her arm around me and smiles. "This is good news."

"Yes," I agree.

We leave the chapel. Kora squeezes my hand. When we get to the waiting room, the Ivanov men are huddled in the corner talking again.

I turn to Kora. "Not what you had planned for your wedding night, huh?"

She dismisses my question and keeps her voice low. "Are you okay?"

I blink away new tears. "I just want to see him."

She nods. "And do you have the answers you needed? Svetlana gave them to you?"

"Yes. Adrian told her he was going to tell me."

She takes a deep breath. "Do you understand why I couldn't tell you?"

"Yes."

"Have your feelings for him changed?"

"No! Of course not. I love Adrian. And what he's gone through only makes me want to love him more," I insist.

She smiles. "I didn't think your feelings would change."

I shift on my feet and lower my voice. "How does Sergey fit into this?"

She glances at the men, speaking in hushed voices in the corner. Anger, revenge, and so many other emotions are on their faces. She pierces her hazel eyes into mine. "I'm going to let Adrian tell you."

A day ago, I would have been upset by it. Now, I can accept her answer. "Okay."

She hugs me. When I pull away, Liam and Killian come into the waiting room. Hailee rises, but they go straight to the Ivanovs.

A nurse comes into the room. "Mr. Ivanov is awake. He's asking for Skylar?"

Relief fills me. I raise my hand. "I'm Skylar."

The nurse smiles. "Follow me." She leads me down the hall and drops me off in front of his room. It's dark, aside from the soft glow of the hallway lights. The beeping of the machines hooked up to him are the only sound. I try to contain my emotions as I approach Adrian, but tears fall down my face.

He's lying on his side, facing the window. Blankets cover him. I go to the side of the bed and put my hand on his cheek. "Adrian."

He glances up. "I'm sorry."

"Shh." I dip down and press my lips to his. "You have nothing to be sorry about. This isn't your fault."

"I underestimated her. She warned me."

"Adrian—"

"You could have gotten hurt or killed. I should have—"

"Stop! Don't do this. I'm fine," I insist.

His eyes harden.

I put the rail down and lie next to him. "Are you in pain?"

"Not a lot. I think I'm still drugged up."

"It's your right side?"

He nods. "Yeah."

I cup his cheeks and kiss him. "I was so scared."

"I'm sor—"

"Stop apologizing."

He stares at me for several moments. "You probably have a lot of questions."

I shake my head. "Not right now. Your mom told me everything."

"My mom?"

I stroke the side of his head. "Yes."

His jaw clenches, and he holds his breath. "What did she tell you?"

"Everything you were afraid to say."

Silence fills the air. I keep stroking his head, waiting for him to say something. When he finally speaks, his voice cracks. "You're still looking at me as if you don't know who I am."

"You're Adrian Ivanov. I've always known what you were capable of. It doesn't change anything."

He swallows hard, and his eyes glisten. "No?"

"No."

He turns away, blinking.

It hits me how much Adrian believed I would run from him. I give him a minute. Then I turn his face back to mine. "No more secrets, Adrian. From this point forward, it's you and me and no more secrets. Okay?"

He scrunches his face and sniffs hard. "Okay, my printsessa. No more secrets."

I scoot closer and put my arm under him so he's resting on my chest. I kiss the top of his head. "Your mom wants to see you. Give me a few minutes, then I'll find out how long they think you'll need to stay here and when we can go home."

He tightens his arm around me. "I feel like I've been waiting forever for you to say that."

I smile against his head. "Get used to it. You're stuck with me now."

He kisses my cheek. "That's all I want."

"Me, too."

29

Adrian

Two days pass in the hospital. Skylar never leaves. Aspen and Hailee bring her a bag of clothes. As much as I want her to get some rest in a proper bed, I feel safer knowing she's near me. Part of me is still in shock when I wake up and see her by my side. I've kicked myself too many times for not seeing that her love for me surpasses anything I could tell her about my truth.

Now that she knows about my past and what I'm capable of, I don't hide anything from her. It's almost as if we opened the flood gate. Over the last few days, I've told her more than I ever thought I would.

The nurse just told us she's going to get my discharge papers ready when Obrecht and Selena come in.

After greetings, Selena asks Skylar, "Want to get a coffee with me?"

"Okay." Skylar kisses me. "I'll be back soon."

"Bogden goes with you," Obrecht insists.

"Yes, sir." Selena gives him a sassy salute, and he stares down at her like she's his dinner. Her face flushes, and they leave.

"Jesus, get a room," I say the moment they are out of earshot.

Obrecht ignores me. "I have news."

My pulse beats quicker. "What?"

He pulls up the chair. "The shooters are at the garage."

A chill runs through me. I start to stand, and he pushes me back down. "Easy."

"Let's go. We'll leave Bogden with the ladies at my place on the way."

Obrecht shakes his head. "No. I'm taking care of this one. You need to rest."

"They're releasing me today. I'm the one who got shot," I growl.

"Don't care. Go home. Enjoy your woman. Besides, Liam has been warming them up for the last day."

"Liam?"

Obrecht nods. "Liam and Killian found out they were hiding in one of Bruno's safe houses. It seems Liam still considers you a pretty good friend."

"What are you talking about?"

"It's like he went into an obsessive trance. He hasn't slept since the shooting. Every second since you got shot, he's hunted those Polish thugs down. He went straight into the house they were hiding out in, put bullets in the other goons around him, and left them for dead. Darragh isn't happy how he went about it."

"Why? What was wrong with what he did?"

"Darragh wanted things planted on the Petrovs to help balance out the war, but Liam wouldn't wait. He went against Darragh's orders. Then he and Killian took the two men responsible for your shooting and were going to take them to the O'Malley's 'garage'," Obrecht says, making quotes with his fingers, "but Boris insisted they bring him to ours. Darragh is going nuts. He threatened to come to the garage—"

"How does he know where it is?" No one is supposed to know. Liam and Killian shouldn't even be there.

Obrecht raises his eyebrows. "He claims he knows and always has."

I scratch my jaw. I have a beard growing from not shaving the last few days, and I can't wait to get home and get rid of it. "Darragh has always claimed to know everything that goes on in the city."

Obrecht's phone rings. "Maksim." His eyes turn to slits. "She should have turned up by now."

My heart pounds harder. Dasha disappeared several hours before her thugs shot me.

"Maksim, we've got a problem with our trackers. How does she vanish if they're doing their job?" Obrecht seethes.

It's a fair question. I've asked myself over and over how it's possible.

"Are our trackers compromised?" Obrecht asks, his face hardening.

Goose bumps pop out on my skin. Over the last year, we've dealt with at least a dozen men working for Petrov or Zielinski in Ivanov employment.

"Can Selena stay with Aspen?" Obrecht runs his hand through his thick, dark hair. "Okay. I'll be there soon." He hangs up.

"Still no word on Dasha?"

He angrily shakes his head. "No. I'm close to pulling the trackers and taking them to the garage to see what I can get out of them."

"Little extreme without any proof, don't you think?" I ask.

Obrecht cracks his neck. "You tell me how they lost her."

"They said they never left the building."

"Then how did she disappear?"

"It happens," I say.

"If you're good at your job it doesn't," Obrecht claims.

"Yeah, well, not everyone is you," I remind him.

"There was no other exit point."

"There has to be."

"No. I went there myself. Sergey was with me before he left for his honeymoon. She couldn't have left unless she went out the front door."

"What about the windows?"

"They were all locked from the inside. I'm telling you, it's impossible unless our guys are compromised or lying about their access point to watch her."

Silence fills the air. I don't want to believe that anyone on my team would be a traitor.

The nurse walks in with paperwork. Obrecht steps back and stays quiet while I sign everything. She rattles off instructions for home and leaves.

There are few people I trust in the world. My brother holds skills no one else does. He's the best, and, as much as I don't like it, if he says it's impossible, then it has to be. The only question is, are our trackers traitors, or were they just neglectful while on duty?

I lock eyes with Obrecht. "Pick them up. Find out what the truth is."

He pats me on the shoulder as Selena and Skylar walk in with four to-go coffee cups.

"The nurse said she gave you discharge papers?" Skylar asks.

I grin and slowly rise off the bed, trying not to wince. "Yep. Good to go."

She puts her hand on my arm. "Slow down. It's not a race."

I grunt. Part of me is pissed Obrecht insists on letting him handle the garage, but as much as I want to carve those two thugs to shreds, being home with Skylar is more appealing. I lean down and kiss her forehead. "Stop being bossy."

She raises her eyebrow at me. "This isn't bossy."

"No?" I try to hide my amusement.

"Nope!"

"Hmm."

"Want a ride?" Obrecht asks.

"Yeah."

I attempt to pick up Skylar's overnight bag, but Obrecht grabs it first. "You don't listen to instructions very well."

"I'm fine."

"Nurse said no lifting heavy objects for a week."

"That isn't heavy."

Skylar puts her arm through mine. "Are you going to be a bad patient?"

I smirk. "Don't give me ideas."

"Okay, lovebirds. Time is ticking." Obrecht leads Selena out of the room, and we follow.

The nurse stops us as soon as I step out of the door. "Mr. Ivanov, I told you we would provide a wheelchair for you."

I grunt and attempt to smile nicely. "Thank you, but I'm good."

"It's our policy."

"Use it for someone who needs it."

"Adrian," Skylar warns.

"What? I can walk."

The nurse rolls the wheelchair over to me. "Please sit, sir."

"Really, I'm—"

"Sir, I could get written up!" the nurse frets.

I sigh. "Fine." I sit in the chair, ignoring Obrecht's amused expression and focusing on my printsessa's happy smile.

We get in the car. They drop us off at the penthouse. When we step inside, Skylar freezes.

"What's wrong?" I ask.

She scans the room. "I um..." She glances around some more. "I'm not sure. Something feels off."

"Everything looks normal to me. Do you think it's because you haven't been here in a few months?"

A big smile appears on her face. She circles her arms around my waist, keeping away from my wound. "I'm sure it's just my nerves from the past few days."

I drag my finger over her jaw. "You know what I want to do?"

"No. What?"

"I want to spend the rest of the day attending to your nerves, starting in the shower."

"You're supposed to rest," she claims.

I lick my lips and fist her hair, tilting her face up more. I lean down so my lips are an inch from hers. "I can't think of anything more relaxing than you sitting on my face. Can you?"

Heat rushes to her cheeks. She opens her mouth, but I slide my tongue in it before she can give me any more excuses about resting. Her hands slide up my chest and lace around my head. She hungrily flicks her tongue against mine, and I groan. "I've missed you so much, my printsessa. Welcome home." I kiss her some more, trying to erase the months of craving every part of her and her body.

"Adrian?"

"Hmm?" I ask, swirling my tongue in her mouth some more.

"I scheduled the movers for tomorrow. I'm having them take anything I don't want or need to the donation center. After that, I'm sending my keys back to my landlord."

I freeze. An uncontrollable grin overpowers me. "So you want to be stuck with me with nowhere to go when you get pissed at me, huh?"

She sweetly smiles. "You said I'm your forever, right?"

"Yeah, my printsessa. Forever. You and me." I kiss her again until she pulls away and takes my hand. She leads me through the penthouse and into the bathroom then turns on the shower. I wince when I remove my shirt.

"You okay?"

"I'll be fine."

"Not what I asked, tough guy."

I drop my pants to the floor. "I'm about to be really good." I cock an eyebrow at her. "Now take your clothes off."

"Spin," she demands. "Let me take your bandages off."

I obey, and she removes them. "Clothes," I repeat, motioning for her to get naked.

She begins to remove her shirt and stops. "Your stuff to bandage your back is in my purse. Let me get it."

I groan. "Later."

She laughs and pats my ass. "Get in the shower and I'll grab it."

"I see your bossy self is back."

"I am not bossy."

I palm her head and kiss her again. "Don't get used to it. You know I'm in charge, right?"

She pushes her hands on my chest, laughing. "Get in the shower."

"Fine," I grumble. "Don't take too long. I have plans for you."

She seductively takes her shirt and pants off so she's only in her bra and panties.

"Fuck, I missed your beautiful self," I say, scanning her slowly from head to toe.

She points to the shower. "In."

"Hurry up and join me," I tell her again and step under the warm water.

She sticks her head around the glass.

"That doesn't look like hurrying," I tease.

"I'm taking my turn."

"Your turn?"

Her eyes travel down the length of my body. She takes a deep breath when she gets to my erection, which is only getting harder by the second. "Spin," she commands.

All right, I'll give you a show if you want one.

"I had a hunch you like to watch," I admit and cockily turn so she can see my backside. I don't allow her to look too long and face her again. "Get your sexy self in here." I step forward, reach out, and cup her sex. "Your hot, wet pussy needs some love, don't you think?"

She glances at my erection again and swallows.

Before she can answer, I slide my fingers inside her underwear and right into her hole.

She gasps.

"So wet, my printsessa. Why is that?" I circle my thumb on her clit and curl my finger inside her.

Her eyes become heavy, and her face flushes. She moves her hips on my hand, and I pull it out. "No more until you get in here with me."

"I'll be right back." She turns and leaves the room.

I call after her, "Hurry!"

Minutes pass, and she doesn't return. The water begins to get cold.

What is she doing?

Skylar's scream fills the air. Chills run down my spine. I grab a towel and dry myself off as I move as fast as I can while screaming, "Printsessa!"

When I step into the bedroom, the glass between the room and balcony is open, and my chills turn to terror. Skylar and Dasha each have their hands on the other's shoulders, wrestling on the wooden ledge. Their cries get louder, and adrenaline fills my cells.

I rush outside, tossing the towel on the floor, and get to them as they roll off the edge. Instinct makes me reach for both of them, and I grab Dasha with my right hand and Skylar with the other.

"Adrian!" They both scream. Their bodies hang in the air over the Chicago streets. Each woman grips the metal rail with one hand.

I only focus on Skylar.

"Stop moving. Stay calm, or it'll make it worse," I order.

Her deep-blue eyes fill with fear. She stops wriggling. Her breath stays short, and her tears fall.

"Adrian!" Dasha screams again. She continues wiggling, which only pulls on my back.

"Stop moving, Dasha!" I cry out, not sure how much longer I can hold both of them.

"Adrian," Skylar cries out.

Dasha doesn't listen. I attempt to pull Skylar up, but it's too much with my back injury and Dasha flapping her body all over the place. She continues screaming my name and telling me to pull her up.

Skylar's hand slips down my arm, and a terrorized shriek comes out of her.

"Stay calm, my printsessa," I remind her. My heart feels like it's going to pound out of my chest.

"Adrian, pull me up," Dasha demands again.

"Adrian," Skylar cries out. The fear in her eyes is something I've never seen before.

I don't take my eyes off her. There is no choice. The moment I met her I would have chosen her. I let go of Dasha's arm and reinforce my grip on Skylar's arm.

Dasha's last screams get farther away as I hold onto Skylar. Her shoulder rips out of the socket, and she screams in agony.

There are no choices. I pull up on her arm until she's halfway on the ledge then grip her under the arms and finish getting her back on the balcony.

I fall to the ground with her in my embrace. She's shaking and sobbing against my chest. I barely feel the cold cement floor as I kiss the top of her head over and over and tighten my arms around her.

"Let me see your arm," I finally say as the shock begins to wear off.

"No. Just hold me."

I look down, and blood is pooling around my bottom.

I need to get off this balcony.

I calmly say, "We need to go inside. Both of us need to see a doctor."

She pulls her head away from me and says, "Oh God, your back."

I wince looking at the bruise forming on her face. "I'm okay."

"Adrian, you're bleeding!" she says in horror, staring at the blood.

"I think my sutures ripped. We need to go inside," I repeat.

She slowly nods.

"Put pressure on your other hand to get up so you don't injure yourself further," I instruct her.

She carefully rises, and I do the same. I lead her to the bathroom and retrieve my phone from the counter, tugging her into my chest. She's still shaking as I rack my brain about who to call first. Everyone is at the garage. Their phones will be off.

Obrecht didn't say Dmitri was there.

The sirens are already filling the air, no doubt from Dasha's fall. I call Dmitri, and he answers.

"I'm about to call 9-1-1. Can you come over?"

"Adrian, are you okay?"

"Yes. Dasha is dead. She fell off my balcony."

There's a moment of silence. Dmitri clears his throat. "Of course. I'll be there in ten."

Something else occurs to me. "Tell Darragh he needs to come."

Dmitri's voice lowers. "Consider it done."

"Thanks." I hang up, kiss Skylar on the head, and call 9-1-1. I pick up Skylar's pants, help her put them on, then wrap one of my T-shirts around her torso, keeping her arms out of them. I have her slide her healthy arm in the sleeve and drape my robe over her damaged shoulder.

I throw on a pair of shorts and a T-shirt.

The paramedics arrive before the police. Dmitri and Darragh show up. The police chief follows Darragh and instructs the other officers to leave.

Skylar's shoulder gets put back into the socket. The EMTs rebandage my back and instruct me to get new stitches.

The officer steps forward. He points to Skylar. "You talk first. What happened?" He points to me. "And, you, don't talk."

I pull her tighter into me and glance at Darragh. He nods, and I do my best to follow his orders and keep my mouth shut.

Dasha may be dead, but she was a Petrov and aligned with the Polish mob. This all needs to be handled with care with the police being involved. The more we keep the mafia out of it, the better. The last thing we need are any more issues with Petrovs or Zielinskis. Zamir may be dead, but any Petrov finding out that I know who Dasha was is not in our best interest. My hope is our problems with Bruno's family are over now that Dasha is dead, and no Petrov ever finds out who Dasha was or that I know.

If only my nagging voice would allow me to believe it. All it wants me to hear is, the mafia never dies, only people.

30

Skylar

My shoulder throbs against the ice pack the paramedics strapped to it. I glance at Adrian. I'm suddenly nervous, but before anyone got here, he told me to tell the truth about what happened and leave any mob stuff out of it. He said if anyone mentioned it to let him handle it.

My chest tightens with anxiety. "Dasha tried to kill me. Adrian was in the shower. I went out to get stuff to bandage him up, and I noticed the doors open. I felt funny when we stepped inside the penthouse, but the doors weren't open when we went into the bathroom."

The officer looks at Adrian. "Were they?"

"No. They—"

"Okay, back to you," the officer addresses me. "Then what? And show me where this happened."

My heart beats faster. The fear I felt comes rushing back. I lead him through the penthouse to the balcony. "I-I stepped outside. Dasha must have been standing against the wall. She charged into my back and we started fighting near the ledge. She tried to throw me over and I grabbed her and tugged her with me. We rolled off. Adrian came running out just in time." I shudder, thinking about how I was hanging over the balcony. Dasha's fall to death could have been me. "We fell over the edge, and Adrian grabbed us."

The officer continues to focus on me. "He caught both of you?"

My pulse beats hard in my neck. "Yes. He told us to stop moving, and Dasha kept screaming and writhing around."

"But you didn't?"

"No. Adrian said I needed to stop moving, so I did."

The officer rubs the back of his neck. "Then what?"

I don't analyze what I say next. The need to protect Adrian consumes me and I lie. It easily rolls out of my mouth. "We both slipped. I held on. Dasha let go."

He cocks an eyebrow, and I don't dare look at Adrian. "She let go?"

I don't flinch. "Yes. I think it was a reflex, maybe. Or the gravity pulling on her body? Have you ever hung off the edge of a building with someone holding your one arm?"

The officer glances over the ledge. A team of police and ambulances are surrounding the cleared-out area where Dasha's body lies. "No, ma'am."

I widen my eyes. "I don't know how long it lasted, but it felt like forever. Gravity is like the devil. It wants to take you."

He nods. "I see. What happened after Dasha fell?"

"Adrian tugged me up and over the ledge. I think I was in shock...plus my shoulder..."

For several moments, my stomach flips as the officer assesses me. He tilts his head and keeps glancing between my shoulder and my face. He finally turns to Adrian. "And this is your version of what happened?"

Adrian's icy-blue eyes pierce into his. In a flat voice, he says, "Yes."

"Do you know why this woman was in your house?"

"She's my ex-wife. She was trying to take my trucking company and money."

"Hmm," he grunts then rises. He smiles at me. "I'm glad you're alive, ma'am. I'm sorry you had to experience that. Please make sure you take care of your shoulder." He spins to Darragh. "I'm glad you called. There was a raid on one of Bruno Zielinski's safe houses. Eight men got massacred. You know anything about that?"

Darragh shakes his head. "No. I don't hang out with Zielinskis."

The officer scratches his neck. "Good to know. If I have any further questions, I'll let you know. You folks take care and make sure you get those stitches fixed." He motions to Adrian.

"Will do."

He leaves, and Adrian, Dmitri, and Darragh talk in the corridor where the elevator is. When Adrian comes back into the room, he's alone.

"They left?"

"Yes." He sits next to me. "Why did you lie about Dasha letting go?"

"I don't know. It flew out of my mouth before I could think. I-I wanted to protect you. Are you mad at me?"

He leans down to my mouth. "No, my printsessa. It was probably the best thing we could tell him. Thank you."

"No one will ever know except us, right?" I ask.

He smiles. "I'd say cross my heart and hope to die, but with our current track record, I'm just going to say yes."

I let out a small laugh.

He strokes my cheek. "Are you okay?"

"Yes. My shoulder is throbbing, but they said it's normal."

He slides his arm behind my back. He tilts his head. His eyes glisten. "But how are you? You scared the shit out of me."

"I'm sorry."

"Shh. It's not your fault. I'm the one who should be sorry. I don't know how she got in here. I have Dmitri and Darragh pulling footage to find out."

My stomach twists. "So there's a breach in your security?"

Adrian's jaw clenches. "Yes. There's no other way."

"Are we safe here tonight?"

"I'll have Bogden do another complete sweep with me and lock us in for the night. I never use the bolt, but I will until we figure this out."

"We should go to the hospital," I tell him.

"No. Our family doctor will come over."

"You have a family doctor that makes house visits?"

His face hardens. "For emergencies."

"Ah. I see. Um...do you have to use the doctor a lot?" I hope this isn't a regular thing. Now that Adrian's letting me in and telling me his secrets, I'm more worried in some ways. Not knowing something creates paranoia. Once you know the facts, real fear can erupt. I'm not scared of Adrian or any of the Ivanovs or O'Malleys, but I don't want anything else to happen to Adrian.

He wraps his arms around me. "No, my printsessa. It's rare." He kisses me again, and I wonder how I survived all these months without him.

"And how are you?" I ask.

"I'm fine. Once the doctor gets here—"

"I meant about Dasha." My heart beats harder.

Adrian's expression turns sour. "I'm glad she's dead. My feelings for her died long before she did. I lost all respect for her the last time I saw her, and she basically stated she was relieved Lev died."

My stomach churns. "What? How could—"

"I'm not sure what all her secrets were, or if we'll ever find out why she targeted us, besides for the money." He leans forward and lightly kisses me. "But I don't ever want us to talk about Dasha again unless there's anything else I find out about her. She doesn't get any more of our time, all right?"

I release a worried breath. "Okay. When will the doctor be here?"

"Dmitri is calling him." He rises and holds his hand out. "I need to stay available right now. Go take a shower."

"Aww." I pout. "I was looking forward to your naked body against mine."

His cocky expression returns. "Don't worry, my printsessa. I'm going to make up for it."

My flutters take off. I shrug the robe off as I walk across the room and glance back. "I hope you aren't all talk, Mr. Ivanov."

"Are you telling me you forgot my skills?" he arrogantly questions and looks at me like he's going to eat me up.

I don't answer him. I only smile and go shower. The warm water hits me, and I spend a few minutes thinking about what happened. Adrian deals with death all the time. I don't, but I feel desensitized by Dasha's demise. When I finish my shower and dry my hair, I'm still thinking about Dasha. I walk into the bedroom with a towel wrapped around me. Adrian is standing on the balcony. His shirt is off, and it looks like the doctor has already come and stitched him up. The night is lit up from the buildings and signs surrounding us. I put my arms around his waist, careful not to touch his wound. "Am I an awful person for not feeling bad about Dasha's death?"

He snorts and spins. His eyes turn icier. "I'm the wrong person to ask, but no. She doesn't deserve any sympathy." He slides both hands in my hair, firmly holding my head. "I forgot to ask you something."

"What?"

"I heard you talking to Selena the night of the rehearsal dinner. This job in New York—"

"I'm not taking it. I already texted Marcus."

"Is it your dream job?"

I shrug. "If I'm working for someone, then maybe. I thought Bowmen was the dream job until I got it and was hit with reality."

"Are you sure you want to turn it down? If it's important to you, then we'll figure it out."

"You would move to New York?"

He breathes deep and slowly exhales. "If it's important to you, yes."

I think about it for a split second. "I don't want to leave Chicago. All our family and friends are here."

"But Bowmen—"

"Is an ass and will always be. It's fine. I'll deal with him."

He twists a lock of my hair around his finger. "There are a few other options, you know."

"Like what?"

He grins. "Start your own label."

I laugh. "We've gone over this. What's the second option?"

"I knock you up and you stay home and do motherly duties."

I laugh again. "Or, I could have it all—create a kick-ass fashion brand and have your babies."

He smirks. "Even better."

"Ha! Funny! Remember I said it costs a ton of money?"

"Yep. I have enough." He holds out his fist. "And since I love you more than life and you're going to be Mrs. Adrian Ivanov, what's mine is yours." He opens his hand. A flawless, princess-cut diamond with a platinum band sits in it. Five rows of round, black diamonds cover the outside and inside of the band. One row covers the sides. Tiny pops of platinum twirl around each black gem. It's gorgeous.

"You..." I gape at the ring and pick it up. "How did you get this?" I know diamonds and jewelry well. It's a rare item. I've never even seen a design like this.

"I had it designed and made for you. You don't deserve a ring anyone else has."

My heart surges. "Wow. Adrian—"

"What do you think, my printsessa? Want to legally be mine forever?"

Tears run out of my eyes. "Yes. More than anything."

He smiles and leans into my mouth. "You'll marry me?"

"Yes."

"When?"

I laugh. "As soon as possible."

His cocky expression that always ignites a fire in my belly appears. His kiss is aggressive and carnal and all things Adrian. It weakens my knees, and he has to hold me tight to him. "Tonight, I'll practice my husbandly duties. Tomorrow, we plan the wedding."

I try to bite back my smile but can't. "What are your husbandly duties?"

His voice, eyes, and entire presence send waves of heat rolling through my body. "It starts off with my mouth getting reacquainted with every inch of your body."

EPILOGUE

Adrian

Six Months Later

"Can you excuse us for a minute?" I save Skylar from a conversation with an intern she hired. His name is Bradley, and he's a tad obsessed with her. Can't say I blame the guy, but I'm glad he's gay. He worships Skylar. She doesn't take advantage of him, but he's super eager to please her. I would be worried about how he's willing to drop anything to be at her beck and call if he didn't blush every time he saw me. Skylar and her friends tease me, saying he has a mad boy crush.

I can't deny it. His face turns red like a bright apple. His usual flamboyant attitude gets more extreme. "Adrian! That jacket is stunning on you!" He touches the collar. It's the jacket Skylar designed for Bowmen before he destroyed it. After our discussion with Chicago's top employment attorney, it didn't take long for Bowmen to cave. She also threatened to sue him with an employment lawsuit for all kinds of things the attorney determined Skylar could go after him for. My printsessa only wanted out of the contract, the jacket's design to be hers, and for him to pull the one he destroyed, off the market. He caved after two meetings. I might have had a talk with him without anyone else knowing about it between those two meetings. There's only one jacket, and I have it. She immediately made it for me, and I love it.

I love everything about my sexy, super-talented wife.

I step back out of Bradley's touching zone. "Thanks. Printsessa?" I nod to the back of the room.

She bites her smile. She thinks it's cute how Bradley is into me. I find it annoying. He's always trying to touch me. Skylar typically makes me bet her how many times he'll feel me up, before we see him.

Within a month of getting engaged, we started her new fashion brand, Skylar Ivanov. Her preliminary pieces have gotten a lot of great press, and she's planning an entire line for fashion week next year.

We just finished construction on her office suite, and we're having a grand opening party. All our friends and family were invited as well as her staff and some business contacts. Most have already arrived. I pull her through the crowd and to the back of her office. I've already pulled the shades, and I lock the door.

"What's wrong?" she asks.

I spin her into the door, caging her against the wall with my body. She looks up at me, and her breath hitches. Lately, all I have to do is look at her and she flushes. I lean into her ear. "I'm getting tired of looking at my hot wife and not touching her."

"Oh? Did I say you couldn't touch?"

I lick her ear then stick my tongue in her mouth, diving in and out until she moans.

"I'm so proud of you, my printsessa. I think I need to show you how much." I run my finger over her dress, and her nipple hardens under it.

"You should. After I tell you something."

I kiss her neck then collarbone. "Yeah? What's that?"

She puts both her hands on my cheeks and pulls my head up. Her blue eyes glisten. "I'm pregnant."

I freeze. My heart skips a beat. "Say that again?"

She smiles. "I'm pregnant."

I open my mouth to speak then shut it. I blink hard. "You are?"

"Mmhmm," she nods.

I kiss her, maybe harder than I ever have before, and she laughs. "How far are you?"

"I don't know. I-well, I hope you aren't upset."

"About what? I'm thrilled!"

"No, not the baby. Umm, I had lunch with your mom and got sick."

"Are you okay?"

"Yes, just morning sickness. Anyway, we went and got a test. So, she knows. I'm sorry, I know I should have told you first. It just happened."

I can only imagine how happy my mom is, and it makes me smile. "It's okay. I'm glad she was there."

"You are?"

"Yes, if I couldn't be, then—"

There's a loud bang on the door, and we both jump. "Adrian! Open up, now!" Obrecht calls out in a frantic voice.

Skylar and I exchange a worried glance and step back. I open the door, and Obrecht's face gives me chills.

"What's wrong?"

"You need to come with me now." He scowls.

"Obrecht, what's wrong?" Skylar repeats.

"He took her."

"Who?" I ask, the hairs on my neck standing up.

His expression is one I only see when he tortures and kills. "Selena. Her bastard ex took her."

READ SAVAGE TRACKER - FREE ON KINDLE UNLIMITED

Wanting anything resembling what I had should suffocate me.

Meeting my neighbor, Obrecht Ivanov, confuses me. The moment he walks through my door, I desperately want him to command me to kneel. I swore I would never return to anything like life with my ex-husband. So why do I feel as if I can't breathe?

Each passing day that I don't cave into my desires, the tension in my soul exponentially tightens. I convince myself to go take care of it and stop the itch once and for all. Just one time and then I'll be fine.

It's bad enough my ex-husband is doing everything in his power to find me. The choice I make puts me in a dangerous and vulnerable position. It's a good thing Obrecht is always watching me.

He's my savage tracker...

READ SAVAGE TRACKER - FREE ON KINDLE UNLIMITED

SELENA
SAVAGE TRACKER PROLOGUE

Selena Christian

Young and dumb is one of my most hated phrases. It feels carefree and implies it's okay to make mistakes, since you have all the time in the world to turn around and fix them. For me, young and dumb can't be my reality. I'm not stupid. No matter what names my ex-husband, Jack Christian, has berated me with, I never believed him when he screamed at me, I was an idiot or declared I was thick as pig shit. He did it so many times, it should have affected my self-esteem, but for some reason, I wouldn't give him that. Buying into the notion that I somehow became stupid seemed to be another thing he wanted to take from me. He stripped me bare of everything I had, but my belief in my brain was one thing I refused to sign over to him.

Looking back, I ignored every warning my family gave me regarding my ex-husband. So maybe I do fit the phrase, but when I think of my situation, I can't help gravitating more toward the phrase, blinded by love, or even young and naive.

When you're barely twenty, living at home with your parents, and waitressing on a small Greek island, the promises of a fairy-tale life from a man like Jack are hard to resist. In my case, it was impossible.

One look at Jack, and I wasn't sure what to do with the flutters in my stomach. There wasn't any doubt he was older, more worldly, and held ridiculous amounts of power. He appeared to have money, but it wasn't something I cared too much about at twenty. Sure, the gifts he bestowed on me for the three weeks he was in town, I accepted with excitement. Everything about him and us was a whirlwind of adrenaline and new feelings I never had before. Every breath he took held confidence I hadn't witnessed in a man before. He could charm anyone with his smile alone. Add in his American accent and dominating presence, and I didn't stand a chance. At the time, I didn't even understand what his powerful aura meant. It made me feel danger and safety all at once. He said he would protect me and never let anyone hurt me. I was his and would always be. If I hadn't been so innocent, I would have understood the balance that needs to exist between a woman and a man when one party has the virility Jack does. Unfortunately, I knew nothing about what happens when you devote your life to a controlling man who doesn't put anyone's needs but his own first.

He made a vow to me. If I moved to the United States and married him, he would give me an incredible life. We would have it all—together. I could barely breathe, contemplating the thought of him leaving and never seeing him again. It was too much to bear. So, against my parents' wishes, I let him sweep me off my feet and away to another continent.

My father was so angry, he wouldn't allow my mother or siblings to come to the wedding. Jack was only a few years younger than my father. My mother begged me not to move and claimed, "You're throwing your life away if you marry him."

Nothing was farther from the truth as far as I was concerned. Jack *was* a life. He represented passion, excitement, and adventure. His world was something I never saw before and probably never would without him. And dating him was unlike any Greek boy I had ever met. He wasn't my first sexual encounter, but I could have been a virgin. Everything with Jack was like experiencing it for the first time but without the awkwardness. He knew what to do, how to do it, and my body submitted to him in ways I didn't know were possible. When he commanded me, I liked it. I assumed it was because he was a real man and knew what he wanted. I never understood why tingles lit up my nerves the first time he made me kneel in front of him. Or how pride swept through me when he taught me how to open up the back up my throat to take all of him in my mouth. If anyone else had bossed me around, it would have offended me. Not with Jack. I couldn't get enough and would have willingly knelt on the floor all night if it made him happy, when we first met.

We got married in the United States since Jack said it was easier to get me a green card if we married there instead of Greece. We had a huge wedding. All of Jack's business associates filled a six-hundred-person ballroom. I knew no one except Sister Amaltheia, a nun from the Greek Orthodox church. Jack allowed me to attend the first six months we were married. I wasn't super religious, but it helped me when I felt homesick. The members almost all spoke Greek. I would go to mass then the luncheon, but Jack soon stopped me from going. He claimed it was cutting into our weekends, and when he wasn't working, my time was his. I was his wife, his property, and he never let me forget it.

Our life was nothing like the world he promised me. We married within weeks of arriving in the United States. The day I vowed to love, cherish, and obey him was bittersweet. It pained me my family wasn't here, but I was determined to have the fairy-tale life Jack promised me.

It didn't take long before Jack's charming, loving demeanor changed. I soon found myself in a foreign country with no money, no family, and a husband who was a monster. The real Jack wasn't kind, funny, or loving. The real Jack was physically violent, into punishments that included mind games, and knew how to rip your heart out and continue to tear it to shreds even when you thought he couldn't destroy it anymore. He didn't use safe words. He controlled everything in my life, right down to allowing me to use the bathroom. And after the first few months of marriage, I never again felt safe.

When Sister Amaltheia had me meet with Kora Kilborn, my divorce attorney, it gave me the courage to divorce him. I still didn't have money and couldn't move out though. Somehow, Kora convinced his attorney to have him stay out of my side of the house, or it was going to hurt his company going public. I'm not sure how she did it. Some nights, he would scream at me through the locked doors while I sat on the other side, shaking. I would call Kora, and I assumed she called his attorney. Jack's phone would ring, and I'd hear him bark out, "Larry."

It was a miracle when Sergey Ivanov swept me away from Jack and gave me a safe place to stay. It was more than I could ever ask for, and when the divorce went through, I bought the condo from him.

I've never had anything that's mine. The amount of money I got from the divorce is more than I know what to do with. Besides buying the condo, Kora wanted me to keep a bodyguard with me when I go out, in case Jack still wanted to come after me. I wasn't sure how to even arrange anything like that, but Kora called and said Sergey had men in his employment who could be my bodyguards if I wanted to hire them. Of course I said yes, thankful I had it taken care of and could breathe again.

My condo is perfect. It's brand new, luxurious, and in downtown Chicago. My building overlooks the river. I'm on a lower floor, but there is also a rooftop. It overlooks all of Chicago and Lake Michigan. It's one of my favorite spots to hang out. Plus, I keep hoping maybe I can meet some new people.

Over the last ten years, I've gotten used to loneliness. When I escaped Jack, I promised myself I'd never let another man control me. But lately, I can't stop the urges I feel to fall into my old role. Several times, I've had to erase my search history, stopping myself from going through with the crazy ideas in my head. They started as seeds, but they've germinated and keep growing.

I'm trying to kill off every vivid dream and urge I have to fall back into anything I had with Jack. Ninety percent of what we had, I shiver in fear thinking about. Yet, the other ten is clawing at me. It's digging into my loneliness, and I'm not sure how much longer I can last. I wonder if I gave in to my desires if I could scratch my itch and then move on with my life.

It's wishful thinking. Stepping into the past can only harm me. How can it not? But all I keep thinking about is how much I need it.

I've tried to distract myself. I've joined my new friends' weekly yoga and brunch routine. I found a few places to volunteer. I even ordered the faucet I wanted to replace. It's the one I wanted instead of what Jack insisted we buy.

When I ordered the faucet, I never knew it would be the catalyst for so many things. The moment it arrives, delivered by the sexiest man I've ever laid eyes on, I feel the earth shift under my feet. The icy-blue, piercing eyes, wavy dark hair, and tattoos covering his neck, arms, and hand scream he's more dangerous than Jack could ever be. His charming smile and dimple barely peeking out on his cheek make his threatening aura seem nonexistent. It's extreme opposites and makes him the most intriguing person I've ever met.

Don't be a fool again. My intrigue with Jack only got me in trouble.

He speaks, a thick Russian accent rolling out of his mouth, and my knees go weak. "I'm Obrecht. This was delivered to my penthouse by accident. Are you remodeling?" His eyebrows lift, and his eyes linger on me.

God help me.

There's nowhere to hide. It's like I have a sixth sense for it. His expression is dominant. It's full of everything I'm craving. I hold the door handle tighter, stopping myself from dropping to my knees and waiting for him to give me a command.

"No." My voice squeaks, and I clear my throat. "No, only the faucet."

Amusement twinkles in his eyes. "Do you have a plumber coming?"

I shake my head, forcing myself to maintain eye contact with him instead of staring at his feet. I admit, "I thought I would call Sergey and ask who he recommends."

His lips twitch. "He'll recommend an Ivanov."

"Oh. Okay." I stare at him, not moving.

"I'm an Ivanov." His lips curve more, and my heart skips a beat.

I tilt my head and, in a teasing tone, reply, "So you live in the penthouse but are the plumber?" It comes out, and my face heats when I realize my voice sounds flirty.

"Nope. Just for you." He winks, making my cheeks blaze with fire.

I'm not supposed to let anyone inside. Jack isn't a man who loses well. Kora has warned me not to let my guard down. "Let me see your ID, please."

He puts his arm around the box and reaches into his pocket. He hands me his wallet. "ID's in there."

Holy mother of all accents.

"Do you always let strange women go through your wallet?" I ask.

His eyes trail over me. "No. Once again, only you."

I breathe through my pounding pulse and open his wallet.

His license reads Obrecht Ivanov, has the penthouse address, and his birth date shows he's forty-five. His picture is just as panty-melting gorgeous as the man in front of me.

Who on earth takes panty-melting photos for their ID?

How is he forty-five? I wouldn't have thought over forty.

I glance at him and open the door wider. "Come on in. I'm Selena. Sorry to be rude."

"Being cautious isn't rude. Don't ever apologize for it," he firmly states.

"Are you Sergey's brother?"

He snorts. "Cousin."

"Oh." I stare at him, and there's a moment of awkward silence. I reach for the box, but he doesn't let me take it.

"I've got it. Is it for your kitchen?"

"Yes."

"Okay. It shouldn't take me too long." He walks past me into the kitchen.

My eyes follow him. My pulse increases as I stare at the way the fabric of his T-shirt stretches perfectly over his taut flesh. And I've never really checked out a man's ass before. If Jack had caught me looking at any man, he would have punished me. I've seemed to have forgotten all my previous rules. I can't tear my gaze off every part of him, including the tattoos on his arms and neck.

He spins and catches me ogling him. My cheeks heat again as he says, "Do you enjoy living here?"

I snap out of it and join him in the kitchen. By the time the faucet is on, I'm in trouble. The air is electric. Every urge I've tried to kill resurfaces like a ripple in the water. It expands until I feel as if I'm about to burst at the seams.

When he leaves, disappointment hits me. The loneliness I've struggled with annihilates me. For hours, I stare at the faucet, thinking about him and what it would be like to kneel in front of him.

That's part of Jack's world. I'm out of it. I cannot go back.

Every time I go anywhere over the next week, I look for Obrecht. When Monday night comes, I can't handle it anymore. I pull out my laptop and look at the clubs I know Jack never goes to.

Just this once. I'll get the urge out of me. Then everything will be okay again.

No one will know me.

The lingerie I bought when I went on a shopping spree for my new post-divorce wardrobe stares at me in the closet. I slowly put it on. The membership I applied for online to get into the club deals with code words. I memorize them all. I give my bodyguard instructions to stay in the car and not escort me inside. He argues with me, and I remind him I'm the client.

"You will get me fired," he says in his thick Russian accent.

I point to the door of the club. I hate being rude, but he can't come in, and I can't chicken out. I need this. "Do not go in there. If you do, there will be consequences."

That's the thing about "if." It represents scenarios that aren't real. The consequences I imagined weren't anything like what happened from leaving him outside.

Every single promise I made to myself to get rid of my itch once and for all becomes impossible to keep. Obrecht Ivanov is part of my "if." He's the equivalent of being on a deserted island and having a lifeline. Once you grab hold, it's impossible to let go until someone makes you.

But I should never have forgotten Jack's threats. For the first time, I wonder if I've become stupid. The dumbest thing I ever did was believe I could escape the wrath of Jack Christian. I should have known how deep his ties with the devil are and that he can reach me anywhere. Maybe I allowed myself to live in a fantasy world because I knew Jack would never stand for another man having me. If I had admitted it to myself, I'd have to let Obrecht go. Seeing each other was a dangerous game. I told him about Jack, but he didn't flinch. He wasn't scared, nor was he willing to let me go. All it did was make him fight harder to claim me.

Once you freely give yourself to someone when you never thought you would, in ways you never imagined you could, unleashing yourself from them is impossible. When someone else comes along and grabs hold of your leash, the thing you cherished suddenly becomes a nightmare.

READ SAVAGE TRACKER - FREE ON KINDLE UNLIMITED

ALL IN BOXSET

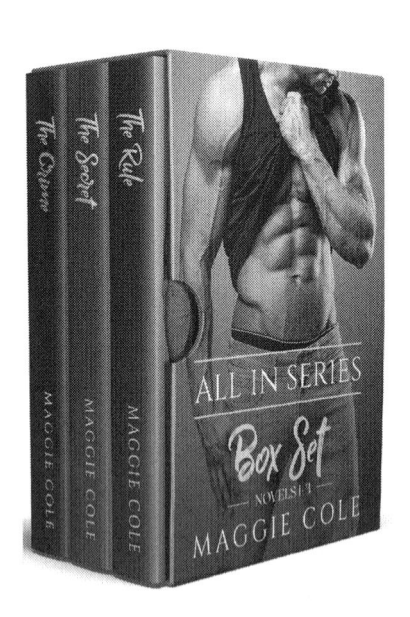

Three page-turning, interconnected stand-alone romance novels with HEA's!! Get ready to fall in love with the characters. Billionaires. Professional athletes. New York City. Twist, turns, and danger lurking everywhere. The only option for these couples is to go ALL IN...with a little help from their friends. EXTRA STEAM INCLUDED!

Grab it now! **READ FREE IN KINDLE UNLIMITED!**

CAN I ASK YOU A HUGE FAVOR?

Would you be willing to leave me a review?

I would be forever grateful as one positive review on Amazon is like buying the book a hundred times! Reader support is the lifeblood for Indie authors and provides us the feedback we need to give readers what they want in future stories!

Your positive review means the world to me! So thank you from the bottom of my heart!

CLICK TO REVIEW

MORE BY MAGGIE COLE

Mafia Wars - A Dark Mafia Series (Series Five)
Ruthless Stranger (Maksim's Story) - Book One
Broken Fighter (Boris's Story) - Book Two
Cruel Enforcer (Sergey's Story) - Book Three
Vicious Protector (Adrian's Story) - Book Four
Savage Tracker (Obrecht's Story) - Book Five
Unchosen Ruler (Liam's Story) - Book Six
Perfect Sinner (Nolan's Story) - Book Seven
Brutal Defender (Killian's Story) - Book Eight
Deviant Hacker (Declan's Story) - Book Nine
Relentless Hunter (Finn's Story) - Book Ten

MORE BY MAGGIE COLE

Behind Closed Doors (Series Four - Former Military Now International Rescue Alpha Studs)

Depths of Destruction - Book One

Marks of Rebellion - Book Two

Haze of Obedience - Book Three

Cavern of Silence - Book Four

Stains of Desire - Book Five

Risks of Temptation - Book Six

Together We Stand Series (Series Three - Family Saga)

Kiss of Redemption- Book One

Sins of Justice - Book Two

Acts of Manipulation - Book Three

Web of Betrayal - Book Four

Masks of Devotion - Book Five

Roots of Vengeance - Book Six

It's Complicated Series (Series Two - Chicago Billionaires)

Crossing the Line - Book One

Don't Forget Me - Book Two

Committed to You - Book Three

More Than Paper - Book Four

Sins of the Father - Book Five

Wrapped In Perfection - Book Six

All In Series (Series One - New York Billionaires)

The Rule - Book One

The Secret - Book Two

The Crime - Book Three

The Lie - Book Four

The Trap - Book Five

The Gamble - Book Six

STAND ALONE NOVELLA

JUDGE ME NOT - A Billionaire Single Mom Christmas Novella

For German Translation go to: https://www.authormaggiecole.com/germany/

ABOUT THE AUTHOR

Amazon Bestselling Author

Maggie Cole is committed to bringing her readers alphalicious book boyfriends. She's been called the "literary master of steamy romance." Her books are full of raw emotion, suspense, and will always keep you wanting more. She is a masterful storyteller of contemporary romance and loves writing about broken people who rise above the ashes.

She lives in Florida near the Gulf of Mexico with her husband, son, and dog. She loves sunshine, wine, and hanging out with friends.

Her current series were written in the order below:

- All In (Stand alones with entwined characters)
- It's Complicated (Stand alones with entwined characters)
- Together We Stand (Brooks Family Saga - read in order)
- Behind Closed Doors (Read in order)
- Mafia Wars (Coming April 1st 2021)

Maggie Cole's Newsletter
Sign up here!

Hang Out with Maggie in Her Reader Group
Maggie Cole's Romance Addicts

Follow for Giveaways
Facebook Maggie Cole

Instagram
@maggiecoleauthor

Tik Tok
https://www.tiktok.com/@authormaggiecole?

Complete Works on Amazon
Follow Maggie's Amazon Author Page

Book Trailers
Follow Maggie on YouTube

Are you a Blogger and want to join my ARC team?
Signup now!

Feedback or suggestions?

Email: authormaggiecole@gmail.com

- twitter.com/MaggieColeAuth
- instagram.com/maggiecoleauthor
- bookbub.com/profile/maggie-cole
- amazon.com/Maggie-Cole/e/B07Z2CB4HG

Printed in Great Britain
by Amazon